PERDITION STREET

PERDITION STREET

LEONA O'NEILL

PERDITION STREET
WRITTEN BY LEONA O'NEILL
PUBLISHED BY QUILL & CROW PUBLISHING HOUSE

This book is a work of fiction. All incidents, dialogue, and characters, except for some well-known historical and public figures, are either products of the author's imagination or used in a fictitious manner. Any resemblance to actual persons, living or dead, or actual events is purely coincidental. Although real-life historical or public figures do appear throughout the story, these situations, incidents, and dialogues concerning them are fictional and are not intended to depict actual events nor change the fictional nature of the work.

Cover Design by Fay Lane

Interior by Cassandra L. Thompson

Edited by Lisa Morris and Olivia Brooks

Printed in the United States of America

ISBN (ebook): 978-1-958228-60-9

ISBN (paperback): 978-1-958228-61-6

Publisher's Website: quillandcrowpublishinghouse.com

For my husband Brendan – my safety, my comfort - and our kids, Daniel, Caolan, Finn, and Maolíosa, my little lights, always guiding me home.

"Through me is the way to the city of woe. Through me is the way to sorrow eternal. Through me is the way to the lost below. Justice moved my architect supernal. I was constructed by divine power, supreme wisdom, and love primordial."

— DANTE ALIGHIERI, INFERNO

CHAPTER ONE

Atlas Bishop wanted just five minutes of peace. Five minutes of no one wanting anything. No questions. No demands. No drama. Nobody to fix. His head was swimming, and his anxiety started to weigh heavy on his chest.

Last night had been a rough one. He looked down at the human bite mark on his hand. The wound was roaring red, and he probably needed a tetanus shot. But it could wait, just like the office could wait. He took a sudden right onto St. Stephen's Green, the clacking of his shoes immediately muffled by fallen leaves.

In his forty-one years on the planet, he experienced few days when his stomach wasn't in knots. He didn't know what it meant to relax. His default setting was hyper-vigilance, and ceaselessly anticipating danger was his constant baseline.

He sensed a panic attack coming. His eyes darted around the park, searching for a place to stand. His breathing was no longer automatic—he had to think about inhaling and exhaling. In his head, he was in a creaky car, holding the metal bar so tightly that his knuckles were white as it climbed slowly toward the top of his mental rollercoaster. Then it tipped over and barreled toward the ground at a ridiculous speed. He never knew where or when it would end, but he was always helpless.

His vision blurred. He tried to blink it away, needing no one to see him like this. This loss of control, this vulnerability, this weakness he could never shake. He thought he might find solace among the silent trees, just for a moment, until the dreaded sensation subsided. He pulled the collar of his trench coat tighter around his neck and started to walk, his steely, blue eyes fixed firmly on the ground.

His fear of losing control in front of others was almost crippling. The sun was shining, but October in Dublin could be brutally frigid. There was absolutely no warmth, and even his hands, clenched tightly in his coat pockets, were as cold as corpses. Lifeless gray windows peered at him from the Georgian houses that wrapped the park in their cold embrace.

Fortunately, his bench was empty. He had been coming here for years and knew this bench, nestled in a quiet corner under the shadow of an old oak tree, was the only one that afforded any real shelter from the elements and, more importantly, from people. If he could reach it without passing out, he would be able to sit and ride out the panic that already had a firm grip on his body.

He flopped down onto the bench and set his palms on its familiar worn and flaking gray paint to ground himself. He closed his eyes and took a deep breath, knowing he would eventually find peace and ease on the other side. That is if he didn't have rabies from the bite on his hand. If that was the case, he could be dead before lunchtime. A bubble of panic burst in his stomach. *Was rabies even still a thing? Probably.* He took out his phone and searched it.

Yeah, it was.

He read the words on his phone screen: *"As the disease spreads through the brain, the patient becomes more confused and agitated,"* and his panicked breath started again. He was definitely agitated. Was he confused? He didn't know. Was not knowing if he was confused a sign of confusion? He read on, his heart beating quicker, his arms heavy, and his head light. *"Rabies leads to coma and eventual death."*

He slammed his phone down on the bench and looked straight ahead, gripping the bench with sweaty palms. *Yup, he was definitely about to die.*

Atlas closed his eyes and tried to remember his breathing exercises. The ones his therapist forced him to look up in a bid to get him to take back control of the anxiety. It was absolute nonsense and never worked, but he had to do something. Anything.

He opened one eye and looked toward the bridge where a collection of tourists were loudly pointing cameras and clicking at anything that moved. Closing his eyes again, he pursed his lips and tried to exhale slowly.

A baby wailed from a passing stroller, stealing his attention again. A couple leaning up against a nearby wall laughed enthusiastically at something in a magazine.

A young woman seated on the next bench, dressed in a dull gray business suit, tapped her shoe heel to a monotonous rhythm pulsating through her earphones. His heart fluttered wildly again, and his hand found his chest as his stomach lurched.

This was it. The moment his heart stopped beating. The moment he was going to die.

He knew it wasn't. *But it might be.*

He couldn't die. *But he might.*

He *had* died before. It hadn't been particularly nice.

Dying didn't scare him. It was this part—the violent head spinning, stomach churning, heart-pounding shaking of the soul free from the body—that he hated.

It was just a panic attack, he desperately tried to convince himself. That's what his therapist had said. But it just didn't feel like nothing this time. This time, it felt like God or the Devil had reached into his brain and was pulling his very soul out through his nostrils.

A passing cyclist rang her bell, and someone bellowed a loud "hello." Atlas spun around violently to throw them a furious look. Couldn't a man even die in peace? People were absolutely ridiculous these days.

He felt his rage rising. Everywhere his gaze landed, someone was deliberately trying to rob him of even two minutes to himself, refusing to let him die quietly in the park from a mystery illness.

Bastards.

His breathing was faster now, nearly gasping out of control. His head spun, his ears rang, and all the moisture disappeared from his mouth. He felt as though he might vomit, or choke, or both. He felt his throat constrict as pains shot across his chest.

A child passing with their mother shrieked with laughter.

"Fuck's sake!" he roared at no one and everyone. Passers-by stopped to look but then hurried on, fearful they might be sucked into the abyss of a strange, angry, shouty man's world. No one made eye contact, and parents put their arms around their children to usher them away from the deteriorating scene.

His mind conjured a memory of his therapist's room: Atlas sitting on the soft, pink armchair in a sunlit room that smelled of scented candles and misery, gripping a novelty furry cushion as he gasped for air. His therapist standing above him, her hand on his shoulder, telling him to "just breathe" as the wild panic gripped him. She had told him that, because of his past experiences, he now feared everyone and was afraid no one would help him because he thought he wasn't worthy of help or love. She had assured him that none of that narrative was real, and he now heard her soothing voice in his head. *"This will pass. Focus on something, a distraction from the physical symptoms."*

She had always told him that anger was an easier emotion to process than fear and that that premise was to blame for his frequent outbursts, that anyone who had witnessed the horrors of his childhood was bound to struggle. He was only human. He had been an innocent child, and none of it was fair. But, she said, he had to stop running from his trauma and face it. That was the only way to heal. He had to release his pain in a safe and controlled manner. Probably not in the park, though. People were staring, and the man on his phone near the bridge was probably calling the police.

Atlas put his head down and surrendered to it, letting it all wash over him. The raging panic, the nausea, the rapid breathing, the heartbeat roaring in his ears, the thought that he would collapse right here in the park, and people would think he was a mad, drunk homeless person and just step over him on their way to work. He would die without anyone's help. And where would his soul go? Up or down? He didn't know. He'd be buried in a pauper's grave because there was no one to claim him. Cold sweat rolled down his face, and he panted furiously, trying to force oxygen into what felt like blackened and diseased lungs.

When his eyes went blurry, and he felt that he was going to pass out, he knew he had reached the peak. He tried to slow his breath and looked up at the last leaves on the trees, trying to concentrate on their slow, peaceful swish in the light breeze.

He forced himself to remember that this had happened a thousand times before, and he hadn't died on any of those occasions. Thinking about dying was stupid for someone like him, as the probability of it happening was extremely remote, given his circumstances and connections. Why was he even worrying about it?

His breathing and heart rate began to slow, and he sighed, long and deep, these sensations all too familiar. He was coming down from the other side of this.

He raised his head and leaned back, running his fingers through his short, jet-black hair, feeling every spiky strand beneath his fingertips. Noticing things was good: it meant his system was regulating, coming back down to earth.

He felt ridiculous, embarrassed by this weakness that he couldn't defeat. He looked around as a couple passed hand in hand, lost in conversation. A child chased a bird on the green, their chubby little hands outstretched to catch it. A man walked past, singing to himself.

Atlas tried to keep the positive momentum going, knowing these distractions might help.

With shaking hands, he reached for his well-worn brown satchel, which he had discarded on the ground when the panic attack had started, and pulled out that morning's newspaper.

A letterbox-shaped picture of a pub brawl spanned the top half of the front page. The camera had captured chairs and tables frozen in mid-air as flying fists connected forcefully with angry, contorted faces. Atlas gazed at it, thinking it had the air of a Renaissance painting. Every single person was doing something different, something violent. He began to read the story underneath.

Four people were stabbed to death, and thirty-six others were injured last night during a brawl at a 50th wedding anniversary celebration in a village pub on the outskirts of Dublin. Locals spoke of their shock at the incident, many of them saying that those involved were good, decent people who had never known to be violent before.

The pub owner, speaking from his hospital bed, said, "People were dancing one minute, then hitting each other the next. I must have been hit, too, because the next thing I know, I'm waking up here in the hospital!"

The police arrested the pub's chef for the murder of three customers. An elderly school principal was likewise arrested for smashing a glass and stabbing the owner of a local flower shop, who died at the scene. The principal then attempted to slit his own throat.

Gardai had to call for backup and a riot squad from central Dublin and spent four hours trying to restore the peace. Most of the pub's patrons were injured, and many were arrested, but no one has any recollection of what happened.

The Gardai Police Commissioner Miriam O'Toole later stated that her officers had never encountered anything like it, adding that "the interior of the pub resembled a scene from a horror film." She concluded that inquiries were ongoing and that her officers had remained behind to process the scene and conduct a full forensic examination.

Atlas sighed again, shaking his head in utter bewilderment at country folk and their weird ways, before turning the page. Anyone else would have been horrified at the violent images and words, but not Atlas. He took a long, deep breath and continued to read.

"Blood On The Streets" screamed the headline at the top of the next page. Another gangland murder: this time, a young father in his twenties was assassinated by a single bullet to the head while he walked his dog in Tallaght.

A pull-out quote stated that sources were linking the murder to notorious criminal gang leader Robert Morrison, someone Atlas knew only too well. The accompanying picture showed a hysterical woman being held back by police as she reached for a sheet-covered body outside a Chinese restaurant. Atlas glumly reflected that the last thing the victim had seen was a flashing neon sign offering two Spice Bags for five euros.

He also noticed two other things, the first of which being that the sheet draped over the victim didn't cover the body fully, and the blood-soaked tennis shoes the victim had spent precious minutes lacing up the morning he was killed were still clearly visible. His feet were exposed in a sickeningly slack and stilted manner, the coagulating red blood contrasting so starkly with the white shoes. Why did the police not think to purchase bigger sheets? It would have prevented a lot of nightmares for both the victim's family and those of a more sensitive disposition who happened to see the article in the paper. Atlas thought it sloppy.

Secondly, there was a small boy in the picture, no more than eight, holding the hysterical woman's hand.

He focused on the little boy as the camera-toting tourists moved their incessant ball of noise and energy to the far side of the bridge. The boy was wearing pajamas, his eyes red and sore from crying. Children shouldn't see such things, Atlas mused. It wasn't right or fair. He looked away and felt another bubble of panic burst in his stomach, thankfully a weaker one this time—the dying grip of this attack. He took another deep breath, set down the newspaper, and tried to focus on something else.

He looked across the lake as a swan floated regally by, the sun's rays giving the creature's soft feathers a mystical white brilliance. He listened to the sound the wind made as it caressed the trees. He noticed the warmth of his palms against the cold bench.

At last, he felt a sense of calmness descend on him, as thick as honey. Another big, deep breath was as clean and soothing as balm filling his lungs. He laughed a little at himself. He hadn't died this time. Again.

"Hello?" said a man's voice from behind.

Atlas didn't turn around.

"Hey you, hello!"

The voice was more irritated now. Insistent.

Atlas kept his back to the voice and sighed.

"Listen, I'm just trying to clear a headache here," he said, not shifting his gaze from the swan. "To get a bit of fresh air. I'm not feeling so good. I just want to read my paper in peace for fifteen minutes before work. Maybe pick another bench, pal."

"You can hear me?" replied the man, who now walked in front of Atlas, blocking his view of the lake. "You can see me?"

Atlas reverted his gaze and looked down at the plaque on the old bench. *Dedicated to Pat, who loved to watch the swans from here.* It was in need of a polish. Everyone who knew this particular Pat was probably dead by now.

Atlas looked above the man's head at the sky, now a cold crystal blue. The sun, as weak as it was, felt nice shining on his face. It promised better, warmer days. He exhaled dramatically.

The man shuffled nervously in front of him, still blocking his view of the lake. "Listen, pal, you need to tell me what the hell is going on!" he said, now sounding more sure of himself.

"Look," said Atlas, lowering his gaze and fixing them on the man's shoes. They were brand new tennis shoes, blindingly white apart from the dark red blood stains. "I don't think I can help you, not right now. I'm not feeling good, and I can't think straight. If you need that particular kind of help, you can head over to my office; it's just across the way there on Perdition Street."

Atlas watched the man place his chin on his chest and sigh heavily, the way men do when they are about to explode. He noticed that the blue designer shirt the man was wearing was still wet with blood. He glanced at the man's hands: they were cold, cadaverous, and blue, reminding him of his mother's hands in her casket all those years ago. That unwelcome thought disgusted him, and he inched sideways on the bench to peer around the apparition and back across the lake.

He felt two bloodshot eyes boring into him and caught the corpse's gaze briefly before stretching his arms across the back of the bench, raising his chin to the sky, and closing his eyes.

"Listen, dickhead," the corpse said angrily. "You have to help me. I followed some kind of light here to you. What. Is. Going. On? Am I... Am I dead...or what...?"

Atlas brought his eyes back to the corpse, smiled sympathetically, shrugged his shoulders, held out his palms, and nodded his head slowly. Some of these guys took a while to catch on.

He stood up, trying to maintain eye contact, but the neat, bloody bullet hole in the front of the dead man's forehead kept stealing his attention.

He scanned the man's face. It always amazed him how the veins seemed to freeze like tiny blue rivers under the skin when a person died. He thought he could make out the whiteness of the man's skull shimmering in the sun through the wound, but he didn't want to be rude and stare.

"Seriously! Are you listening to me?" the man shouted, poking an icy finger into Atlas's shoulder.

Atlas studied the bullet hole, trying to determine what caliber bullet had passed through the corpse's brain. He wondered what that felt like.

"He used a silencer, didn't he?" Atlas asked, nodding towards the wound on the dead man's forehead. "A .22?"

The dead man stared at Atlas for a second, his mouth slightly ajar. "What?" he said after a pause. "A silencer? How the fuck would I know? I'm dead. Jeeeesus!" He raised a porcelain-like hand to his head, touching the wound with trepidation, before throwing his hands out again towards Atlas.

"All I know is that I woke up on some street, and no one could see or hear me. My wife and son turned up and started screaming. Everyone was screaming. Everything was in slow motion, and I could see myself lying there, with my brains splattered all over the fucking ground. And then there was this light, and it was as if it was calling me. I thought it would be like in the films, and it would lead me to Heaven or some other nice place, but instead, it led me to this stupid park and to you, some dickhead who can't even answer simple questions."

Atlas sighed.

"Are you... Are you God?" the dead man asked, slowing his rant momentarily before taking off again. "You better be God or somebody important, man, or I am going to absolutely lose it right now. I am literally on the brink; I'm on the fucking edge here! One more thing, and I swear to God..."

Atlas put his hands in his pockets and stared across the park, tuning the man's voice out. At the other side of the lake, a young boy and his father were throwing bread from a loaf bag into the water for the swans. They took turns dipping their hands in and lobbing the bread into the water, cheering each other on and laughing as the gathering swans fought over the wet bread.

"What is going on here?" shouted the dead man, snapping Atlas's attention back to him. "What the fuck are you looking at? Are you even listening to me? I'm freaking out here, like I'm having an actual mental breakdown right in front of you, and you're daydreaming! I swear to God, I'm going to punch you so hard in the face."

Atlas considered the dead man and laughed gently before finally answering.

"I'm not God, Caliber .22," he said calmly, gathering up his satchel and the newspaper. "I'm a Soul Binder. I send souls to Heaven and Hell. I'm presuming, according to this article here—" He patted the newspaper. "—that it was Morrison who shot you. I've bound seven souls to him already. They are with him daily, screaming in his ears, clouding his vision, whispering, tormenting, sucking the joy from his existence. I hear he hasn't slept in years. But he's strong, the strongest I've ever seen. He is damned to Hell but is taking his sweet time going there. I have no idea why.

"I *will* bind you to him, for that is my duty. But you have a duty as well. You must want this; you must desire it. You must have rage and hatred in your heart, strong enough to take that soul of his all the way down to Hell. Seven before you have tried, and they've all failed. And after they had exhausted their rage, they were left with only their own sorrow. Not even the weight of their sorrow is enough to drive their killer mad. You need to do better and push him right over the edge. For only then will Hell reclaim his soul, and your soul will be free to enter Heaven."

The dead man stared at Atlas, slack-jawed at the unexpected information overload.

It took them so long, sometimes. Even when they were standing with holes in their heads and vengeance in their hearts, it took them an age to process what was happening.

"Sorry, what?" said the corpse. "What the fuck is this? Are you insane? What do I have to do? What are you again? You're still getting punched right in the face."

Atlas looked across the lake again as the father and son walked away from the bank, hand in hand. He let his information sink in with his new client. It often took a few minutes, sometimes as long as an hour. He watched the dead man's expression change from bewilderment to anger and eventually to resignation.

"Right," he said, almost whispering, and leaned against the railing. "So, I am dead then. Like just gone, as in dead, as in forever, as in not living anymore. There's no going back from this, is there?" His voice trembled for the first time, and he looked away towards the traffic outside the park, sniffing loudly.

Atlas could see the other side of the park through the hole in the dead man's head. He puffed his cheeks out with another violent sigh before standing up and setting off toward Perdition Street. The dead man followed, asking a series of desperate questions that Atlas largely ignored. He hoped the dead man wouldn't cry. He hated it when they cried.

Caliber .22 started to cry.

CHAPTER TWO

Atlas's office spanned the first floor of a beautifully restored Georgian house on Perdition Street, nestled among dozens of tall, imposing houses, now converted into offices by the city's many lawyers and accountants. These were no soulless buildings: they were alive with ivy and expansive dark windows that reflected the beautifully ornate wrought iron railings cordoning them off from the rest of Dublin.

No one paid much attention to the gold plaque on his building bearing his name and the title Private Detective. Very few read Latin these days, so the inscription *Opus Dei In Terra*—God's Work On Earth—just looked like some pretentious inspirational quote to those passing by.

He didn't get much passing business anyway. His offices were paid for jointly by the Gardai Siochana on both sides of the Irish border as thanks for his services in solving cold cases and by the Vatican for ensuring that the murderers and victims were dispatched to Heaven and Hell, as appropriate.

He had known nothing of this arrangement until a few years ago. Two days after awakening from a near-death experience, a stranger in a suit had arrived and sat at the bottom of his hospital bed. Atlas had thought him a doctor or consultant, as he had an air of confidence and authority about him. Instead, he said that he was the Angel Gabriel. He told Atlas that he had been spared from death, but in exchange, he was now in the employment of God and was one of one-hundred-and-ninety Soul Binders scattered across the world.

Atlas, head still fuzzy from the concussion that had rendered him unconscious for forty-eight hours, had stared silently at the man because he wasn't sure if he was actually there. He thought perhaps the stranger was someone who had possibly gotten lost on their way to a psychiatric appointment or was a figment of his addled, bruised, and drugged-up brain. He'd been having a few problems like that since he drove his car into that wall at seventy miles per hour.

He listened as Gabriel, who proceeded to devour a packet of cheese and onion potato chips that had been on Atlas's bedside table, savoring them like they were Michelin Star fare, told him that he now had a special power gifted by God himself. He stated that Atlas could now see the dead, well, more specifically, the murdered, and it was now his job to help those poor souls find peace in Heaven by sending their killers to Hell. He casually added that he would be working alongside hell's representative, a Mr. Smith, but they would get to the finer details of that arrangement later. For now, he needed Atlas to get his strength back, get out of bed, and get to work because the souls were piling up, and it was causing major problems.

Atlas remembered pressing the nurse call button by his bed frantically as Gabriel munched on an apple that he declared he had taken from the unconscious patient next door, babbling about how much better the food "down here on Earth" was. His mouth full of masticated fruit, he concluded that Atlas was replacing the last soul binder, who had met a rather unfortunate end when his head was removed from his body. Bad timing for him, Gabriel had observed, but a fantastic business and life opportunity for Atlas. It was either that or dead. There were no other boxes to choose from.

A nurse had then charged into the room, asking if Atlas was okay while quickly pressing buttons on the beeping machines by his bed, indicating his heart rate was dangerously high.

In hindsight, Atlas hyperventilating, pointing manically, and blathering loudly about the angel sitting on his bed eating his chips, stealing apples, and talking about God—when the nurse saw nobody—probably warranted the high-dose sedative that he subsequently received. He woke only intermittently over the next twenty-four hours. When he finally came around, he opened his eyes to be greeted by the sight of his dead mother at his bedside. Later, in the middle of the night, he saw a man with half his skull and an eye missing, coughing softly from a seat in the corner of the darkened room.

The doctor had told him that the hallucinations would cease when the swelling in his brain went down. But they didn't, and by the time he was released from the hospital, he had a whole collection of "hallucinations" following him home.

He had sat in his living room, trying to ignore them and their incessant chattering and horrifying injuries, focusing instead on the television. He took some painkillers, drank some whiskey, and passed out on the sofa. They were still there when he woke up ten hours later. They were always there. His mother was the only one who never spoke but just sat there, staring straight ahead, her face consistently creased with worry.

By the time Gabriel returned—sitting down at the kitchen table with Atlas as he held his head in his hands one evening—Atlas was ready to listen.

Gabriel had told him that he was to be Ireland's next Soul Binder. He was to work for Heaven, alongside his counterpart, Hell's Mr. Smith, to ensure the free and equal flow of souls both upstairs and down, as had been agreed in an ancient sacred pact. He would have to sign all the paperwork and vow to dedicate his life to this sacred duty, to bind the souls of the murdered to those who had murdered them using Holy instruments that harnessed the power of Heaven. He was to "defend Heaven for the Innocent and Banish the Guilty to Hell," as Gabriel had said. He would work with specially selected and trained police officers—those with the necessary experience and skills to deal with tricky, hard-to-solve cases—to obtain true justice that would have eluded them without divine intervention. Never mind jail: those were the divine rules of the universe. He would be guided and supported by God's representatives on Earth at the Vatican. Gabriel insisted that he was doing God's work, regardless of how nasty, violent, and bloody it got. Bad people deserved Hell, not mercy, he had assured him. Life was not a game.

This was an important job, Gabriel had warned, and one Atlas had been specially chosen for, as he knew the pain of brutal loss and the sense of revenge that radiated from the very depths of a broken being. This was his chance to gain the vengeance and justice that had eluded him thus far. It was his opportunity to do good things, to ensure he went upstairs when the time came and not down to the fiery depths. Not a lot of people had that choice handed to them. He had a free pass to make bad guys pay.

Gabriel had then presented him with a rope and some runes and told him that he was practically bulletproof but to keep his head on his shoulders and his blood inside his body because there were some things that even angels couldn't fix.

His first binding had been the worst. He had awakened one morning, blinking and bleary-eyed, to discover a sopping wet little girl with sunken eyes and a tattered dress at his bedside. She looked to be about six or seven years old and had waited silently, while he had pulled on a hoodie and some shoes. She led Atlas through his living room, past all the other corpses he'd accumulated, her ice-cold hand soft and delicate against his own. He quickly slung his bag containing all the items that Gabriel had given him over his shoulder before they headed out of the front door. They had walked for two hours along streets of opulent, ivy-covered Georgian houses, sparkling expensive cars, and trees lush with leaves. They walked along bustling city center streets alive with car horns and accents from all over the world, all the while the cold from the little girl's hand constantly radiating through Atlas's palm. They passed into the inner city, with its unkempt streets and graffiti-covered walls, and he had watched people's expressions get harsher and heard their accents harder, unseen burdens weighing heavily on their shoulders. The bird song of the suburban streets was replaced by the sounds of angry shouting, riddled with expletives.

They had eventually stopped outside a terraced house with a chipped, peeling red front door and a broken windowpane. Atlas had looked around the garden, where a dirty doll's house was discarded by the fence, its only company a pink girl's bike with the front wheel missing.

"Is this where they are?" he had asked the little girl, looking down at her. "The one who killed you?"

She had looked up at him and gripped his hand tighter, her large, hazel eyes sad and beautiful. She had nodded, and Atlas had felt a familiar anger start to bubble inside him.

He had tightened his hand around hers and opened the gate, held together with thick rope, before knocking hard on the front door.

A voice had shouted from inside to fuck off, but he had knocked harder, and the door had finally swung open to reveal a skinny, stubbled man in dirty tracksuit bottoms and a stinking red t-shirt.

He had asked what Atlas wanted. Was he the police? Had they found his daughter, or was she still missing? Atlas had looked down at the little girl, and she had nodded her head slowly, the terror clear to see in her eyes.

Atlas had dropped her hand and grabbed the man by the scruff of his t-shirt, pushing him noisily back into the house. He had kicked the door closed behind him as they had wrestled along the hallway, through a sea of empty beer cans and takeout containers, before toppling into the kitchen. The man had been as light as a feather, and Atlas had hurled him over the messy kitchen table, dirty plates and glasses crashing to the ground along with him.

Atlas hated people who hurt children and women and had beaten the man until he was almost unconscious. It was then, while raining down blows on the man's head as he pleaded for mercy, that he realized Gabriel had been right. As he extracted his own personal vengeance on those who had stolen the lives of others, he liked it.

He liked it far too much.

Throwing the bloodied man onto a chair, Atlas unfurled onto the table the runes, rope, and roll of parchment that Gabriel had given him. He had slapped the man hard in the face to rouse him—he wanted him to see this—and then read the holy words while holding the stones. Having felt a surge of power rush through him, he had instinctively thrown the rope to the ground and called the little girl to him.

The man's swollen eyes had widened in horror at the sight of his dead daughter. He had staggered from the chair, not believing what he was seeing. The man had then spoken words that Atlas had heard escape terrified mouths thousands of times since, that it couldn't be true. That he was seeing things. That this wasn't real. Atlas quickly found that murderers were not fond of facing the consequences of their actions in the cold light of day.

Atlas had watched as the little girl climbed on her father's back, wrapping her stick-thin, bruised arms around his neck before joining her hands in front of his chest. On any other day, it would have looked like a doting father giving his daughter a piggyback ride, but not today. She wrapped her skinny legs around his waist and screamed in his ear as the man lost control of his bladder and began to shake uncontrollably, frantically trying to shake her off.

The faces of the guilty, the expressions of horror and terror, were always the same.

Atlas had cracked the rope off the kitchen tiles and swung it around his head like a lasso, enveloping the father and daughter in its bright golden embrace.

"Take your vengeance, precious girl," he had told her. "And make it brutal."

He had packed up his things and walked away, not looking back at the sickening scene. Instead, he stumbled down an adjacent alley, where he puked up the pizza he had eaten before going to sleep the previous night. He then returned home and broke the seal on a bottle of Bushmills Whiskey, downed its entire contents, and passed out on the sofa in the living room.

That had been only the start of it. He had bound thousands of souls since then.

Today's client, the miserable Caliber .22, walked slightly behind him down Perdition Street. Fallen leaves from the trees had formed a stunning blanket of earth-tone colors beneath their feet, but the passing Dubliners in their dark business suits, sipping their morning coffee or talking on their phones, didn't notice it. Nor did they see the eighteen-hour-old corpse with a gaping hole in his forehead, blood-stained shirt, and raw red eyes as he struggled to keep pace with the surly private detective.

Atlas took an unannounced sharp left and trotted up the well-worn concrete steps to his office door.

As his shoes sank softly into the thickly carpeted hall inside, he breathed in the rich scent of mahogany and books, their sweet aroma blocking out the rancid smell of the city and immediately making him more at ease. This was his safe place. Everything felt familiar here. He could feel himself settle.

He looked down at his hand. It was still trembling and probably would for a while, a combination of a lack of whiskey and the aftereffects of the panic attack. He could sense that the dead man was following closely behind him, now having caught up. His soul would be his shadow now until he was bound to the man who had taken his life.

He never asked clients their names. It felt too personal, and he didn't like that type of attachment. He didn't want to know anything about them, he didn't want to get to know them, and he didn't want to know anything about their families or others they had left behind. He wanted nothing to do with their lives, their loves, or their losses. They were just clients, just numbers, that were to be turned around and bound to their killers as quickly as possible. This was just a job, he told himself. Instead, he gave them nicknames, usually linked to what had brought about their end. That was why the dead man now following him up the stairs to his office was Caliber .22.

He opened the heavy door to a bright, airy office.

"Good morning, Mr. Bishop," chirped his secretary from behind her desk in the spacious reception area.

"Good morning, Elsa," said Atlas. He noticed that her hair had been recently styled, the loose curls falling around her face a lighter blonde than before. It was nice, he thought. "I trust you had a good weekend."

"Oh, you know," she said, tucking an errant strand of hair behind her ear. "A reasonably quiet one. Only sensible drinking and moderate sinning." She winked and flashed him a cheeky smile. He couldn't help but smile back.

He looked at Caliber .22, who was staring at the framed Bouguereau depicting Hell, then back to Elsa's smile.

"Very good," said Atlas, trying to remain professional.

"Varie has sent you over one of those tricky case files," she said, her smile fading. She handed him a faded blue folder with the usual Garda Siochana "Under the Official Secrets Act 1973" stamped on the front.

"So I see." He frowned, taking a sideways glance at the dripping-wet woman sitting on the waiting room sofa, her saturated brown hair stuck to her face. She was missing a pink stiletto heel, and the strap of her impossibly short sequin neon dress was hanging off a pallid shoulder. Her stomach was swollen as if pregnant. Around both of her wrists was a dirty blue, frayed piece of rope that had snapped where it had once bound her hands tightly together. She was sobbing softly into a clenched fist.

Elsa picked up a gold cross from around her neck and kissed it, whispering a prayer under her breath.

"I'll be with you in a second, Miss," said Atlas softly, opening the file. "I see. Drowned. Tragic. Two weeks ago. No leads. Well, we'll have to see about that. Just make yourself comfortable for a few minutes. I have to sort a few things out with Caliber .22 here, and then I'll be with you shortly."

Elsa blessed herself and looked out across the empty office. "God bless her!" she declared with the air of an American preacher.

"I have another client here, Elsa," said Atlas, glancing at the man standing to his left. "I'm pretty sure it's a Morrison case."

Elsa kept her eyes fixed firmly on her desk and gripped her pen with both hands like it was a protective holy relic.

"Is he here now, Mr. Bishop?" she asked quietly.

"Yes, right here," said Atlas softly. "Don't fret, Elsa. I'll take care of it. He'll be gone soon."

As he moved to open his office door, he wondered what type of person would feel comfortable working in such odd conditions. He was glad that he had found Elsa. She was the niece of a priest he had once worked with, a parish exorcist from County Meath he had once helped with a job. Elsa was discreet, sweet, and had a good heart. She was smart, understood the seemingly unimaginable, and very caring, always praying for the souls they encountered even though she could not see them, no matter who they were or how they had met their end. She also bound her womanly form in too-tight dresses and skirts, a welcome distraction from the corpses that followed Atlas around all day.

He liked her very much and thought she liked him too, but despite facing the worst kind of human beings imaginable without fear every day of his working life, the thought of asking her out absolutely terrified him. There were times they had gotten close to something, but he could never let his guard down, not even for her.

"A triple espresso when you get a minute, Elsa," he shouted from the hall while wrestling with his keys. "On second thought, make it a quadruple."

His doctor had told him to stop drinking coffee because it led to his heart racing. But Atlas figured that his heart raced most of the time anyway, so he kept drinking it. And if he didn't drink coffee, he would have nothing to mix his whiskey with. His doctor had also said that he should do more of what scared him in a bid to combat his sometimes-crippling anxiety, so he thought drinking too much coffee, against his doctor's strict orders, was as good a place to start as any.

He loved his office. He had never dreamed that he would ever have a place he could call his own, somewhere that felt like home. All manner of books lined his shelves, from expensive, leather-bound tomes to shiny new paperbacks and dusty, ancient ledgers that he had picked up at second-hand stores. They were all methods of escape. He had read every one at least once, some of them multiple times.

The stern eyes of stoic Belfast dockers stared down from several paintings on his walls. He didn't know why he related so much to the gruff, tough, tattooed, flat-capped men who said so much without speaking, but he picked up a Terry Bradley painting every single time he saw one. It was like an addiction to him. *The Kiss*, a classic depicting a talon-nailed blonde kissing a docker that his ex-girlfriend Varie had bought him the Christmas before she dumped him, hung on the wall directly in front of his desk. It sometimes made him believe that he might feel love again someday.

He sighed, hung his trench coat on the stand, and walked over to the window.

He pulled out his leather chair and sat at his expansive mahogany table. Placing his palms flat on the table and bowing his head, he took several deep breaths in through his nose and out through pursed lips. He wanted the comforting smells of his office to be absorbed into his very lungs and give him ease. He was at the tail end of his panic attack now, the part where he just felt exhausted and shaky.

A soft knock at the door caused him to open his eyes.

"Come in," he shouted. Elsa entered, her red-tipped fingers wrapped elegantly around a steaming mug.

"Thank you so much, Elsa," he whispered gratefully. She walked out of the room, the ghost of her perfume lingering in her wake.

Caliber .22 was pacing up and down in front of him, and Atlas could see that he was getting agitated. Such was the course of these matters. Denial and sadness first, then some grief and anger, followed finally by an unquenchable thirst for revenge. He welcomed the final stage, for they needed that desire, or the binding wouldn't work.

"Caliber .22, sit down!" shouted Atlas. "I have to make a call. I need to check my official channels."

The dead man's energy was making Atlas edgy again. He needed peace to rebalance himself: he could feel the acid begin bubbling in his stomach.

He reached over to the end of his desk and fumbled for a concealed button, a small drawer sliding silently open in response.

Atlas reached for the Bushmills whiskey bottle inside and, with a resigned grimace, unscrewed the cap. The sound it made was familiar and comforting. He needed something to get him through this neverending morning.

Caliber .22's sunken, red eyes glared back at him from the sofa.

"What!?" snapped Atlas. "You're stressing me out with all that pacing and fist wringing and mumbling. Would you ever just sit down and shut up?"

"I didn't say anything," replied the corpse blandly. "It's none of my business if you want to start the day with a drink."

"That's right," growled Atlas. "It *is* none of your fucking business!"

He put the cap back on the bottle without taking a drink and threw it back into the drawer with a clatter. The dead man had taken the pleasure out of it. "It's not like you could tell anyone anyway, the state you're in. Half your head is missing," he sniped.

Atlas felt bad the second the words had left his mouth. He looked down again into the drawer, this time at the battered Bible next to the discarded whiskey bottle. He picked up the Bible and opened it to a page where a well-thumbed, black-and-white photograph sat of a small, smiling boy and a beautiful woman, posed hand in hand. He always felt such sorrow for that little boy, for not knowing what horrors lay ahead.

He took a swig of his coffee to dispel the dark thought and set the picture back down on the Bible.

"I'm sorry," whispered Atlas. "I shouldn't have said that, Caliber .22. Forgive me. I get terribly stressed out at times, and I've had a terrible morning."

"What do I care?" snapped the corpse, cutting him off. "It's probably a hangover you have. I can't believe *you* are my only hope of getting into Heaven, a fucking drunk with an anger management problem, and God knows what else. I'm totally screwed."

Atlas rolled his eyes, picked up the phone, and hit redial. "Hello, it's me." His voice was soft, deep, and calm, not wanting the person on the other end of the line to detect his distress. "How are things?"

He took another drink of coffee and smiled at the response.

"Glad to hear it," he said, pausing again. "Yeah, I know, she found me. She's here. Two weeks out and no leads? Look, I'll get her sorted, no problem. I'll find out who ended her, but I have another client with me here this morning. One of Morrison's, I think. I haven't got the full details from him yet, but I will. I know it was him."

He swiveled his chair to face the window. He didn't want to look at Caliber .22's mangled head anymore, not when he had his beloved Varie at the end of the line.

Outside, city workers were rushing to offices and shops, swinging plastic lunch bags or purses while swigging their takeaway coffees. The street was already starting to seize up with traffic.

"I don't need to wait for a file for this one," he said, reverting his attention to the call and lowering his voice. "Look, Varie, he's only been here thirty minutes, and he's already driving me crazy. He's about to blow, so I need to get him bound soon. Everyone knows it was Morrison who did it."

He put his feet up on the windowsill.

"What are you talking about? The dogs on the street know it was Morrison, Varie!" he laughed. "When have I ever got it wrong? My equipment will lead me to Morrison. It has never let me down before. Email me the details you have now if it makes you feel any better, and I'll send your people the bill. But I'm not waiting on you. He's sitting here in my office. I don't get a minute's peace as it is, and you know what I'm like when..."

He took his feet down from the windowsill and spun around to his desk again, her last words sharply refocusing his mind.

"Can you be sure?" he demanded. "The last few sightings got her hopes up so much, and it broke her heart when they came to nothing."

He listened intently, again picking up the photograph of him and his mother from its resting place atop the Bible.

"In a hospice? Does he match the description?" he asked. "Even the accent?"

He flipped the old photo around and silently read the words on the back of it—*Defendere Caelum Pro Innocente, in Exsillium Agere Noxios Inferno*—Defend Heaven for the Innocent, Banish the Guilty to Hell.

"No, I won't tell her this time," he said, resting his forehead on his hand. "I'll tell her if I definitely find him. Her energy is fading, and I need her to have the desire for revenge and the binding when the time comes. Did your source say if I have much time?"

He nodded at her response and took a deep breath.

"Thank you," he whispered. "I will see to it when I complete these cases. Hopefully, we will have more concrete information, and that bastard will still be alive."

He ended the call, stood up from his desk, and walked to the window again. He stayed there for a few minutes, concentrating on his breathing. In through the nose, out through the mouth. In for four seconds, hold for seven, and out for eight. Turning, he inhaled the dust from the old, leather-bound books that lined his bookcases, he inhaled the stale smell of coffee from an old mug on his desk, and he exhaled stress, worry, and fear. Or at least, he tried to.

Shaking his head to clear it, he marched to the adjoining bathroom and washed his hands with lemon soap, concentrating on the space between his fingers, much like a surgeon would before an operation. He then grabbed his trench coat off the stand and walked to the door.

"Come on," he said to the corpse in his office, now sullenly reclining on the sofa. "I need to get rid of you two."

CHAPTER THREE

Atlas skipped down the office steps and onto Perdition Street, his light footfall not betraying the fact that he now had a thunderous headache. He cupped his hand over his mouth, lit a cigarette, and tried to ignore the pain, simultaneously glaring at Caliber .22, in case he had any notions of telling him off for smoking, as well as drinking, in the morning. The drowned woman stood behind him as Atlas dragged hard on his cigarette and surveyed the pair of corpses, a sorry sight in the cold light of day. He fished his sunglasses out of his trench coat pocket and put them on. His hangover was kicking in, and his body was starting to scream for more alcohol.

He nodded for the corpses to follow him and took off towards Grafton Street. The city was alive now, people pulsing through its many veins. They joined the throng of people going about their day, Atlas wondering what they would say if they could see the corpses now amongst them. Would they scream or just go back to scrolling on their phones?

"Where are we going?" shouted Drowned, trying her best to keep up. Atlas tuned into her accent: was it Russian? Ukrainian? "Why this walking and walking?" she pleaded. "Why must we walk so much? I have been walking for days already. I don't want to walk anymore."

Atlas stopped and spun around to face her, trying to hide his irritation. "Take off your shoe," he said, pointing at the sole stiletto she was wearing. "You're walking with one shoe, all up and down. That's why it's hard. Take that one off and throw it away. It will make walking easier. We have to walk to my car, which is not far. But I have a headache, and I'd like to get there without making it any worse."

Atlas could hear Caliber .22 grumbling behind him and turned to glare at him. "Would you like to register a complaint also?" he scowled. "What's your problem, apart from the obvious?" The dead man rolled his eyes and continued to mumble.

Atlas started walking again, registering the steady slap of Drowned's bare feet on the pavement as they passed wheel-heeled couples in designer gear in the shadow of Dublin's most opulent stores. The sparkle of diamonds drew his eye toward a lavish jewelry store on a corner, and he caught their surreal reflection in its window as they trudged past it. He needed a shave, and the two corpses dragging their earthly bodies along behind him needed to be gone.

He looked down Duke Street towards Gilligan's, his local pub. He could smell the sweet aroma of wood, whiskey, and cigarette smoke, even from here. It might have been his imagination conjuring up the smell, but he licked his lips and slowed, pulling his sunglasses down to see if Mick the barman had put the sandwich board out on the street yet, signaling opening time. A double Bushmills would immediately cure the headache that was currently creeping across his skull. He could hear the clink of the ice on the side of the glass and feel the soft bounce of the green leather seats as he sank into one of them. He could hear Mick humming and feel the comfort of the cozy nook that allowed him to watch Dublin silently pass him by outside.

"What are you doing?" asked Caliber .22, breaking into his line of vision. "Are you in some kind of trance? It's like nine o'clock in the morning. Do you need a drink that bad you can't even wait until lunchtime? Some fucking detective you are. All you can find is the pub."

Atlas pushed his sunglasses further up the bridge of his nose and walked on, the pain in his head pulsing with his heartbeat, angry that he was letting a dead man dictate what he could do with his time and his liver.

The delicate smell of fresh flowers filled his nostrils, emanating from the flower stalls beside the luxury Westbury Hotel. He was immediately taken back to his mother's kitchen on a quiet Saturday morning. Standing at the kitchen sink, she filled a slim white vase with water to place three pink roses she had cut from the back corner of her overgrown garden. They bloomed once a year, and he recalled that she checked every day to see if they were ready. When they finally were, it made her so happy. She had smiled down at him, the angry black and purple bruise on her face reflecting the sun shining through the window, serenading him with a song about promising a rose garden.

He shook the memory from his head and stomped on, the two corpses at his heels. As they turned the corner onto College Green, the imposing gothic majesty of Trinity College rose up to greet them. This was old Dublin now, the city's former banking district a testament to old money and opulence from another era.

They walked beneath the shadows of imposing, ornate gray stone structures—banks that had once held the riches of the Dublin aristocracy. Some still housed money behind their pillared and plinthed facades, others were now expensive restaurants and designer stores.

Atlas navigated the busy street, weaving in and out of groups of chattering tourists fresh from Temple Bar and Dubliners going about their day, all oblivious that the recently deceased walked among them. The pungent aroma of coffee reached his nostrils from one of the many cafes, and he drank it in as buskers sang songs of love and lust. As he passed it, he gazed longingly in the window of Il Fornaio Caffe at their sweet pastries, his mouth watering. He looked back at Caliber .22, who was shuffling along a few feet behind him, the still oozing gunshot wound immediately putting Atlas off any inkling for sweet treats.

"Up here," he gestured, turning onto Trinity Street. They followed the curve of the formidable Gothic Pen Corner's shop window, staring up at the ornate clock on the shop's stone turret. It was almost 9:45 am. Gilligan's Pub would definitely be open on the way back, he hoped.

He clicked the car keys inside his coat pockets, and the lights of a vintage, black Jaguar XJ8 flashed to life.

"What the fuck is this?" asked Caliber .22.

"My wheels," said Atlas, surveying his pride and joy. "Don't even think about saying anything. I swear to God I'll leave you here."

Caliber .22 snorted. "What year is it? It's like something my grandfather would drive. An old banger! We'd be quicker walking. You'd think with the money you pull in, you'd be able to afford something fancy."

Atlas scowled at him, his patience wearing thin. "And where's your car, dickhead?" he snapped. "Is it in the same place as the rest of your head? Shut up and get in."

The traffic was heavy—nearly at a standstill. They certainly would have been quicker walking, but as his car softly rumbled in the shadow of Christ Church Cathedral, Atlas figured he could use the time to read more of the report on the drowned woman currently dripping half of the River Liffey all over his back seat.

He hit the button on the glove compartment and it fell open, throwing empty cigarette packets and two bottles of Bushmills Whiskey onto the floor, one empty, the other with maybe two mouthfuls left in it. Keeping his eye on the road, Atlas rummaged around until his hand emerged, clutching a small, ornate metal box.

He met Drowned's gaze in the rearview mirror.

"This is a Quaesitor," he said, holding it between his finger and thumb. "It helps me find killers who don't want to be found. It lights up the connection between them and you, like a thread that takes me to them. You place your hand on this, and it will tell me where your killer is."

She did what she was bid, and the metal box omitted a gentle, infrequent hum. It was one of the more modern tools of his job. Developed by his friend and fellow Soul Binder, Austrian priest Jack Gertenberg, it was the perfect mix of old-school craft and cutting-edge technology.

Gabriel had brought him to Austria around two months after he had started his new role. Atlas had been having a hard time dealing with the deluge of corpses arriving in his world—including his living room and bedroom—and had been heavily self-medicating with painkillers and whiskey. The problem was, when he opened his bloodshot eyes in the morning—or, more likely, the afternoon—his problems had often doubled, sometimes tripled.

Gabriel had arrived early one morning and found Atlas sitting on the cold bathroom floor in his underwear, sweating profusely after having vomited the entire contents of his stomach. All the while, an American woman he had met either in Gilligan's or maybe on the way home slumbered in his bed.

The angel had sat down beside him on the floor.

"The folks upstairs don't think you're coping very well," he had said. "They think you need to pull yourself together."

"I want to die," groaned Atlas.

"Unfortunately, I can't facilitate that," said Gabriel. "It's not your time, and you still have work to do."

"I don't want to do your work," Atlas had said wearily. "I've had enough. I don't care where I go. The here and now is a bollocks, and anything is better than that."

Gabriel had looked at him sympathetically, drawing his knees up and leaning his elbows on them.

"I promise you will find reward in this work eventually," he had said. "When you can see through the dark clouds. This is just a transition time. It takes time to get used to the dead, all the blood and gore and injuries, the sadness, the pain, the anguish in dealing with people who have been broken by someone else, seeing the very worst side of humanity every day. You genuinely will get used to it —everyone does—and your reason for doing it will eventually outweigh all the horrible stuff."

Atlas had shook his head vehemently, his stomach churning.

"I'll never get used to this," he had said. "The little innocent kids brutalized, the women beaten and killed by the men they loved, the lives of good people stolen by bastards who don't deserve to breathe. This will never feel normal. I hate it."

Gabriel had lit a cigarette and handed it to him.

"I'm taking you to see someone," he had said. "Someone who can help you see the good in all of this."

"I'm not going to see a shrink," Atlas had growled.

"Put some trousers on," said Gabriel. "Or I'm taking you there in your boxers."

They had met in the kitchen five minutes later, Atlas now fully clothed. Gabriel had stretched out his hand in greeting and Atlas took it. He blinked, and when he opened his eyes again, they were in the middle of a small courtyard with tall, bright white windowed walls on all sides of them. Gabriel had gestured for them to walk through an archway that led to an arcade and then a busy street beyond thick church-like wooden doors.

As they had emerged, Atlas had recognized the Romanesque and Gothic amalgamation that was St. Stephen's Cathedral in Vienna. He had only ever seen it in pictures, and even that had been impressive, but it was nothing compared to real life. He had gazed upon the double-headed eagle mosaic on its roof as they had crossed the road and taken in its immense tower and spire piercing the morning sky above Stephansplatz. It had taken Atlas's breath away.

They had then joined the crowd of people milling around the square, following the church's wall around and through heavy, ornate wooden front doors. An old man in a flat cap had stopped and stared at Gabriel as he passed, even though nobody else could see the angel. Gabriel had stopped, smiled, and spoken to the man in German, telling him not to worry and that he would see him soon. The man had smiled back as if relieved, nodded at Atlas, and walked on into the morning sunlight.

They had walked on into the church, Atlas's senses immediately engulfed by a symphony of light, color, and beauty. A cavernous nave stretched out before them, with rows of towering columns that seemed to reach towards the heavens. The lofty ceiling, adorned with ornate frescoes and intricate Gothic tracery, created an illusion of infinite space. Sunlight filtered through the stained glass windows, casting kaleidoscopic patterns of vibrant hues across the polished stone floors.

They had walked on, the air filled with the soft murmur of prayers, the echoes of only Atlas's footsteps reverberating against the ancient stone. The flickering glow of candlelight danced upon the gilded altar as they neared it.

Father Jack Gertenberg had turned to greet them as they approached, his creased face lighting up as he embraced Gabriel like a brother. Atlas had looked at those kneeling in silent devotion in the pews surrounding the altar. He had hoped none of them saw the eighty-nine-year-old priest hugging thin air.

They had sat in his vestry, drinking tea out of delicate china cups. Gabriel had devoured the scones provided like he had never set eyes on food before, nodding his head enthusiastically and waving his hands when Jack spoke.

Jack had sat on a purple armchair, the sun streaming in the window onto his hairless head. The crevices on his face were deep with age, his hands weathered and etched like ancient tree bark.

"I, too, struggled with the task when it was first presented to me," he had told Atlas. "I had been a priest for almost thirty years but lost my faith and found gambling, drugs, drink, women, and despair. I had no family to speak of. Eventually, Gabriel appeared to me in the Bockshorn Irish Pub as I hunched over my pint, contemplating suicide. We talked for hours over freshly poured Guinness about God's work and the good that could be achieved by combating evil."

Jack had looked at Atlas and said he had known horrors, too.

"My entire family—my mother, father, two older sisters, an uncle, and my grandmother—were murdered in the concentration camps of war-torn Germany. I was the only survivor. I had a hard life, a brutal one, in and out of orphanages all over Europe until I joined the priesthood. I gave my bitterness, hatred, and anger to God to carry. I tried to carve a good life."

He had sipped his tea and told Atlas that his trauma and pain were always there in the background.

"I had had no closure, no justice," he had said. He waved his knotted hand in the air. "I could be walking down the street and greeting the man who killed my family and destroyed my life but wouldn't even know. It haunted me."

He had looked Atlas in the eye and said that the pain of knowing their killers were allowed a normal life had eaten away at him for years.

"Gabriel's 'career opportunity' gave me the chance to get revenge. I bound lost souls and searched Europe for the men who killed my family, Gabriel allowing me to bind their souls to these monsters and drag them down to Hell. I felt my burden lift and knew that this was my calling. I've never looked back."

He had told Atlas that it was hard but rewarding work.

"God called me to this role, and he has now called you. "We aren't here by accident; our spirits have led us. It is grueling—I understand that—but to survive, you will need to erect an emotional barrier to protect yourself from the horrors. Treat it like a job, and distance yourself. Otherwise, it will break you."

Jack had gotten up and strode sure-footed to a large mahogany desk and pulled out a drawer. Atlas had studied him—he had the look of an elderly man but the sprightly air of a much younger one —and wondered how he handled the more reluctant recipients of soul bindings.

Jack had smiled, his eyes cheeky, bright, and excited, as he handed Atlas a small metal box. He had said it was a Quaesitor—a seeker, a searcher—developed when he worked in the Sacred Innovation Department of the Vatican vaults.

"All human souls created by God are divine," he had said. "And every moment in time with a person forms a sacred connection, big or small, good or bad. I have created a way to recognize that thread and find a way back through it. These little boxes have revolutionized soul binding."

Atlas had looked at the small metal puzzle box, then back to Jack.

"Get your spirit to place their hand on it, and it will find the last sacred Earthly connection—that of them and their killer," he had said.

He had put his hand on Atlas's shoulder. "Don't doubt yourself, Mr. Bishop. You are strong enough to do this job. There are bad people out there who need to be dealt with, and there is no better, fiercer heart to do it than yours. You will find your father one day and make him pay for what he stole from you, what he destroyed. Make that the driving force in all that you do."

#

Atlas looked down at the Quaesitor, making the familiar, comforting humming sound on his car's passenger seat, and smiled a little, remembering the many times he had gone back and visited Jack and that Vienna Irish bar he was so fond of.

The traffic in Dublin remained gridlocked as Atlas glanced again at his passengers. Drowned's hair was dripping water all over his seat while Caliber .22 was leaning, with what was left of his shattered skull and exposed brain, against a headrest. They were both making a mess that Atlas knew his handheld vacuum wouldn't fix. He tutted irritably, knowing he would have to get the car valeted again on the weekend, even though it would look perfectly clean to everyone else.

He glanced away from the grisly scene across at another car idling alongside him. The male driver and his female passenger were arguing animatedly, their toddler asleep in the child seat in the back. Normal life. Atlas wondered what that must be like.

"Drowned," he said, shifting his eyes to her notes. "Who killed you? What was his name?"

"Why you say that?" she snarled, her accent thick and menacing. "Why must you say Drowned for me in place of name? Why you call this man with a hole in his head Caliber .22? We are dead, but we have names! Show some respect!"

"It's just a thing I do," said Atlas, not meeting, but feeling, her piercing gaze. He thought she had clearly accepted her fate—death—and was now in the angry phase of transition. "Look, it makes it easier for me. I see death and murder every day in my job, and it wears me down sometimes. I see so much horror, so this is how I protect myself from the terrible things I have to process. There's no offense meant to you; I hope you understand that."

The words came out of Atlas's mouth, but he knew them not to be entirely true. He had tried to erect an emotional barrier, but the horrific sights and details of each case still did something to him. Something only the numbing whiskey took away. He had felt barely anything for years. His psychotherapist had told him that it was a trauma response and was not a healthy place to stay. He told himself these people meant nothing to him, that nothing meant anything to him. This was just a job. It had to be. He was an empty shell—one that rattled with pills and whiskey and regularly shook with anxiety—most of the time just lumbering through the motions of this life.

"I want to help you," he continued. "I *will* help you. Now, this person who killed you: who was he?"

"My boss, Roland," sniffed Drowned. "He is a bastard. I told him I was pregnant, and he did this to me."

"You were pregnant." Atlas sighed. A lot of these cases were like a hammer to the soul. He would definitely need a drink after this binding to take the edge off a horror show that never seemed to end.

He knew that the drowned woman was right, that he needed to be a little more emotional about things and not stone-cold all the time. The corpses said that to him a lot. It was what normal people did, he supposed—felt something. He forced himself to be normal, tried to bring up these elusive emotions.

"It's really sad about your baby and what happened to you," he said, catching sight of his attempt at a sympathetic smile in the mirror and recoiling in horror. He immediately straightened his face. "I'm sorry for your troubles," he added, looking away. "Do you know how the binding works?"

"How would I know that?" she spat, glaring at him. "I think this is the first time I have died, no?"

Caliber .22 snorted in laughter.

Atlas pursed his lips to stop himself from smiling. He was glad she was angry. He placed her accent as from Moscow. He once had a job there, a nasty enough business. Someone had fled there and then wasn't too interested in being consigned to Hell. He thumbed the thick dagger scar on the side of his neck as he remembered their encounter

Drowned sank further down into the seat, folding her arms like a sulky teenager. "I understand nothing of this," she said. "I am wandering streets for over a week in one shoe. I walk miles and miles, then I arrive back at the place where he threw me in the stinking river. I cry and I cry and I cry like a baby. Then, I see ball of light in the dark. It moves, and I go too far into this stinking city. It takes me to your office, and I am here now in the back of your stinking car with this man with a hole in his head. How am I to understand this mad shit? Tell me!"

Atlas took a deep breath and looked out towards the Liffey, moving swiftly and fiercely, unlike the traffic.

"The police couldn't find any evidence against him—your boss," Atlas began. "They let him go because he had an alibi."

"But he took my life!" Drowned screamed. "He said he was drowning me like a dog because that was what I was. That I was of no use to him pregnant. I couldn't fight him off; he was too strong! He is a nasty, stinking bastard!"

Caliber .22 sat up taller. "Fuck, he sounds like a right bastard," he exclaimed, his anger rising. "What are you going to do to him, Captain Amazing?"

Atlas ignored him but was relieved that the female corpse was showing some real anger against her murderer. She would need that when she and Roland became reacquainted.

He could sense his anger rising, too. There was nothing he hated more than men who hurt women and children. He felt a burst of excitement, the adrenaline coursing through his veins. He loved to make bad bastards pay.

The humming from the device on the passenger seat suddenly became louder and more frequent.

"Drowned, this is your chance for revenge," Atlas explained, turning a corner into an alleyway strewn with rubbish and overflowing bins. The whirr of a fan thundered above their heads.

"He will murder again!" he shouted as the humming became more urgent. "He does not value life in any way. He sees humans as nothing more than animals to use and abuse. He sold your body to strangers and discarded you when you became pregnant and useless to him. He's a monster."

The dull thump of rave music from a nearby club joined the din of the fans. The morning sunshine hadn't yet reached this place. Atlas slowed the car to a stop, the Quaesitor now chirping urgently like an alarm from the passenger seat.

"This was not your destiny," yelled Atlas over the din. "Your destiny was to raise your son in Moscow and live a long and happy life. This man robbed you of that."

"Bastard," Drowned cried out. "*Mʊ'dak* (asshole)! He robbed me of life! He robbed my baby of a life!"

Atlas slammed on the brakes and turned to face her in the back seat.

"I will bind your soul to his, Drowned," he shouted over the sound of the Quaesitor, now squealing at an ear-splitting level. "And when I do, you must steal his sleep and his sanity. You must make him doubt himself, fill his every moment with your deathly cries, take away every joy he has in life, torment him, torture him, haunt his dreams, and reside in his nightmares. Make him pay for what he did to you and your baby. Life for life."

Atlas looked out of his car, his eyes darting from one door to another in the alley, then back to the Quaesitor, before finally returning to Drowned.

"You must strip him of everything and drag his soul to the gates of Hell. For it is only then that you and your child will receive the gift of Heaven and be free. Now stay here and let me do my work, and I will call you when I'm ready."

The Quaesitor rose to a crescendo and emitted a single, excruciating tone as Atlas threw open his car door, immediately hit by the pungent stench of rotting food from the bins. He stood waiting as a door was flung open, and a man landed face-first in a rancid puddle at his feet. The Quaesitor had never failed him, not once. Atlas kissed the pendant around his neck, whispered a prayer, and bounded towards the man.

"Roland?" shouted Atlas as he neared him. "Roland, is that you?"

He was a short, round, greasy bald man with an unshaven face and rotten teeth, complemented by yellow fingers with black fingernails. He was wearing red flannel trousers stained from crotch to ankle and a disgusting t-shirt that failed to cover a hairy belly that hung low over his waistband. He reeked of body odor.

Roland staggered to his feet and squinted at Atlas. "Who the fuck wants to know?" he slurred.

Atlas grabbed him, pinning him to the wall by the throat. "The name's Bishop, Roland. Atlas Bishop and I have some unfinished business that we need to resolve."

Roland struggled to free himself, but Atlas's iron grip was solid. "What do you want? A woman?" he gasped. "I have plenty of those. Cheap whores, cheap prices for a good time. I'll get you a good one."

Atlas released his grip on Roland's throat and punched him hard in the stomach. The fat man doubled over in pain before Atlas caught him with an uppercut, splattering his nose all over his face. As he tried to stagger away, Atlas grabbed him with both hands and threw him against the wall, crushing his chest with his arms.

"I want to talk about a woman, yes," said Atlas, twisting his thumb into Roland's eye. The other man roared in pain but could not escape Atlas's grip. Blood poured from his nose and down the back of his throat, causing him to choke. Atlas leaned in so he could whisper into Roland's ear. "A woman you murdered like a dog. I fucking hate men who hurt women. You're going to pay for what you did to her, you waste of oxygen."

He grabbed Roland's testicles and twisted them as hard as he could. Roland roared, then whimpered, as agony overtook his capacity for screaming.

"You know what I always find with these men who hurt women?" Atlas asked calmly as he twisted some more. "That they have no balls."

Atlas, seeing Roland gag, let go and moved backward just in time to miss the spray of vomit from his victim's mouth, all color drained from Roland's face.

"Look at you," Atlas sneered, slapping him hard on the side of the head. "You are a sad and pathetic bastard. You disgust me. You will pay dearly for what you have done. Life for life."

He pulled a package from his inside pocket. "I take it you know Agneska Avenkov?" he asked as Roland groaned in pain.

"Awh!" spat Roland, through blood and vomit. "You're a cop! I told you pigs everything I know. I don't know no slut called Agneska. Dead or not. Nothing to do with me. She probably slipped and fell into the water, the stupid bitch."

Atlas kicked Roland hard between his legs, causing him to collapse in a heap on the ground, where he writhed in agony, intermittently crying and gagging.

Atlas rolled a cloth out onto the hood of his car. He saw Drowned inside, waving her hands to the heavens and screaming in Russian. Caliber .22 sat with his arms folded beside her. She was almost ready.

He started the car and backed out of the alley, leaving the sorry sight of Roland behind. One more customer to sort out, and then he could go and find that bastard who called himself his father.

CHAPTER FOUR

The sun bounced off Varie's blonde hair like it originated from there. She was slightly ahead of Atlas on the path. He touched her shoulder, and she turned to face him, her piercing green eyes fixed fiercely on his. She looked at him lovingly. He liked that.

"Atlas," she murmured, and he admired her lips, teeth, and tongue navigating his name.

"Yeah?" he replied, moving closer. He wanted to kiss those lips so badly. She felt like home.

"At," she repeated.

"Yeah?"

"Atlas! Wake up, for God's sweet sake!" she screeched.

He pulled back and looked at her. She sounded strange.

"At, you really have to stop drinking yourself into a coma with that bloody whiskey!" she shrieked. "If I've told you once, I've told you a thousand times: those damn spirits you drink like water will be the death of you!"

Confused and disorientated, he opened his eyes to see his mother's ghost leaning over him in the gloom.

"Bloody hell, Ma, can I not have some privacy?" he grumbled, pulling the coat he had used as a blanket up to his neck. "You scared the life out of me there. If I want to fall asleep drunk on my own sofa. I have every right to."

"Get up and go to bed, son," she scolded, ignoring his protestations. "You'll get a hump on your back lying there like that. Drunk. Again."

He looked at his mother's face: her skin so pallid and blue; her eyes sunken, dark and sad, yet still so beautiful. Her light had been fading consistently over the last two years to the point where she barely glowed at all now.

She had once been a fierce working-class Dublin woman who would have taken anyone's head clean off their shoulders for giving her cheek, but he was her favorite boy, and she loved him fiercely: she had always told him that. She had a voice that could raise the birds from the trees in alarm but was still so soft when she tucked him into bed at night. She could be cross—there was no doubt about that—and stern when he did wrong, but he knew without a shadow of a doubt that she loved him.

It had always been her and him together, and they only had each other, until she was taken away from him.

As he groggily sat up, he caught glimpses of her in blue light still flashing from the television he had fallen asleep watching. She was wearing the same sunshine yellow dress she had died in, the one she was wearing the evening her husband—his father—had stabbed her in their kitchen as they sat down to dinner. A dark, circular bloodstain now covered the front of her favorite dress, and when she first arrived back with him, he would often have found her in the kitchen, panic-stricken and looking for bleach to clean it with. It never worked, and he knew she hated that. She had always taken so much care with her appearance—fixing her hair and hiding her bruises—and now she was forced to walk around with a bloodstained dress and the evidence of his father's brutality forever on show. No one could see it or her but him, of course, but she still felt it.

She flopped down into her armchair, the one she had claimed as her own when she had come home from the hospital with him after the accident six years ago. The one she had sat on every night since, just staring into the darkness until the sun came up. She had stopped weeping a few years ago, thankfully.

"I see you have a new friend," she said softly, nodding at the other sofa. Atlas looked over to see Caliber .22 slouching on his couch like he owned the place.

Atlas rolled his eyes. "I *had* forgotten about him," he grumbled. "I tried all day to find his killer, but to no avail. I got nothing. I really hope he isn't going to stick around."

"No offense," he added, looking at the corpse.

"None taken," Caliber .22 retorted, stony-faced. "I hope you don't think this is fun for me either, dickhead."

"It's hard, son," Atlas's mother said gently to Caliber .22 "It's such a big change in your life. You know, your death."

"Yeah, you don't say, Missus," he snarked, sitting up and putting what was left of his head in his hands.

"You'll get used to it," she said, looking from him to her son, concerned. "Are you feeling low?"

"Am I feeling low?" he gasped incredulously, looking from Ma to Atlas and back to Ma again. "Low, like? Am I depressed, you mean? Are you fucking serious? I have actually been murdered, love. I'll never see my family again, and I'm sitting here with some kind of freak who talks to the dead and his dead ma. I'd say 'low' is a serious understatement at this juncture, Missus, no harm to you."

Atlas snapped. "Who are you calling a weirdo? And don't speak to my ma like that."

"I actually said freak," the corpse shot back "And *you* is who I am talking about."

Atlas rubbed his eyes. He was pretty sick of this shit. Day in and day out. All of it. It was relentless, and he was very, very tired.

"I want to go to my funeral," announced Caliber .22 announced suddenly.

Atlas looked at him in amazement. The guy was actually serious. "No, absolutely not. No. That is definitely not a good idea."

"Why not?" Caliber .22 demanded.

Atlas didn't actually have an answer for that because, generally, the dead didn't hang around long enough to see their funerals. The more he thought about it, he didn't particularly want to watch dead people crying and wailing at their own funerals. It wasn't his scene. All that unbridled emotion flying around made him seriously anxious. He reached for the elastic band he wore around his wrist, pulled it, and let it snap against his skin. He felt sick just thinking about it and fished a stomach tablet out of his trouser pocket.

"Because I don't want to take you," he heard himself saying irritably.

"Atlas!" his mother said sharply. "This young man wants to go to his own funeral. He has been through a lot in the last few days. Do you know what it's like to be murdered? No, you don't. We do. You will take him."

"No, Ma. I won't." His stomach was churning now.

"You will," she warned ominously, in a familiar tone he remembered from his youth, the authoritative one that meant she meant business. It was almost menacing, particularly when it was paired with the stare. He saw a flash of the old her. "You will, son, and you will be happy about it or else you'll have me to deal with."

"Happy about it?" he laughed, but his mother's stare wiped the smile straight from his face. "Oh, for God's sake," he said, exasperated. "You two will be the death of me. I'm going to bed."

"I'll wake you at 9:00 am, son, for the funeral," said Ma, the softness returning to her voice along with the smile. "Goodnight, son; that's a good boy."

Atlas collapsed on top of his bed, the taste of whiskey and stomach acid still festering in his mouth. He was asleep within two minutes.

The funeral was in a small church overlooking the sea, just outside Dublin. Atlas and Caliber .22 arrived before the funeral cortege.

They sat silently in one of the back pews as soft organ music wafted upward and evaporated into the rafters. Caliber .22 had wanted to go up to the front where his family would be, but Atlas said it was here or nowhere. He had a banging headache, an insatiable thirst, and serious fatigue and wasn't willing to deal with the dramatics that would no doubt ensue when the dead man saw his grieving loved ones.

"There's not that many people here," said Caliber .22, deflated. "I thought there would have been more people here. I was a young man taken down in my prime; you'd have thought people would have turned out for me."

An older woman sat down beside them, took off her leather gloves, and dabbed her eyes with a tissue. "They are bringing him in now," she said to Atlas. "Poor fella."

Atlas nodded sympathetically. The woman sobbed into her tissue.

"Who the hell is she?" Caliber .22 said, pointing a thumb at her. "Who is this woman? I don't even know her! Why is she crying? Listen, I think we might be at the wrong funeral. It mustn't be me; I don't recognize anyone here. Well, there are a few up front I know. Marty from the bar, there's Bottler, and Danny from the gym. Oh, there's John and Anne, but I think those two go to every funeral. It's like a day out for them; they're only here for the sandwiches and booze after the burial."

"Shhhh, now," whispered Atlas.

The woman looked at him quizzically.

"Did you know him long?" she asked, rummaging about in her handbag for, presumably, more tissues. "The poor man."

"Not long," replied Atlas somberly, looking at Caliber .22, who was scanning the woman's face for even a hint of recognition. "Just recently, really. Did you know him well?" he asked, attempting to engage in polite conversation.

She looked up from her bag. "No, I didn't know him at all. I just love a good funeral," she said, flipping open a compact mirror and checking her make-up. "It's a good place to meet sad, single men." She gave Atlas a sly wink that turned his blood to slush.

The corpse lost it and dramatically threw his arms in the air.

"What the hell? Are you serious?" he shouted in the woman's face. The sound bounced off every wall in the chapel, but Atlas knew only he could hear it.

He turned to face the front of the church as Caliber .22 stood up and roared. "Who here even knows me? What kind of funeral is this?" He put an icy hand on Atlas's shoulder before continuing his tirade. "No, I definitely think we're at the wrong funeral. This one is packed with hangers-on, people only interested in the sandwiches afterward, and old tramps like this doll here looking to get off with sad, desperate men. Let's get out of here."

Just then, the organ piped up, and the congregation stood as one. The doors opened, and a French bulldog wandered down the aisle, tongue hanging from its drooling mouth. "Awh Jeez naw—it's Roger, look!" wailed Caliber .22. "My dog! He never left my side, ever. He was my best friend. I was walking him when I was shot. Roger!"

The corpse went suddenly silent and watched aghast as the wooden box containing his earthly body was carried up the aisle by four solemn men. Atlas had a sure, sinking feeling it wouldn't be long until things went very swiftly downhill.

"Natalie!" Calibre .22 shouted when his partner came into view. "Rory!" He clambered across the pew to stand in front of them. "It's me!" he called out. "I'm here! Don't cry! Don't cry, Rory. Daddy's here. It's okay. *I'm* okay."

But his hands could not touch them, and they couldn't hear his reassurances. They just walked slowly on towards the altar, with the bizarre sight of Caliber .22 running alongside them, shouting that he was there, that he loved them, that he was right there, and could they not see him?

Atlas thought it best to just let him get on with it and get all of the emotion out of his system.

As the casket was placed at the altar and the family filed slowly into their seats, Atlas looked at the dead man's crestfallen face.

Yeah, he thought. *Things are about to go off.*

Caliber .22 stared hard at his closed casket, then his family, then Atlas before letting out an almighty, animalistic roar.

That'll be the denial, thought Atlas.

He grimaced and put his fingers in his ears.

"You alright?" said the old lady sitting beside him as the shouting at the front of the church intensified.

"Sorry, what?" asked Atlas, rather too loudly. He could hear nothing except Caliber .22's howling. "He's just so bloody loud, and I have a banging headache."

The woman looked alarmed, and mourners turned around and glared at him in disgust.

"Sorry," he whispered, gesturing with his hands to those in front of him. "I'm sorry... I'm a bit deaf."

Caliber .22 was now on his knees, hugging his own casket, wailing at the top of his voice, and crying loudly.

That will be the grief, thought Atlas. The wails became louder and louder, more dramatic in fashion. Theatrical almost.

"Awh, Christ, give me patience!" groaned Atlas, turning heads again. He formed his hands into a prayer and looked up to the ceiling until they went back to their own business.

He then excused himself, asking the older lady to let him pass as he needed to get out. She placed her hand on his bottom as he navigated his way over her handbag and coat on the ground. He flipped her lecherous hand away. He needed a cigarette badly. He had told his mother this was going to be a nightmare, but no one ever listened to him.

There was no point staying in the church, as there was no way he could have gone up and fetched Caliber .22 without looking like he was a crazy person. He would have to wait until it was all over and the corpse had worn himself out. Until then, Atlas sat on a low wall in the graveyard and smoked three cigarettes, one after the other.

An old man in a heavy tweed jacket sat smoking a pipe at the end of the wall. He was all beard with knotted hands and kind eyes. He looked like an old fisherman, Atlas thought. Wise and calm. They nodded at one another, and Atlas heard him say something about the weather. He didn't quite catch the old man's words, whether he was raving about it or complaining, so he answered in a typical Irish generic fashion, which covered all the bases. "Awk sure, I know."

They sat in silence for another few minutes before the old man spoke again. "Terrible business about that cinema," he said, louder this time.

Atlas inhaled his cigarette enthusiastically, pulling the smoke deep into his lungs. "What's that?" he said. "What cinema?"

The old man's eyes widened. He was clearly delighted he had found someone who hadn't heard the news. "The cinema in Bray. Last night. Didn't you hear about it?"

Atlas exhaled and shook his head gently. "I haven't, no," he said, hoping against hope that this wasn't some long and boring story that Irish folk loved to tell about happenings no one was interested in, involving people no one knew.

The old man shuffled up a bit along the wall, and Atlas was hit with the aroma of whiskey and pipe smoke that instantly caused a fresh wave of his hangover to wash over him.

"Well," the old man began, and Atlas just knew that from the tone of that single word, this was indeed a man who loved to drag a story out. "My nephew works in the bar across the road from the cinema, you see. The Plaza, it's called. The bar, not the cinema. He's nineteen years old and on a year's break from university. He's doing biomedical science. It's tough enough going, but he wants to be a pharmacist or something."

Atlas stared hard at the man, his expression no doubt relaying that he would like the story to move at a faster pace, with the more important details at the forefront.

The old man sat up straighter.

"Anyway," he continued, "James, that's his name, said that the police were called for the 10:00 pm show at the cinema. It was Terminator or some romance film or an action one; I can't remember the name now. I think there might have been a big monster in it. You know what the young people are like with their films, especially those monster ones. They are mad about them. What was it called, now?"

Atlas turned his head away and rolled his eyes, wondering if he would be better inside watching the amateur dramatics of his newly dead friend.

"So, there were about fifteen couples in there, and they all watching the film, whatever it was called. And then they all started fighting with one another. All of them. Punching and scratching and biting. Fighting with each other, fighting with other couples, fighting with the staff, the staff fighting one another. A big brawl, just. Police were called, and a couple of ambulances too, but they all fought with the police too, even the women. It spilled out onto the street, them all beating the hell out of one another. All of them were arrested, even the staff. That's mad, isn't it?"

Atlas nodded his head. It was strange, for sure. He put his cigarette out with his shoe, and the pair sat in silence, looking out over the church car park and the field beyond. Atlas wondered what would make thirty complete strangers attack one another in a cinema of all places. He recalled a documentary he had watched one time about subliminal messages in films, but that was to encourage people to smoke cigarettes, not try to kill one another.

He was enjoying the silence. The only distractions were the man sucking intermittently on his pipe and a seagull squawking overhead. He closed his eyes and breathed in deeply through his nostrils, feeling the calm descend on him again after having watched Caliber .22's meltdown in the church. He lifted his head to the sky. The sun's rays had finally broken through the clouds, and its light caressed his face. It felt good.

"Godzilla!" shouted the old man urgently, making Atlas jump.

"Jesus Christ!" gasped Atlas and dropped his cigarette.

"That's what it was called," exclaimed the old man triumphantly. "The film they were watching before all hell broke loose. It was Godzilla."

Atlas looked at him as he rose to his feet, smiled, and shuffled back toward the church. He looked forlornly at his still-smoking cigarette lying in the dirt and rummaged in his pocket for another one.

"Do you know my Daddy?" asked a little voice beside him.

He was shocked to see a lad of around eight standing at the wall. He hadn't even noticed him come over. It was Rory, Caliber .22's son. He recognized him as the hysterical child from the newspaper and from his dead father dancing around him, trying to comfort him as he had walked beside his casket in the church.

"I do, yeah," replied Atlas. "I mean, yeah. Yeah, I did."

"Were you best friends?" he inquired in the way only a child can.

"Um... I suppose, maybe we might have been, perhaps," said Atlas. He didn't want to tell the little guy he thought his dad was the most annoying corpse he ever had the misfortune to meet, that even the very sound of his breathing made him murderous, that his big stupid head made him want to puke, and those judgemental, bloodshot eyes made him want to lash out.

The little boy made him uncomfortable. He really didn't like knowing client's stories, seeing their lives and the devastation left in the wake of their passing. He never met their families; that was just too much. Seeing that kind of thing every day would wear you down. All that terror, horror, and heartache would drive a man mad. He had put up an emotional barrier like Father Jack had advised, but the little guy in front of him was presently knocking on it with his chubby little hand, and Atlas didn't like it one bit.

"Should you not be inside, boy?" he asked him. The child was making him increasingly nervous. He was around the age he had been when his own mother had died.

The little boy glanced at the church and shook his head. He looked so small and innocent.

Atlas took out another cigarette and lit it, exhaling loudly into the crisp morning air. He knew this was going to be a bad idea, bringing a corpse to his own funeral. Didn't he say it was going to be a bad idea? But neither of them would listen. Now, all Atlas could hear was Caliber .22 screaming and shouting from the church like a banshee.

The little boy began to sob quietly, and Atlas winced, looking around desperately for other adults to deal with the situation. There were none to be seen.

He got up from the wall and stood near the child. Moving his hand to hover over the child's shoulder, he awkwardly tapped it with two fingers and muttered, "There, there now."

The little boy suddenly embraced him with both arms, held on tightly, and cried harder.

Atlas stood rigid for a moment, softened, flicked his cigarette away, and placed a hand on the sobbing child's head. "Rory, isn't it?"

The little boy looked up and nodded, tears rolling down his cheeks.

Atlas knew words were needed here. "Listen, Rory. I know you're, I suppose, sad." He took the boy gently by the shoulders and extracted himself from the child's grip. "These types of things will make you sad, for sure," he continued. "But your daddy is going to Heaven. I'll make sure of that, and he'll be able to look down on you throughout your life, watching you grow up to be a big, strong man."

The little boy shrugged off Atlas's hands. "I'm going to kill the man who killed my daddy," he said, a look of resolve hardening his small features. "That will make him proud."

"You don't need to do that, Rory," said Atlas. "You don't need to worry about that at all. Let me sort out that bad man. I promise you I will. He'll be sorry he crossed your daddy when I'm finished with him. He'll be really, really sorry. That I can guarantee."

The church door opened, and a man shouted the boy's name. Rory smiled and ran to him.

Atlas leaned back against the wall and watched the boy disappear back into the church. He had a strange feeling in his stomach, like butterflies or sadness. It might have been sympathy, but it had been so long since he had experienced it that he wasn't quite sure. It might have been a determination to do the right thing for the little boy. It also might have been the sausage sandwich he had eaten on the way here. He didn't like it, whatever it was, and shook his head to dislodge the feeling.

By the time the funeral cortege had reached the graveside, Caliber had expended all of his energy and was a broken man. He stood subdued at his own graveside as his partner and son wept, oblivious to his presence. Atlas watched the family cling to one another as mourner after mourner hugged them and mumbled empty words of comfort before leaving them alone on the hillside.

"Mammy, that man said he was going to kill the man who killed my Daddy," said Rory, tugging at his mother's coat and pointing toward Atlas. The woman he had heard Caliber .22 call Natalie turned to face him.

"What?" she asked. "What did you say?"

Atlas moved forward. He had forgotten that she couldn't see her dead partner, and it was just him and the grieving mother and son left in the graveyard. "No, no," said Atlas softly. "No, I'm not going to kill anyone. No, I was just talking to your little lad outside his daddy's funeral. I think he picked me up wrong."

"You said you would sort him out," said Rory obstinately. "The man who killed Daddy. You said you were going to make him very, very sorry he had crossed my daddy."

Natalie stared at Atlas. He could tell that she could not compute what was going on.

Caliber .22 poked Atlas in the shoulder.

"I need to tell her where the money is buried," he said. "Tell her I buried it beneath the window in the kitchen, in the flower beds."

"What?" said Atlas. "What money?"

"What are you talking about, money?" asked Natalie. "Who are you? Did you know..."

"Tell her!" shouted the corpse.

"Look, Natalie..." said Atlas.

"How do you know my name?" she interrupted. "How did you know our son's name? Do I know you?" She seemed afraid and clung to her son.

"I need you to listen to me, Natalie," Atlas said firmly. "Your husband, he told me something, and I need to tell you. There is some money buried he wants you to have. It's beneath the kitchen window. In the flower beds."

"Tell her it's in a blue sports bag," urged Caliber. "There's nearly a million euros in there."

"How much?" asked Atlas, turning to the corpse. "Where... where the hell did you get that much money?"

"It was a deal," mumbled Caliber. "I am Morrison's accountant. Well, I was his accountant, I suppose, given the circumstances. He's probably got someone else by this stage. We were making a deal with another gang over drugs, and I was to give them the money in the bag. But I stole it instead and told Morrison that they had robbed me. He believed me at first, but I guess..."

"What the fuck?" shouted Atlas. "Are you stupid? No, don't even answer that. Jesus Christ, what were you thinking?"

Natalie looked at Atlas in horror. She frantically scanned the graveyard, terrified, clasping her son to her body to protect him from this obvious madman.

"Who are you talking to?" she demanded. "Is there something wrong with you? Are you sick or something? Are you mad? Look, I really don't need this, today of all days. Please just go away and leave us alone."

"The money is in a blue sports bag, Natalie," Atlas said, calm again. "There is nearly a million euros in it."

Natalie glared at him like he was insane. "Now I know you're joking," she sneered. "You're sick. We don't have that kind of money. Look, this isn't funny. Why would you do this to me?"

Caliber .22 grabbed Atlas's arm. "Tell her I got it for her," he said. "Tell her I love her, and I want her to buy a new BMW with it and take Rory on a holiday. Tell her she can buy a house too if she wants."

Atlas stared at the dead man, unable to fathom the stupidity of stealing from Dublin's most notorious gangland leader.

"Do you realize what you've done?" he insisted, staring at the corpse. He knew as soon as the words had left his mouth that the dead man before him, with a hole in his forehead, probably did grasp the enormity of his actions.

"I just wanted a better life for us," he said sadly, looking at his partner. "I didn't want it to end like this. I just saw the money, it's more than I could ever dream of having in my life. We never had anything—we always struggled. I just wanted to be able to give my son a better life, so I told Morrison that they robbed me. He must have found out I was lying. I thought I could get away with it, go away somewhere, start again, be happy, and get away from this place. Now the funeral is over, he will be coming to get it back. I know I shouldn't have..."

Atlas grabbed Natalie by the arms. She stiffened immediately and started to scream. "Listen!" he hissed, stopping her scream in its tracks. "Listen very carefully to me. Go home and, if Morrison's men aren't already at your house, dig up the sports bag, take the child, and get as far away from here as possible. Start a new life somewhere else. Your husband stole that money from Morrison, and he will have no qualms about killing you and the boy to get it back."

Natalie whimpered while Rory clung to his mother's coat as Atlas released her. "I'm sorry," he said. "But you need to go, it's not safe here."

Natalie straightened herself and looked at Atlas. "What is going on? How do you know all this?" she whispered. "Who are you talking to? Is it him? Is he here?"

Atlas hated things like this. Why did people have to be so bloody emotional? All. The. Time. "Yes," he responded, exasperated. "He's here. He's there," he said, pointing to the gravestone.

"Can you tell him we love him," she asked, sobbing now. "Can you tell him that? That me and Rory love him? Can he hear me?"

Caliber .22 now had tears streaming down his deathly pale face.

"We love you, Stephen," she began. "Please...come back. I can't live without you." She turned to Atlas. "I don't care about the money. Tell him that. I will give it back, all of it. I just want him back. Can you bring him back?" she pleaded. "Can you make him come back? My boy needs his daddy."

"Daddy?" sobbed Rory. "Please come back to us. I don't want to have no daddy."

"I can't come back," Caliber .22 bawled. "I wish I could. I don't want to leave you. I love you, and I'm so sorry."

Atlas stepped back from the scene for a moment. The emotion was too much, and he thought he might puke. People loving one another and showing affection made him feel uncomfortable and dizzy. He took a sharp intake of breath to steady himself. Sadness was an emotion that didn't sit easily with him. Anger, however—he could deal with that. Anger was a more comfortable, safer emotion for him. He spied a stone on the path in front of him, and he kicked it hard, sending it flying across the graves and smashing a flower vase.

"For fuck's sake," he raged as if it was someone else's fault. This day was just too much for him. He walked away for a while, lit a cigarette, and turned back to watch the grieving woman and her son sob while an invisible dead man tried to comfort them. It was tragic.

"Natalie," Atlas called to her after a time. "Go home. Get your stuff. Get out. Never, ever come back. Tell his parents, tell his brothers. Nobody is safe from them. Your husband stole drug money from one of Dublin's most notorious and dangerous criminal gangs. You can't do that and live. These people are not to be messed with. They will kill you all. Go."

"Thank you," she mouthed and hurried away, clasping Rory's hand in hers. "Thank you so much."

The pair hurried down the hill, stopping only once to glance longingly back at the grave before disappearing.

Calibre sat with what was left of his head in his hands by the freshly dug grave.

"Come on, you," Atlas called to him. "You menace. I fucking told you this was a bad idea. Let's go home."

CHAPTER FIVE

"What is wrong with this bloody thing?" shouted Atlas, shaking the Quaesitor enthusiastically. "It's completely dead! It's totally useless!"

Atlas looked at the corpse standing in front of him in his office and laughed softly. "Sorry, no offense," he said. "I didn't mean..."

"No skin off my nose," said Caliber .22. He walked over to the window in a huff and morosely gazed out of it. He had been in a mood ever since the graveyard and was totally sullen, depressed even. There was no way the soul binding would work like this.

Atlas's mother was wrong and he had been right. Caliber shouldn't have gone to his own funeral. But Ma wouldn't hear of it. She and the corpse would sit up at night talking. Atlas could hear them from his bedroom. The corpse would cry, and his mother would try to soothe him. This had been going on for over a week now. He hoped he wasn't going to be stuck with Caliber .22 long term; the guy was no fun at all and was always there, hanging over Atlas like a black cloud.

"Come over here and put your hand on this again," he called to the dead man. "One more go."

Head down, Caliber .22 dragged his feet across the carpet and held out his hand. Atlas placed the Quaesitor in it.

"Nothing," muttered Atlas.

"Maybe you need to change its batteries," said Caliber.

Atlas snorted. "It doesn't run on batteries, friend," he said, examining the tiny instrument.

"Friend?" Caliber looked up, smiling slightly for the first time in a week.

Atlas looked away, embarrassed. "It's just a figure of speech," he said awkwardly. "I don't mean we're friends. How can we be friends? You're dead, and I'm, well, I'm not."

"Jesus, you're a bundle of laughs," said the corpse. "From what I can see, you don't have any actual living friends. From here, you look like a bit of a sad loner."

Atlas could feel his anger rising. His stomach was beginning to churn, and he could feel his chest tighten. "What are you talking about?" he snapped, walking toward his desk. "I do have friends, and you're one to talk about being miserable. You've been moping around after me all week."

"I'm fucking dead!" shouted the corpse. "You horrible bastard!"

Atlas pulled open the drawer and screwed off the top of his whiskey.

Caliber .22 looked like he might cry. "Oh, there you go! Straight for the whiskey," he accused. "You're going to drink yourself to death, Atlas Bishop, and maybe we can be friends."

"Shut up!" shouted Atlas. "You sound like Ma, and you're giving me a sore head. Sit down and shut up so I can figure out a way to get rid of you."

Caliber's bottom lip trembled, and Atlas rolled his eyes. He could not deal with people's emotions, living or dead. Why did they have to throw them all around the place, disturbing everyone else's peace and making everyone else feel bad?

Atlas swung his chair around to face the window and took four deep breaths—in through his nose and out through his mouth, as his psychotherapist had advised him. He chased that exercise with three gulps of whiskey—in through his mouth. He closed his eyes and waited for the amber liquid to take the edge off.

His cell phone vibrated in his jacket pocket. Pulling the phone out, he saw Varie's name blaze across the screen. He swung back around to his desk, sitting up taller in his chair.

"Ha! There you go, asshole, an alive friend," he gloated, shaking his phone at Caliber .22. He let it ring another few times before answering, not wanting to seem too eager.

"Hey, Varie," said Atlas, with a self-satisfied air. "How are things?"

"I'm good, At. I hope you're okay," came Varie's reply.

Atlas listened, loving how his name sounded in her voice. He had loved her since he was twenty-one years old and had never stopped, even when she had. They had been together for ten years. Those years hadn't been all sunshine, but every fiber of his being jarred ceaselessly when away from her. She had wanted to get married, but he had been afraid of them ending up like his parents. He had bought a ring but had never found the right moment to ask her. The ring was still in his bedside drawer, taunting him every morning when he opened the drawer to search for painkillers to kill his constant headaches.

She was the only one who understood him. He had felt happy with her for the first and last time in his life thus far. He hated himself for not having been the man she needed.

"Yeah, things are good here," he said. "I'm still having trouble shifting Caliber .22, but I'll hopefully get him sorted soon. Ma and him are best friends now, swapping hair and makeup tips, gossip, and the like."

Varie laughed. "Well, that's not so bad they're friends," she said. "Have you told her about the sighting of your Dad?"

"I haven't told her anything yet, no," he replied. "I want to wait for confirmation. I have Elsa on the case, inquiring about me in all the local hospices. There can't be too many old Dubliners in that part of the world. He'll have given a false name, too, no doubt. But as soon as I know for sure, I'll go."

Atlas conjured her face in his head, the way she always fidgeted with something when she spoke. She discussed the recent spike in the city's crime statistics, about large groups of people fighting for no apparent reason, like in the pub outside Dublin and the cinema in Bray, and how all of those involved had no recollection of events when later questioned by detectives. She asked if he had heard anything on his alternative networks. He said he hadn't heard anything more than what she'd just told him.

"Only that some old guy, a fisherman, told me about the cinema in Bray, just," he said, recalling the conversation at Caliber .22's funeral.

"A fisherman?" she asked, laughing. "How very random."

"Yeah, never mind," he had replied. He noticed how his voice changed when he spoke to her. It was calm, gentle. She was his peace, and he had fucked it up.

"Yeah, the fisherman told me about the fight at the cinema, and I read about the brawl at some party outside Dublin in the paper while I was sitting in St. Stephen's Green one morning last week."

Varie sighed softly. "Are the anxiety attacks bad these days, Atlas?" she said. "Sitting in the park helps, but have you been back to the doctor?"

"No, I'm okay. The doctor just tells me to change my lifestyle, but I have a great lifestyle."

Atlas listened as Varie softly lectured him about looking after himself, about not getting too stressed, and laying off the whiskey because it wasn't good for him. She cared for him. She just didn't love him enough not to be married to someone else.

"I know," he conceded. She was right. Everyone said it, but when Varie did, it was different. "I will, Varie," he said. "Yeah, I promise. What have you got for me?"

"The police up in Belfast have a case they can't crack," she said, returning to business mode. "A young man was killed by paramilitaries outside his house, in front of his mother. The whole thing was witnessed by around thirty people in the street. But you know how these things go, not one of them will make a statement, they are too scared."

"Belfast?" he asked. "Yeah, I remember seeing it on the news. Terrible business. The fella wasn't out of his teenage years, wasn't he?"

"Yeah," she sighed. "He was only a boy, nineteen years old. The dogs on the street know who it is, but the cops can get nothing concrete to get him on. It's sad, all these years after the peace deal up there, these terror groups still have such a grip on communities. Witnesses have been threatened, and nobody will nail this guy. It's very frustrating. But I know you'll do it justice."

Atlas leaned back in his chair. "I'll see what I can do, but I can't promise anything. My equipment is playing up."

"Yeah, that's what you say to all the girls, Atlas," she quipped.

He laughed out loud. A sudden flash of her face came into his head, sweaty and flushed, underneath him on the bed.

It was always awkward ending their conversations, and he hung up reluctantly. Her voice always made him mourn for how things used to be. He had messed everything up by being a nightmare to live with by refusing to deal with his demons. She said he wasn't "emotionally available" and that his head would continue to be fucked up, that he would keep hurting everyone around him if he didn't grow a set and deal with his past. At least, he thought that was what she had shouted at him when she had slammed his front door for the last time six summers ago, calling him a dickhead through his letterbox. That had been clear enough through her sobs. He had definitely heard that.

They had talked it over many times since, and every time, Atlas felt like she had taken his heart from his chest and kicked it around the room like a football. The conversations around her new boyfriend, who had become her fiancé, and then her husband were especially difficult. He just wanted her back; she just wanted a quiet life with a man who didn't constantly fight with the shadows in his head.

"Fancy a trip to Belfast, Caliber?" asked Atlas.

The corpse sat up. "Aye, I suppose I've nothing else to do."

"That's the spirit," said Atlas, grabbing his phone. "Let's go."

The sun was setting in the car's rear-view mirror as they left Dublin. Caliber .22 looked out the passenger window, staring glumly at nothing in particular.

"Are you alright?" asked Atlas. He inquired, not because he cared, but because he didn't want to sit the entire way to Belfast in silence.

"What do you care?" the corpse replied gruffly. "I'm just an inconvenience to you. You can't wait to get rid of me. And also, am I alright? Are your eyes working? I've a hole in my head. I'm dead. I completely fucked up my life and the lives of my family. I'm as far from alright as any person could possibly be. So it's kind of a stupid question."

Atlas looked over at him. He was a sorry sight. Blood-stained shirt. Hole in his head. His color was fading, and he was starting to really look dead. And dead miserable.

"Look, I'm sorry," said Atlas. "I have a very stressful job. It gets to me sometimes, and I have a short fuse. I have my own problems, too, you know."

He frowned at the corpse but, seeing his solemn demeanor, softened his expression and attempted a different approach.

"I spoke to your boy outside your funeral," he said. "He seems like a nice lad. I would be, I suppose, sad to leave him too. It must be tough. I didn't mean to hurt your feelings."

"Okay," said the corpse, sighing. "I suppose I didn't mean to say you have no friends, either. Or that you are a dickhead. Or a weirdo. Or a freak, or a sad bastard, or a..."

"Yeah, alright," interrupted Atlas irritably. "Look, you're probably right. My job consumes a lot of my time. People, dead people, come into my life, and I have to get them sorted. It's just a job to me. It has to be. I make very few connections. I live with my dead Ma, and there aren't a lot of people who would get that. It probably makes me a bit of a dickhead at times. And not a lot of people would understand my life and the mad stuff that goes on, let alone tolerate it."

"Except Varie. She gets it, doesn't she? What's the story between you two?"

"Ah, it's a long story. A long and probably boring story," Atlas demurred.

"Am I going anywhere, mate?" asked Caliber, shifting in his seat. "Shoot."

Atlas gripped the steering wheel and looked ahead at the road. He didn't like sharing anything about himself. It was too much like letting his guard down, like giving people power over him. But the corpse would be gone in a few days, so he supposed it didn't really matter.

"She and I met when we were at university," he began reluctantly. "We were both at Trinity College studying criminology. We met and became friends in our last year. I was in love with her completely from the first minute I met her. She made me feel..." he trailed off, looking at the corpse. He felt stupid.

He shoved his feelings of awkwardness down and continued. "Anyway, she was always a challenge, always just out of reach. We finally got together two summers after we graduated. We were together for ten years and joined the police together. We were going to get married. Well, she talked about getting married. I just kind of...well, I felt...I didn't want to... I was..."

"And how did you mess that one up?" asked the corpse.

"And why would you think it was me who messed it up?" snapped Atlas. "She left me. She walked out one day. Said I was like a brick wall and had no emotions, which is ridiculous. She said she couldn't handle my moods, that I was shut off from the world and running away from my trauma, so she couldn't unfold me. I told her she was talking shit, I was perfectly normal. I had, you know, emotions and stuff."

Caliber laughed. "You have the emotional range of a toaster. In fact, that is actually an insult to toasters. You have literally no emotions whatsoever. You get angry. But, apart from that, you actually are a brick wall. No feelings. Just cold. Ice cold."

"I'm not cold!" said Atlas, raising his voice. "I feel stuff. I feel angry right now, so fuck off!"

"See? Anger and nothing else. When was the last time you even cried?" asked the corpse.

Atlas knew, but he wasn't going to say. Instead, he glanced over at the patchwork fields out his window. The sun was dipping low beneath a mountain.

"Come on," said Caliber. "It's not a hard question."

Atlas lit up a cigarette. "Leave it now. Just stop. I don't want to talk to you anymore. No more talking until Belfast."

"No," replied Caliber .22, rather obstinately. "You need to talk about this. It will help you. Varie is right. You need to stop running away from your pain. After my daughter died, I went to counseling. It destroyed me, but it helped. It's good to talk. Talking about it makes you think about things differently. Come on, it will help you, honestly."

"I went to counseling," snapped Atlas. "It was a load of shit."

"Come on, Atlas, it will help you to talk." The corpse wasn't giving up.

"Help me?" Atlas sneered. "Help me how? Be more like you? Standing at your own grave crying like a big baby?"

"Stop being a hateful bastard, Atlas," said Caliber .22, turning away again. "Seriously, you really are such a dickhead! It's no wonder you have no friends. You just shove everyone away by being an asshole all the time. You can't help yourself."

Atlas exhaled his cigarette smoke dramatically. "The last time I cried I was under the kitchen table in my childhood home, alright?" Caliber nodded, and an uneasy silence hung between them until Atlas spoke again.

"Ma was lying on the floor beside me," he continued, looking straight ahead, "trying to breathe, gurgling, her blood all over the kitchen floor. Blood was coming from her mouth, and I was trying to wipe it away with my sleeve, but it just kept coming. My Da stabbed her with her bread knife—got her in the heart. She was looking at me with terror in her eyes, gasping for air, grabbing me like she was drowning, and then she just stopped. She just... stopped. Stopped gasping. Stopped reaching for me. It was just her eyes staring at me, dead, nothing. Total silence. I can still smell the gravy she had been making to have with dinner that had burnt to the bottom of the pan on the stove. I can still smell the iron from her blood, the shampoo from her hair. I cried then, alright? I was eight years old, and I haven't cried since. I can't cry; I literally cannot physically cry. There's something wrong with me. I feel nothing; I'm numb. Does that make you happy? Now shut up about it."

"That's rough, man," said Caliber. "That's rough for an eight-year-old to see."

"Yeah, it was. But it didn't affect me. I was totally fine afterward."

"Yeah, you are fine," said Caliber, smiling sympathetically. "You're perfectly fine. You are an alcoholic with an anger management problem who is afraid to show emotion or open up to anyone. You fly off the handle at a moment's notice and have to do deep breathing exercises—at least, that's what I think you're doing—to stop you from having panic attacks. It doesn't work because you have panic attacks every day and you shout in your sleep, did you know that? At the top of your voice, roaring like a fucking madman. You also speak to murdered people all day long and live with your dead mother, who you watched being murdered. But you're fine? Jesus Christ, Atlas. You are not fine. None of that is remotely fine."

Atlas snorted, putting his elbow on the car window and rubbing his forehead. "When you put it like that, you do make me sound like a weirdo," he said.

"Has your dead mother been with you since you were eight? The teenage years must have been awkward."

"No," said Atlas. "Just for the last six years. I suppose I went off the rails a bit when Varie and I split up. I hit the bottle hard and took a bit too many risks. I don't know why I'm telling you this."

"Keep going; you're on a roll," the corpse urged. "I'm telling you, it's good to talk. You'll feel better."

Atlas stared at him. "What are you, my counselor, now? This is weird. It feels like an episode of Oprah fucking Winfrey here. Let's change the subject. It makes me feel like shit talking about this stuff. I don't like it. This is why I don't like counseling. This shit right here."

"No," said Caliber. "It's good to chat; it lightens the burden. What else are we going to do? We've another hour on the road. Come on."

Atlas took another drag of his cigarette. "Jesus, this is ridiculous," he moaned. "Alright then, Oprah. I'll play your game."

He took a deep breath and began again. "I suppose back then, after Varie dumped me, I wanted to die, really. She had made everything in my life better, everything easier, lighter even. My life had been foster homes, juvenile detention centers, and fighting my way through school. I pulled myself up and got into university, got a job, and met Varie. She made the world softer. Everything was brighter, more colorful, and less scary. Less hostile. But the darkness was never far behind me, and no matter how hard or fast I tried to run to get away from it, at times, it swallowed me whole.

"I never had anyone to call my own, who loved me, until Varie. And no one since. So when she dumped me, it just affirmed every notion I had about being a worthless human being. I knew that everyone I ever loved would leave at some stage, either by themselves or taken by someone else. Because that is what happened every time.

"I crashed my car into a wall one night outside Dalkey, full speed. I can't remember the moments before it or if it was on purpose or not. But thinking back, it probably was. I wanted to die.

My life meant nothing to me. When they got me to the hospital, I was in really bad shape. I died on the operating table, and they brought me back, but when I woke up, Ma was standing at my bedside in the dress she died in. I told the doctors I could see her, that I could hear her talking to me. They said that it was because of the head injury I sustained. A hallucination. They gave me medication, but she didn't go away. She never left me after that.

"And that's when I met Gabriel. You know, the angel? He told me that I'd been given a second chance, but I had to work for it and help people find peace. People like you.

"When I left the hospital, I saw more murdered people. They would come to me at all hours of the day or night, asking for help. I'd wake up and they'd be at the end of my bed, just like standing there. It took me a while—and Gabriel and Ma nagging ceaselessly—to realize that it could be something good. It could be a gift, or a curse, or whatever you want to call it, and that I could help people, do something good.

"So I suppose, yes, all of that stuff makes me a bit of a dickhead at times," Atlas finished and sighed.

Caliber .22's eyes widened. "That's a really mad story there. I know I get mad about being dead and all, but I also know I had people who loved me in life. Your father being a bastard, your mother being taken from you, Varie walking away. No wonder you get pissed off sometimes."

"Yeah," said Atlas. "It can get a bit heavy to carry, but it's grand. It doesn't affect me that much. I just get on with things. I'm fine."

Caliber smiled, an oddly unnerving sight. "Do you feel a bit better sharing it?" he asked. "I always think it's better to get things off your chest, things that are bothering you. Things like that just eat you up from the inside if you don't let them out. I think you've done good work here; we've maybe even bonded a little. Do you feel a burden has lifted?"

Atlas gripped the steering wheel again, his face darkening. He had that poisonous feeling again, coming from his core. "No," he replied firmly. "What do you want me to do, fucking cry or something? That would make you happy, wouldn't it? Me sitting here sobbing like you. Then we can hug. What about that? Big hugs all around. Maybe I can tell you I love you, and you can say it back. You'll be going for Oprah's job next. You'd look great on the screen with a big hole in your head. Just shut up about it, alright?"

Caliber rolled his eyes and turned his head back to the window. "Honestly, Atlas, you're such a dickhead."

They traveled on, not speaking for the rest of the journey.

"We're here," Atlas said abruptly about an hour later, piercing the silence as Belfast's bright tapestry of mesmerizing, twinkling lights came into view. The moon hung round and heavy over Belfast Lough.

Atlas pulled over and took out his phone, searching for the article about the dead teenager's funeral. Dollops of rain hit the windshield as they sat in the shadow of the iconic Harland and Wolff gantry cranes. He looked out the window at the mammoth structures, their rustic hues of yellow and brown still bright in the night skyline over the city. They were the giants of this post-conflict city, having spent decades standing tall, weathering the elements, and looking down on a city emerging from the darkest days of violence and hatred.

The corpse didn't speak as Atlas took off again, navigating the dark and rainy streets. They passed rows and rows of terraced houses, the eyes of gunmen staring down at them from gable walls, a throwback from the Troubles era. They sped past other murals of smiling children painted on other walls—more friendly, colorful attempts to look to the future. People walked hurriedly through the streets, heads down and hunched over against the elements. Despite it having been twenty-five years since the paramilitary ceasefires, Atlas always thought Belfast's inhabitants looked strained, like some invisible force weighed them down. Maybe it wasn't them; perhaps it was because he was incapable of seeing the good in anything or anyone anymore and always gravitated toward the grim and the dark.

They drove over an ornate Victorian-style bridge, across the River Lagan that weaved like a ribbon of darkness beneath them, and into the city proper, through clusters of high-rise buildings standing tall like luminous sentinels, their windows aglow with a multitude of colors. They passed late-night revelers, arms around each other, singing, laughing, and shouting their way to the next pub. There was a vibrant energy pulsing through the heart of this city, Atlas mused. But there was always some asshole waiting in the wings to try to drag it back to the bad old days of death, darkness, and misery.

The rain poured down ceaselessly, only reinforcing Atlas's sour mood.

"How will you know where this guy is?" asked Caliber. "How will you find him?"

"Where would you have gone if you hadn't seen my light?" asked Atlas.

"I don't know. I probably would have followed my family," he replied. "Or the graveyard. It's weird. You kinda know you're dead, but you're not quite sure. Seeing your body in the ground is a dead giveaway, but you still think it's not real. It's been more than a week since this guy was killed. He probably went to his own funeral, too."

Atlas took his eyes from the road and looked at the corpse.

"Don't even say anything about that," warned Caliber. "Don't you dare say a fucking word, dickhead."

"I wasn't going to say anything," replied Atlas mildly. "I was just hoping you weren't going to cry again."

The dead man tutted, rolled his eyes, and sighed.

"Heartless bastard," he said. "And there was me thinking we had made some kind of breakthrough back there, with our heart to heart. I shouldn't have been so stupid."

Atlas started. "You tell anyone what I said, and I'll..."

"What?" asked the corpse, smiling. "Kill me?"

"Yeah," said Atlas. "And I'll do it right this time."

Caliber .22 snorted.

They approached a weathered, moss-covered stone arch that framed a vast cemetery. As they drove along its winding driveway, the car's headlights danced over ancient gravestones that rose like crooked teeth from the earth.

Perched atop the solitary hill, the headlights carved a sandstone church out of the darkness. Its spires stretched skyward, punctuating the heavens and meeting the rain before it reached the ground.

The headlights and the rain combined to make the stained glass windows shimmer.

Atlas switched off the engine, and the cloak of darkness returned. It was silent, except for the rain on the window and his tense breathing.

"What are we doing now?" asked Caliber nervously.

"We'll go to the grave first," Atlas replied. "We have to start somewhere."

In the darkness and pouring rain, the church and graveyard felt ominous and unfriendly. Atlas could see less than ten feet in front of him before the gloom consumed everything. As if in a concerted attempt at creating an utterly foreboding atmosphere, the wind howled bitterly outside the car's windows.

"Are you coming?" Atlas asked.

Caliber grimaced and peered up at the church spires.

"Don't tell me you're afraid of the dark?" said Atlas, turning to look at the corpse. "Wait. Are you really?"

"No," he replied defiantly. "I'm just going to sit here. I don't want to get wet. It's raining horribly out there."

"You're dead," said Atlas. "You have a hole in your head. You won't feel the rain."

Caliber reluctantly began to take off his seatbelt. "You always have to keep rubbing it in my face, don't you?" he snapped, swinging open the passenger side door. "You can't leave a dead man in peace, can you? You're always saying something horrid."

Atlas was already walking up the steps toward the church. The rain was harder here on the hill and the wind had picked up, roaring down the more modern graveyard behind the church towards them. Atlas checked the mammoth wooden doors, the brass handles freezing to the touch. He knew they would be locked.

He pulled up his collar against the wind and walked toward the graveyard, the corpse following along behind him, muttering under his breath.

"The fresh graves are somewhere up here," Atlas said, taking off at pace into the darkness. "There! I can see a big patch of undug grass: it'll be around there somewhere. Let's see if we can find him. Otherwise, it's back to his Mum's house, and that could be awkward."

He took off, jogging past the simple headstones, then along stone pathways between lines of larger, more elaborate headstones, under which the more affluent rested in the cold soil. He then traversed a baby graveyard in which teddy bears and flowers did their best to keep their heads up against the howling wind. They arrived at an area where mounds of fresh earth were settling over newly-occupied graves.

Atlas held his hand up and gestured for Caliber to stop. Up ahead, an unnatural blue light illuminated a newly erected gravestone.

"Wait," he said. "We don't want to spook him."

"Spook him?" said the corpse, barging past Atlas. "Are you serious? He's dead. I'm also dead. You're... I don't know what you are. But I think he'll be past the point of no return in that particular area."

Atlas caught up with Caliber, and together, they approached a man sitting with his head on his knees beside a freshly dug grave.

The young man was tall and well-built, his body honed by the gym. He had recently cut hair, short at the sides and a little wavy at the top, albeit drenched in the rain, a strong jaw, and a heavy brow. His snug purple hoodie lay open, revealing a once-white t-shirt that was now stained blood red.

"Hello," said Atlas softly, but the wind and the rain carried his voice away.

"Oi!" shouted Caliber, and the dead man looked up, startled.

"Don't be alarmed," shouted Atlas, pushing past Caliber again and walking toward the dead man. "My name is Atlas Bishop. I'm here to help you."

The dead man stood up quickly, his faded jeans also stained with blood. His stature exuded youthful confidence, yet beneath his casual attire was vulnerability, fear, and sadness. His face was bruised and looked sore. "Can you see me?" he shouted, staring earnestly at Atlas.

"Yes," roared Atlas, battling to be heard over the building wind. "I know what happened to you. You are no doubt afraid, confused, and angry."

Caliber poked Atlas in the arm. "Hey! How come you didn't say any of that to me?" he said. "You told me to fuck off!"

Atlas looked disapprovingly at him, then back to the other dead man. "I am a Soul Binder," he roared. "You are stuck. I want to find the man who did this to you, make him pay, and send you on to Heaven and peace. Is that okay?"

"Can you bring me back to life?" he asked, moving forward excitedly.

Atlas shook his head. Why did they always ask him that? "No," he replied. "I can't do that, but I can make the man who killed you suffer. Do you want him to suffer?"

"Yes, I do," said the dead man sadly, then more determination, "I do."

He walked nearer to them, and Atlas could see the wounds on his chest and neck, his collarbone shining in the blue light of the orb floating beside him. "You were hit with a shotgun blast, yes?"

"Oh, here we go!" sang Caliber .22, throwing his hands into the air.

"Yes," said the dead man in a thick Belfast accent. "Blew me right down my hallway like a bomb blast. And now my body is in the ground, down there, under all that soil."

He turned around and looked at his grave. "Just there, under all of that," he said, his voice growing quieter. "There's no air down there, no light or anything. It's, like, really dark. I'm probably getting eaten by worms or something."

"Okay, Shotgun," said Atlas, noticing the trauma in the young man's tone. "There are no worms. Your body is in a cozy casket, so nothing will be able to get in. Look, we want to help. Come with us."

"Where do you want to take me?" he asked.

"We are going to find the man who murdered you," said Atlas. "Come on; it'll be alright."

The rain was falling sideways now, hitting Atlas hard on the face as they began walking back down the hill toward the car.

The two dead men shook hands and exchanged introductions as Atlas walked on ahead, looking over Belfast's blanket of lights below. He hoped that he would be able to find the dead man's killer, as he wasn't keen on collecting corpses. He longed for the day when he wouldn't have one hanging around him at all. He might actually get five minutes of peace then. But for now, death was a constant companion.

He reached the car and opened the glove compartment, fishing out the Quaesitor. He looked to the heavens, murmuring a silent prayer that it would work this time.

"Hey, Shotgun," he called. "Come here and put your hand on this."

The dead man did what he was told. The Quaesitor lit up and Atlas breathed a sigh of relief as it emitted a slow, steady hum.

"Okay," said Atlas, his spirits rising. "Get in the car. This hopefully won't take long."

The trio tumbled into the car, and Atlas turned on the ignition. He was soaked through. He looked in his rear-view mirror at the young man's face. Although it was battered, bruised, and swollen, he could tell that he was, or had been, very young.

"How old are you, Shotgun?" he asked.

"I'm nineteen," he said solemnly. "Well, I was nineteen when I was living. I suppose I will always be nineteen now; is that how it works? Do I stay nineteen forever? Or do I still age, now that I'm..." He trailed off.

Atlas stared at him. There was no way this sad kid would be fit for the binding in his current state. He needed him to want revenge more than anything, that all-consuming desire to clamber onto his murderer's back and stay there until the bitter end.

"Who killed you?" asked Atlas. "Who did this to you?"

Shotgun looked down at his blood-stained shirt. "It was a gang of men who beat me up," he said. "They told people I was breaking into houses, but I never did that. I would never do that. I had a job: I'm a welder; I had my own money. I went out with one of their ex-girlfriends, but I didn't know she had been seeing him. She called it off with him a few weeks ago, and then we got together. I saw him in the bar, and he started a fight. I'm a boxer, see, so I can fight. I got the better of him—embarrassed him in front of the whole bar. He hated that, the skinny prick.

"The next night, they kicked in my ma's door, threw her on the ground and beat her, then beat me. Five or six of them. I got a few digs in, busted a few noses and heads, and pushed them back out the door. Nearly had them, too. And then this specky prick Jonny comes in with a shotgun and blows me down the hall. Last thing I remember is my back hitting the stairs and my ma screaming.

"I woke up in the hospital. Well, I didn't wake up, but I got up. Everyone was around my bed crying and wailing. My ma, she was making this noise; it was like an animal, almost. It was really scary. My family couldn't hear or see me, no matter how loud I shouted. I walked home and sat in the corner of my ma's living room during the wake. That was really weird, sitting there looking at myself in a casket, everyone in there gawking at me. And then I went to my own funeral. I never thought I'd do that. That was the worst bit. Very weird."

Atlas and Caliber shared a glance and looked back at Shotgun.

"People were coming in and telling my ma they were sorry.

People I hadn't seen in years, people I didn't even like. Some people I didn't even know!"

"That's rough, brother," Caliber interjected. "I know where you are coming from. I hear you."

Shotgun sighed. "And then I just stayed here, day and night for ages. What else could I do? And then you came. That's my story, I suppose. It's tragic, isn't it?"

Atlas nodded. "Right," he said. "What was the name of the prick who shot you?"

Time to poke the bear.

"His name is Jonny Hallahan," said Shotgun. "He's one of the bosses of a paramilitary gang near my housing estate."

Atlas rolled the car across the gravel driveway. "Well, let's go and get him then," he said.

The young man laughed softly. "I don't think you understand," he said. "He's untouchable. You'll not be able to get anywhere near him. He's dangerous, and he's always got a crowd of henchmen around him with guns. They're thugs. He doesn't give a fuck, he'll kill you too."

Atlas smiled. "No, he won't, son. I have powerful friends on my side. My job is to get revenge on this bastard for what he did to you, and nobody, absolutely nobody or nothing, is going to stop me."

Shotgun perked up a little at this, sitting up straighter in the back seat. "Who are you?" he asked.

"As I said before, I'm Atlas Bishop, the Soul Binder. I am going to take you to this Jonny, and I'm going to bind your soul to his. Life for life. You are going to torture and hurt him like he hurt you, and you are going to drag his sorry soul to Hell because that is where he belongs. And then you, my young friend, are going to Heaven. No more sitting in rainy graveyards for you. Heaven is beautiful, full of blissful and gentle things and the people you loved who went before. Full of happiness and love. You deserve to go there."

Atlas had never been to Heaven. Heaven had only ever come to him in the form of Gabriel, but he had talked about it over pints in Gilligan's, and that's what the angel had said it was like. He hoped to see it one day in person himself.

Caliber .22 stared at Atlas, confused.

"What?" whispered Atlas.

"That was like, really nice, Atlas," he whispered back. "I think you're growing."

"Shut up," growled Atlas.

Shotgun smiled from the back seat. "Right," he said. "Let's do this, then."

CHAPTER SIX

"Do you hate this man?" asked Atlas, pulling out of the church driveway and back out onto the rain-soaked street. "This man who stole your young life away."

"Of course I hate him," said Shotgun. "I can still see his face as he pulled the trigger. He was laughing, the bastard."

"Bastard!" shouted Caliber, joining in.

"If he was here now in front of you, what would you do to him?" asked Atlas as the humming from the Quaesitor got a bit louder.

"I'd kill him," said Shotgun without missing a beat. "With my bare hands. I could take him too if it were just me and him. I beat him the first time."

"He took your whole life away from you," said Atlas. "Nineteen years is no age to die. You had your whole life ahead of you. All those life adventures, all that partying, all those girls, all those nights out. All those laughs. Having kids of your own, getting married, growing old. That bastard stole it all while laughing in your face."

"It's just tragic," said Shotgun. The humming from the Quaesitor was getting louder, the divine thread pulling them ever nearer. Atlas was concerned the anger wasn't intense enough, the thirst for revenge not nearly as strong as it should be. The binding wouldn't work at this level.

Caliber .22 seemed to pick up on this concern and winked at Atlas in his rear-view mirror.

"What did this bastard do to your mum?" he asked. "Did you say he beat her? Your poor mother. She'll probably never get over that and losing her son. That will just break her poor heart."

"The fucking prick!" Shotgun shouted, startling Atlas. "He and his cronies got my ma on the ground and were punching and kicking her. You should have seen them; they had no mercy. Her glasses broke, and they cut her eyes! She couldn't breathe! That's when I knew I had to get up to fight back. There were three of those bastards on me, and I got the strength to get up and get those bastards off her and out the door."

Through the veil of rain-streaked windows, the streets of Belfast unfolded before them. The road glistened like orange diamonds, reflecting the street lights. Each droplet of rain danced upon the windshield, distorting the world outside into a surreal dreamscape.

The car turned into a housing estate. They passed a group of youths standing around on a corner laughing and a woman and her child rushing home in the rain. Atlas stared out the windows at colorful painted walls depicting Irish dancers and the Titanic. Six imposing tower blocks pierced the velvety night sky as the humming grew louder from the box on the passenger seat.

Caliber shook his head, drawing his fists into a ball. "You need to make this fucker pay for what he did to your mum," he said. "And to you. Your mum did nothing wrong, and he ruined her entire life. He broke her poor heart! She'll never get over you. And he laughed when he shot you? He'll not be laughing when we're fucking finished with him."

Atlas grimaced. He didn't realize he and Caliber were now a team, but he could see the dead man's nostrils flaring. He was angry as hell, and Atlas was grateful for it.

"We're here," Atlas announced, switching off the engine. They were at the foot of an immense tower block. Atlas counted twenty floors before it disappeared into the clouds.

Caliber .22 opened his door, and Atlas caught his gaze in the mirror. "I'm coming too," he said. "I want to see the cowardly prick who shoots teenagers and beats up mothers."

Atlas grabbed the Quaesitor and got out of the car, hoping Jack's box wouldn't let him down.

The trio walked into the brightly lit lobby. It was clean, barring a few graffiti scrawls about the IRA on the muted, otherwise inoffensively painted pastel-colored walls. The stark brightness from an overhead light reflected off Caliber .22's skull as he stood there smiling. Atlas looked away and pressed the elevator button, and the door opened immediately. He pressed numbers 10, 11, 12, and 13. The Quaesitor would tell him on the ascent when he was close. The two corpses got in. He could see the rage in Shotgun's sunken eyes now, Caliber's words having done the trick. Atlas smiled wryly at him, and he winked back.

Atlas checked his reflection in the lift mirror. He badly needed a shave, and his eyes had bags beneath them. He ruffled and fixed his spiky hair at the front, looking this way and that at his strong jawline, stopping only when he caught Shotgun's gaze in the mirror. The kid looked like he had spent a week in the graveyard.

The humming got louder the nearer they got to the top floors, becoming constant at Floor 13, where he walked out. He stood in the middle of the hallway and waved the Quaesitor at the four doors facing him, the box leading him to the one in the far corner.

"Are you going to knock on the door?" asked Shotgun. "It'll be a security door, and there are probably about ten of them in there. They'll be on drugs and might have guns."

Atlas looked at him. "Don't lose your nerve now, Shotgun," he said. "They can no longer hurt you. You are safe, so do this for your mum. You've absolutely nothing to fear or lose."

Atlas reached for a gold cross around his neck and bowed his head to recite the prayer Gabriel had gifted him for strength and protection in these circumstances.

"God, grant me your Heavenly vigor to battle evil," he whispered. "Gift me your power and protect me so I may do your divine work. Grant me courage."

He felt a warmth wash over him from above, spreading down his head and face, covering his chest, and then passing down his legs to his feet. He felt strong, invincible, and brimming with power.

He held his hands in prayer, looked above, and whispered, "Thank you; amen," before blessing himself.

Atlas rolled his shoulders and cracked his neck, one side, then the other. "Right, let's go get this fucker!" he said and marched towards the door purposefully.

His boot crashed against the door, taking it off its hinges and sending it sliding down the hallway, knocking a man who had been standing there off his feet.

He could feel the divine power coursing through his veins now, like pulsating white light.

He stormed into the apartment as two burly men came running up the hall from the kitchen. He ducked and dived, swinging heavy and powerful punches that connected with their skulls. He grabbed one man's ear and smashed his head into a picture frame hanging on the wall, letting him fall to the ground unconscious as two more bounded towards him. The first of their noses to reach him was met with the palm of his hand. Atlas laughed maniacally as he heard his nose break. He enjoyed violence far too much, and having divine power that made him stronger made it far too easy. His dread had been replaced with adrenaline, and he loved the feeling of it racing through his veins. He ducked as the second man threw a punch before pinning him to the wall with his forearm and squeezing his testicles, twisting them almost 360 degrees with his other hand, causing the man to pass out and crumple to the floor. Atlas cackled at the sight of him on the ground.

Another man fired a gun at him, but he effortlessly dodged the bullet and ran at the gunman. He laughed while rugby-tackling him, hurling them both into a concrete wall, knocking the man unconscious.

"Is that one of the thugs who hit your ma, Shotgun?" he asked.

Shotgun nodded.

Atlas kicked him hard in the stomach, stepped over him, and strutted into the kitchen, where two more thugs were protecting a smaller man, their fists raised. Two more sat around a table covered in white powder, at the end of which a beaten and bloodied man sat tied to a chair, barely conscious.

"What the fuck is this?" shouted the thin, bespectacled man from in between his two burly bodyguards. "Where are the rest of them?" he said, frantically looking over Atlas's shoulder, expecting a rival gang to have caused this level of carnage.

"It's just me, dickhead," snarled Atlas. "And my imaginary friends. And you'll fucking see that I'm enough."

One of the bodyguards ran towards him. Atlas punched him hard in the throat, lifting him off his feet, and he collapsed in a heap, gasping for breath before passing out.

"Who the fuck is this guy?" shouted one of the men at the table, standing up. "Marty? John?" He rattled off a few more names, his voice diminishing to a whimper as none of them answered.

"They're all having a wee sleep in the hall," replied Atlas, smiling menacingly. "Thugging, shooting teenagers, and snorting cocaine is exhausting business, evidently."

"You!" Atlas shouted at the last man protecting his target, turning to point at him. "Sit down. It's him I want."

"Fuck you!" shouted the remaining bodyguard and lunged at him. The other two jumped up from the table, one armed with a bread knife. Atlas floored them all with ease, not even breaking a sweat, before throwing the breadknife at the wall, where it stuck.

"You!" he yelled at the bespectacled man he had been protecting, "Are you Jonny?"

"What the... What the fuck is this?" asked Jonny, moving between being petrified and angry. He was still trying to look tough, but his brain couldn't compute what he was seeing: every one of his foot soldiers lay incapacitated on the floor, groaning in pain.

He had a goofy look about him, not what Atlas had expected from the leader of a terror group that had command of an army of steroid-bulked thugs. He was wearing skinny jeans and a tight t-shirt that hugged his minuscule muscles.

"Fucking shoot him!" Jonny shouted at his men, his voice shaking. But they didn't move. They couldn't move.

The man tied to the chair gave out a low groan.

Atlas moved forward. "I asked you a question, dickhead!" he snarled. "Are. You. Jonny?"

Jonny looked from his unconscious friends and back to Atlas before nodding his head.

Atlas swung the tall freezer door beside him open and hit Jonny square on the head, breaking his glasses and dazing him. He then punched him hard in the stomach. Jonny fell to the ground, curled up in the fetal position, and Atlas kicked him repeatedly until his anger slightly abated.

He moved to the man tied to the chair, pulled a knife from his back pocket, and sliced through the rope that bound the man's hands together behind his back. He opened his eyes and closed them again, his eyeballs rolling back in his head.

"Who's this poor fucker?" he asked Jonny, who was still writhing on the kitchen floor, holding his stomach. "Someone else who beat you in a fight?"

Atlas saw fresh cigarette burns on the man's arms, something his father had used to do to his mother. He felt the anger rising in his chest and slapped the man in the face. "Wake up," he shouted. "I want you to see this."

The man came around, raising his hands to his face, awaiting more pain. "It's okay," assured Atlas. "I'm not going to hurt you." He turned to Jonny. "But I'm going to fucking hurt him, and I want you to watch."

Jonny had risen shakily to his knees and was attempting to pull himself up to the kitchen counter. Atlas strolled over and kicked him again, his boot connecting with his head, sending him spinning onto his back.

He bent down beside him, gripping his shirt in clenched fists and pulling his bloodied face to his. "Not so tough now, big man?" he snarled. "You seem to have lost your nerve without your gun and your men."

He pulled him up to his feet. "Shotgun! Caliber!" he shouted into the hall. "Come in here".

Atlas stared into Jonny's bloodshot eyes as the man he had murdered walked into the kitchen. He loved seeing the shock on their faces, loved to see bad people suffer. He didn't know if that was sick or not. He didn't know if he cared.

Jonny's face dropped, and his eyes opened wide and wild. He tried to form words, but his rapid breathing wouldn't allow him to talk.

Shotgun sauntered into the kitchen, surveying the battered men scattered all over the floor. The harsh overhead fluorescent lighting was unforgiving, and Shotgun looked terrifying, a week in a rainy graveyard having done his complexion no good at all. His sunken eyes were bloodshot and raging, his nostrils flared, and the blood on his shirt and in his wounds shone bright in the light.

Jonny shook in terror, tears in his eyes. Atlas looked down to a puddle of urine that was gathering at his feet and stepped back in disgust. Caliber .22 walked in behind Shotgun, the glaring hole in his head still bleeding.

"You!" Atlas snarled at Jonny. "Don't you fucking move." Jonny wasn't about to, being paralyzed with fear, only his eyes moving as they darted back and forth between Atlas, his friends, and the corpse of the man he had shot, now glaring at him from across the kitchen.

Atlas looked back at both of the corpses. They were indeed an impressive and terrifying sight, as was evidenced by Jonny's shaking, crying, and pissing himself. The imminent binding rendered the undead visible to him and anyone around him. Atlas allowed himself a smile.

"Which one of you pricks hit his ma!" shouted Caliber, grabbing a whimpering, barely conscious thug by the scruff of the neck. He opened his eyes and screamed. With wide eyes and a frothing mouth, Caliber continued. "Tell me now, you pathetic fuck! Look at my face! Because I am going to haunt your dreams forever more. You're all going to Hell, and I'll be waiting there to flay you alive and turn you inside out!

"You had to shoot this boy to stop him from defending his poor ma. His ma! Cowards! You will writhe in pain in the Lake of Fire, and I'll be there to watch and laugh!"

The thug passed out again. Caliber laughed maniacally as Atlas rolled a cloth out onto the kitchen table.

"I hate you, Jonny Hallahan," seethed Shotgun. Atlas could feel his rage fill the air. "You are going to pay for what you did to my ma, what you did to me. I am going to drag you to Hell. They'll enjoy you down there."

Jonny whimpered, openly sobbing now.

"What the fuck is this?" he cried. "Is this the drugs? Am I hallucinating?"

Atlas scoffed, then raised two large, sand-colored stones above his head.

"Tua actiones, pace tu juri perdiderunt," he declared loudly. *"Quod furto tenes animam tuam, et in aeternum vives in tormentis antequam infernum vindicat."*

By your actions, you have forfeited your right to peace. Your soul will be bound to that which was stolen, and you shall live for eternity in torment before Hell claims it.

The fluorescent lighting in the kitchen exploded overhead, cloaking them in darkness, as sparks flew from the open freezer door.

Atlas clasped his hands together, and a thunderous clap blew the glass in the kitchen window outward. The microwave exploded, sending white sparks everywhere.

"Shotgun," said Atlas calmly, placing the stones in his pockets.

"Do your worst. Heaven awaits you. You deserve peace. He does not."

Shotgun went toe-to-toe with the now babbling Jonny. Atlas unfurled his luminous rope and whipped it once, slicing the fridge door in half. Shotgun wrapped his arms around Jonny as if to embrace him, his mouth at his murderer's ear. He began to whisper as he climbed onto Jonny's back. The souls always did that instinctively, thought Atlas as he whipped the rope around them and spoke again.

"Ligatus in aeternum, usque ad Caelum et Infernum sua debita."

Bound forever, until Heaven and Hell claim their dues.

Jonny sobbed loudly as the rope's light faded and the kitchen returned to darkness.

Atlas lowered his face close to Jonny's. "You will never hurt another innocent again," he snarled. "Hell always claims its dues."

He then turned and considered the men on the floor, who were starting to wake up. He picked up the bread knife from the table and plunged it deep into the leg of the nearest goon, who roared in pain. Atlas slapped him hard in the face, and he stopped and stared at him, petrified.

"Look at me!" he shouted. "Look! You tell these fucks I'll be back for you all real soon. For all of you pricks who live by the sword. You're all going to Hell," he growled.

Atlas couldn't leave the man who'd been tied to the chair, so he hauled him up and over his shoulder in a fireman's lift. Glass crunched under his feet as he marched out of the kitchen and down the hall. He took the stairs this time, even with the extra weight, as he wanted to run off some of the energy that was still coursing through him. Caliber .22 ran after him, struggling to keep up.

Atlas threw the injured man in the back seat of his car, and they sped off, tires squealing.

"That was brilliant," said Caliber excitedly. "I mean, totally brilliant. Did you see how scared they were?"

Atlas looked at him before pulling out onto the main road. Caliber was practically buzzing. It made him smile as he realized he kind of liked this guy. "What was that about turning them inside out in Hell, skinning that guy alive?" Atlas asked, laughing.

Caliber laughed back. "I don't know!" he said. "It just felt right. I saw it in a film one time. It was good though, wasn't it?" He turned in his seat to face Atlas. "I saw you smash that dude's head into the wall," he continued. "It was crazy good! You're a badass! Why were you laughing?"

Atlas stared at him in amazement. "Because it's fun, obviously," he deadpanned. "I like hurting bad people. I try not to kill them, just hurt them a bit. Help them to know what it feels like to be powerless, vulnerable, and afraid, like their victims. Before they go over the edge and murder someone. Hurting them helps me get the anger out. It's my version of counseling, I suppose. Violence. Some people do yoga; some go to the gym. I hurt people. I'm better at it than talking, at least. Hurting bad people makes me feel better for a while." His voice trailed off as he contemplated this burst of introspection.

"Anyway," concluded Atlas, "you were brilliant, I'll give you that. You were absolutely terrifying."

Caliber .22 smiled proudly. "I was, wasn't I? And so were you. You were psychotic! Laughing while you twisted that guy's balls. Even I was scared!"

There was a groan from the back seat.

"Oh, shit. I forgot about him," said Atlas, looking in the rearview mirror. "We need to get him to the hospital."

He slammed on the brakes, spun the car around, and headed west toward the city's Royal Victoria Hospital, where they dropped their new acquaintance at the front door. Once done, they left Belfast, the rain, and the paramilitaries behind them.

CHAPTER SEVEN

Elsa looked worried as she entered Atlas's office. Her face had a completely different appearance without her smile.

"Excuse me, Atlas," she said softly. "I have tried forty-two hospices in Normandy and Brittany. None of them have a Dublin resident. I'm so sorry. I think Varie's source might have been mistaken."

Atlas turned his chair to the window, as he didn't want her to see him annoyed. He had been searching for years for his father and was sure that, this time, he had finally tracked him down. But he always thought that.

"Thanks, Elsa," he replied quietly.

"I'm sorry, Atlas," she said, backing out of the door. "Can I get you anything?"

"No," he said, not taking his gaze from the park across the street, from the trees, from where his bench was, where peace was. "I'm fine. Thank you."

But he wasn't fine. Every sighting got his hopes up. Every disappointment winded him. He knew he had been given this gift, this curse, this ability to damn souls and save souls because of his mother and his ability to relate to those who were taken so brutally. The one person he didn't want to see escape unscathed was that bastard who called himself his father. But he always seemed to be one step ahead of him.

It was times like these he recalled flashes of him pinning his mother to the wall in the hall while screaming at her, his disgusting whiskey breath all over her beautiful face. Her, so delicate and vulnerable in his strong grip. He had slapped her face so hard that she had fallen, spilling a casserole over the wall and carpet, all while his father screamed at him to be quiet. His mother had always blocked his path when he was in a rage and wanted to take it out on young Atlas. She had been so brave, so warm, so beautiful, even with the bruises, while his father's face was always contorted with anger.

He remembered his mother being thrown onto the kitchen floor, the sickening sound of bones thudding against the hard tiles. She would sit sobbing at the kitchen table, counting out the few pennies that hadn't been spent on booze to buy a tin of soup for them. He remembered his father plunging a kitchen knife deep into her chest at 6:11 pm on a Sunday evening, his eyes darkened by rage and hatred. He remembered the fear that he would be the next to be killed. His father had always hated Atlas and loved to see him in pain.

Atlas felt his chest constrict now, unable to take a deep breath. Was he like his father? He liked to see people suffer, too. Not little kids, though, just bad people. His heart rate quickened, and he felt dizzy. Without turning around, he fumbled for the drawer with the whiskey bottle in it.

"Don't, Atlas," said Caliber .22, getting up off his seat and walking toward the window. "You don't need that stuff. Take a deep breath. In through your nose, out through your mouth. The feeling will pass. Work through it. It's okay."

Atlas thought about telling him to fuck off but knew he was right.

"Are you my counselor from beyond the grave now?" he asked

wearily, his voice soft and void of the usual rage when whiskey was brought into the conversation.

"Talk to me," said Caliber. "It will go no further. After all, as you keep reminding me, you'll be getting rid of me as soon as you can."

Atlas rested his head back against his chair. "I need to find my father," he said. "I need to bind my mother's soul to him before he dies, which I believe will be soon. If he dies without being bound, my mother will have to walk this earth forever, and she does not deserve that torment. Can you imagine that? Her being here long after I go, not being able to speak to anyone, ever? No one able to see or hear her, roaming the earth, no end to her loneliness. Everyone who knew and loved her gone. God knows how she would end up. She would never be at peace. She'd go mad. I couldn't bear it. I couldn't bear to let her down again. I have to find him and finish this."

"And you will, Atlas. You will find him. You are the best at what you do."

Atlas looked at the corpse.

"I certainly hope I find the bastard," he said. "Because roaming this world alone would be a fate worse than even death."

Atlas got up and walked into the bathroom, washed his hands, and then washed them again. They were clean but busted up—his knuckles raw red and blistered from punching the thugs in Belfast. The cold water soothed them for a second. He looked in the mirror. His reflection stared back at him, tired and weary. People often called him handsome, but he wasn't so sure. Varie said he had a vacant look about him at times, and he found that more believable. He had his father's jawline, strong and proud, and his black hair. He hated that. But he had his mother's blue eyes and her smile when he used it. He hadn't seen either of them smile—truly smile—in a very long time.

He needed to get outside to grab a coffee and some fresh air.

"I'm going for a walk," he announced. "I need a..."

"Coffee?" said Caliber. "Not whisky. I'll come with you."

They stepped out into the sharp morning air, and Atlas tried to ignore the tension in his body and the feeling of impending doom. He jogged off the pavement and walked across the street to the St. Stephen's Green Shopping Centre, in all its 1980s-does-Victoriana glory. The huge glass and white steel structure glimmered in the sunshine. It always reminded him of a wedding cake—a wedding cake that sold good coffee.

He walked under its huge glass dome, glancing up at the mammoth clock—its hands as tall as a man—and passed boutique shops, small glass kiosks selling all kinds of everything, and lush, green foliage that softened the grand iron arches that held it all together. It was an odd place: beautiful but odd.

His mind raced as he stood in the queue for the coffee shop. He thought the walk would have cleared his head, but the whirr of the coffee machine and the relentless chatter of other customers provided him with no comfort at all.

Atlas looked around and noticed many of the coffee shop's customers were glued to the television on one end of the room, listening to the breaking news about an incident at a Dublin supermarket that had left several people dead. Early reports said that there were gunshots; several people had been stabbed, and a man had been knocked down and killed outside the store. The news anchor said that there were reports of two apparent suicides at the location and that Gardai now had the area sealed off. There were fears it might have been a terrorist attack.

The small, super-friendly barista's chirpy greeting pulled Atlas's attention away from the screen. "Hi, Atlas! What'll it be today?"

"A decaf cappuccino, please," he requested.

She replied with a cheery, "No problem," and began asking him about his day.

He recognized her face. She had worked here for a while and had told him her name before, but he had forgotten. They had gone too far down the road now for him to ask again—it would be far too awkward—and her name badge was covered by a tea towel.

"Yeah, it's going good," he lied. Where would he even start to tell a barista about his life?

He turned his head to the television again, then back to the barista who was telling him about her weekend.

"What's the point in drinking that muck?" asked Caliber, standing at his side. "It's like non-alcoholic beer. You don't even get a kick out of it. If I could still taste stuff, I'd be totally drinking quadruple espressos and beer at lunchtime and eating burgers all day long because now I don't think..."

"Do you ever shut up?" blurted out Atlas and the smile immediately left the barista's face.

"No!" stuttered Atlas. "I didn't mean you!" But she had already turned her back on him to finish his drink hurriedly.

She slammed it down on the counter in front of him, spilling a third of it.

"I honestly wasn't... Thank you," Atlas mumbled and sighed. He walked away, feeling worse than when he had come in.

He and Caliber groused at each other all the way through the park and back to the office. Atlas didn't much care that he looked like a mad man to the ordinary person on the street, appearing like he was talking to himself, intermittently stopping and shouting, and pointing back toward the coffee shop.

On his way up the stairs, he complained that he would never be able to go back to that coffee shop ever again. The barista must hate him now.

"Wait!" said Caliber, stopping and searching in his pockets. "I think I have my tiny violin in here somewhere. I'm sure it was here in my jeans. Just hold on a second. I really want to play a tune for you."

Atlas rolled his eyes and was about to pour his coffee over his dead acquaintance's mangled head when a voice called out to them from the floor above.

"Hello? Hello there, can someone help me?"

Atlas looked over the banister to the next floor up and saw a small woman peering down at them.

"Yes, madam," he called. "I'll be with you now."

Atlas took the stairs two at a time, Caliber .22 following close behind him. They approached his office door to find a woman in a supermarket uniform, whose neck was purple with bruising, and a man sitting on the stairs with his head in his hands.

"Can you hear me?" asked the woman. "Can you see me?"

"I can," said Atlas gently. "I can. Now come in, and I'll see if I can help you."

He touched the man on the shoulder and he lifted his head. Atlas could see that his once light blue t-shirt was now red with wet blood, as was most of his trousers.

"Sir," he said. "Come into my office, and I'll explain all."

The man looked at Caliber .22 in horror, who weakly smiled back at him. He jumped up from the stairs and scrambled to get in the door and away from him.

"Elsa, I have a few cases here I'm just going to bring through," Atlas announced as he passed her desk.

"A few?" asked Elsa, looking fearful. "That's unusual. Well, more unusual than what usually goes on here. Am I... Can I get you anything?"

Atlas shook his head. It was indeed unusual. Apart from when he had first started, he had only ever usually received one case at a time. There was always a first time for everything.

"Come in, come in," he gestured to his new guests. "Sit down. Make yourselves comfortable."

The woman flopped down onto the sofa, her handbag clutched across her chest like she had just come in from a night shift and was about to unpack the day's happenings with her flatmate. The man lingered just outside the doorway, shooting Caliber terrified glances.

"Please, sir," said Atlas. "Come in. It is alright. I can help."

The man took tentative steps into the room, found a chair, and threw himself in it, pulling his knees up to his chest and hugging them.

"We've got a real worrier here," whispered Caliber, nodding at the man.

Atlas looked at the pair. A sorry sight they were too. He let the worrier settle and addressed the woman.

"What happened to you, Miss?" he asked.

"Well," she began. "I think..." She stopped, laughing nervously. "I'm sorry, it's a bit ridiculous. But I think that I might be... I think... I don't know for sure...but I think I might be dead."

Atlas nodded his head. "Yes, I think you're right."

She nodded back. "I thought as much." Her smile faded.

Atlas sat on the edge of his table. "Can you tell me what happened to you?" he asked again.

She gripped her handbag tighter and took a deep breath. "I had just finished my shift," she started. "It was the last of a five-day run. I had my bag packed, my coat on, and was walking through the aisles to go home. There was a man walking towards me. He had just abandoned his shopping cart, and he looked really angry. He wasn't a druggie or anything. He was dressed well enough and had diapers in his cart, family stuff, you know? He just grabbed me and started squeezing my neck. I couldn't breathe! He squeezed harder and harder. His eyes were absolutely crazy. He didn't say anything, either. It was like he wasn't all there, like something had taken control of him. It wasn't normal. I tried to fight him, but I blacked out. When I came to, I was standing over my body. The man who strangled me was also lying there. His throat was slit, and I don't know if he did it himself or someone else did, but there was a knife beside him. Then there was this light... It just appeared, and it felt warm and nice. It was so cold on the supermarket floor. I haven't warmed up since. So I followed it, and it brought me here." She paused and relaxed a little.

"I met this man on the stairs," she continued, gesturing at the man who was now rocking back and forth on the chair. "He doesn't say much."

Atlas nodded. This was complicated. There was no soul to bind her with since her murderer was already dead. "What will I call you, Miss?" he asked her. He looked at Caliber and back to the woman. "What is your name?"

"Anne," she said sadly. "My name is Anne or *was* Anne when I was alive. I don't know if that changes when you're dead. Do you get given another name then, or can I keep the one my mother gave me? Oh, my mother...my mother is going to be so upset with me being dead." She began to sob, and Atlas patted her hand awkwardly.

"There, there," he said.

Caliber smiled encouragingly and gave him a thumbs up. Atlas ignored him and turned his attention to the man in the chair.

"What happened to you, sir?" he asked.

The man just shook his head and buried it in his knees.

"Can you tell me what happened?" asked Atlas again. "I want to help you."

The man didn't budge. Didn't lift his head. Didn't make a sound.

Atlas got up, walked across to his desk, and sat down at his laptop. He pulled up a Dublin news page and looked at the headline. "Seven Dead In Shocking Dublin Bloodbath." Atlas clicked on the link and read about a thirty-two-year-old supermarket worker who had been strangled, and a forty-five-year-old man shot dead outside the same shop. He read further down the page: the man called Joseph had been shot as he had used an ATM machine by a man who had then turned the gun on himself. Another unnamed man had slit his own throat in the store, and reporters were trying to establish the identities of the other victims.

"Joseph?" said Atlas, addressing the man. "Your name is Joseph?"

The man looked up and nodded his head quickly.

"Okay," said Atlas. "This is what is happening. You are both dead. You have been murdered, but you probably already know that."

Joseph began crying, too.

"I'm sorry, Joseph, if you weren't fully aware of the situation thus far," said Atlas. "I am a Soul Binder. The light you saw? That draws you to me so I can help. At the moment, you are stuck. Your soul is stuck here on Earth, for whatever reason. You might have missed the window of opportunity, you might not be ready to go, you might need justice or revenge on the one who took your life, or you might be in denial." He looked directly at Joseph, who was still sobbing into his hands, all folded up in the chair.

"My job," said Atlas, turning to Anne, "is normally to find the person who murdered you, and bind your soul to theirs. Your job is normally to torture them just by your presence. Weigh them down with guilt and remorse and eventually help deliver them to Hell where you will be set free and your passage to Heaven secured. We find ourselves in a bit of a pickle, however, if the people who murdered you are also dead themselves. But we'll work it out. Do you understand?"

Anne nodded as if Atlas had just given her directions to Tesco, and she was about to set off in that direction, while Joseph buried his head in his knees again. Atlas sighed loudly. The last time he had three souls to save at the same time was when he first started, and he'd never had souls with—if the news articles were correct—no definitive person to bind them to. He didn't really know where to start, and he was worried about their souls. He had an inkling that they would be stuck here forever, but he had to try. He thought he might begin with Joseph, as the corpse's nervous energy was beginning to make him irritable.

Atlas opened the bottom drawer on his desk and fished out his Quaesitor.

"Joseph," he said. "Come here and put your hand on this device, please. It will tell me where the person who murdered you is. If he is still on earth, we can find him. We can bind you, and we can get you on your way to a better place, to Heaven."

Joseph didn't lift his head, so Atlas got up and went over to him.

"Put your hand on this, Joseph," he said, standing over him. "Come on now. I need you to work with me on this."

No movement. Nothing.

Atlas took the corpse's hand and pressed the Quaesitor into his palm, but it didn't make a sound. He took it back and shook it beside his ear, before placing it back in the corpse's hand. Nothing.

"Anne," he said, walking quickly to the other seat. "Give me your hand."

She did as she was bid, and Atlas placed the Quaesitor onto her outstretched palm. Again, nothing. No sound. No movement.

"It must be out of battery, Atlas," suggested Caliber

"It doesn't run on batteries, Caliber," Atlas snapped. "I've already told you that. They have worked perfectly fine for six blasted years and have just stopped working this week." He walked across to the window to look at it in the better light. "I need to think," he mumbled. "Let me think, for God's sake."

Caliber .22 fell back onto the sofa and folded his arms in a huff.

"Give me your hand, Caliber .22," said Atlas suddenly, marching towards him. "I want to see if it works on you."

Caliber ignored him and stared out the window instead, still insulted.

"Oi! Hand!" Atlas shouted.

The corpse stretched out his hand without taking his gaze from the window. Atlas placed the Quaesitor in his palm, but it remained as dead as when it had touched the others. Atlas walked back to his desk, sat down, and put his head in his hands.

For six years, the Quaesitor had been his only tool for finding those who had wronged souls. Without it, he was powerless to find and bind souls, unless they knew the exact address of their killers, which was rare. Sometimes the link was just too weak for the Quaesitor, and the threads that bound the souls together snapped. Sometimes he just couldn't find the killers to bind. If people were going around killing others and themselves, he had a serious problem. A problem with excess souls and nowhere to put them.

"Let me think," he whispered, for the moment ignoring the three corpses staring at him. But all that was whirring around in his brain was that if he didn't sort this out, he would have to spend his life with three dead strangers and his dead Ma, as well as any other deceased stragglers who wandered into his office. He would never get a minute's peace ever again. "Let me think," he repeated, sighing dramatically. He could feel himself starting to sweat through his shirt. His mouth was dry, his thoughts overwhelming.

A sudden commotion from Elsa's office broke his concentration. A man shouted, a woman raised her voice in anger, and someone screamed, "Everyone, shut up!"

Atlas jumped up from his desk and ran to the door, swinging it open. "What the hell is going on here?" he roared as a crowd of eight or nine people, all talking loudly or shouting at one another, stood with their backs to him.

"Jesus Christ, Atlas!" Elsa gasped from her desk, her hand to her chest in shock. "You scared the life out of me! Why did you shout like that? Have you taken leave of your senses? Dear God, you scared me half to death!"

The crowd slowly turned around, and Atlas realized why Elsa couldn't hear or see the chaos. Three gunshot wounds, four stabbings, and a guy with what looked like tire marks up his t-shirt all surrounded him, hitting him with a barrage of questions.

"What is happening? Why are we here? Can you hear us? How can I get back to life? What the fuck is going on? Am I dead? Are you dead? He's definitely dead; I can see through his skull. Is this Heaven? Can you tell my family I'm alright? Is this Hell? I have children! This can't be happening. What happened to me?"

"Everyone shut up!" Atlas thundered, and Elsa cowered in her chair, eyes fixed on the ground. She kissed a holy medal on a chain around her neck and blessed herself, sinking low in her chair and covering her head with her hands.

Atlas clapped his hands. "Everyone, zip your mouths and come with me into my office," he said. "I'll see what is going on. No one talks. Right? Right."

One after another, the corpses trailed into his office. They stood beside his desk, they sat on the edge of his sofa, they stood beside his window, and when at last the final corpse was through, Atlas closed the door. The room immediately looked and felt drastically smaller. He felt claustrophobic, and his chest started to tighten. He hated people around him. Dead people, especially. There was too much energy in the room, and none of it was positive.

"What the hell is going on?" he asked aloud. The corpses all opened their mouths to speak. "Aaah! No!" he shouted. "That was a rhetorical question."

He looked around to see if he could find a sensible-looking person.

"You," he said, pointing at a woman in a nurse's uniform. "Tell me why you are all here."

She moved forward, fixing her hair behind her ears. "Well," she said, "I don't really know. I was in Mullen's Supermarket on Bruton Street. It was really busy—the queues for the registers were ridiculously long. I remember seeing a man come in—he looked kinda familiar: I think he was one of those gangland guys who's always in the paper. One of the criminals who's always in court. He dresses very well. There's a girl at work, you see; she's married to his brother, but he's okay. She's always talking about him. Anyway, he looked weird, like his eyes were all black, just black.

"Then everyone started fighting. Like *everyone*, even mothers with babies in strollers. People were punching and kicking and biting, pulling shelves down on one another, hitting each other with saucepans... I heard gunshots too from outside.

"I felt myself get really, really angry. It came over me like a wave. I think I hit the woman who was serving me. I remember wanting to kill her! And that's not like me. I am a nurse! I help people. The man behind me in the line had bought some kitchen knives. He stuck one in my chest, here," she said, pointing at her name badge, from where a mammoth blood stain had spread. "I woke up, and there were bodies everywhere. I looked down at myself, lying over the belt at the register. It was so weird. I tried to do CPR on myself, but I couldn't do it. I was gone."

Atlas nodded sadly while even Caliber's face creased in empathy.

"The woman who I attacked—the shop worker—she was dead

too. She had killed her boss, then slit her own throat. She was standing there, looking at herself. Then there was this big thing. I don't know how to describe it; it was a horrible creature. It grabbed her and took her away, as well as a load of other people. Then I saw a light, just there, above the newspapers. I went to it, it moved, and I followed it here."

"A creature?" asked Atlas. "Like a dog? A wolf?"

"No," she said, shaking her head. "It was much taller than a man, with big, gangly legs, enormous black eyes, and a scary white face—white as bone. It was disgusting."

Atlas eyed her suspiciously. He had never heard of such a thing.

"Are you sure?" he asked. "Did it speak? What did it do? Where did it go?"

"Yes, I'm sure," she said, sniffing. "I saw it with my own eyes! Big terrifying thing. It growled more than spoke. It just scooped up people and bounded out the door, taking half the door frame with it."

"I saw it too," said another dead woman in gym gear. "It moved in a really weird way, like, so unnatural."

Atlas moved his attention to her. "Did it say anything? Was it a man or a beast?"

"It was a beast, I think," she said. "Its breathing was really heavy and loud. It took my friend, just grabbed her body, but it left me. She had...she had killed a man in the cereal aisle with her pen knife. She had stabbed him in the neck with it and then killed herself. A man who worked at the deli counter killed me, and it took him too."

Atlas narrowed his eyes. "So it only took the people who killed others, but it left those who were killed without harming someone else?"

The two women nodded their heads in unison.

Atlas puffed out his cheeks. It was some story. "Who else got killed at Mullen's Supermarket?" he asked. "Hands up only: no shouting."

Two more people put their hands up. "What is going on?" he asked, looking at Caliber, who only shrugged his shoulders.

"Where are the rest of you from?" asked Atlas. "One person at a time."

A man walked forward wearing exercise gear and a bicycle helmet.

"I think a lot of us came from the shorefront at Dalkey," he said, his eyes darting from one corpse to the next. "Yes, I recognize that man and that woman. I was out for a bike ride and had stopped at the coffee dock on the promenade. It was so strange. I was standing there one minute, totally relaxed, petting the dog of the man in line ahead of me, and the next minute everyone was trying their best to kill each other. A little old lady came at me with a spike, like one of those things at a barbeque. What's it called? A skewer? She was like a mad woman. The man with the dog got me in a headlock and choked me—presumably—to death. I say presumably, but I mean definitely. I'm pretty sure I'm dead; like, my smartwatch is showing no pulse right now. All the other people here were killed there too." He pointed at the other corpses in turn. "Stabbed, strangled, hit with a brick on the head, the old woman got him with the skewer. I've never experienced anything like that. Being murdered, I mean. It was crazy.

"Then, as that lady said, there was a little ball of light. Some of us followed it, and we arrived here. Others didn't. It's all very surreal, and I don't really know what to think about it, to be quite honest with you."

Some of the other dead nodded their heads in agreement. Atlas walked to his desk and sat down. He now had eleven corpses to bind, no one to bind them to, and a malfunctioning Quaesitor. Someone spoke, and he put his hand in the air to stop them. "I need to think," he said, putting his head in his hands. "Let me think."

Caliber .22 came to his desk. "Is this normal?" he asked, and Atlas looked at him through his fingers.

"No, Caliber," he replied. "It most definitely is not normal. I have never seen anything like this in all my years doing this. I have no idea how to deal with it."

Caliber sat on the windowsill behind Atlas and sighed. "I guess this means it will be a lot harder to bind me if you are overrun with dead people."

Atlas looked at him. "Yes. Tricky indeed... I need to work it out, but I have no idea how. I was overwhelmed with three souls to bind, and now I have eleven, with complications."

Caliber fell silent. The whole room was silent, apart from the heavy breathing of a larger corpse sitting on the sofa beside Anne.

"Can you stop breathing so loudly?" Atlas snapped at him. "I'm trying to think over here. It's not like you even have to breathe at all. You're actually dead. you know. Breathing is no longer required."

"Atlas," whispered Caliber, standing up. "Take it down a notch. You're being a nasty bastard again. Everyone here is trying to cope with new experiences. Take it easy."

Caliber clicked his fingers at the corpses. "Right," he said authoritatively, "everyone out. Let's give this man a chance to think. We'll move into the kitchen."

When the last of the corpses had shuffled out, Caliber turned back to Atlas, who still had his head in his hands. "We'll give you some peacc, Atlas, to work this all out. I know you can do it."

Atlas just stared at him, this man with a big hole in his head and a big misplaced sense of faith that he would be able to turn this mess around. Caliber smiled sympathetically and disappeared through the door.

Atlas's head was swimming. He had a horrible feeling in the pit of his stomach, an almost claustrophobic sense of foreboding eating away at his insides. It was one of those emergency situations where people frantically look around for someone to help—an adult, a responsible person—only to discover they are the most adulty adult, the most responsible one there, and they have absolutely no clue what to do. Panic rose in his stomach, and he looked at the drawer holding his whiskey.

He leaned back in his seat and exhaled dramatically. He needed advice, help, and someone to tell him what to do with eleven corpses.

He picked up his phone and dialed a number.

Gabriel had introduced him to Walter D'Arcy a few years back. He owned and ran the Bittlesburn Funeral Home on the edge of the city. He had a gift: the dead whispered and he could hear them. He wasn't a Soul Binder, but kept many secrets and heard many things. He would have been overrun these last few days.

Atlas often visited him if he hit a brick wall on cases when all else had failed. Sometimes the binding did not work, or the thread was too weak or broken. Walter heard things others didn't, couldn't, and he often acquired pieces of the jigsaw that helped police solve cold cases. People took their secrets to the grave, but Walter heard their confessions before they got there.

An elderly woman, lying dead on his table, had whispered that she had washed her son's bloody clothes after he killed a man in Dublin docks thirty years previously. Atlas was able to bind both killed and killer's souls three days later.

"Walter," he said, sitting up straighter. "Can I come and see you?"

After the hurried call, he threw on his coat and headed for the door.

"Caliber," he shouted firmly in the direction of the kitchen. "Come with me. The rest of you stay here."

CHAPTER EIGHT

"Where are we going?" asked Caliber as they drove through Dublin's back streets.

Atlas peered through the windshield at the ominous sky. A black cloud, pregnant with rain, was about to burst. "I need advice," he said finally. "Something weird is going on and I need to know what it is. Walter will know the answers. He always has the answers. The dead whisper to him."

"Walter? Walter who?" asked Caliber. "That doesn't answer my question."

"You'll see," replied Atlas.

They navigated the labyrinth of city streets along the River Liffey, history and modernity blending seamlessly. Georgian facades stood proud in the night, the narrow alleys between holding hidden gems. Laughter and music drifted from the cozy pubs that peppered the city's streets.

They passed beneath the shadow of Dublin's General Post Office, its building commanding attention with an imposing neoclassical façade and grand granite pillars that still bore the scars of rebellion. Stopped at traffic lights and lost in thought, Atlas gazed up at its clock, a silent witness to his city's evolution, and wondered what the hell was going on.

He drove far too fast to the outskirts of the city, heading toward the seaside commuter town of Castlerock.

Caliber occasionally squeezed his eyes shut as Atlas passed cars and broke the speed limit. He grasped the hand grip above the door for dear life, even though he was dead. When Atlas raised an eyebrow, he told Atlas that he was once almost killed in a car accident, and would he mind slowing down? Or maybe he just shouldn't drive when he was overly stressed. Atlas eventually did slow down—just in time to drive under an ornate wrought iron sign that read "Castlerock Crematorium" before a more modern one welcoming them to "Bittlesburn Funeral Home."

Under the shroud of night, a mansion loomed before them like a specter against the inky black sky, its imposing gothic silhouette rising from the darkness. Ivy tendrils clung to its weathered walls, and the moonlight cast eerie shadows across the lawn. It couldn't have looked more haunted.

Atlas gazed at the gargoyles perched atop the pillars at the bottom of stone steps leading up to the house, their forms frozen in perpetual vigil.

"Holy moley, that looks like a big, old haunted house right there," exclaimed Caliber. Atlas said nothing, his head whirring with possible explanations for recent developments, none of them good. He knew he wouldn't be able to settle until he found out what was going on.

He got out of the car and took the stone steps before the house two at a time, Caliber close behind. He rang the bell, and a deep voice boomed, "Yes?" through a speaker.

"I need to speak with Walter; it's Atlas Bishop," he said, and the door buzzed and slowly opened before them.

They were met in the hall by a short, gray-haired octogenarian in a leather apron. One of his eyes was pure white. He gestured for them to follow him, and they walked through the old house, past viewing rooms and vast spaces filled with empty seats and walls adorned with painted portraits of humorless characters. With dark red velvet and sad flowers everywhere, the mansion felt very heavy.

At the back of the house, the old man walked ahead of them through a door with a metal plaque that stated "Preparation Room." And there was Walter D'Arcy—an old man with a shock of wild gray hair and a face with crevices so deep one could lose a finger in there—dabbing a recently departed old woman's face with flesh-colored paint.

"You have a visitor, Mr. D'Arcy," said the old man.

"Yes," said Walter slowly, without looking up. "Welcome, Mr. Bishop. Welcome, young Stephen. I trust you are adjusting to your new life or, rather, death."

Walter could see the dead. He could hear the dead.

Caliber opened his mouth to speak but Atlas cut him off. "Why are there eleven souls in my office, Walter?" Atlas said, skipping the small talk. "Why are people killing one another on my streets? Why is my bloody equipment malfunctioning?"

Walter peered at Atlas over his spectacles. "Something strange is afoot," he said. "I'm glad you called. I have been hearing whispers, and wanted to converse with you about these rather strange things."

"What things?" asked Atlas, impatiently. "Tell me, Walter."

"These people are talking," said Walter, pointing at the corpse on his table, his words falling from his mouth painfully slowly. "They speak of Mr. Smith."

The mention of Mr. Smith's name made Atlas's skin crawl. He was Hell's version of him and collected the souls of the Irish murderers that he bound. It was the only thing they had in common.

He had first met Mr. Smith on neutral ground, in the Brazen Head Bar on the banks of the River Liffey. They had met there to sign a contract stating they agreed to work together peacefully to populate Heaven and Hell.

Atlas had been nervous going to the meeting on that particular

Saturday morning, and had asked Gabriel to wait when they got close so he could smoke one more cigarette. He had stood looking at the lush floral baskets hanging around thc front of the brown-bricked building and the people milling around the large empty whiskey barrels in the sunshine enjoying a drink and wondered if they knew Heaven and Hell were congregating inside.

"There's no need to be nervous, Atlas," Gabriel had said. "It's just a formality. "

He had walked into the bar, the oldest in Ireland, and saw it had the air of a quirky, overpacked antique shop. The faces of Irish rebels stared down from a mismatch of pictures on the wall adjacent to a wall clustered with pictures of famous actors and politicians. Another wall had dollar notes pinned to it. In the corner, a coat of arms stood guard.

"Ah!" said Gabriel. "There they are." He motioned to a blazing fireplace topped by a heavy mahogany mantel, decorated with candles, musical instruments, and an old wireless radio.

The two walked toward the fireplace and two deep wine-colored leather winged armchairs facing one another in front of the grate, a round table between them. An ornate, wooden mirror hung above the mantel, reflecting Atlas's worried expression back at him, while the eyes of Irish revolutionary, soldier, and politician Michael Collins peered down on the proceedings from an adjacent frame on the wall.

A sullen man, dressed all in black, with sunken cheekbones and dead eyes stood silently behind one armchair.

A taller man with the poise of a predator lounged in the armchair, his legs crossed. His tailored suit fit like a second skin, draped over broad shoulders, accentuating his commanding presence. Dark eyes, sharp as flint, pierced through the smoke-filled air. His hair was slicked back with precision, revealing a face etched with scars. His jawline, chiseled and firm, smacked of unyielding resolve. Atlas looked at the "No Smoking" placard that sat on the round table between the two chairs and noticed the cigarette hanging languidly from Mr. Smith's lips, a symbol of his defiance against the world. His aura screamed power and control.

"Ah, Moloch!" shouted Gabriel, his hands as wide as his smile. "How fantastic to see you again, my friend!"

Hell's representatives did not respond or alter their dour expressions.

"Atlas, sit, sit," said Gabriel, gesturing to the empty armchair. "Let's get to know one another a little better. Atlas, this is Mr. Smith; Mr. Smith, this is Atlas Bishop. Let's get some bonding going here! No? Okay..."

Atlas sat with his hands on the arms of the chair, his legs wide in a power pose as Mr. Smith stared back at him, like a boxer before a fight, slowly smoking his cigarette. Atlas, his heart racing, hadn't backed down and didn't speak first. He just stared back at him. He already hated Mr. Smith, and he suspected the feeling was mutual. They sat in silence for five minutes before Gabriel finally interjected.

"Okay!" he said cheerily. "So, we know why we're here. Atlas has replaced Frank Doyle, our last Soul Binder, who unfortunately had his head removed from his shoulders by, well, we don't know for certain, but we suspect one of your staff, Mr. Smith."

Mr. Smith moved his eyes from Atlas to Gabriel for twenty seconds, then slowly returned them to Atlas.

"But we will say no more about that," Gabriel continued, aware that he had pricked a nerve. "These things...they sometimes happen in business: misunderstandings and the like. So we have now appointed a new Soul Binder, a Mr. Atlas Bishop, here present, which means we need to renew our contracts with regard to the fair and equitable distribution of souls and the renewal of respect, collaboration, and promises. It's just a formality, but it keeps everything in order."

Gabriel produced a blindingly white piece of paper and a white pen from out of thin air. He leaned over and set them on the table in front of the two soul binders.

The writing had been so small Atlas couldn't read it in the dim light, and he didn't want to start going over the small print now. He had known most of what he was signing, since Gabriel had drip-fed the information about the pact to him since he started on his journey.

Over pints of Guinness in Gilligan's Pub, he had said that centuries ago, the protocols were non-existent and that Hell had just stolen souls at will. Heaven had tried to bring them back, but each was claiming them as their own. Conflict arose, and Heaven, embodying purity and righteousness, wanted to guide souls to eternal bliss. Hell, driven by temptation and darkness, wanted to snare them in eternal torment. Obviously, a row ensued, which had then escalated into an all-out war.

He had said that the war had intensified, with each side employing elaborate schemes and divine interventions to sway mortal decisions, souls becoming pawns in a cosmic power struggle, their destinies uncertain. It was brutal and bloody and had almost destroyed everything.

Angels and demons had clashed as a battle for supremacy raged, shaking the very foundations of reality. As the fate of the universe, and indeed human existence, hung in the balance, one side called for a truce, they negotiated a pact and an uneasy peace formed between the two. Heaven and Hell then appointed Soul Binders and Soul Collectors to enact the pact worldwide.

The pact simply meant good people went to Heaven and bad people went to Hell. It meant that there was no crossover or confusion. Soul Binders, like Atlas, made bad people feel the pain and anguish they had caused others. Soul Collectors, like Mr. Smith, picked them up at the gates of Hell and served eternal damnation on them. Heaven's souls were then released to go above, and everyone was happy. Well, apart from Mr. Smith, who looked positively murderous all the time.

Gabriel had said that while there were a few little blips on the road, and it was always a delicate peace—an uncomfortable alliance—it mostly worked well.

A grandfather clock chimed gently in the corner of the Brazen

Head and pulled Atlas back to the room, Mr. Smith, and the sacred agreement in front of him.

Atlas had pulled the piece of paper over, picked up the pen, and scrawled his name at the bottom. He trusted Gabriel that it was nothing bad and that he wasn't signing his life away.

Mr. Smith had lit another cigarette and blown the smoke in Atlas's face. Atlas hadn't flinched.

Mr. Smith had then slowly raised his hand, and Moloch placed a black pen into it. Atlas noticed he moved like water—so smooth—as he reached over and made a mark on the page. Once done, he flicked his cigarette at Atlas, got up, and strode out of the bar without a word.

They had met several times since. Mr. Smith became more obnoxious with the passing of time, and Atlas more adept at hiding his nervousness.

"Walter," Atlas said. "What are the dead whispering to you?"

"The dead," Walter slurred. "Those who died by their own hands this day and last, last week: they say Mr. Smith has a plan, a dangerous and horrible plan. It involves hatred and violence as you have seen in recent events. The plan involves Hell being overrun by innocent souls duped by the Devil into evil deeds and Hell's minions roaming the earth."

Things are starting to make sense now, Atlas thought.

Walter put down his tools and took off his glasses. "There have been rumblings. The dead know; they have told me things. This is about power and nothing else. Mr. Smith is collecting souls for Hell, and he has ideas about building an army. He's intent on bringing the Devil back to walk the Earth. You will have seen strange happenings, innocent people being overcome with rage and attacking others, dozens brawling, humans being cruel to other humans. That is his work. The brawl in the pub on the outskirts of the city. It was a dummy run, as was the cinema, the supermarket, and the other events. The death toll is rising, no? He is testing the dark power, testing his limits. More death and destruction will come. The more people he can get to commit dark deeds, the more they will populate Hell. He has something big planned. He is cruel and brutal and doesn't care who is harmed—man, woman, or child. I don't know what he is planning, but he will not be content with ten or twenty murderous souls. He wants thousands, millions.

"He has some very bad people working for him, Atlas. Half of the criminal gangs in Dublin are with him. He has some very dark plans."

Atlas felt a shiver run down his spine. Mr. Smith was an obnoxious and arrogant bastard. He worked for Hell, after all, and you didn't get there without the right credentials. There was nothing good about him at all.

"But the pact..." started Atlas.

"He cares about nothing," interrupted Walter. "Nothing except power and money. He will take the consequences of breaking the pact, even if it destroys the world. His heart is pure darkness."

Mr. Smith had pushed the boundaries before. He was, as Walter said, power-hungry. But the pact had always brought him back. It was a sacred, binding contract. Everyone from the top to the bottom in Heaven and Hell had to abide by it, with no exceptions. Everyone knew what was at stake if the contract was broken. All Hell would break loose—literally.

Atlas had to remind him before how important it was to avoid war and the wiping out of human existence.

"Atlas," called Walter as he neared the door. "This is more serious than your other quibbles. This is deadly. From what I am hearing, Mr. Smith wants to either recruit you or kill you. This is not a joke. He will offer you your heart's greatest desire. You will be tempted. He wants the souls of the innocents here in Ireland. But that is only the start: others will join him if he is successful, and it will spiral. This will end in war.

"He wants you now because you can bind souls and decide their destination—Heaven or Hell. If you don't do his bidding, he will kill you and steal your power. He has found a way to control people, to have them do his bidding, and to block all your seeking devices. That's why you have a build-up of souls. He will have also rendered your protections useless. I've never seen him like this before: he is absolutely crazed. Hate is spilling out into the world. They are becoming more powerful. The world is out of balance. It could tip off its axis should the balance of power be knocked over. I am fearful for the first time in my existence. This is serious, Atlas. You need to protect yourself. He wouldn't think twice about taking your lifeblood and stealing your sacred instruments."

"I have protection," said Atlas, fumbling with the pendant around his neck. "With this, I can't be harmed."

"No," said Walter firmly. "The whispers have told me that he has stripped down your protections in order to get to you, to weaken you, make you feel vulnerable and unsafe, to get you to join him or die. They know your power. But those protections will not save you now, Atlas. They are useless. Mr. Smith and his men have grown immensely in power. He wants to be the Devil's own right hand. He will try either to recruit you or get you out of the way. He wants the power of the Soul Binder; can you imagine that? Binding and collecting souls at will, with no care if they are innocent or guilty? War will come again: do you understand? Your life is in imminent peril. This *world* is in imminent peril. I'm surprised you haven't been hit by now. You won't survive this, Atlas, not if he doesn't want you to, not even with that sacred pendant."

Atlas rubbed his eyes. His first thought was to wonder if this day could get any worse. His second thought was that yes, it could. It very much could.

Walter shuffled over beside him.

"Listen, Atlas," he said gently, "long before you, James Le Fondre was a Soul Binder. He died in 1912 and is buried in the catacombs under Christ Church Cathedral.

"He was the finest soul binder that ever lived... No offense.

There wasn't a murderer he couldn't find. There wasn't a soul he couldn't bind. The previous Mr. Smiths hated him. Tried to kill him countless times, but to no avail. He lived until he was 109 and died peacefully in his bed of old age."

Atlas exhaled impatiently. "Why am I getting a history lesson here, Walter?" he asked, trying not to exhibit any visible signs that he was miffed by Walter's "finest soul binder" quip. He thought he was pretty damn good himself.

Walter smiled. "I knew James," he said. "I knew him very well."

Atlas stared at Walter. "You knew him in 1912?" he asked. "What the hell age are you, Walter?"

Walter ignored his question. "I believe he was in possession of some manner of special protection. There is no way he could have done what he did without it. No Mr. Smiths could ever touch him, and I think that's why they hated him so much. I had heard rumors of an amulet called the Silver Praesidium, but it hasn't been seen or heard of since the turn of the century, and I think it's because James had it and still does. It wards off evil and malice like nothing before. I think it could be with him in his final resting place in the wall of the catacomb. I haven't told another single soul, living or dead, this information in all my years. If that doesn't tell you we are all in peril, I don't know what will.

"You need to get that amulet, Atlas. You need to get it tonight. Don't waste a single second more. I believe your very life depends on it; *all* our souls depend on it. The very world depends on it."

Atlas sighed dramatically. He had eleven souls in his office, and the Devil's most powerful minion wanted him dead and was possessing folk with murderous rage. Right about now, he didn't much care if the Devil, or anyone working for him, killed him. He was so tired of this shit.

"Atlas," Walter whispered, moving closer and gripping his arm. "Now is not the time to give up. If Mr. Smith kills you, he takes your powers, and all souls, whether innocent or guilty, will go to Hell. Young Stephen here. Your dear beloved mother. Burning in the fires of Hell for all eternity. Innocent souls damned forever.

First Ireland, then the world. This dark power will be infectious. You can't let it happen."

Atlas nodded slowly and gathered himself. "You know I would never let that happen, Walter," he said, turning on his heels and marching back outside with Caliber close behind.

CHAPTER NINE

Atlas sat for a moment, staring at the steering wheel of his car as if it would magically conjure up solutions to his current problems. He laughed quietly when he realized what Walter had just done. It was exactly what Caliber had done with Shotgun in Belfast: stirred his emotions by bringing up his mother. No matter about anyone else, his mother was not going to spend eternity in the fiery pits of Hell. She had endured that pain and much more on this Earth with his father.

Atlas sighed. He longed for a normal life, one that didn't involve murders and murderers, souls and lords of the underworld looking to annihilate him. He wondered when that day would come. He wondered why he kept doing this job. There were times he hated it, and there were times when he loved it. Helping people get justice and peace was what fueled him. He felt alive doing this job, even though it would probably kill him.

From his vantage point, he looked down at the lights of the city, over the rooftops of houses, and thought of other people in their homes tonight, worrying about mortgages and troubles with kids, dealing with horrible people at work, and he envied them profusely.

From the passenger seat, Caliber opened his mouth to speak, but Atlas raised his hand, and he shut it again.

A large black crow landed on the hood of the car as Atlas turned the ignition. He switched on the window wipers to scare it away, but it sat there, staring at him as he drove slowly back down the dark driveway.

Atlas rolled down his window. "Get off, you stupid bird!" he shouted, but it didn't budge. "Get out of my way!" He threw a cigarette box at it, but still, it didn't move.

"I don't think it speaks English, Atlas," muttered Caliber from the passenger seat, still anxious about speaking aloud.

Atlas sounded his horn and the crow lifted off, and they watched as it disappeared into the darkness.

Atlas turned his gaze back to the driveway and accelerated away, straining his eyes to try to see the gateposts or crematorium sign. The lights from the city had disappeared. As they moved closer, the mist swelled into a black tornado. Driving closer, they realized it was a spiraling mass of birds sucking in gravel and branches until it formed a gigantic being with mammoth limbs and fiery red eyes.

The creature was wrought from the essence of a thousand crows, a macabre symphony of sleek feathers and twisted sinew, a monstrous amalgamation that moved with the eerie grace of a shadow cast by the moonlight. Once completely formed, it bounded toward them.

"It's made of fucking crows, Atlas!" shouted Caliber from the passenger seat. Atlas ignored him, trying desperately to see out the back window as he reversed at speed back up the driveway.

The avian abomination, the harbinger of the Devil's will, still came at them. Its ebony plumage shimmered with an otherworldly sheen, its eyes reflecting the light of Hell's fires, and the talons that adorned its monstrous limbs swung wildly at the car.

"Bloody hell, Atlas!" shouted Caliber. "Go faster!"

Atlas slammed on the brakes and shifted into gear, spitting gravel everywhere. The ground shook with each of the beast's mammoth steps.

The creature stretched out one of its gargantuan wings, pounding it onto the hood of Atlas's car and sending it somersaulting into the air. Atlas intermittently saw the crematorium's lights in the distance as they spun around like the contents of a washing machine before the car hit the ground again. Everything went black.

His face stung. Blackness again. More stinging.

"We need to get out, Atlas!" yelled Caliber, slapping him hard in the face. "Get up!"

Atlas shook his head to gather his bearings. They were upside down. He could see the creature soaring low over the grass toward them, but his head hurt so much. His face was wet, and he could taste the metallic wetness of his own blood. He closed his eyes for just a second before Caliber's renewed slapping jolted him awake again. Walter was right: his protections were useless. They needed to run.

He crawled out of the car and saw Caliber calling him from the edge of a thick forest area. "Come *on*, Atlas! Run!"

Atlas picked up the pace and they disappeared into the darkness, Caliber running ahead, Atlas trying to keep up. His head pounded in tandem with his heartbeat, his pulse nearly deafening.

The creature crashed into the forest after them, the trees slowing it down due to its girth. Each time it met resistance, screeching crows flew from its form to seek them out before being sucked back into the swirling vortex again.

Atlas and Caliber charged through the trees as moonlight struggled to pierce the thick canopy. Spectral glimmers cast upon the gnarled roots seemed to writhe like serpents beneath the loamy earth.

"He can't see us in here," panted Atlas. "Move quietly, slowly. We need to get out of here."

The nightmarish creature, an infernal fusion of a thousand avian souls bound together in a macabre dance of feathers and malice, moved slowly, hunting them like a prowling cheetah. Its disjointed form undulated and pulsed, a writhing mass of caws and shrieks that echoed through the tangled labyrinth of the forest. Branches groaned and twisted as it moved.

Atlas, his head still spinning from the initial collision with the creature, crept backward, keeping his eye on it. He stepped on a branch, its sharp snap echoing through the woods, and the creature spun its head towards them.

Its caws crescendoed into a cacophony of terror, drowning out its prey's desperate gasps as they stumbled blindly again through the undergrowth, trying to find a way out. A flurry of talons and beaks descended on them with unerring precision, tearing Atlas's flesh in a savage ballet of carnage.

His head and face bleeding profusely now, Atlas ran while batting away the marauding birds tearing at his skin. Just when he'd about lost hope of eluding the beast, he glimpsed a stone wall in front of him and heard traffic beyond it.

His heart pounding like a drum, he sprinted toward the wall, his only hope of escape. He didn't know what was on the other side of it, but anything was better than where he was.

Adrenaline surging, he clambered over the wall, defying gravity's grasp and feeling the rush of wind against his face. Time slowed, each heartbeat echoing in his ears, as the ground rushed up to meet him, hard and unforgiving. His muscles strained, absorbing the impact, and he rolled to disperse the force. Highway traffic thundered past him, taking his breath away.

He rose swiftly, stealing a glance above and catching another glimpse of the grotesque silhouette framed against the moon. With renewed urgency, he bolted, an approaching semi-truck swerving out of the way, missing him by mere centimeters.

The creature crashed to the ground behind him, sending large fragments of stone and cement everywhere. It was immediately struck by a speeding double-decker bus, which then swerved and spun, narrowly missing Atlas before hitting the wall beside him. The screeching of crows was deafening as they fought to get away but were sucked back into the creature's central mass again. The entity took another step forward but was mown down by several other vehicles in a cataclysmic pile-up. The few surviving crows flew away with an almighty din into the night.

Atlas, his back to the highway wall, gulped in a lungful of frosty air. Curious, alarmed bus passengers peered out its steamy windows at him and pointed. Seconds later, Caliber poked his head over the wall.

"Are you alright there, chief?" he asked. "Or are you one of us now, the undead?"

Atlas was sure that he had met the first of Mr. Smith's friends. "Yeah," he said, panting. "Only just. Jesus, that was close, several times over."

Caliber jumped down to join him on the road as people started emerging tentatively from the wreckage of their vehicles. Thankfully, nobody appeared to be too seriously hurt.

"What the hell was that?" Caliber asked, looking at the blanket of dead birds and feathers strewn across the road.

"What *from* Hell was that, more like," Atlas replied, wiping his brow.

Atlas heard sirens in the distance, and he really didn't want to explain to the police why he had jumped onto the road, or why he was so banged up, or how a huge flock of now-dead crows had caused a multi-vehicle collision.

"We need to get to Christ Church Cathedral right now," he said.

They weaved through the static traffic to the other side of the road, climbed a wall, ran through a schoolyard, and emerged onto a suburban street. He recognized the area: Varie had grown up a few streets away. Her mother still lived in the house.

As they walked past the neatly lined houses, Atlas examined himself. He looked like he had been through a shredder, his face a mess of blood and muck. That said, Caliber still looked worse.

Atlas glanced through the windows they passed at life going on inside the suburban houses. Lights shone from living rooms, exuding a sense of quiet contentment and serenity, their façades bathed in the warm glow of street lamps.

Picket fences delineated boundaries between each carefully tended yard, and Atlas looked up at a window as the curtains closed on a warm, golden room. There was a peaceful serenity and wholesomeness that stood in stark contrast to the duo walking down their street.

Atlas suddenly felt vulnerable to the underworld for the first time in years. He was startled by every noise, suspicious of every passing person, and the realization unsettled him.

"That was a close call, Atlas," said Caliber. "You were very nearly dead like me! I wouldn't want that to happen to you, partly because you wouldn't be able to help me move on to the other place and partly because we'd be stuck together forever. Two dead dudes roaming the Earth with no prospects. That would be truly awful."

Atlas looked at the dead man and managed a smile. "Thanks for your help back there. You're right. If you hadn't woken me up, I'd be dead right now."

He turned to see a bus rumbling down the street. "Come on," he said, starting to jog. "We'll be walking for hours. We need to get this protection amulet, get my equipment working again, and get you and the rest of the souls sitting in my office sorted."

"I think I might miss you when I move on," Caliber said, running behind him. "This is the most fun I've had in my life or death. Whatever. That creepy Nostradamus guy in the crematorium, the big monster thing... It's been good."

The bus stopped, and the pair climbed on board, the driver surveying Atlas's bloody face and tattered clothes with horror as Atlas fished loose change from his pocket. He looked along the aisle and was met with the frightened faces of elderly women hugging their shopping and people in business suits recoiling. He thought for a moment that they could see Caliber but then realized that they were actually frightened by *his* appearance.

He smiled in an attempt to appear normal and friendly as they sat down, Atlas next to the window. He looked at Caliber and smiled. The corpse had proved himself useful and always had his back. He was actually good company. Atlas wanted to say something meaningful about all this and opened his mouth to speak, but he was so awkward with expressing emotions, embarrassed by them. He couldn't think of a thing to say, so just nodded instead.

They got off at Portmarnock Railway Station, a Victorian-style fusion of past and present, frequented by city workers who preferred the suburbs.

They walked beneath ornate ironwork and embellished, sweeping archways and into the station, where digital departure boards and sleek ticket kiosks blended with polished wooden benches and vintage signage.

The smell of freshly brewed coffee wafted towards them, and Atlas's stomach growled. He paid for his ticket, and they made their way to the platform to catch the next train into the city center. It was bright, noisy, and packed with revelers. Atlas positioned himself with his back to a wall to prevent a surprise attack from behind.

The adrenaline had worn off, and he started to shiver, his tattered suit jacket unable to keep out the cold. He had left his winter coat in his car, his beloved vintage car that had been destroyed by a giant creature made from birds and branches. He wondered how he would explain that to his insurance company. Caliber sat quietly on the ground beside him. He seemed melancholy, but Atlas didn't want to ask him. He just wanted a moment of peace—to gather himself and regain his strength.

A woman's boisterous laughter brought him back to the present moment as a crowd of women wearing crowns and fairy wings ambled down the platform. He was glad to see the train trundling slowly into the station.

"Are you ready, Caliber?" he asked, nodding toward the platform. Caliber got up, and they filed in behind the bachelorette party, who were all wearing "Team Bride" emblazoned t-shirts. Intermittent squealing from the group jolted Atlas from his thoughts.

"What the hell is that?" shouted one of them as the train came to a stop in front of them. She was pointing up at the night sky. "Is it birds? It's so weird."

"I dunno," said another. "And I don't care either; get me to the pub!" They all giggled and cheered.

Atlas looked from the sky to Caliber. "We need to get on that train," he said urgently. "I don't like the look of that."

Caliber nodded in agreement.

A huge mass swirled above them, black against the midnight blue sky, moving like a murmuration of starlings.

The train doors swung open, and the bachelorettes started to move into the carriage. Atlas's gaze never left the black mass. He pushed forward a little and hoped the women would hurry up.

"My heel is stuck!" shouted one of them, laughing as she bent down to free it and causing everyone behind her to stop.

Atlas watched as the mass stopped mid-flight and began to descend, hurtling towards them.

"Move, move, MOVE!" he shouted, shoving the remaining women into the carriage. People fell over the stuck woman and landed on the ground, angry yells ringing out as Atlas pushed everyone ahead of him and followed closely behind. The stuck woman was crying, and her boot heel had lodged in the doors, rendering them unable to close. Atlas unzipped her boot, pulled out her leg, and pushed her back into a seat, kicking the boot so hard out of the door that it landed on the adjacent platform.

The woman got up and shouted in his face about her boot as he frantically pushed the button to close the doors.

"Dear God, please close, please close," he whispered as he began to hear a buzzing noise over the train's engine. "Close all the doors! Now!" he yelled up the train.

The doors began to glide shut as the lights of the station were eaten up by darkness. A train station employee came out of his office to see what the commotion was, and Atlas saw the expression on the man's face turn to terror as the train doors closed and thousands of winged insects swarmed the station, suffocating everything.

The train chugged forward as the screaming started. The bachelorettes huddled in their seats, the woman with one boot clinging tightly to Atlas's taut arm as he recoiled in horror at the sight outside. The lights inside the train car flickered, and he dearly hoped the driver would put their foot down and get them away from the hellish platform.

The windows were alive with disgusting spiders and centipedes. There was nothing Atlas hated more: he was terrified of spiders and centipedes. They had far too many legs. He looked away and swallowed hard to stop himself from throwing up, smiling weakly at the one-booted woman. He looked at all the legs again and gagged. As the train picked up speed, the spiders and centipedes were blown off. By the time they had reached their Lord Edward Street stop, only a few of the more persistent ones were still attached.

"We need to hurry, Caliber," urged Atlas, stepping off onto the platform. Behind them, the one-booted woman moved towards Atlas with purpose. He looked at her feet as she hobbled across the serrated, concrete platform, her remaining boot in her hand.

"What are you doing?" he asked her, bewildered. "Look at your feet! They're bleeding! You've stood on..."

He moved just in time to avoid the heel of her boot hitting his head. Her friends were screaming at her from the train to come back as the door alarms beeped to alert passengers that it was about to move off, but she ignored them.

She lunged again, and Atlas grabbed her arm. She had a glazed look in her eyes. He asked her again what she was doing, but she wasn't there.

"Stop! Stay away!" he shouted, pushing her back, but she kept coming at him.

The train station manager came towards them, a portly man whose hat hid a bald head well. As he approached, Atlas started to tell him what was happening. The woman's heel made contact with Atlas's head as he was distracted, and the manager placed his hands around Atlas's neck and began to squeeze. He couldn't breathe and was about to pass out as the woman kept assaulting him with her boot. He could hear Caliber shouting and pulling at his arm. He mustered whatever strength he had left to knee the manager hard in the groin. He dropped Atlas immediately, who broke into a stumbling jog, heading for the stairs and exit.

A woman with a stroller stopped walking, abandoned her baby, turned, and lunged at Atlas, who pushed her to the ground. A man reading a paper on a bench got up and struggled with him until Atlas punched him in the throat and broke free. They kept coming at him from all angles. A woman at the newsagent stand raced at him with her scissors, and he broke her nose with a swift jab. A man serving at a coffee kiosk watched him approach and ran at him, but Atlas swept his feet from under him, sending him tumbling to the ground. A van's tires screeched to a halt, and the driver got out and shoved Atlas against a wall before trying to choke him out. Atlas headbutted him and wriggled free, leaving his suit jacket sleeve with his attacker.

He ran out of the station and onto the road, where a taxi swerved out of its lane and drove straight for him. He dodged an oncoming semi-truck and stopped on the other side of the road to catch his breath. They were still coming at him—more and more of them. Crazed, hate-filled people, some holding weapons, and all wearing blank expressions.

"Atlas!" shouted Caliber from behind him. "Watch out!"

An elderly woman walking her Labrador lunged at him with the dog's leash in her hand and wrapped the leash tightly around his neck as her miserable dog could only watch. Atlas tumbled to the ground, throwing her over his back as a double-decker bus screamed to a halt, the passengers all piling out and running at him. Atlas ran into the shadow cast by Christ Church Cathedral as an army of the murderous and seemingly possessed gave chase.

He climbed the railings of the closed church at speed and jumped down into the grounds, the impact of his feet hitting the ground causing him to roar in pain. He frantically looked for a window he could smash to get in. Finding one, he picked up a big stone and threw it through a window barely large enough for his frame to squeeze through. As he did so, he cut his arm badly on a shard of glass and fell on the cold stone floor beneath.

Caliber was already standing beside the door. "This way, Atlas; come on," he said, nodding at the door.

Adrenaline was now coursing through Atlas's veins. A cut on his head was bleeding badly down his face, and blood from the wound on his arm was turning his shirt crimson. He felt dizzy and disorientated but knew that he had to go on.

The pair found themselves in the main church.

Streetlight filtered through stained glass, casting warm, kaleidoscopic hues upon ancient stone pillars. High vaulted ceilings soared overhead, adorned with intricate carvings and delicate ribbing. The nave unfolded before them in graceful arches, revealing a sacred space where history breathed. The air was infused with incense and reverence. It was so quiet, vast, and serene, standing at odds with what was happening outside its doors.

There was a sign on the wall pointing to the Catacombs.

"Catacombs this way," said Caliber, running in front of the altar. "Come on!"

A large stained glass window disintegrated in front of their eyes, and a brick skidded across the floor towards them. Atlas unhooked the rope from a gold barrier post around the altar and ran after Caliber with it, closing and barricading doors as he went. They ran down winding stone steps to the catacombs.

Descending into the catacombs, they stepped into a labyrinthine underworld of ancient stone passages, their walls bearing the weight of time. The air was heavy with the scent of earth and dampness, while the only sound was the echo of their footsteps reverberating against the cold stone.

Sporadically placed torches flickered, their firelight casting eerie shadows that danced across walls adorned with cryptic inscriptions and fading frescoes. Rows upon rows of niches, like silent sentinels, cradled the bones of the departed. In this subterranean realm, time stood still, the boundary between the living and the dead blurring into obscurity.

"Find James Le Fondre, Caliber," Atlas shouted. "His coffin is buried in these walls; his name will be engraved somewhere. Quickly!"

The pair ran along the walls, scanning the names of bishops and archbishops.

"Here," shouted Caliber after what seemed an age. "James Le Fondre!"

Atlas could hear voices from above and realized that it wouldn't be long until they were trapped in this small space with hundreds of murderous individuals. He would never survive. He ran at the wall, swinging the barrier post like a baseball bat, causing the stone to crack. He could hear shouting from not far away and swung again. The crack lengthened. Another swing with the metal post and the stone fell away, a coffin falling to the ground and breaking apart. A skeletal arm flopped out onto the ground.

"Forgive me, James," whispered Atlas, pulling the coffin's wood apart. "This is an emergency."

Shadows of people flickered along the walls.

"Hurry, Atlas," said Caliber breathlessly. "I don't want to die twice."

Atlas rummaged under the skeleton's shirt until his hand hit the cold metal of a chain.

The first of the crazed attackers burst out of the small tunnel, with more and more following, like ants bursting forth from an anthill. Atlas recognized the one-booted woman from the train.

"Atlas!" shouted Caliber, turning to fight. The marauding masses just ran through him. A man charged at Atlas with a knife held aloft.

Atlas yanked the silver chain from the skeleton's neck and pulled it clumsily over his head. He held it against his heart, feeling warmth, light, and a still calmness filling his body.

The man with the knife stopped suddenly and dropped it, his hate-filled expression vanishing. The attackers stopped running and stood, bewildered by their surroundings. The one-booted woman asked Atlas what was going on and where her friends were: she was supposed to be in the pub as she was getting married next Saturday. Atlas ignored her.

Caliber was bent in two, hands on his knees like he had just finished a marathon.

"Jesus Christ, Atlas," he said, panting. "You nearly gave me a heart attack right there. Seriously!"

"You and me both, friend," said Atlas. "That was insane."

Atlas put his arm around the dead man and limped through the bewildered crowd out into the night. Atlas looked down at his arm. He was losing a lot of blood and was beginning to feel light-headed.

"I swear this fucker is going to be the end of me, Caliber," he said.

"You just called me your friend!" replied Caliber with a triumphant look on his face.

Atlas groaned.

CHAPTER TEN

"I'm afraid you're going to need stitches, Mr. Bishop," said the genial nurse. "In your arm and your head. I'm just going to grab some things I need. Lie back and try to relax; I won't be long."

Atlas leaned back, trying to shoo away the feeling that the sterile white walls were closing in on him. The clinical scent of antiseptic that permeated the air was making him nauseated. He sank into the narrow, stiff treatment bed as much as it would allow. Beyond the blue curtain's edge, the steady rhythm of Emergency Room activity echoed.

He closed his eyes to the stark overhead light above him. The adrenaline had worn off and he was utterly exhausted, devoid of any energy, barely able to lift his hand to his face. He dozed off and woke again to cold hands on his chest.

"Nurse, do you need me to take off my shirt or anything?" he said without opening his eyes. He felt a tugging at the chain around his neck and immediately sat up, pushing a young male doctor's hands away.

"What are you doing?" demanded Atlas, swinging his legs off the bed.

The doctor stared at him blankly without speaking.

"I asked you a question!" said Atlas firmly.

"Mr. Smith requests an audience," the doctor finally said, his unnaturally deep voice filling every corner of the tiny cubicle. "Hellfire Club. Tomorrow night, 9:30 pm."

The nurse swung open the curtains, focusing on not dropping her tray of instruments. "Right," she said cheerily. "Let's put you back together then, shall we, Mr. Bishop?" She looked up and saw the doctor still standing there.

"Oh! Are you okay, Dr. Devlin?" she asked the doctor, whose gaze hadn't left Atlas. "It's just stitches with this one; he doesn't need anything else. I can sort him out; it's fine. Are you okay? You look a bit tired."

The doctor looked at her blankly and walked away without answering. She rolled her eyes and tutted. "Honestly," she said, exasperated. "Some of these young doctors. They have absolutely no manners."

Atlas blew cigarette smoke high into the air. He was in the dimension beyond exhaustion now. His head hurt, his arm throbbed, and he just wanted to crawl up into a ball and forget everything that was happening. He looked up to the bright sky. He hadn't realized he had been inside the hospital for as long as he had: it was almost 11:00 am.

Daytime was less dangerous, he convinced himself. But the incident with the doctor had spooked him. How did Mr. Smith always know where he was? He didn't even want to think where he would be without the protection amulet.

A car horn beeped, bringing him back down to earth. He jumped in.

"I'm sorry for texting you like that, Varie," he said. "But I didn't know who else to contact. There was trouble."

Varie put her hand on his bloodied head. "You don't say, Atlas," she said, looking worried. "Are you okay? What on earth is going on?"

He scanned her face as she spoke, admiring her softly curved nose, skin like butter, and lips imbued with the hue of ripe berries. Her eyes were luminescent verdant pools framed with lush and thick mascara-laden ebony lashes. Cascading locks of honeyed blonde hair fell below her shoulders like waves of silk. She was wearing a faded Nirvana t-shirt and skinny jeans and still looked classic, timeless. Her wrists were adorned with crystal beads, as usual. She felt like home, like peace. Atlas exhaled loudly.

"I've just had a bad night, Var," he said.

Approaching ambulance sirens signaled a hasty move away from the front door of the hospital.

"I'm really sorry about texting you," he said as they pulled out of the hospital grounds and into traffic. "I didn't have anyone else to call."

She looked at him sadly and then back to the road.

"No one who understands, anyway," he added, trying to redeem himself in her eyes. He didn't want her to think him pathetic. "My car was destroyed by this big creature made out of crows."

Varie looked from the road to Atlas with a concerned look on her face. "Crows," she said slowly and looked back at the road.

"Yeah," he said. "I've never seen anything like it. Then there were all these insects. Jesus, Varie, you had to see the amount of them. Spiders, centipedes..." He wretched, gathered himself, and continued. "They attacked the train we were on. I fucking hate spiders."

Varie looked at him again and back to the road, saying nothing. She looked worried.

"And then, the worst. I was attacked by all these crazy, possessed people who wanted to kill me, and I had to break into Christ Church Cathedral to steal a necklace from the body of a long-dead Soul Binder."

Varie looked straight ahead. "Atlas, what is happening?" she said. "Surely that's not normal?"

Atlas laughed out loud so hard it hurt.

"Nothing I do is normal, Var," he said. "But I agree with you, this is absolutely not normal."

Varie looked from Atlas to the road and back to Atlas again as if searching for an answer. "Listen, I am still a police officer," she said. "Don't be telling me about any illegal stuff you're doing—breaking into churches, stealing stuff, and the like. I can't know that stuff because I might have to arrest you."

Atlas laughed again and looked out the window.

He had told Varie about his new line of work a few weeks after he had first met Gabriel, and he was one hundred percent certain he wasn't a hallucination. She had visited him in the hospital. The nurses said that she had come in straight after he was brought in by ambulance and every day that he was unconscious. They said she had cried over his bed.

She had come to see him when he woke up and held his hand but had said she couldn't go back to him, that he made her too sad, made her cry too much, that she was afraid of being consumed by his demons too. She had said she was sorry but had to move on.

They had met a few weeks later in St. Stephen's Green: him on crutches, her in heels. They had sat on a bench beside the serene lake, sipping coffee and watching the swans glide by. He had said that he wanted to tell her something and needed her to listen but that he wasn't mad.

"When I woke up in the hospital," he had begun, "I saw the ghost of my mother. She was right there. I see other people, too, murdered people. They come to me for help."

He had given her a moment to process this information as she had looked at him like he was mad. But he had wanted her to know—to know him—he didn't want there to be any barriers between them knowing one another completely, the good and the bad, the way it always was.

"So," he had begun, because this is where it got complicated. "The Angel Gabriel, he came to the hospital, and he..."

"Atlas, for fuck's sake," she had shouted. "Stop this..."

Atlas had put his hand over hers, then took it away again awkwardly. "Varie, please," he had pleaded. "I know this sounds completely mad—that I sound completely mad. But I now bind the souls of the murdered to their murderers, I'm Ireland's Soul Binder. Other Soul Binders work with police on cold cases and to bring those who can't be nailed to justice. Our kind of justice—we make them pay. We deliver them to Hell."

Varie had scanned his face for a smidgen of humor. "Why are you doing this to me?" she had begged, her eyes filling with tears. "Why? You have lost your mind. I can't, Atlas," she had said, standing up. "I can't do this anymore. I'm sorry."

She had walked away, her cream coat billowing in the wind, blonde hair bouncing along behind her. He had watched her go over the bridge and out of sight. He continued sitting in the park, finished his coffee, then went to Gilligan's and drank himself stupid.

A week later, he had arrived at Finglas Garda Station with the corpse of a murdered man and asked for her at reception. She had reluctantly brought him into an interview room and brought the file he had instructed her to get, rolling her eyes as he told her that the victim had been killed by a man he had been talking to at a party.

"How do you know that, Atlas?" she had asked him irritably. "This guy was found on wasteland at the docks, totally clean. We only found out his name this morning. We have no leads, and you mean to tell me you know who killed him? What, are you a psychic now? I really don't have time for this."

"He's standing here beside me, Var," he had said, his face stern and serious.

"At, you're not well," she had said. "Please, don't do this. I hate seeing you like this."

"Varie," she said. "His name is Barry Malloy. He's standing right here."

"How do you know his name?" she had snapped, eyeing him

suspiciously. "We haven't released that yet. Atlas, you better tell me. How do you know?"

"Because he's standing right here," he said, pointing his thumb to his right. "He was strangled," he said, looking up at the corpse. "It looks like the guy used wire because his neck is cut right back to the bone. He was almost decapitated."

"How do you know this, Atlas?" Varie insisted. "There was only me, Robin, and Gerry on that case and the coroner. I haven't even written up the notes yet. None of it was made public. Who told you this?"

"Varie," Atlas said gently, leaning over the table towards her. "He is standing right here with me. The guy who killed him cut off three of his fingers on his right hand—must have been for a souvenir, the sick bastard."

Varie, her face unable to hide her shock, had looked over Atlas's shoulder and around the room.

"He says he met this guy at a party in Glasnevin, says he had a Welsh accent," Atlas looked around as the corpse spoke. "Sorry, he says it was a Scottish accent. The guy had told him he worked on a building site in Drumcondra, a shop complex. Said his first name was James. He was of stocky build, had black hair, and had a Manchester United tattoo on his right arm. I'm going there now, and I'm going to bind this guy's soul to him. He will make him pay for what he did and will drag him to Hell. He won't be spending any time in jail, I'm afraid. But it's still justice, whatever way you look at it."

Varie had taken a while to process the deluge of information. But three days later, she had arrived at his front door and informed him that police divers fished the body of a Scottish man called James Snell out of the Liffey. They had gone to his house in Drumcondra and found a scribbled note confessing to the murder, along with notebooks full of hate, far-right ideologies, and murderous plans.

Varie said she was listening.

Atlas had told her about his work, how he had struggled with it, and how he hoped that one day he might be able to bind his mother to his father and put his demons to rest. He had wanted her to say that she would take him back, that she would help him, that she would be there for him, that everything would be alright. But she had just smiled, kissed him on the cheek, said she'd see him again soon and left.

Over the next six years, she had slipped him cases the police couldn't solve, and he would find the perpetrators. He had never stopped loving her, and she had never stopped keeping him at a safe distance, well away from her heart.

He looked at her now in the car, her brow furrowed, trying to navigate the Dublin traffic and get him home.

"Do you remember I told you about Mr. Smith?" he asked her. "Hell's version of me."

"The smoking man, the guy with the attitude?" she replied, pulling out onto a divided highway.

"Yeah," he replied. "Him. It seems he is planning something bad, something that could threaten the very fabric of the universe."

Varie turned to him, looking frightened.

"Yeah," he said. "It's bad. I think he has something to do with the mass brawls, the mad stuff happening with people beating the hell out of one another and then not remembering anything about it. He seems to have gangland figures working for him, spreading hate and anger. I think he's making these people murder, but I don't know how. He's possessing them, and I think he's trying to kill me. The people who were coming at me last night, Varie—they were deranged. Mums with strollers and little old ladies trying to strangle me with their dog leashes...just glazed expressions, but rage in their eyes. I think he's trying to scare me, intimidate me, show me what he's capable of.

"The people I'm talking to say he's planning something with huge numbers. I don't know how he does it, but everyone just goes insane. They fill up with hate, and they just start killing one another. He takes the murderers' souls straight to Hell, and I think he wants the innocent, too. I think he has notions of taking over the binding so he can fill all Hell with their souls, and that will mean war between Heaven and Hell."

Varie stared at him, shocked. "Why would...?" she stuttered. "What?"

Atlas shrugged his shoulders, which he soon realized was a very painful move. The painkillers the nurse had given him were wearing off rapidly.

Varie looked at the road ahead. "There was an incident last night in a church in north Dublin," she said. "A brawl at a vigil Mass. Twenty-four people injured, and four senior citizens dead. They were killing one another in there, Atlas! We had to send in the riot squad! Even the priest was arrested for beating a man with a candlestick! It was utter mayhem. I bet it was these guys. Everyone at the station is scratching their heads about these incidents, and no one can explain them, not even those actually involved in them. It makes no sense whatsoever."

Atlas nodded. It also hurt when he moved his head. "The incidents all over Dublin—he's ramping it up," he said. "We have an agreement, Heaven and Hell. We had to sign a contract. If he breaks that contract, I don't even want to think what would happen. This is the end of the world stuff here, Var." He continued, "We are meeting tomorrow. I will remind him that our contract is binding, that it can't be messed with."

Varie gasped. "You're meeting with the man who is trying to kill you? Atlas, you can't. Look at the state of you! He almost killed you tonight."

Atlas's head was pounding. He looked out the window and away from her, remembering how Varie's voice went up a few octaves when she was angry. He remembered her angry voice could cut through steel. He was hungry, needed coffee, and didn't want to listen to screechy voices right now, even if it was Varie's. He rubbed his eyes, then his temples, and then exhaled loudly and dramatically.

"You're hungry," said Varie. "You always do that loud sighing thing when you're hungry. Let's grab some breakfast. We can talk about all of this madness. Maybe you'll be more rational when you eat something. Andrew's gym gear is in the back seat. You guys are the same size, and he won't mind if you borrow a T-shirt. It's in the bag on the back seat. Put it on."

Atlas bit his lip. He didn't particularly want to wear Varie's husband's clothes, but he looked down at his own blood-splattered t-shirt he was wearing and reluctantly reached around for it. It smelled of expensive aftershave.

Varie had met Andrew at work: he was a police officer as well. Atlas wanted to hate him because Varie loved him, but he was a nice man, and he treated her well. He didn't drink himself into stupors, disappear for days on end, and pick fights because he didn't feel comfortable when things were going well. Varie deserved a man like that. He just wished he was that man.

He pulled his bloody t-shirt over his head and put Andrew's on.

Varie pulled her car down a narrow street and navigated the vehicle into a tiny parking spot with expert precision, leaving no more than two centimeters front and back. She looked at Atlas for some semblance of praise as she turned off the ignition.

"Nice parking," he said eventually, managing a half smile even though it hurt.

They found a seat in a busy bistro, all red brick and bohemian furniture. The place radiated an eclectic charm, its walls adorned with vintage posters and signs about coffee, allowing people to make bad decisions quicker. Wooden tables, worn with age, were scattered across the mosaic-tiled floor, each adorned with mismatched chairs. Soft melodies of folk music intertwined with the aroma of freshly brewed coffee. A chipper blonde teenager with a nose ring took their order and brought them some coffee, which Atlas drank like it was water, and he was fresh from the desert. Everything hurt, even his very hair.

"Atlas," Varie said gently, leaning over the table to him. "Please, let me help you. How can I help with this? I don't want anything to happen to you." She put her hand on his. "Please, Atlas. Is there another way to sort this out? Do you have to go to him?"

People under umbrellas at the outdoor tables were laughing and chatting, and Atlas was extremely jealous of their ignorance of what really went on in the world.

"Atlas, I'm really worried about you," she said again. "We are friends. Am I not allowed to worry for you? Why won't you let me in? You keep me at such a distance, always. Come on! We've known each other long enough to still care about each other. You said not five minutes ago that you couldn't trust anyone else."

Atlas thought about what Caliber had said, that he had the emotional range of a toaster, that he needed to trust people more, and suddenly felt bad. "Varie, listen," he said. "I have protection, and I will be okay. I'm always okay. Don't be worrying. Everything will be fine."

He sat back as the waitress set a full Irish breakfast down in front of him. He could feel his mouth watering and looked from the brown sauce bottle to Varie; her eyes were wet.

"Hell has never wanted you dead before, At," she said. "This is new stuff. I'm scared."

Atlas sighed again. He was so tired and so hungry. He just wanted to eat something and sleep. His brain wasn't capable of deep thinking at the moment.

Varie dabbed at her eyes with her napkin, and he forced a smile, placing his hand on hers. He was almost faint with hunger. "I'll be okay," he insisted. "I will be. I promise." Her hand felt so warm under his, her skin so soft, and he could feel her energy pulsating through his flesh. As they looked at each other, for a moment, there was no one else in the bistro.

Atlas sighed. "I've been thinking these last few days about stuff," he said, his thumb rubbing the top of her hand. "I dunno, I have this new friend, and he's all deep and into, I dunno, talking, emotions, feelings, and stuff. Anyway, after we broke up, I blamed you for everything, and I'm sorry. None of it was your fault. It was mine. I messed up. You were always so happy, you always looked out for me, and I was just too fucked up to realize how good I had it."

He looked around the bistro as he spoke, finding it easier to speak honestly when he didn't have to make eye contact.

A man dressed in a long black leather coat walked in the door.

"You know that feeling good, feeling happy was hard for me," he continued. "It doesn't seem real, almost. You know, the bad stuff happened to me when I was a kid, and from that time, my counselor says I just kept looking for that hurt over and over again. It's like there's a part of me that wants to feel hurt. I don't know. It's what I have always known, you know? It feels normal. It's hard to explain, I suppose.

"I wanted you to know it wasn't your fault, any of it. I find it hard to...you know...look, I'm sorry for everything I did or didn't do when we were together, Varie. I struggle with showing...you know... Look, just I suppose... I wanted you to know, really, that I...really loved you." He continued scanning the room.

"I thought it was better, safer, to keep you at a distance so you wouldn't get hurt by all the bad stuff inside. I wanted to keep my hurt to myself. It's like a poison. I didn't want to contaminate you with it, too, because you are good, just a good person. I'm really sorry about all that. I'll always be sorry about that."

Atlas looked back at Varie, who was now staring at him blankly. He had expected some form of emotion since he was spilling his guts out to her, but her eyes were dry. He at least thought that the speech might have brought a tear to her eye. It was the most profound speech he had ever made.

Across the room, he heard a glass smash and someone shout.

"Varie?" He tried to recall what he said to see if it had included anything that might have offended her. "Are you listening?"

A fight suddenly broke out across the bistro floor. Two men were punching one another, bumping into tables and other patrons. A well-dressed woman smashed a glass on the table in front of her and jabbed it at her friend across the table. Waitresses were rolling on the floor, pulling each other's hair and screeching. A teenager swung a silver tray at an older man's head with a sickening clang. It had the air of a bar room brawl about it, except the participants were wearing Rolex watches, Italian shoes, and Pashmina shawls.

"What the hell is this now?" shouted Atlas, standing up. Every bone in his body ached. "Jesus Christ!"

Varie stood up behind him. Atlas felt a sharp tugging at his neck, and when his eyes returned to her, she was brandishing a large kitchen knife in one hand and his protective amulets in the other.

"Oh, no, Jesus, no, Varie!" he shouted as she jabbed it at him. He ducked as a glass flew at his head from the melee two tables down.

She jabbed it at him again, nicking him on the arm. "Varie!" he exclaimed, blood pouring from the wound. "Snap out of it, woman!" Her eyes were blank and dead.

The bistro's front window smashed, and two brawling men spilled out onto the street, their arms and legs flailing.

Atlas sucked his stomach in as she jabbed at him again and again, contorting his body with her every strike. Adrenaline was coursing through his veins now, a strong painkiller. He looked around for something to protect himself with.

An older man ran at him, arms outstretched as if to strangle him, but Atlas felled him with a vicious punch. Varie growled at him in an animalistic manner and lunged at him with the knife. She wasn't a weak woman, and fighting her was starting to wear him out.

Everyone in the bistro was now fighting with each other, some of them starting to head toward Atlas.

Varie lunged again, and he wrapped his arm around hers, pushing the knife outwards and away from his body. She growled some more and hissed at him. "I'm really sorry, Varie," he said, sticking his fingers up her nose and pulling hard. She screamed. He threw her to the floor and knelt on her knife-wielding arm as she punched him in the face, causing pain to sear through his already bruised brain. His head spun wildly as she scratched, bit, and spat. Finally, Atlas wrestled the knife from her hand and sent it skidding across the kitchen floor under a fridge. He pulled Varie up by the scruff of the neck just as a waitress jumped on his back and tried to gouge out his eyes with her fake nails.

Atlas threw the waitress over his shoulder onto the ground before spinning around and throat-punching a man who was about to attack him with a tire iron. Varie launched herself at Atlas, screaming like a banshee until his palm connected hard with her nose. She recoiled, blood pouring down her face. He used the distraction to grab his protective amulets and put them over his head before rugby-tackling her, forcing her into a fireman's lift, and making for the door. On the way, he clambered over a man who was straddling another man he had just stabbed in the chest. The assailant stood, blocking Atlas's path, pulled the knife from his victim's chest, and plunged it into his own, smiling maniacally as he fell to the floor—dead.

Atlas crashed through a line of tables and chairs and climbed through a large broken window out onto the street. Varie's nails tore at his back as she tried to kick herself free. He broke into a run, her feet still flailing wildly, connecting more than once with his groin. He ran farther and farther away from the bistro. By the time he got back to the car, the flailing and scratching had stopped, and Varie was sobbing uncontrollably.

"I'm going to put you down now, Varie," he said, panting. His heart was pounding, and he felt sick and dizzy. "I want you to remain calm."

He set her down, and she stood crying, tears mixing with the blood from her injured nose. "What the fuck, Atlas?" she sobbed. "My nose is so sore. What happened? Why am I covered in blood? Why are you covered in blood? Jesus Christ, we just went for breakfast. Why is it that this always happens with you? Why can't nothing be normal with you, ever!"

Atlas sighed dramatically. He looked down at his arm, which was still bleeding. "I don't know, Varie. I don't know what happened. One minute we were talking and the next thing the whole café was killing one another. It was bizarre. It has to be something to do with Mr. Smith."

He looked down at his feet.

"You attacked me with a knife, Varie," he said quietly. "I had to disarm you. I've seen some disturbing things in my time, but that is definitely up there among the top three. Genuinely."

Varie stood open-mouthed. "Atlas, I would never..." she began. "I wouldn't hurt you."

He shook his head. "It wasn't you," he explained sympathetically. "It was like you were taken over by something, by pure rage. It was pretty wild."

Varie touched his arm. "Did I do that?" she asked. She put her hand to her nose, which had bled all over her face and shirt. "What happened to my nose?"

"Listen," Atlas interjected. "I got you out of there, and here we are. They are probably still killing each other in there. You'll need to contact your police station, as a matter of urgency, and get in there. I saw one woman stabbing another with a broken bottle. And there was a man who stabbed his friend and then himself. It was crazy."

Varie called the incident in, then hung up, a look of confusion settling on her face. She wiped her nose on her sleeve, which just made the mess worse. "I don't remember any of it, At," she said, shaking her head. The last thing I remember was you telling me you'd be okay if you met Mr. Smith."

Atlas rolled his eyes.

"Did you not hear the rest?" he asked. "All the stuff about years ago? How I'd changed? I was pouring my bloody heart out for once." He muttered expletives under his breath as he opened the car. "I'll drive," he said. "You're covered in blood."

Varie took the keys from him. "No, I'll drive," she insisted, smearing more blood over her face with her hand. "You know I always drive."

Atlas handed her the keys. He wasn't in the mood to argue, not after what he had just seen. They drove in silence to his office, where Varie switched off the ignition and turned to face him.

"That," she said, "was crazy."

Atlas nodded. She should have seen it from his perspective—her running at him with a big butcher's knife, murder in her eyes. "It was, yeah."

Varie grabbed his hand. "I want you to be alright, Atlas," she said. "I don't want anything bad to happen to you. Will you promise me you'll be careful?"

Atlas nodded again. He was shaken up, exhausted, and just didn't have the capacity for anything more taxing than finding a quiet corner and sleeping right now.

"Listen, I am going to go in," he said. "Make sure you wash your face before you go home. I don't want your husband to think I put you forward for a boxing contest this morning. And I don't want you to worry. I have protection and people looking out for me. I'll call you tomorrow or the next day, yeah? It's been a crazy day. Go and get some rest."

Varie reached across and kissed him on the cheek. Her face smelled of blood, but her hair smelled delicious. He loved Varie more than he loved anyone in the world and felt a pang of sadness so strong it made him almost nauseated. He wasn't sure if it was the medication, the moment, the lack of food, or the loss of blood.

"Be careful, Atlas," she whispered. "Come back in one piece."

Atlas closed the car door and ran up the stone steps to his office. Once inside, he heard the din and knew it would not be the best place to sleep. However, if Mr. Smith's people were following him, he didn't want to lead them to his mother in case he wanted to use her as a bargaining chip.

CHAPTER ELEVEN

Atlas opened his office door to discover it was standing room only. Many more souls had arrived in his absence. He saw a few senior citizens that he presumed were from the church Varie had just told him about. There were a few well-dressed individuals he thought might be from the pub brawl and a few from the cinema. He saw a lady wearing a Pashmina that was definitely from the bistro they had just left. Caliber was standing on his desk, trying to calm everyone down. Atlas stood for a moment in the doorway, watching the dead man tell everyone everything was going to be fine, that Atlas would sort everything out, that if they needed anything—whatever dead people could possibly need—he would sort it out.

He was going to miss him when he crossed over, he thought, as he tied a tea towel tightly around his arm to stop the bleeding from Varie's attack.

Caliber saw Atlas at the door and jumped down from the desk. "There he is," he said, smiling, his grin failing as he took in the sight of him, bleeding. "He's back."

The corpses turned to Atlas, and all started talking at once, hitting him with a flurry of questions. "What's going on? Why am I here? Am I dead? I can't be dead; I'm only twenty-four! Why can't my family hear me? Why am I so cold? Who are all these people? I was only at Mass, and now I'm here; what's going on? I only went out for lunch, and my friend attacked me. Why have some of these people got holes in their heads? I want to be alive again; can I be alive again?"

Atlas rubbed his eyes. He literally couldn't take this anymore. He was unable to process a single word. He still needed food, and he needed sleep.

Caliber noticed his distress. "Right. Everyone, back off!" he shouted. "Atlas needs to rest. Everyone out! Out onto the stairs, the other office, anywhere. Atlas needs peace and quiet and time to think. Out! Out! Out!"

He was so glad for Caliber, at that moment, that he patted him affectionately on the arm. "I need to sleep, Caliber," he said wearily. "I need someone to watch over me. Mr. Smith seems intent on taking me out; even the doctor at the hospital was working for him. Varie almost stabbed me just now."

"What? Jeez," said Caliber .22. "Listen, you can tell me about it later. Get some shut-eye, and I'll stand guard. I'll get the other members of our deceased community out on watch. You sleep."

Atlas half-walked, half-stumbled over to the sofa, and collapsed into its softness. Within seconds, he was asleep. Caliber closed the door gently behind him and instructed the corpses to man the stairs and shout at the top of their voices if they sensed danger.

Atlas awoke to Caliber gently shaking his arm. "Atlas," he whispered. "Your secretary is here in the front office. I thought you might want to wake up now. It's 7:00 pm."

Atlas looked at Caliber. "Jeez, you're not getting any prettier," he mumbled groggily.

Caliber smiled. "Yeah, you need to take a look in the mirror at yourself, pretty boy," he said.

Atlas sat up and rubbed his forehead, yelling in pain as he did so.

Elsa rushed in.

"Atlas!" she said breathlessly. "Are you okay? Oh my God, what happened to your head? Why are you covered in blood? Oh God, Atlas! You look terrible. You're in pain!"

Atlas got up, swayed a little, and sat back down again. "I'm okay, Elsa," he said. "Honestly, it looks worse than it actually is. I just had a little run in with, well, with a few bad guys. They look worse than me."

Elsa sat down on the sofa and put her hand to his head. "It looks so painful, Atlas," she said gently. She removed a silk handkerchief from her bag and tenderly began rubbing blood from his forehead.

"Poor Atlas," she said, wiping his cheek gently. "Who could do such a thing? Your poor face."

She put the handkerchief to her red lips and wet it with her tongue. Atlas could smell the perfume from her wrists as she gently rubbed it on his temple.

"What can I do?" she whispered, rubbing his lip. "Tell me how I can help you, Atlas."

She cared for him; he knew that. But this was something else. She dropped her hand, and they stared hard at one another. At that moment, he wanted to kiss her.

"Atlas," whispered Elsa as he moved closer. "Please, I..."

He put his hand on her cheek. Her skin positively radiated heat. His thumb brushed her lips, and he pulled her face towards his. They were centimeters apart, and he could smell the coconut scent from her neck, feel her breath on his skin.

Varie's face appeared in his mind, and he blinked. He looked at Elsa and smiled wistfully, even though it hurt. He wished he could let Varie go. He wished he could let Elsa in. Varie was a constant barrier to living life. He just couldn't move on. Atlas dropped his hand from her face and looked away.

"I'm sorry, Atlas, I just... I didn't mean to... I just really came in to pick up a file," she said quickly. "I wanted to work on it over the weekend, try to catch up with some..." She looked at the ruffled cushions on the sofa and the sleepy look in Atlas's eyes.

She straightened her skirt and fixed her hair, settling back into professional mode.

"Atlas, there is a strange atmosphere out there," she said, pointing out the door. "I felt it as soon as I walked up the stairs. It's worse in my office. It's like a real suffocating feeling. Heavy. Creepy almost. Is there a lost soul out there?" She blessed herself and kissed the holy medal around her neck.

Atlas looked out to her office, which was wall-to-wall corpses. There were three women sitting on her desk, dangling their feet over the edge, several more sitting on her sofa, two fighting over a chair, and several stretched out on the floor.

"Yeah, Elsa," he said, standing up. "We had one or two come in over the weekend. Don't worry, I'm going to sort it out. Things will be back to normal on Monday. I promise."

He looked at her pleadingly. "I'm really very sorry about all of this," he said. "It's been a little crazy lately. I've been a little crazy. I'll make it up to you; I swear I will. I want you to know I appreciate you so much for everything that you do for me here. I would honestly be lost without you. I really think that you and I...."

"Thanks for saying that, Atlas," she interrupted. "There are times I think... I dunno. Listen, I'll go now and leave you..." She looked at his bloody sleeve. "...to it. I'll see you on Monday."

Caliber smiled from his chair across the room before Elsa had even left the room. "What the fuck are you doing, mate?" he asked.

"How long have you been there?" Atlas snapped as he heard the front door close.

Caliber shook his head. "You have a beautiful woman there who is totally into big, nerdy freaks with undertaker energy. She's there, wanting to plant the lips on you, and you go all weird on her. Jesus Christ, man, what is wrong with you?"

Atlas snorted and tried to settle back into the softness of the sofa. He didn't spend enough time relaxing. It was like he always had to be uncomfortable to punish himself.

He liked Elsa. He liked her a lot, actually. She was beautiful and funny, wise and caring. He felt so at ease in her company. Well, more at ease than he usually did. She was perfect. The only thing wrong with her was that she wasn't Varie, and he hated himself for thinking that.

"Anyway, do you think you will be able to sort this?" asked Caliber, interrupting his thoughts.

Atlas looked over at Caliber lounging on his chair, his head back, staring at the ceiling. "I really hope so. Mr. Smith is a very volatile character, and we stand in opposition, but that is why it works. The agreement we have is sacred and binding, and I hope we can get this ironed out and get back to normal. Get all of you on your way."

Caliber sat up a little. "I really hope so, as well, Atlas," he said. "Although I'll miss my life here, my partner, and our boy, there is nothing I can do now to change that. I royally screwed up, but I think Heaven will be grand. Our daughter is there."

Atlas stared across the room at his friend. "I'm sorry, Caliber. I didn't know that."

The dead man nodded. "Yeah," he replied. "She died three years ago, a few days before her first birthday. Louisa. She was just a baby. Such a beautiful baby; she had these beautiful blonde curls. She got sick with sepsis, and it took her in a matter of hours. It was absolutely out of the blue. She just had a sore throat, normal stuff, and then we were rushing her to the hospital. There are days I still can't believe it, and then there are other days it hits me like a truck. My partner tried to take her own life about a month afterward. She left me a note saying she wanted to go take care of Louisa. But now I suppose I can. So, if I think on it, that's one positive thing in all of this shit."

Atlas nodded. He felt desperately sad. These emotions were new to him and seemed to revolve all around Caliber. "I'm so very sorry," he said. "You have had so much pain in your life, and there was me going on about my own woes. Jeez, you must think I'm a right dickhead; well, more of a dickhead than usual. I am going to make it my mission to get you back to your little girl. I'm going to get all of this sorted. Find Morrison and bind you to him. You will see Louisa again."

Caliber smiled sheepishly. "Thanks, Atlas. I'd really love that. I have had my fair share of heartache, yes, and I've had to work through that. I think that's why you and I get on so well. We know what pain—brutal, unforgiving, merciless, raw pain—feels like. We really know what that suffocating darkness feels like. We are kindred spirits. Our lives haven't exactly been easy. And I don't think you're a dickhead."

Atlas smiled back. He had talked more to Caliber in a few days than he had to anyone in his whole life. "I think you're right, my friend," he said. "I think I will miss you when you move on."

"There you go!" sang Caliber. "Look at you being all emotional, and look at that—you didn't explode, and you didn't die! You're growing!"

Atlas laughed. He knew he was right. He got up off the sofa, weaved his way through the gathered corpses in reception, stepped over those sitting in the hall, and went to the kitchen to make himself a cup of coffee. He searched in the cupboards for cups and coffee before opening all the drawers, looking for a spoon. He realized he had never actually made himself a cup of coffee for as long as he had been there. He managed. He stood proudly with a coffee made all by himself, chewing an out-of-date granola bar Elsa had left in the cupboard, and looked out of the window over the busy Dublin street below.

He wished he could call his mother, as he desperately wanted to speak to her to make sure she was okay. He knew she would be worried about him not coming home last night, but there was no way to contact her. The dead couldn't answer phones.

He wanted to tell her he was sorry that he had failed her, that he couldn't protect her from his father, and had been unable to do anything. He wanted to say how sorry he was that he had let her die there on the kitchen floor because he was eight years old and didn't know CPR or how to stop bleeding. In the six years her spirit had been with him, they hadn't once talked about that night.

He didn't know what was happening to him—perhaps it was the several near-death experiences he had had in recent days or the very real threat to his life—but he felt like time wasn't on his side anymore, and he wanted to be real and tell people how he felt before it was too late. It was a strange sensation but not one he was altogether hating.

He sipped his coffee and called his mechanic, telling him to try to salvage what was left of his beloved car from the lawn at the crematorium.

"Yeah," he said. "I was drunk at a party, and I flipped it."

There were questions from down the line.

"Yes, Frank, a party at a crematorium," he muttered defensively. "Have you never been to a party in a crematorium? Look, it's on the lawn anyway, upside down. See if you can knock it back into shape, and be gentle. Also, could you send a courtesy car to the office, please. A Jag, if you have any to spare."

Atlas listened and nodded his head as Frank's laughter taunted him from down the other end of the phone line.

"Yes, that's fine; thanks, Frank," he said. "Yes, yes, I'll let you know when the next party is at the funeral home. Very funny."

He hung up and leaned back in his chair, looking out the window again at the street below. The sun was dipping below the skyline now, hues of amber and gold rolling over the buildings. The street beneath his window, adorned with a mosaic of cobblestones, glistened in the fading light. Shadows danced, elongating the figures of passersby, shuffling through the bustling thoroughfare to get home to the things and the people they loved most.

Atlas could almost hear the city exhale a collective sigh, transitioning from the vigor of day to the serenity of dusk. In this moment, he could hear Dublin's heartbeat echoing through the narrow alleys and broad avenues, a symphony of urban life under the canvas of the setting sun.

This, this city, this life, this human existence, this balanced universe, he couldn't let anything happen to knock that sideways. Maybe all those years ago, when Gabriel was talking about him finding his *why*—why he did this job, why he didn't just give up—this was it. This moment, the moments to come.

"Atlas," said Caliber softly. "It's almost 9:00 pm; we need to go."

Atlas reached into the top drawer and removed his protection pendant, the one he always wore. He knew it no longer worked, but he pulled it over his head and its metal clinked reassuringly alongside Le Fondre's amulet, which he hadn't taken off since he had found it.

He bowed his head and whispered a protection prayer as Caliber stood in the doorway.

> "O mighty guardian, envelop me in your shield of light,
> Grant me courage to face the darkness,
> Strength to stand tall in the fight.
> With each step, let your armor of righteousness be my guide.
> As I march into battle, let justice and truth be by my side.
> May your divine presence shield me from harm's wicked grasp
> And lead me safely through the chaos with unwavering courage, I ask.
> In the name of valor and honor, I raise my voice in prayer:
> Protect me, Lord, as I venture into warfare.
> Amen."

He had been brought up a Catholic beside his devout mother in church every Sunday and had, as a young boy, looked up wide-eyed in Mass at a broken and bowed Jesus on the cross, his feet and hands nailed to the wood. It had terrified him.

The eyes of religious figures had stared down from the walls of their house, and his mother had taken him on a tour of the statues in the cathedral every Saturday, stopping to pray beneath each one, her rosary beads wrapped around her hands clasped in prayer, her head bowed.

She had pinned religious medals to the inside of his school uniform and told him to pray to St. Anthony when he lost something. She had told him to give his burden to the Lord, and he would help him carry it and had knelt beside him as he prayed before bed every night.

At her funeral, he had wondered why God hadn't helped his mother escape from a violent and brutal man who had made her life a misery. With the amount of praying she did, he thought he might have at least let her live. He asked his Aunt Mary, and she said that God took his mother because he only took the good people, and he needed her in Heaven. As he sat on the cold wooden pews, gripping his prayer book in his small hands, Atlas vowed never to be good again. He didn't want God coming for him, too.

He had lost his faith in a God that would strip a child from his mother and allow him to navigate care homes that left him broken and bruised. In his teenage years, he only shouted at God when he was drunk. In his twenties, he had mostly ignored him but still found himself sitting at the back of churches around Dublin every Christmas Eve, a flask of whiskey in his hand, absorbing the twinkling lights and gentle vocal devotion of Midnight Mass. It gave him comfort. It reminded him of his mother and afforded him a moment of peace.

He didn't wear his faith on his sleeve, but it was always there in the background, there to lean on when things got bad. And when Gabriel arrived, he at last had something physical to believe in: it wasn't just blind faith any more.

Atlas tapped his pen on the table in front of him. He didn't know what he was going to meet tonight, but he wanted to make sure he was taking every precaution possible to protect himself. If Walter was right and the power had indeed gone to Mr. Smith's head, things could get very dangerous indeed. He was so close to finding his father; he didn't want to fail now and let his mother down.

Frank, the mechanic, had left a slick, black Jaguar XF outside his office. Being on the payroll of the Vatican had its perks, for sure. It was a beautiful machine, but as he walked toward it, pressing the key fob and bringing it to life, he felt a pang of longing for his crushed car that he had loved so much and had served him so well.

"Nice wheels," said Caliber, getting in. "Really nice."

Atlas didn't acknowledge the compliment as he fastened his seatbelt and adjusted the mirrors.

"Did the mechanic say that your old banger of a car could be saved, or did he not think..."

Atlas raised his hand. "I don't even want to speak about it," he said, pulling out into traffic. "It's a real sore point at the moment."

He weaved his way through the nighttime traffic, his car's smooth engine barely audible. The city took on a different vibe at night. Neon signs danced as they passed busy city center streets. They turned, and the historic Dublin Castle loomed into view, resplendent on the hill in the warm glow of street lamps. They drove down past the River Liffey, a liquid canvas reflecting the city's luminance, then sped past narrow cobblestone lanes and strong, imposing buildings from another era and headed for Montpelier Hill. Dublin's skyline retreated in the rearview mirror and into distant memory, swallowed by the ink-black night. The city's bustling energy gave way to a serene stillness beyond their windows as they drove deeper into the countryside. The car's headlights pierced the darkness, casting fleeting glimpses of shadowy buildings as the road grew steeper.

Atlas looked up at the canopy of stars that unfurled above them, a celestial tapestry strewn across the velvety night sky. The stars were never visible from Dublin. He had almost forgotten how beautiful they were. The moon bathed the landscape in a silvery glow, illuminating the rolling hills and verdant fields spread out before them.

"Caliber, I don't know what I'm going in here to," he said as they spun around bends and climbed higher above the city. "This guy, Mr. Smith, is an asshole at the best of times, but Walter says he has now taken leave of his senses altogether. I think it might be best if you wait outside."

Caliber shook his head. "No way, Atlas," he said firmly. "I have your back. I don't want anything to happen to you. I can't be a big help, but I can be of some help. I can be your eyes at your back. I won't say a word."

Atlas looked across at him sitting in the passenger seat. He had grown accustomed to his injuries now. He hardly even noticed them, especially when the dead man wore the old beanie hat Atlas had dug out of his desk drawer. He couldn't see through his skull now, which was a welcome blessing.

"I could die here tonight," Atlas said. "And I don't know where I will go if I do. Hell could claim me if Mr. Smith bids it. I don't want to get all soppy here, but I just want you to know that it has been great, really great these last few days. You have been a good friend to me, and I'll never forget that, even if I don't make it out alive."

Caliber grinned from ear to ear. "You've gone from being a cold, heartless freak to a big, old, soppy romantic in a few days, Atlas. I'm so proud of you. And I love you, too!"

Atlas laughed. "I wouldn't go that far, dickhead! Take what you're getting! We're friends; that's all I'll say."

The car glided along another dark, winding road through tunnels created by immense trees, their twisted branches entwined in a haunting canopy, casting eerie shadows on the deserted road below.

Atlas was quiet, thoughts swirling around his head. He thought he would have felt more anxious than he did, but the anxiety had left him, as it always did in times of peril. It would be back with a vengeance in a few days' time when he'd had time to process all the weird things that had happened and how close he had come to dying again.

Gabriel had told him long ago that Heaven and Hell could not themselves get directly involved in disagreements on Earth, lest they tip the delicate balance, and that the representatives here had to work out any issues themselves. That made things more difficult and the pressure more intense.

He didn't trust Mr. Smith. Hell, every time he met him, he treated him with absolute disdain, hostility, and loathing. He would be relying on a dead man's protection pendant and his own ability to negotiate with him, but everything was uncertain.

He slowed the car a few times, pondering whether to turn around and go back to Dublin, but something propelled him on. He needed to know what was going on and how—and if—he could fix it. He had so many lost souls in his office who needed to be moved on, and his big fear was that Mr. Smith really was planning something on an epic scale. He needed to prevent that, to talk him down.

He put his foot on the accelerator and sped past dark fields and over stone bridges as Dublin spread out below them like a carpet of twinkling lights. They went higher and higher into the Wicklow Mountain range until they reached Montpelier Forest. A dirt track took them to the edge of the forest, where William Connolly's old Hunting Lodge stood—immense, eerie, dominating the very darkness that enveloped it.

He had learned about the old lodge in school. Dating back to the 1700s, it had been constructed as a hunting lodge for the Speaker of the Irish Government, William Connolly.

In 1723, Connolly had ordered his workmen to demolish an ancient neolithic tomb nearby in order to use the stone from its cairn to build the lodge. Legend had it that the Devil had been so enraged that he had blown the roof off the building, which Connolly had simply replaced with more stone from the grave. Hence the reason why it was a thick, clunky, unusual, and unwelcoming building. The air was always thick around it, the energy dark and angry.

Dangerous people had long gravitated toward this place. It hadn't been called the Hunting Lodge since 1753 when those prone to black magic and devil worshiping had met high above Dublin for nights of debauchery, sex, and Satanism. Its current name was the Hellfire Club, and some more superstitious patrons swore they saw the Devil there. Atlas didn't doubt that for a second.

It stood cold and silent in the darkness, casting an ominous silhouette against the starlit sky. Ivy crawled up the sides and pulled the lodge back down to the earth. Atlas shuddered.

This was where Atlas and Mr. Smith had conversed many times about the pact or about difficulties that had arisen. Sometimes Mr. Smith summoned Atlas simply so Mr. Smith could be rude, arrogant, and feel that he was in control. It was always business, and Atlas never enjoyed it. But he had never felt dread in his stomach like he did now.

"Are you ready, Caliber?" Atlas asked. He wasn't too sure if he was ready himself.

"I was born ready," said Caliber as they got out of the Jaguar. "And I suppose I am dead ready, too."

The imposing stone mansion stood in complete darkness as a sudden wind whipped about their faces. It was always colder here on the summit of Montpelier. Atlas looked down across Dublin. It was majestic, beautiful, warm, and inviting from this vantage point, and he wished he was there, bathing in its orange glow. He turned his face toward the biting wind and walked on, slowing as he neared the lodge.

"Are you okay, Atlas?" asked Caliber. Atlas could tell he was scared.

He nodded. "We wait here for admission," he said. "It's okay. It's all going to be okay."

A skeletal top-hatted man emerged from the lodge and bounded down the path toward them, his flesh stretched impossibly tight across his bones.

"Who requests entry?" he boomed in an unnaturally loud bass tone. Atlas looked from his impossibly shiny shoes, skinny trousers, and dusty tailcoat to his skeletal face and sunken eyes, made even darker by the rim of his top hat. He was almost cartoonish.

"Atlas Bishop, Soul Binder," he said confidently, almost cockily, not breaking his gaze. The key with these people was not to show any semblance of fear. They could smell it.

The top-hatted man stared at Atlas for longer than was comfortable. It was clear something was computing somewhere. "Enter," he announced eventually and motioned for them to walk ahead of him.

Atlas walked forward through a veil of what felt like a spider's webs. He looked at the old mansion, transformed now, lit up with dozens of fire torches on the walls. Hundreds of people thronged the site, spilling over onto the grounds outside, and he could hear loud and slow Balkan folk music float across the grass towards him. He turned to their guide, whose flesh appeared to have now abandoned him entirely, his bones shining in the moonlight, looked into his fully exposed eyeballs and asked him which way.

"The Great Hall," he growled.

Atlas felt for the amulets around his neck. They were still there. He took his protection pendant between his forefinger and his thumb and kissed it. "Lord, protect me, bless me, and keep me safe," he murmured before marching swiftly up the steps of the house, past ladies with Venetian masks and haunted-looking men.

The music inside was loud and hypnotic. He could feel himself becoming intoxicated by it. Perfumed air swirled with the heady scent of exotic oils and incense, tantalizing his senses. Lush cushions beckoned reclining guests, casually draped in silken robes that barely concealed their desires. Laughter mingled with the music's rhythmic cadence as naked bodies entwined in a symphony of indulgence, writhing at the end of every gaze. Fat men on thrones gorged on food as circus performers juggled and cartwheeled past Atlas and Caliber. Beautiful people paraded past on all sides, and Atlas desperately wanted to follow them.

"Atlas!" shouted Caliber, snapping him from his trance. "Concentrate."

Atlas headed toward the grand staircase, stepping over couples lost in lust, and entered the Great Hall. He had never seen this place so alive in all his years of coming here.

The Great Hall was a symphony of Gothic elegance. Tall, arched windows adorned with intricate patterns filtered the moonlight, casting ethereal patterns upon the polished marble floor. Ornate and opulent chandeliers suspended from lofty ceilings and dripping with crystal prisms scattered kaleidoscopic light across the chamber. Carved gargoyles leered from darkened corners, their stony visages frozen in perpetual angst. Crimson draperies cascaded from vaulted ceilings, framing elaborate frescoes that depicted scenes of brutality, pain, and debauchery.

The music was at its loudest here, mesmeric folk music keeping those swirling around on the dance floor in a permanent state of enthrallment.

Bodies swayed like reeds in a strong breeze, caught in the ebb and flow of the rhythms. The air was alive with the fervent strumming of guitars, the plaintive wail of violins, and the enticing beat of tambourines.

Atlas looked at the revelers, their eyes glazed over, transfixed by the spellbinding harmony, their souls surrendering to the intoxicating cadence. He felt himself falling again, enchanted by a barefooted woman, her long, dark hair cascading over her shoulders, her lips plump, silk dress falling off her shoulder to reveal her breast. Her eyes, wild with passion, beckoned him and pulled him to her. Time lost its grip, and the world faded away until there was only the two of them and the music's pulsing, pounding, perambulating rhythm pushing him deeper into desire.

"Atlas!" shouted Caliber again. "For fuck's sake, man! Focus!"

Atlas shook his head and ran his hand through his hair. "Sorry," he said, nodding for them to keep walking. "Jesus, this place."

He could see Mr. Smith in the distance, his arms stretched languidly out over the back of a red velvet sofa.

Cloaked in the darkness of an all-black suit, he cut a commanding, sinister figure. Each tailored line spoke of sophistication and danger, of his formidable presence, and of his sinewy strength. His demeanor was always as sharp as the cut of his attire, exuding an air of confidence, power, and control. With a flick of his hand, he waved away the two half-naked women who had been entertaining him.

He lit a cigarette and drew hard on it as Atlas strode with purpose toward him, his gaze piercing through the smoke-filled haze and locking onto his adversary.

Atlas drew nearer, his demeanor composed, a mask of unrivaled confidence. With a nod, he acknowledged the presence of his foe, a silent recognition as he prepared for the impending clash.

Mr. Smith didn't speak, his countenance even darker in this dimly lit room, an unsettling blend of charm and malice. Eyes of burning embers smoldered beneath a furrowed brow, their intensity piercing through Atlas as he stood before him. His lips curled into a sly smirk, barely concealing the abyssal depths of his intentions.

"So Atlas Bishop still walks among us," he growled. His voice was both magnetic and unnerving. Two thunderous-faced goons stood behind him, glaring at Atlas, who said nothing.

Instead, Atlas sat down on a nearby red velvet upholstered chair and leaned back, attempting to exude confidence. He knew that Mr. Smith could smell fear—he enjoyed it—so he wasn't going to give him anything to use against him.

"Mr. Smith," he began impatiently. "You requested a meeting. What do you want?"

The air was thick with tension, charged with the imminent threat of violence. Atlas knew it, but his demeanor remained cool and collected, a veneer of calculated composure masking the turmoil within.

"I have a business proposal, Mr. Bishop," Mr. Smith replied slowly, the words rolling menacingly off his tongue.

"I'm listening," said Atlas. Caliber moved to stand behind him.

"I know what your heart desires, Mr. Bishop," he smirked. "You are darker than you would have Gabriel believe. I like that. You are more like me than *you'd* like to believe. Come and work for me. I can give you what you want."

Atlas tilted his head and sighed. "I'm nothing like you, Mr. Smith," he said, holding his stare.

Mr. Smith smiled. Atlas had never seen that before, and he found it unnerving. He shifted uncomfortably in his seat.

"Come and work for me, and I can give you love, peace, happiness..."

"Those things are in big supply in Hell, are they?" interrupted Atlas.

"...money, power, fame, adoration," Mr Smith continued, unfazed. "I can make your lady love you again. I can bring your mother back to you; I can give her life. I have the means."

Atlas wanted to tell him to fuck off, but he knew that the fate of this world could weigh on his words right now. He sighed, knowing he must navigate the delicate balance between diplomacy and defiance. His voice, a low rumble laced with authority, carried the weight of experience and determination. In this high-stakes negotiation, every word could become a weapon.

"I feel compelled to remind you, Mr. Smith, of our sacred agreement," said Atlas, holding his nerve. "I feel compelled to..."

"Work for me, Atlas Bishop," Mr. Smith interrupted smoothly. "I can make *her* love you again: that's what you want, isn't it?"

"Mr. Smith," said Atlas, more insistently. "The pact is ancient and binding. Your actions over the past few days have not been conducive to a harmonious agreement. You need to step back."

"If you don't work for me, Mr. Bishop," said Mr. Smith, not breaking his stare, "I will kill you, stamp over your corpse, steal your binding rope and your soul, and take them back with me to Hell." Mr. Smith's smile hardened into a grimace.

Atlas glared back at him. He believed every word of the threat.

"What are you doing, Mr. Smith?" he asked.

"I am claiming dominion," he replied, casually lighting another cigarette. "Call it insatiable ambition, a burning desire for absolute power; call it whatever you want. I will shape Hell's infernal realms in my own image and overthrow the current occupant of its throne."

He sat up straighter, pointing at Atlas with a cigarette between two fingers. "We have been lenient for too long with you people," he seethed. "The Supreme Leader has let Heaven dictate our destiny—a weak-minded thorn in my side—but no more. My infernal desire burns brighter, and I will reign supreme. I am building an army that will take over Hell's realm and then the world. Join me or die."

Their eyes locked in a silent exchange, each gaze a challenge unto itself. Around them, the air crackled with tension, charged with the weight of their shared history and looming conflict. Atlas could hear the intoxicating music floating through the room and tried to block it from his mind before speaking again.

"The reason that Hell has souls, that Hell exists, is because of the sacred agreement, Mr. Smith. You can't go rogue, wanting power for yourself, no matter how big your desire. This will start a war that will destroy everything, even you."

Mr. Smith laughed in response. "Yes, legions of souls will rally under my banner, Mr. Bishop," he snarled. "First in Dublin, then the world. There will be an army of souls that you and I can collect together. Heaven will not win this cataclysmic clash of divine wills. Join me. Be on the right side of history for once."

Atlas shook his head and stood up, and Caliber moved swiftly to his side.

"I have people—hungry and heartless people—" said Mr. Smith, also standing, "who are more than willing to kill the innocent to fill our ranks. I can make others do my bidding, but I need you and your binding rope. With them, my soul collecting would be simply unstoppable. I can have the bad and the good: it makes no difference to me what color their souls are."

Atlas tried not to let the rising fear reach his face. "This will not stand," he said, his voice clipped.

In a second, Mr. Smith was nose-to-nose with him. "Who are you to tell me what will stand, little man?" he growled. "You are a pathetic creature. I could crush you like a cockroach right now.

"You are a weak, sad, broken human, Bishop. You will never be able to stop me. This world is ours. Our time has finally come, and in a few weeks, the world will bow before me, the Master of Hell. Darkness and hate will envelop this land—all lands—and your world will be gone forever, just like that. Darkness will consume the light, so join me, or die."

Mr. Smith stared suddenly at Atlas's chest, recoiled, and hissed. "You have Le Fondre's amulet," he snarled. "That is the only thing between you and eternal damnation this night, Bishop. Be sure of that."

At that very moment, Varie came into Atlas's head, and he shook the unwelcome thought away.

"I can make her love you again, Mr. Bishop," whispered Mr. Smith as he circled around Atlas. "You can have anything you want, even her. I can click my fingers, and she will be in your bed. That's what you want, isn't it? That's all you want. You need only say the word.

"I can make your life easier, Mr. Bishop. You work so hard for Heaven, but you get no thanks. They just take, take, take, and you are eaten alive by anxiety and depression. I can make it go away, give you peace." He turned to face Atlas again and motioned behind him.

"I have men working for me on the streets of your Dublin, creating new murderers, collecting souls. I believe you have some souls in your office. I can take them off your hands and bring them to Hell. As for my men, well, I have promised them eternal life for their collection efforts. You might know some of them. Say, Morrison here, perhaps?"

Robert Morrison appeared from an alcove and walked to Mr. Smith's side.

Atlas heard Caliber inhale sharply.

"Atlas," he whispered. "That's him."

Mr. Smith eyed Morrison and then Caliber. "Morrison is out on the streets taking lives, collecting souls, and bringing them to Hell. Because of the pact, I have a few irritating production issues. You see, Heaven-bound souls generally resist Hell, so your binding rope would significantly speed up my purgatory production line. That's what I want. You can come with it or not. I care not."

"There is no way in Heaven or on Earth I would work for you, Mr. Smith," Atlas said firmly. "Our arrangement still stands. My innocent souls will go to Heaven, and black-souled murderers, like Morrison here, you are more than welcome to. Now if you don't mind, I have an innocent here I need to bind to Morrison."

Morrison laughed, and Atlas could hear Caliber breathing loudly behind him, knowing he would explode soon in a mess of emotion. Morrison lunged toward Caliber.

"You cried like a little bitch when I shot you," he sneered. "How's your little boy, now that he has no daddy? I bet he's..."

There was a loud bang, and Morrison collapsed to the floor. Mr. Smith stood behind him, his Kumbley and Brum pocket pistol still smoking.

"Nooooooo!" screamed Caliber. "You fucking asshole!" He lunged for Mr. Smith but went through him, hitting nothing but air. He sank to the floor, his body shaking with sobs.

Mr. Smith ignored him.

Atlas glared at Mr. Smith.

"Choose your side, Bishop," said Mr. Smith slowly. "And choose wisely. Because I will either give you your heart's desire or destroy everything and everyone you hold dear to get to your rope."

"Fuck you," said Atlas.

Mr. Smith nodded and strode away towards a large wooden door.

A sinister horde gathered around Atlas. Ghouls, their gaunt forms twisted by hunger, slunk from the shadows with bared fangs and hungry eyes. Beasts with matted fur and eyes gleaming with primal aggression snarled in anticipation. Among them, slobbering humans, driven by base instincts, joined the macabre fray. Their collective breath hung heavy with malice, filling the air with a suffocating dread. They closed in, the atmosphere crackling with an unholy fervor, a symphony of growls and guttural cries heralding the imminent onslaught—a nightmarish tableau of teeth, claws, and savage hunger. They took swipes but were pushed back by an invisible force as if burned.

The amulet was working.

"Caliber, let's go," said Atlas with as much urgency as he could muster.

Caliber was still kneeling on the floor, sobbing uncontrollably as the ghouls turned their attention to him.

"Leave him!" shouted Mr. Smith from the doorway. "We'll take the rest, this one is destined to wander the earth forever."

He smiled menacingly at Atlas. "And Atlas Bishop is to blame for that destiny like he is to blame for his poor mother's demise. You could have saved her Atlas; you could have helped her. She died because of you, you sad, little man, and I'm going to drag her to Hell. Let those facts eat away at your little black heart. You think you're going to Heaven when it's your time? I don't think so. Think about that during your little panic attacks. We'll see each other soon."

He winked and disappeared through the door.

Atlas grabbed Caliber by the scruff of the neck and marched him past hissing ghouls and grotesque monsters, running down the stairs and out into the night. They didn't stop running until they got to the forest, where Caliber again fell to his knees on the ground, sobbing.

"I'm stuck here forever like this," he sobbed. "I'll never see Louisa again, nor my family. I'm to roam this earth lonely forever, a tortured fucking soul. On my own."

He slapped the ground and sobbed harder than Atlas had ever seen him so far, tears streaming down his face.

"It was all I had," he sobbed. "All I was hanging on to, to get me through this shit. To see my little girl again somehow. To go to her, to hold her in my arms again. What have I got now? Nothing!"

"I'm so sorry, Caliber," said Atlas, unsure of there being any words big enough to meet the moment. He was pacing up and down, unable to form a clear thought in his head. He had destroyed someone else's life and death and felt utterly useless. "I'm so fucking sorry."

Caliber put his head in his hands. "Just leave me here," he said. "Go on without me. I'm no use to anyone, living or dead. I'm going to just stay here. In this forest. I'm going to haunt this forest, screaming at people. A tortured soul. Forever."

Atlas held out his hand. "Take my hand and get up," he said. "We have really important work to do here. We can't allow Mr. Smith to hurt others as he has wounded you. We have to protect these souls, and I can't do this without you. You and I are a team. We are fucking invincible. No one will break us. Come on."

Caliber stopped sobbing and looked up. "I can't, Atlas," he whispered, wiping his eyes with the back of his hand. "I can't go on. Just leave me here. I have nothing to go on for."

Atlas looked at him, his hand still outstretched. "These bastards," he said, pointing up towards the mansion, "won't stop until every soul on this earth is hellbound. Innocent men, women, and children. Your wife. Your little boy. Your mum. He won't stop until he takes them all and tortures them for an eternity. You have to protect them, Caliber. *We* have to protect them. Gather your strength, gather your courage, and get up on your feet."

Caliber thought for a moment and accepted Atlas's hand. He stood for a minute, and Atlas pulled him into a hug, thumping his back.

"Things didn't work out," Atlas said. "As we planned, I mean. But we just get a new plan, a better plan. We'll figure something out, Caliber. I promise."

Caliber sniffed.

"We need to get to my mother. I think he will try to take her. Are you with me?"

Caliber nodded, less enthusiastically than Atlas had hoped, but he nodded all the same.

"Let's go, then," Atlas said. They both took off through the forest to his car, which Atlas hoped was still in one piece.

CHAPTER TWELVE

"Ma!" shouted Atlas, searching the rooms of his house. "Ma!"

The television was on in the living room, but he couldn't remember if he had left it on before he had last headed out. She was not in the kitchen either. "Ma!" he shouted again.

"Atlas?" she shouted from the balcony. "Is that you?"

Atlas exhaled for what seemed like the first time since leaving Mr. Smith. "Yes," he said, walking toward her voice. "It's me!"

He wanted to hug her but stopped short when he saw her face, which looked like thunder.

"Where the hell have you been, Atlas?" she roared. "No phone call, no message! You didn't come home for nearly two days! I was worried sick!"

Atlas took a few steps back. "Ahhh..." was all he could fit in before she started again.

"I thought you had been killed!" she screamed. "I thought something terrible had happened. Where have you been, and why is your head busted up like that?"

Atlas pulled her into a hug regardless and waited for her to run out of steam, which took a few more minutes of ranting. He wished her hugs didn't feel so cold. Her skin was like ice, and the coldness seeped from her into his chest. Still, it was better than nothing at all. He broke apart from her eventually, holding her gently by her shoulders.

"Ma, it's really important that you listen to me now," he said softly. "We are all in great danger. Hell is planning to take over the world somehow. They have been possessing people, making them kill innocent folk. And some of them have spent the last two days trying to kill me, hence the reason I couldn't come home. I didn't want to lead any of them here. To you.

"I need you to come with me right now so I can get you to safety. I don't want anyone taking you to Hell because I might not be able to get you back. We are going to walk out that door, get into my car, and we are going somewhere where I can protect you before the Devil's men claim your soul."

"Oh," said his mother quietly. "Okay."

The lights were on in Atlas's office, and the front door was wide open. As he crossed the threshold, he could see what looked like claw marks on the door. There was broken glass on the ground in the hall and picture frames scattered in pieces on the stairs.

"Stay close," he said to his mother as they climbed the stairs. "Don't leave my side."

He pushed open the door of his office. The reception area had been trashed. Elsa's files were everywhere, and her computer screen had been smashed. He walked into his office, which had been ransacked.

"They were looking for the binding rope," said Atlas. "Mr. Smith's meeting was a ruse. They wanted us away to get in here." He had a sudden sinking feeling and frantically looked around. He rushed to the boardroom, then to the library and the kitchen. "The souls!" he shouted out to Caliber, who was five steps behind him. "They are all gone! Every single one!"

He trudged back into his office and sank down on the sofa,

which had been ripped open. He raised his eyes to Heaven. "I can't believe I fell for it. He's taken everyone."

A noise from his bathroom made him stand up. "Stand back, you two," he said, marching toward the door. "Caliber, protect Ma."

Caliber, who hadn't said a word since they had left the Hellfire Club, moved in front of her.

Atlas swung open the door and adopted a boxer's pose. Inside, two female corpses—one dressed in a business suit and the other in a supermarket uniform—were huddled together, whimpering.

Atlas's mother pushed past him to the women. "There, there, now," she said. "You're okay; come on. It's safe now. Come on out."

The women followed her to the sofa and sat down, still clinging to each other.

"What happened?" asked Atlas, standing over them. "Where is everyone?"

The women in the business suit spoke. "They took them," she said. "Monsters. Big, tall, ugly, brutal, slobbering animals. Sheet-white faces, big black eyes. They burst in here—horrible, horrible vile creatures, climbing up the walls. They were like dogs, or wolves, standing on their hind legs." She sniffed.

"They grabbed people and tore them limb from limb. I didn't know souls felt any pain, but it was awful. They put...they put poles through people, like stuck them right through their eyes, like they were collecting them on sticks. They skewered them through their chests and stomachs, too. They dragged people down the stairs and into this big black carriage and threw them all together in the back. It was like an old-fashioned horse and carriage thing. We could hear them screaming from the back of it. It was awful! We hid here in the bathroom. I didn't think souls...that we could feel pain. But the screaming was horrible. I can still hear it..."

She broke down in sobs.

"There, there," said Ma. "You're safe now. Atlas won't let anything happen to you."

Atlas sighed. He wished people would stop telling folks that. Caliber had promised the very souls who were crammed into the demonic carriage the very same thing not five hours ago. Now, they were someplace with poles through their eye sockets being stabbed by burning pitchforks or force-fed lava.

Atlas slumped into a seat. The souls had sought him out to find peace. What peace was this he gave them? He couldn't protect them. They were burning in Hell. He shouldn't have trusted Mr. Smith.

He put his head in his hands. He had failed them like he had failed his Ma. Everything he touched turned to shit.

He looked over at Caliber, who was slumped in another chair, totally despondent, like his fight had left him, like a deflated balloon. He looked to his mother—his beautiful, kind, caring mother—with her arms around the two weeping corpses, whispering words of comfort despite her own anguish.

He remembered Mr. Smith's words. He would give him everything he wanted or take everything that mattered to him away. Everything that mattered to him, except for Varie, was in this room.

The burden of his responsibilities weighed heavily on his shoulders, pushing him further down in his seat. He now had only four souls to protect. A bubble of panic burst in his stomach. He threw his head back onto the chair as if staring at the ceiling would somehow give him a solution to a problem that was getting bigger and more dramatic by the minute.

His gaze moved to the ornate ceiling medallion around the crystal chandelier in the middle of his office. He hadn't noticed the detail before. It depicted St. Michael the Archangel wielding his sword in various battles, the Latin words *Fortitudo* (Bravery) and *Fidem* (Faith) embossed on it.

Atlas sat up in the seat and pulled out his cell phone, scrolling down the names until he got to Aidan Sweeney, the brother of Mick Sweeney who owned Gilligan's Bar.

"Aidan," he said urgently. "It's Atlas Bishop from Gilligan's. Have you bought St. Michael the Archangel Church yet?"

"Yeah, hi, Atlas," came the reply. "I bought it six months ago; it's had a total refurbishment. It looks amazing! We're opening next month with a big music night. You going to make it your new local? Mick says you keep his lights on over there."

Atlas didn't laugh. "Aidan, listen. I need a big favor. This might sound strange. Can I rent it from you for a week or so? I have some business that I need a bar for. I need it all to myself for at least a week. No workmen, no nobody. I'll give you ten thousand euros."

"Yeah, I mean, sure, Atlas," said Aidan. "You can wire me the money before the end of the week. We have a deal. When do you need it?"

"In ten minutes," came the reply. "I'll meet you there then, yeah?"

Atlas hung up. Aidan had turned an 18th-century church into a modern bar and restaurant. More importantly than that, the sacred ground would afford the dead souls some protection from Hell's beasts.

Atlas turned to the rest of the room. "Right. We are going to the church," he said, trying to sound confident. "This office is no longer safe. I need to protect you all, and I need holy ground. Come with me."

Atlas marched to the door and swung it open to be greeted by three corpses standing in reception.

"Why was I drawn here?" said one bewildered-looking young man with a knife in his back. "I was just walking into a coffee shop, and I got hit in the back with something. I blacked out, and I walked here. What's happening? Am I dead?"

Atlas looked from him to the two others: a middle-aged, bearded hipster man with blood all down his barista apron and a female traffic warden with a gunshot wound to her head. "Listen, I will explain everything when we get to safety. Yes, unfortunately, you are dead, but I need you all to come with me now, calmly and quietly." One of the trio opened their mouth to speak. "And without any questions for now," added Atlas.

He put his arm around his mother and held her close to him as they walked, knowing no one could penetrate the protection afforded by Le Fondre's amulet. He hoped it would extend to her, too. Caliber dragged his feet sadly behind them.

"Let's go," Atlas said, muttering a protection spell under his breath as they bounded down the stairs and piled into his car. He put his mother into the passenger seat beside him, and the corpses doubled up on each other's knees in the back. He spared a glance at his mother before he pulled out into traffic. She looked worried: the depiction of Mr. Smith's beasts ripping souls apart had not been pleasant to hear. "It'll be alright, Ma," he said quietly. "I'll make sure nothing happens to you. I promise."

She smiled that sad smile she used when she didn't really believe what was being said. Atlas's stomach flipped as he remembered again the last time something happened to her, and he couldn't help. He didn't need to look at her blood-stained dress; the visions were never really far from his mind, playing over and over again like an old film stuck on a specific scene.

He drove much too quickly across the city. They sped past Dublin Castle, its formidable gray stone exterior commanding attention, its turrets and towers rising majestically towards the sky, and ornate windows punctuating the fortress walls. They trundled down cobblestone streets, past quaint restaurants and bars that were still asleep, and raced along the banks of the River Liffey.

They glided past buildings from another era, brought back to life by Dubliners who adored the history of the city, and sailed past the Ha'Penny Bridge, its graceful, white lattice arches leaning over the river and cast iron frame bathed in the soft glow of the street lamps. Atlas looked at a happy couple navigating its weathered wooden planks, stopping for a kiss.

He hoped that what lay ahead would not destroy all mankind.

He screeched to a halt outside the converted church in Jervis Street, got out of the car, and shook Aidan Sweeney's hand. Aidan handed him the keys and left.

Atlas gestured to those jammed into his car to follow him, opened the passenger door for his mother, and together they walked over the threshold of the church. Atlas felt peace and calm wash over him immediately.

Transformed from a sacred space into a beacon of conviviality, the bar was a harmonious blend of former reverence and future revelry. At its heart, a massive, polished, round wooden bar stood in the open expanse of the former nave, encircled by tall, tan vintage leather chairs. Bottles of warm amber and crystal clear liquid shone on immense glass shelves, and wine glasses sparkled from racks above the bar. The scene exuded modern sophistication amidst the historic setting. Majestic balconies overlooked the scene, their wrought iron railings framing views of stained glass windows that painted the interior with kaleidoscopic hues.

Aidan's contractors had taken meticulous care to preserve features from the church's original incarnation. A winding iron staircase led to upstairs rooms. Repurposed pews lined the walls. A large Baroque stained glass window dominated one wall, perfectly positioned to allow the early morning light to caress the golden pipes of the original organ on the opposite wall. A large marble plaque affixed near the baptistry proudly proclaimed that both the playwright Sean O'Casey and revolutionary Wolfe Tone himself were baptized in the church's ornate wooden font.

Atlas locked and bolted the door, even though he knew it would not prevent the type of people who would come from getting in.

He whispered a protection prayer on the front and back doors and windows on the bottom floor.

"Lord, envelop this Church in your protective embrace.
Banish darkness; ward off evil's grasp.
May love, peace, and safety dwell within these walls.
Strengthen our bruised spirits; shield us from harm.
Let your guiding presence be our fortress, now and always.
Amen."

He then returned to the corpses who had gathered in a huddle beside the bar.

"We are safe here for now," he said. "This is still holy and sacred ground. The devil's beasts cannot come in. Others *will* come, so we must be constantly on our guard. Please make yourselves comfortable so that I can do my work." He looked at the newcomers. "My friend Caliber will explain what is happening and will put your mind at ease."

Caliber, who had taken a seat at the bar, looked up sadly, then back at his hands.

Atlas climbed the staircase to the second floor, whispering his protection prayer as he went, touring all corners of the building. When he was satisfied he had protected every vulnerable place, he retired to Aidan's office and closed the door.

He fell to his knees, bowed his head, and made the sign of the cross on his head and chest.

"Dominus custodi me," he said, *"et animas perditas custodio. Ego in periculum et auxilio opus est."*

Lord, protect me and the lost souls I watch over. I am in peril, and I need help.

"Gabriel, ego tuo ducto opus est. Placet, da mihi audientiam," he continued.

Gabriel, I need your guidance. Please grant me an audience.

He blessed himself, got to his feet, and walked over to and leaned on the desk, folding his arms, head bowed. Waiting.

"Atlas," said a voice behind him.

Atlas smiled sadly. "Hey, Gabriel," he said, moving over to the seat in front of the desk. "Thanks for coming."

Gabriel possessed an arresting presence, his chiseled features reminiscent of classic Hollywood allure. His eyes were piercing, almost electric blue. Sculpted cheekbones framed a charismatic smile that hinted at both mischief and sincerity, while blonde, tousled hair added a touch of rugged charm to his suave demeanor.

He was wearing a white suit today, fitting the angel stereotype well. With an aura of effortless elegance, Gabriel's tall, lean frame moved with grace and poise towards Atlas.

"You have a big issue, At," he said, sitting on the edge of the desk. "It's the talk of upstairs."

Atlas nodded.

"An issue is one way of putting it, yes," he said. "Mr. Smith has broken our agreement. He is possessing innocent people, turning them into murderers, and taking them to Hell. He has tried to kill me. He says he's putting an army together to take over. He has stolen a number of my innocent souls and has ripped others apart. I know you're watching. And I know the rules: you can't interfere. But this is getting beyond the capabilities of...well, of me. You need to help me."

Gabriel looked in Aidan's drawers and pulled out a packet of dry roasted peanuts. "Awh! I love coming to Earth and tasting everything," he said. "Food tastes like fresh air upstairs. I like this place. It's a bar, yes? I wonder have they got the Guinness tapped up yet? Lord above, I'd love a pint of Guinness."

Atlas glared at him.

"So, yes, sorry the boss wasn't happy with you losing those souls," Gabriel said. "I mean, he still loves you; he loves all his children equally. But he was cross. You know he didn't smile or joke at all earlier. It just wasn't like him; he wasn't his usual self. Everyone was saying it, and it was because of that, because of those lost souls."

Atlas had never met "the boss." He'd only met Gabriel on Earth. All communications came through him and the Vatican, but Gabriel was his only contact from above. He hoped he might visit Heaven one day. On his bad days, he hoped he could go there and stay in peace so that soul binding would be someone else's problem.

"Look, Gabriel," Atlas said sternly, unsure what to think about God being pissed off at him. "I'm not sure what else I could have done. I tried to persuade Mr. Smith to pull back from the edge, but he tricked me. He is planning some kind of spectacular event. There is talk of *thousands* of souls being lost. I lost the souls, yes, but I was duped by someone that you, he upstairs, and I have had a long-standing agreement with. I don't know where they were taken, and of course, I want to get them back. They were shipped out in some kind of carriage."

Gabriel nodded, munching on the peanuts. "They've gone to

Hell, At," he said. "Once there, they are very, very difficult—indeed almost impossible—to retrieve. It's not like you can just walk into Hell with a list and get them back. There are rules in the agreement that we can't encroach on each other's territory. Also, you can't go to Hell unless, well, you belong there. Like, when you've taken a life, and that's where you will be punished. It's a lost cause, I'm afraid."

Atlas sighed. "But they are *innocent*, Gabriel," he argued. "How can it be that they can do that, drag innocent souls to Hell?"

Gabriel looked up from his peanuts. "It's kind of what they do, At," he said, stray, half-chewed peanuts falling from his mouth. "They are evil. They do bad stuff. They do the awful things that turn your stomach. Horrible, horrible stuff. We might just have to write off those souls and leave them there. We did our best. There's nothing really we can do for them, sadly. There are laws—ancient holy laws, written before you and I—that can't be broken. Hell is for murderers and bad, awful people. You don't want to go anywhere near that place. It's not nice. In fact, it's the most awful spot; wouldn't recommend it at all."

Atlas shook his head. "No!" he insisted. "I can't let him take them! Some of them were just kids, teenagers. What about the laws Mr. Smith is breaking? Are they not ancient and unbreakable?"

Gabriel nodded. "Yes, they are, and if I'm hearing you right, Hell is going to get a lot busier if you don't stop Mr. Smith."

Atlas looked confused. "If *I* don't stop him?" he asked. "*Me*? Gabriel, I'm going to need help here. This is the Devil's right-hand man we're talking about. And a flipping army, as well as the might of criminal Dublin. They are planning something big, and I need reinforcements."

Gabriel screwed up his face. "Yeah, listen. You know we can't help," he said. "Sorry, Atlas. We really can't be seen to be stepping in on Earthly issues. It could spark a war. That's why you guys are employed all over the world to sort this stuff out. We absolutely cannot get involved. It's written in the agreement, and the man upstairs is a real stickler for the rules." He shoved another handful of peanuts in his mouth.

"Also, if we did that, then people would think we should step in on everything. You know, all the Earthly wars and the natural disasters, people getting sick and dying. People would get to thinking we should help them out personally, and there are seriously big regulations governing that. We just can't, unfortunately." He lobbed the empty peanut packet into the corner trash can and grabbed another packet from the desk drawer.

"I bet the Devil isn't messing with this stuff either. I bet there's distance being kept on that side of things, too. Could you imagine God appearing on Earth to sort something in this age? He'd be all over social media in seconds, and he doesn't like the attention. So you see, that's why we have representatives on Earth. You guys do the groundwork—the digging, the dirty work, so to speak—and we get to keep our hands clean and handle the upstairs side of things. I suppose the Devil does the same, handling the downstairs stuff. It just makes everything so much more clean-cut. It's how it's always been done; it's how it always will be done."

Atlas stood up. "I can't fucking believe this," he said, holding his hand to his now throbbing head. "I am on my own with this? Jesus Christ, Gabriel!"

Gabriel opened his second packet of peanuts and put another handful in his mouth. "I'm afraid he isn't allowed to help either, At. It's very complicated. You wouldn't believe the paperwork; it's a nightmare. We used to have a crisis management team upstairs to step in when needed. Some people would even make appearances on Earth to calm matters, but that crew hasn't been in operation in centuries. He likes it that way."

Atlas puffed out his cheeks, exhaling slowly, and shook his head, disbelieving what he was hearing.

"You are *beyond* useless to me in a fight," he snapped. "I have to do this all myself? There are people actually killing one another on the streets of this city after being possessed by Mr. Smith, and you tell me you can't help me. Can you at least put some protections on this building so we are safe? Also, I need to pay a man ten thousand euros for rent. You need to sort that out."

Gabriel nodded enthusiastically in agreement. "I'll get admin on it right away. And good thinking with the holy ground idea. I can up your security, no problem."

He clasped his hands in prayer and began muttering.

"Domine, da hoc terrenum locum tuum divinum ac ultimum praesidium, et custodi malum terminis suis, et animarum recta perdita huic loco sacrato, et aditum ad solos invitatos da, et tegere illum cum summa luce."

Lord, grant this Earthly place your divine and ultimate protection, keep evil at its boundaries, direct lost souls to this sacred place, grant access to only those who are invited, and cover it with your sovereign light.

As he spoke, a shimmering golden dome of light fell over the old church. "Done," he said. "Now no one can come in here unless you personally invite them in, At. Any lost souls will be redirected here instead of your office. Happy to help."

"Yeah, cheers, Gabriel," replied Atlas sarcastically. "A great help. I appreciate it so much; I really do. It'll take about five minutes for the place to be completely overrun with souls."

Gabriel tilted his head.

"Look, I know this is hard," he said. "Frustrating. But what we can't have is this escalating into an all-out war between Heaven and Hell. We have complete faith in you that you will be able to handle this issue calmly and quietly out of the public eye and everything will just return to normal, no harm done. I realize he seems to have gone rogue this time, and that is not good. People have gotten lost in the melee, and that's unfortunate. No more need to be lost. I think us stepping back a little here will really help you to grow as a Soul Binder. It builds character, you know? You'll sort it out. We believe in you."

Atlas looked at him standing there with his thumbs up, smiling, peanut crumbs all over his suit. "Gabriel, I cannot impress upon you enough that this is radically different from any of our spats," insisted Atlas. "He is different now. Changed. His men are killing innocents across Dublin quicker than I can keep up. He is causing people to kill. He has spent the last two days trying to kill *me*. He wants me to work for him or die just to get my bloody rope. Heaven will be empty of souls if he has his way. The Earth will be Hell's kingdom!"

Gabriel clasped his hands together in prayer at his heart. "Atlas, yes, you must stop him," he said. "You have been given God's work to do on Earth. I know you can do this. Gather your courage; be strong of heart. *Ite fauente Deo, anima ligante. Non nocere.*"

Go with God's blessing, soul binder. Do no harm.

He winked at Atlas, who crossed his arms in a huff, bowed his head, and directed his gaze to the floor. When Atlas looked up again, Gabriel was gone, and only the smell of dry roasted peanuts remained.

Atlas walked down the stairs, dragging his feet. He had absolutely no idea how he would fend off Mr. Smith, get the lost souls back, and basically save the world. He stood at the bottom of the stairs and looked around. His mother was in one of the booths, comforting a sobbing Caliber. The two corpses who had been saved from Mr. Smith's soul snatch were in another booth, still clinging to each other. The three new souls who had arrived as they were leaving his office sat at the bar, talking quietly amongst themselves.

Atlas felt lost and alone. His head spun. He needed to think.

CHAPTER THIRTEEN

"Oi!" Atlas shouted, getting the corpses' attention. "Everyone, I need you to listen carefully to me. This church has strong, divine protections around it now, and you will be safe here within its walls. Do not go outside; do not let anyone in. More souls may arrive, so make them welcome. I am going to my office to pick up some items I will need in this fight. Stay here. Stay safe."

He nodded at his mother and smiled reassuringly. She smiled back. He had an uneasy feeling in the pit of his stomach, and it was growing. He walked to the front door, kissed his protection pendant, and whispered, God protect me, bless me, and keep me safe," before bounding out onto the path, straight to his car, and across the city to his office.

The office was still a mess. He had texted Elsa and told her to take the week off as he wasn't sure if it was safe for her to come in. He told her to relax, that he would sort everything out, and that he looked forward to seeing her next week. His finger hovered over the "x" button before sending, uncertain if he should put a kiss at the end. He wrote and deleted it several times, eventually sending it without the kiss.

He would hate for anything to happen to Elsa. As he picked up the files he needed from around her desk, he thought he might, after this was all over, *if* this was ever over, finally ask her out for dinner and stop being so closed down. Caliber was certain that she liked him, and he liked her too. She was beautiful and kind and sassy when she wanted to be, and above all, she made him laugh. His head felt it was time he forgot about Varie, although his heart wasn't so sure. He compared every woman he met to Varie. It was a curse.

Varie was beautiful; she was strong and feisty. He pictured her face in his head: it was perfect—she was perfect. She took no nonsense from anyone, had a serious attitude, and was one of the most opinionated people he knew. He absolutely loved that about her, although it often got her into trouble. He loved how they could have argued for hours about subjects, then fall into bed together with the same passion and fire.

But he made her sad, made her cry, and made her worry, and she hated that.

The practical side of him knew she was married to someone else now, and he had no chance of getting back what they had. That moment had passed. They were both completely different people, and it was time to move on. That is, of course, if the world wasn't taken over by darkness and they all died horrible deaths.

He opened the door to his office and was immediately overwhelmed by the mess. He had no idea where even to begin cleaning up, so instead, he sat at his desk, spun his chair around, and looked out the window towards the park. This was where he always did his best thinking.

A noise from reception broke his concentration, followed by a soft knock at the door. He hoped Elsa hadn't come in. He had told her it was dangerous, although he would be glad to see her. Maybe they could talk in case he didn't have any time left. There was an urgency, he sensed, in telling people how he actually felt, and there was no harm in having more feelings and more people to talk to.

The door slowly opened, and Varie walked in.

"Varie," said Atlas, surprised by her presence. "What are you doing here? It's not safe."

She didn't answer him. Just held his stare, smiled, and walked over to his bookcase, running her fingers along the books still on the shelves. She was dressed for a night out. Her tight, red skirt clung to her curves, her hair was curled, and her heels were high. Her lips were blood red, and Atlas could smell her perfume from across the room.

"What's going on, Varie?" Atlas asked again, confused. "It's not safe here, you shouldn't stay."

She looked at him from across the room, her eyes a beacon of allure, radiating a magnetic pull. Her gaze was like a siren's call, drawing him closer, igniting a fire within.

"Your face healed up well," he said, not breaking her stare. "I'm glad what happened didn't leave any black eyes or bruising. I was kind of worried about that. I thought your husband might punch me."

He thought the mention of her husband might remind her that she was married, but he had wanted a moment like this for six long years. He felt himself ensnared in her web of seduction, unable to resist the intoxicating spell she was casting with her eyes alone.

In their silent exchange, worlds collided, passions ignited, and the air crackled with anticipation about what could be. She looked at him lustfully through hooded eyes and thick lashes, and he remembered that look well—had dreamed about it often. He wanted it to be true, but he also knew not to be so stupid.

"Var," he said, laughing nervously. "I'm not sure what's happening here..."

Varie walked to his desk and bent over in front of him. He could see the lace of her bra hugging her breasts. "Don't question," she purred "Just let it happen."

Atlas wished he could have her. The longing was almost nuclear, so painful was it that he was rendered speechless. She walked around to his side of the desk and straddled him in his chair.

Although he wanted her so badly, she wasn't his to have. "Varie," he started, "I don't think this is a good idea. You're..."

The rest of his words were lost in Varie's mouth, her soft lips parting his. He felt a rush of helplessness, a surge of lust, and let go, putting his hand on the back of her neck and pulling her into him. Six years of sexual tension playing out had her chest pressed to his and her tongue in his mouth. She pulled him closer, knotting her fists in his shirt, kissing him harder, more urgently. His fingers wound themselves in her thick, soft hair. He wanted her so much and pulled her closer.

They broke apart, glaring at each other like warriors, and without warning, she began tearing at his buttons as he pulled her blouse over her head. He held her and stood up, laying her across his desk. He took off his shirt as she pulled urgently at his zipper.

"Why don't you take those off?" she whispered as Atlas moved on top of her, kissing her hard on the neck.

"What off?" he breathed. "What do you want me to do, Var?" He had forgotten how soft her skin was, how perfectly her body fit with his, and kissed along her collarbone as his memories flooded back.

She pulled at his pendant and the amulet. "These," she whispered. "Take them off, Bishop."

Atlas stopped and stood, his lust evaporating, and stepped back from the table, ensuring the amulet was safely around his neck. His hair was disheveled, and his trousers barely stayed up.

"Bishop?" he muttered, staring at her in confusion.

"What?" asked Varie. "What's wrong?"

"You called me Bishop," he said.

"So?" she said. "Come on, I want you so badly."

"Who are you?" he demanded, zipping up his trousers and buckling his belt. "I knew this was too good to be true. Who the fuck are you? Show yourself."

Varie stood up and fixed her skirt. "I'm the love of your life, Bishop," she demurred.

Atlas shook his head. "No. You never call me Bishop; it's always At. You're not Varie. Who are you? Reveal yourself."

Varie walked towards him and attempted to put her hands in his hair, but he pushed her away.

"Reveal yourself. Now!" Atlas snarled.

Varie tutted, rolled her eyes, and transformed immediately into a fat, balding, greasy, middle-aged man with bad teeth. Atlas looked on with utter disgust as the man's hairy belly protruded over Varie's red mini skirt, folds of flab and armpit hair bulging out over her bra straps. His furry legs were stuffed in strappy stilettos and looked very much like overstuffed sausages. Atlas felt sick. Varie's red lipstick was smudged all over the man's stubbled face, which Atlas had, not two minutes previously, been kissing passionately.

"Oh, Jesus Christ!" he said, feeling like he was going to puke. "What the fuck? What the fuck is this? Who the fuck are you? This can't be..." He choked back the bile rising in his throat, his mouth suddenly tasting disgustingly tainted.

The man grunted, shrugged his shoulders, picked up his silk blouse from the floor, and staggered on his high heels toward the door.

Atlas threw up in his mouth and spit into the trash can near his desk. "What the fuck were you eating?" he screamed at the man.

"I had two sausage rolls before I came up here," not-Varie grunted back, sniffing loudly. "And a cigarette."

"Jesus! Get the fuck out!" roared Atlas, running at him and pushing him out the door. *"Get out!"*

He slammed the door so hard after him that the only remaining picture frame fell off the wall and smashed on the floor. A fresh, hot rush of vomit raced up Atlas's throat and spewed out of his mouth onto the floor.

He grabbed some tissues off the coffee table and flopped down on the sofa in exasperation. He couldn't believe he had been so stupid as to let Mr. Smith get into his head in such a big way. He wiped his mouth, pulled out his cell phone, and called Varie.

"Hey," he said. "Are you okay?" She didn't answer, just asked him if he was alright, and that she had been worried.

"I'm fine, yes," he said. "But I need you to come to a safe place. Remember I told you about Mr. Smith? He knows who you are, and you're in danger. I'm so sorry."

There was silence on the other end of the phone.

"I'm sorry, Varie," said Atlas. "But this is urgent. I need you to come to the church on Jervis Street. It's the only place where I can keep you safe."

"How does he know about me, Atlas?" she asked quietly. "This man from Hell."

"Look, it's a long story, but I..." he started.

"How does a man from Hell know about me?" she asked again, more insistent. "This man who is killing people all over Dublin. How the hell does he know about me?"

"Look, Var," Atlas sighed. "He told me he would kill me and destroy everything I held dear, and you came into my head. I'm sorry."

Varie sighed at the other end of the phone. "What about Andrew? Is he safe? Should I take him to this church as well?"

Atlas thought about that for a second. "No," he said. "Andrew will be alright. These people want me to work for them and will be using the things I love to persuade me. They will know Andrew has no leverage with me, so he'll be safe, but you're not. Because they know that I...well... You need to get here now."

She hung up the phone without saying goodbye. Atlas sat looking at his phone for a moment, stunned. Everything he loved had turned to ash and dust, and everything he touched turned to shit. He had fucked up Caliber's soul binding and was still fucking up Varie's life, even though she wasn't with him anymore. He was poisonous.

When he walked back into the church, he still had that awful taste in his mouth of sausage roll, cigarette, sweat, and unexpected hairy man chest. Atlas leaned up against the gable wall and gagged again as he tried to shake the thought from his head. He also tried to shake the vision of Varie lying back on his desk and the serious heat between them, even though it wasn't her. Mr. Smith was messing with his head, and he hated it. He needed to concentrate on fixing this situation.

Caliber smiled weakly at him as he walked in. "Hey, Atlas," he said quietly.

Atlas sat down beside him. "What's going on here? Is everyone okay?"

Caliber nodded. "Yes, all's as good as can be expected from a room full of recently deceased individuals. I think we're all doing well. Your mum and I had a good chat. I'm feeling a little better about everything. There's not really anything I can do about it, so I'm not going to turn into one of those tortured souls. I've seen them in horror films, running around wailing and scaring people, hiding in wardrobes and basements. It's not a good look. It's not me. I'm going to try to be positive about things. I'm going to make a difference. It's what Louisa would want, what Natalie and my boy would want. I'm not going to let them down." He sighed wistfully.

"We have had another eight souls come in. I gave them the chat, and they are all okay or will be. Nothing strange has happened. We tried to get the TV to work, but we couldn't lift the plug to put it in the wall."

Atlas smiled grimly. "What about the other souls?" he said. "What are their stories?"

Caliber glanced over to a large booth in the corner of the bar, where a group of corpses had gathered. "Three stabbings, four shootings, and a woman strangled, all thanks to a fight in a police station," he said. "Mr. Smith's work, of course. That woman has three children; her youngest is just a new baby. She's on her own, her kids are being taken into foster care, and she's finding it very difficult. Your mum is there, as always, holding her up. Your mum is great, Atlas. She's been helping them all. I think she's enjoying the supporting role. You're lucky to have her around. She's absolutely amazing."

Atlas smiled. "She really is; she's one in a million."

Atlas looked at her, with her arm around a weeping corpse, talking gently to her. He looked back at Caliber, opened his mouth to speak, but then closed it again.

Caliber tilted his head to the side like a dog who had heard something strange. "Go on, Atlas," he said. "Say what you were going to say."

Atlas puffed out his cheeks, stuck his hands in his pockets, and shuffled his feet. Emotions made him so uncomfortable.

"I just don't know how I'll be when we have to say goodbye," he eventually said. "To my mum, that is. I mean, I had to say goodbye to her the first time around, but I was only a child. I didn't really understand. At the funeral, one of our neighbors told me the casket acted like a rocket ship and took her up to Heaven. You can imagine the dreams I had as a kid." He raked his fingers through his hair and sighed.

"I never got to say goodbye, really. When she was on the kitchen floor, she was trying to say my name but couldn't get the word out. I didn't say goodbye then. I was just crying, really. I mean, properly say goodbye, the heartfelt goodbye you say when you know you will never, ever see that person again. The things you want them to know, the things you want to stay with them forever. The deep, meaningful, profound stuff. I thought about it when you were talking about your family and not being able to go to your daughter. I know that kind of pain.

"When I was growing up, I had forgotten what my mum looked like over the years, which terrified me. I had forgotten the sound of her voice. And then she came back. She was back just as I remembered her, the same voice, everything. When I was little, I prayed every single night that I would do anything if God gave her back to me. And then...there she was.

"And I've been dreading the moment we have to part again from the minute she came back to me. But I can't think about that now. I need to figure this whole mess out."

Caliber nodded sympathetically. "Any ideas on that side of things?" he asked.

Atlas shook his head. "I went to my office to think, and..." he trailed off.

"What?" asked Caliber. "What happened? Come on, Atlas; you have to stop bottling things up. You always feel better when you get it out."

Atlas couldn't bring himself to say that he had been duped by a hairy middle-aged man in a mini-skirt. "Mr. Smith sent someone to me," he said instead, awkwardly. "He put some kind of illusion on them or on me, I don't know. He made someone look like Varie and..."

Caliber sat up, more interested now. "What happened?" he asked. "Did you get it on with some lady you thought was Varie?"

Atlas cringed a little more. "Just forget it now," he said. "I'll tell you about it later when there is more time. I need to figure out how to stop Mr. Smith because this can't go on. We can't live here forever, in a pub. We have to stop them from killing innocent people. Any ideas?"

Caliber shrugged, and Atlas rolled his eyes. There was a loud knock on the front door.

"I think that's Varie. I told her to come here to be safe."

Caliber grabbed his arm. "Be careful it's the real one, Atlas," he warned. "What we don't want is to invite some evil minion in here."

Atlas walked to the front door and looked through a small window, where Varie stood outside looking worriedly at her phone. He opened the door.

"Hey," she said. She looked irritated. "I'm here; now what?" She tried to walk in, but Atlas put his hand up.

"Wait," he said. "There are protections around this place. Just wait. I need to make sure that you are you."

Varie looked confused. "That I am me?" she asked, her annoyance even more evident. "Come on, At, it's freezing out here. Let me in, for God's sake."

Atlas looked at her. He wished he could stay away from her, that he could forget her. Every time he looked at her face, he felt pain, which was worse now because of the heated fumble with not-Varie earlier that afternoon. The thought of it still made him queasy.

He cleared his mind. "Varie," he said. "What was our song?"

She held her head, and he could see the bruise on her forehead where she had hit the ground at the bistro. "What?" she asked. "What are you on about?"

Atlas maintained his most serious face. "What was our song, Varie? When we were together."

She looked at him sternly before replying. "Hawkmoon 269, U2. What is this about? What's going on?"

Atlas opened the door for her. "I invite you in," he said. He was relieved he didn't have to deal with another fake Varie. She walked past him, leaving the ghost of her perfume in her wake. He shook the flashbacks of them together from his head, locked the door behind her, and followed her into the bar, which was now full of chatter. Another five souls had arrived, and Caliber was standing on a bar stool giving them the "everything will be alright" pep talk.

"Sorry about the noise," he said to Varie over the din.

"What noise? she asked, totally bewildered. He watched her look around at, for her, a completely empty bar. "At, how long do I have to stay here? I'm worried about my own safety and for Andrew."

"Look," he said. "I'm sorry. This place is protected. You'll be safe as long as you stay here."

"I can't live here, Atlas," she snapped. "I have a life, a husband, and I..."

She stopped, looked at her hands, and fiddled with her wedding ring. She always did that when she was nervous.

"It's okay, Var," said Atlas. "You'll be alright, here, I have..."

"I'm pregnant," she blurted out. "I wanted to tell you the other day, but we got distracted. I'm having a baby. Andrew and I, we're having a baby in the spring."

Atlas was struck dumb. He could feel physical pain in his chest, and his stomach sank. He looked to Varie's face, then down to the hand that was on her belly.

"That's news," he eventually choked out, hoping his face didn't betray the fact that he was rocked to his very core. His Varie, having a baby. With someone else. "Good news, I mean. That's good news, Varie."

Varie stared at him. "Oh, At," she said. "I don't really know what to say. This is all very weird for me. This, what you're saying, all the weird stuff happening these last few days, finding out about the baby. I don't really know what...it's all a little hard to take in, a bit overwhelming."

Atlas watched her as she spoke, and genuinely wished he could move past her, could see past her even. She cast the biggest shadow over his life, and now he was going to have to watch her have a family with another man. The family that should have been his had his demons not chased her away.

Over her shoulder, he could see someone in the alleyway outside. He tried to focus as Varie continued to speak. "We've been trying for four years," she said. "We thought it wasn't ever going to happen; it's a miracle. I know this might be a shock to you, as you always thought we might...you know...I mean, we will always be close. We shared something really special for many years. There were times when it was great. There were other times when, well, not so great. In fact, it was fucking awful. I mean really, really bad. I never want to feel pain like that again. But listen, our hearts will always be entwined. You will always be my..."

"Ma," shouted Atlas. "Ma!" He ran to the front door and started unlocking it. "Why is Ma outside, Caliber? She can't be outside! It's not safe!"

Caliber and Varie ran to him, both talking at the same time. "Wait, stop talking," he said to them both. "I need to get her back in here. Don't move, you two. Stay in the bar."

Varie looked around her, bewildered, as Atlas unbolted the last lock and ran out into the alleyway where his mother was talking to what looked like a bloody corpse.

"Ma!" shouted Atlas, running towards her, "Ma, come inside!"

"It's fine, son," she shouted back. "I'm just trying to get Jocelyn here to come inside. She's scared."

As Atlas neared, he could see that Jocelyn was not an innocent lost soul but rather a slobbering Hell beast, a grotesque combination of nightmarish features. Its twisted form, encased in putrid, oozing flesh, writhed with malice. Its eyes were ablaze with unholy fire, and it glared malevolently at him, fangs protruding from a mouth that dripped a vile black ichor. A symphony of guttural growls and sinister snarls emanated from its cavernous maw.

"Ma!" shouted Atlas, running forward. "Move away! Come to me; it's not what you think!"

He could hear the riotous clattering of horses' hooves crashing on stone as a black carriage thundered down the alleyway. It raced towards him, an elegant relic of a bygone era, its lustrous ebony frame intricately adorned with ornate filigree, its polished brass fittings glittering in the sunlight. It rattled over the cobblestones, its immense black wooden, wrought iron-wrapped wheels rolled with a rhythmic cadence down the alleyway. A canopy of midnight velvet trimmed with delicate lace housed a wooden bench on which a black-cloaked figure sat, whipping his steeds. With eyes ablaze like smoldering embers, four sinewy, sleek, black horses harnessed the infernal chariot, their hooves striking the ground like thunder, echoing the dread of eternity's march.

Atlas ran faster, shouting for his mother to come to him. The slobbering beast grabbed her by the waist, hooked her into the carriage, and they were both swept along in a cacophony of pounding hooves, screaming, and maniacal laughing.

His mother's terrified eyes searched for her son as she was shoved ungracefully into the back of the carriage. Atlas ran after it but couldn't keep up. His mother pulled back a black lace window curtain and screamed his name, but he could do nothing but watch her and the carriage disappear out of the alleyway and out of sight.

CHAPTER FOURTEEN

Atlas threw his clenched fists at the stone wall so hard he broke the skin on his knuckles and drew blood.

"At," said Varie softly.

He kicked a wooden trunk on the floor beside the door and yelled at the top of his voice. Once he had expelled all the air in his lungs, his chest tightened, refusing to allow him to take a breath in.

"At, I'm scared," said Varie. "What is happening? What's wrong?"

He flopped down on top of the chest and put his head in his hands. He tried to regulate his breathing, but his heart was trying to beat its way out of his chest. He could barely hear her voice over the sound of his heart pumping in his ears.

Varie spoke again. "At, I..." But Atlas put his hand up to silence her.

"A minute, Varie," he said breathlessly, his voice strained. "Just leave me..."

The chest pains had started, and he was feeling dizzy. His lungs felt like they were seizing up, his throat closing over. He realized he was hyperventilating but couldn't stop himself. His eyes widened with terror, and he gasped for breath, gripping the wooden chest so hard his knuckles almost burst through his skin. He threw his head back as the tears streamed down his face.

"They've taken my mother," he gasped. "Hell's beasts. They've taken her soul."

Varie stood open-mouthed, looking first into the bar and then out onto the street.

"I don't know how to fix this, At," she said. "Can I call someone? What should I do?"

Caliber crashed into the room. "Atlas, what the fuck? Where are they taking her?"

Atlas looked at Caliber with bloodshot and panicked eyes, sweat beads rolling down the side of his face, which was now an ashen gray.

"They've got her, Caliber," he sobbed. "I've failed her again."

Caliber hunkered down in front of him. "Atlas, you need to breathe," he said gently. "Look at me. Just at me. Everything will be okay. Just slow it all down. Breathe with me, Atlas."

Atlas stared at Caliber with terror in his eyes. "I almost had her," he gasped. "But they snatched her away from me." He could barely get the words out.

Varie knelt down beside him.

Caliber moved his hand up and down in mid-air, encouraging Atlas to breathe with the motion. Tears spilled down his cheeks as he groaned and breathed and breathed and groaned.

"I need to find out where they took her," he gasped. "I need to get her back."

"It's okay," whispered Caliber. "All we have to do right now is breathe. That's great. Now, let's do that again."

With each breath, he could feel his chest loosening up and the pain easing until he was able to take a deep breath again. The panic that had rushed over him like waves from a raging ocean was now settling.

"Thank you," he said to Caliber, gripping his shoulder. "I'm sorry."

Caliber nodded.

Varie stood up. "That's okay," she said. "I didn't do anything, really. Why did you call me Caliber?"

Atlas had forgotten she couldn't see him.

"Varie," he said, wiping his forehead, nose, and eyes with his sleeve.

He found it hard to look her in the eye. Thinking that he was dying had made him feel vulnerable, stupid, and weak.

"I need to get to Ma before they take her to Hell," he said, sighing. "I'm sorry. I wish you didn't have to see all that just now. I didn't handle it that well. I don't like being vulnerable, showing you..."

Varie interrupted him. "Atlas, you forget who was there in the middle of the night when you would wake up screaming at the top of your lungs. You forget who was there when you would drink yourself into a stupor, and I'd have to pick you up outside some bar you'd been kicked out of. You forget who was there when you would get drunk and nasty and fight with anyone and everyone around you, including me. You forget who was still there in the morning after the awful nights. You forget your darkest moods. You forget I hid with you under the covers when you couldn't get out of bed. I've seen you vulnerable more times than I care to remember. I've seen you completely broken. I tried to fix you. You just forget. I don't."

Atlas looked at her and said nothing. She was right, of course. And she was better off without him. She was better with Andrew, living a nice life, with a nice family. He was poisonous. He couldn't even protect his own mother's soul.

He stood up, but his legs shook. The adrenaline that had been pumping through his veins was wearing off.

His legs remained unsteady under him, but he managed to make it upstairs, gripping the banister for fear his legs might collapse under him. He stumbled to the office and threw himself into the chair. He couldn't get his mother's face out of his head, how panicked she had looked as she peered out of the back of the carriage.

He needed to get her back, but he needed to know where they had taken her.

He got up and walked to the window, feeling sick at the thought of what they would do to her. He looked out onto the street as if that might provide him with some answers. The sun had gone down on Dublin, and twilight had descended upon the city streets. The once-bustling thoroughfare around the church had adopted an eerie stillness. Shadows stretched and contorted, concealing sinister figures.

Demonic beings with twisted human forms and eyes gleaming with malevolence skulked in the darkness, their presence palpable yet unseen by unsuspecting passersby. But Atlas could see them. In shop doorways and in alleyways opposite the church, in the places that the streetlights didn't reach they waited and watched.

They dressed in black human clothes, but their faces—ashen and mottled skin, sunken eyes, and skeletal forms—gave away their otherworldly origins. Whispers of chaos and despair clung to their ethereal forms, infecting the air around them with a sense of dread.

Gabriel's protections would hold: Atlas didn't doubt that. He watched one demonic being step out of the shadows and raise his head to where Atlas stood at the window. They locked eyes, but Atlas stood firm. The demonic being, towering and imposing, exuded an ancient malevolence, its eyes black and ablaze with infernal light.

A man in a suit turned a corner and walked determinedly down the street. The demon smiled at Atlas and turned his head slowly to the man.

Atlas banged on the window to alert him, but he had earphones on and didn't hear the din. The demon reached out a gloved hand and placed it on the man's head as he passed. The man turned to dust, disappearing in the breeze.

"Fuck!" shouted Atlas, banging the glass.

The demon raised a black-gloved hand, pointed his finger at Atlas, and gestured for him to come out. Atlas used his middle finger to provide an answer and stormed away from the window, pacing up and down, cursing the demon, Mr. Smith, and his own blasted life.

He stopped mid-pace and looked to the window again, an idea forming in his head. He rummaged in his bag, grabbed a few things, and stormed out of the office and across the balcony, shouting to Caliber below to meet him in the storage room at the back of the building.

He headed for the ornate spiral staircase that descended to the ground floor, holding on to the cool steel banister, each step strong and unyielding. He picked up the pace and ran to the back door of the church, swinging it open dramatically.

He stood in the street light, producing his cigarettes slowly from his pocket, before pulling one out of the packet and cupping his hands over his mouth as he lit it. He sucked in the nicotine and exhaled loudly into the night sky.

Demonic beings began to emerge from the blackness of the shadows, their statures an unsettling fusion of human and infernal essence. With sinuous grace, they converged upon the church gate, their black eyes gleaming with twisted hunger. The invisible shield that enveloped the sanctuary held, an ethereal barrier warding off their malevolent intentions. Undeterred, they encircled the protective veil, their sinister murmurs reverberating like an ominous hymn. As they lingered in the shadows, they brought a palpable tension that hung in the air.

Atlas stared at them as they paced, unable to cross the barrier. The one who had gestured to him from the window walked towards the church's gate. In the moon's pallid glow, the demon, humanoid yet grotesque, walked back and forth like it was hunting prey. With every step closer, shadows coiled around its form. Their eyes locked, a silent exchange laden with primal instinct and foreboding. The demon's visage contorted into a twisted smirk, relishing the fear it thought it instilled.

Yet Atlas stood resolute, a flicker of defiance in his gaze.

"You wanted to speak to me, dickhead?" Atlas called, hands in his pockets, cigarette hanging off his lip. "What did you want?"

"You," the creature growled.

"Well, here I am," he said. "Come and get me."

The demon fixed its gaze upon Altas with a chilling intensity, its eyes seething with hatred. Its human-like features contorted into a horrible grin, revealing rows of jagged teeth glistening with anticipation.

Every movement it made was a calculated dance of predatory instinct as if savoring the impending feast before the first bite. Within its stare lay an abyss of darkness, swallowing hope and stirring primal fear.

"We've got your mother," it hissed. "She was screaming for you. You should come here and get her."

Atlas glared at him as he moved closer, waiting for him to stand apart from the others.

"Fuck you," snarled Atlas. The demon smiled wider, walking ever closer.

Atlas unfurled his binding rope, and with a swift flick of his wrist, it crackled through the air like lightning. With precision born from years of practice, the rope wrapped around the demon, snagging it in a taut embrace. Atlas tugged the rope hard, pulling the demon through the protective barrier. The rope had it bound like a stiff statue, its arms and legs pulled so tight they were almost fused to its body. He grabbed it by the hair and dragged it into the church and the storeroom where Caliber was waiting.

"What the fuck, Atlas?" shouted Caliber. "Why are you bringing that thing in here?"

The demon wrestled against the rope, spitting and hissing when it found escape was impossible. It growled, a low, guttural sound that reverberated and bounced around every tile in the room and glared at Atlas through dark, murderous eyes.

Atlas looked around the room. Still holding the demon by the hair, he grabbed a chair from a dusty corner with one hand and pushed the demon into it with the other. He pulled another chair over to rest across from the demon and sat down in front of the beast.

"See this?" he said, holding his protection pendant in his hand. "I just need to touch you with this, and you'll explode. Just a little tap, and that will be it. It won't be pleasant. There will be demon brains and guts everywhere, and it will be a total fucking nightmare to clean up. But you make one wrong move, and I'll do it. Are we clear?"

The demon growled at him in response. Atlas looked around the storage room again and spied a box labeled "Spare Bar Tools." With one eye still on the demon, he walked over, rummaged around in the box, and withdrew an ice pick.

"Where is my mother being kept?" he asked calmly as he returned to sit eye-to-eye with the demon.

It stared into Atlas's eyes. "Your bitch mother is being ripped limb from limb." Atlas got up, kicked the chair back, and plunged the ice pick deep into the demon's leg. It roared like a lion.

"Tell me where she is!" shouted Atlas, pulling the ice pick out and immediately thrusting it into its other leg.

The beast began to laugh. "You think this will make me talk, human? Torture me. Don't stop now! Keep going! What's next?"

Atlas threw the ice pick to the floor and pushed his thumbs into the demon's eyes. It writhed and screamed in agony, fighting against the rope to break free. Atlas removed his hands and walked away.

"Awhh, don't stop!" shouted the demon, its eyes bleeding. "I want more! I love it!" It began to laugh maniacally.

Atlas looked at Caliber, who moved forward. "I bet this fucker wouldn't want to go to Heaven, Atlas. He wouldn't fit in up there, I'd say," said Caliber. "He'd stand out like a sore fucking thumb. You can make that happen, can't you?"

Atlas smiled and rummaged in his pocket for a crystal with runes etched on one facet. "You see this?" he said firmly, leaning over the demon, and slapped him hard in the face. "Look at me! Do you see this?"

The demon looked through bloodied eyes at him and nodded.

"Two words and a wave of this, and you'll go straight to Heaven, forever."

The demon laughed again, spittle flying from his mouth.

Caliber gasped. "You mean you can just send people to Heaven, just like that? Why didn't you send me? Or your mum, for that matter?"

Atlas glared back at him, tilting his head and widening his eyes. The stone he held in his hand was used mostly to calm inflammation and cure migraines, it had no more power to send people to Heaven than Atlas's shoe. But the demon didn't know that. And Caliber was ruining the vibe of his bad cop act.

"We'll talk about it later," snarled Atlas through gritted teeth.

Caliber slumped back against a wall, and Atlas turned his attention back to the demon in the chair, who was snickering at the exchange.

"You think I don't mean what I say, dickhead?" snarled Atlas. "You will go to Heaven where everything is beautiful and people are sweet and peaceful. There is no anger there; there is no violence. You will be stripped of everything. That's what I can do to you, you insignificant prick. Right now. It would take just one second, and you'd be surrounded by bliss. Nothing you can do about it—just absolute bliss and happiness. All. Day. Long."

The demon squirmed a little in its seat.

"Lord, have mercy!" shouted Atlas, and the demon winced in pain, hissing and gagging.

"Haha!" Atlas laughed at it. "You don't like that name, do you? In the name of Jesus Christ, tell me where my mother is!"

The demon shook its head and growled, the skin on its face starting to burn.

"You can't even hear the Lord's name without gagging. Upstairs, you'll meet the big man himself. Jesus actual Christ!"

The demon shook its head violently.

"Yes!" shouted Atlas. I will send you up there and you will meet Jesus Christ, and you will endure every good thing there is. Kindly little old ladies, offering you boiled sweets all day long, for an eternity. The sun shining constantly. There is beautiful, peaceful music everywhere you go, even outside. Harp music, the stuff you hear in elevators, except worse. There are beautiful things everywhere. Lovely flowers and stuff. And they sing! Angels. They sing all day long. What is it they sing, Caliber?"

Caliber looked bewildered. "I dunno," he said. "I think it's 'Abide With Me.' They sang that at my funeral."

Atlas nodded. "They sing 'Abide With Me.' Let's sing it now. Come on, everyone, join in! *'Abide with me, fast falls the eventide,"* he sang. The demon winced. *"The darkness deepens. LORD! With me abide.'"*

"Come on, sing!" he shouted, and Caliber joined in. "'*When other helpers fail, and comforts flee. Help of the helpless, oh, abide with me!'"*

Atlas sang loudly and enthusiastically.

"'Swift to its close ebbs out life's little day. Earth's joys grow dim, its glories pass away. Change and decay in all around I see. O Thou who changest not, abide with me.'"

The door swung open, and Varie walked in.

"What the hell, Atlas?" she exclaimed. "What are you doing standing in here singing hymns to yourself? Have you lost your mind?"

The demon growled, tried to stand upright, and moved as if to run at her. Atlas ran in front of it, waving the pendant. "I swear to God, demon, I'll blow you up right now. Don't tempt me."

The demon growled, breathing angrily through its nostrils. It backed up and sat down, its chair scraping violently along the ground.

Atlas turned to Varie. "It's fine," he said sharply, softening as he took her face in. "I'm just letting off a bit of steam here. I need you to go back into the bar so you're safe. I'll be there in a minute."

She closed the door quietly, and he turned to the demon in the chair again.

"You're going to Heaven, Hell beast!" he roared. "It's a beautiful, glorious, happy place. It is just lovely and you are going to absolutely hate it. The Lord himself knows you will love it!"

The demon shook his head violently.

"Yes!" shouted Atlas. "Yes! That's where you're going! It is! Up there! Everyone talking about the Lord and how great he is. Making sure you're warm enough. Smiling. Playing harps. There is so much harp playing. So much. The Lord loves harp playing. Everyone praising the Lord through harps!"

The demon was sweating profusely now. "No!" it hissed desperately. "Stop saying his name. I don't want to go there. No smiling! Not harps. I fucking hate harp music!"

Atlas had cracked him. "Yes!" he shouted. "Yes, there will be! Harps everywhere. I think Jesus plays a harp, too, and what do you call those other things?" He looked at Caliber for inspiration.

"Pan pipes, Atlas," the dead man replied.

"Yes! Pan pipes! Everyone is so beautiful. Everything is so peaceful. Everyone loves Jesus, and you will love Jesus too! The Lord will love you!"

"Noooo!" screamed the demon.

"Yes!" Atlas screamed back. "Everyone will be laughing and happy. The happiness is almost at sickening levels. And the peace is unbelievable. Big peace."

Atlas was screaming so much a blood vessel was visibly pulsing in his temple.

"Yes!" he roared. "There will be absolutely no screaming, no pain, no torture. None whatsoever. People love each other. Like really love each other. Everyone will want to be your friend. Even Jesus Christ. You will love people. Love is everywhere. The Lord is everywhere!

"And," added Atlas, "there's Mass all day long, every day. Twenty-four-hour Masses. Mass that has no beginning and no end; they go on forever. They love praising the LORD!"

"No!" shouted the demon, openly weeping now. "Stop! No more! I'll tell you what you want to know!"

Atlas smiled at Caliber, who winked back at him. "Tell me where she is."

The demon sniffed. He was a shadow of his former self and seemed smaller in stature. Atlas had broken him. "They are in the old, abandoned Kane Street Police Station in Bray," he whimpered. "At the portal to Hell."

Atlas nodded to Caliber. "Let's get this piece of shit out of here," he said. He tugged the rope and pulled the demon to its feet, grabbing it and dragging it along the corridor to the back door.

He threw it out into the night, the binding rope still attached as it fell to the concrete ground. Atlas pulled the demon to its feet and shoved it through the gate and beyond the barrier.

"You are not welcome here!" he shouted, pulling the binding rope back.

The demon spun around as it unfurled and grabbed the rope with its fist just as the last of it was floating back to Atlas.

They locked eyes, and a tense pause ensued—a silent exchange. The demon pulled its features into a smile, baring its teeth.

Atlas pulled hard on the binding rope, and the demon fell forward into Gabriel's protection veil and incinerated, golden sparks floating up into the night sky.

CHAPTER FIFTEEN

Atlas stomped up the stairs and into the office. He blessed himself, mumbled a few words in prayer, and shouted. "Gabriel! Get your arse down here now!"

Gabriel appeared on the seat across the desk with a knife and fork in his hand.

"For fuck's sake, Atlas!" he raged. "I was in New York there, in a restaurant. The waiter was coming over with my steak on one of those sizzler plates. I could see him; he had it in his hand. Do you know how long it has been since I had a steak dinner, Atlas? I'll tell you, it's been..."

"Shut up!" roared Atlas. "Mr. Smith has taken my mother as leverage. He is planning something huge, to take thousands of souls. You and the boss upstairs either give me the means to fight these fuckers properly, or I'm out of here, and it's your problem."

Gabriel sat up straighter in his chair. "Well," he said, putting his cutlery down and adopting a more diplomatic tone. "I need to see what we can do. I'd need to put in a request to the holy relic department. They might have something."

Atlas pulled his runes from his jacket along with a crystal, a golden relic from his back pocket, and a leather bracelet from his wrist and slammed them on the desk. "I quit, Gabriel. It's your problem now. There are at least forty souls downstairs to process, along with the thirty or so we lost to the demons—wherever they are—and the volume of slobbering, demonic beasts outside waiting to pounce is increasing by the hour. There is a gang of seemingly immortal Dublin criminals running around, making people murder one another so as to build a ghost army for Hell. As I said, they are planning a huge mass murder event. Best of luck with it all."

Atlas started for the door.

"Wait!" shouted Gabriel. "Wait, Atlas. You were chosen to do this. You can't just walk away."

Atlas stopped. "Why?" he demanded. "What's to stop me?"

Gabriel stood up to face him. "If you break the binding contract, you die."

Atlas looked back at him, expressionless. "Is that all?" he said. "I die?"

Gabriel nodded. "It's written in the contract you signed. You forfeit your right to life. You only live this life to serve God. You were chosen for this role. If you walk away, then you die."

Atlas laughed. "Gabriel," he said. "There have been many times I wished I had died the night I was supposed to, on that dark country lane, in the car, when I drove into that wall. Do you honestly think death scares me? I would almost welcome its embrace at this stage. What the fuck do I have to live for? My only motivation was to help my mother, and they've probably ripped her soul to pieces by this stage."

He put his hand on the handle of the door and opened it. Gabriel raised his hand, and the door closed again. "Atlas, wait! I can help you," he said.

Atlas turned to him. "How, exactly, Gabriel?" he sniped. "With a few stones and a fucking amulet? That is not going to cut it this time. You have no idea what I'm dealing with here."

Gabriel fixed his face firmly to a sympathetic pose. "Give me just five minutes, Atlas, please," he begged. "Just five minutes until I can get you what you need. I promise you we can do this. We need you. Without you, Dublin, then the world will succumb to darkness in days. You can't walk away now. Too many are depending on you. You are being tested, so stand strong."

"Five minutes," said Atlas, looking at his watch. "Not six or five and a half. Five. Be back here with a plan, ammunition, an army: I don't care what. But a workable plan and some backup. I need things that can blow up demons, and I need the means to fight. Do you understand me? You need to sort this out, or I walk."

Gabriel nodded silently and disappeared, and Atlas flopped back into his chair.

"You told him," said Caliber. "I'm glad to see you got your fight back."

Atlas leaned back in his chair and looked at the ceiling. He sincerely hoped his mother was okay, or as okay as a dead woman could be. He hoped they would try to use her as a bargaining chip and that they would keep her intact. The adrenaline from his earlier panic attack had worn off, and he was now totally exhausted. He felt deflated but knew this was no time to rest. He looked at his watch. Three minutes down. Gabriel would need to show himself soon. He stood up slowly and walked shakily to the window. The sun was coming up, bathing the buildings before him in a warm orange glow.

Four minutes.

"Atlas," said Gabriel from behind him. "I want you to come with me."

"Where exactly, Gabriel?" he said. "We haven't got the luxury of time at this precise moment."

Gabriel smiled. "Trust me," he said gently, stretching out his hand. "Come on."

Atlas reached out his hand as if to shake Gabriel's. He felt his eyes shut heavily, like a slow-motion blink. When he opened them again, he was in a mammoth warehouse, with hundreds of desks housing switchboards and operators, ringing phones, and a wall of chatter that reached a vaulted ceiling humming with frenetic energy.

"Where are we?" asked Atlas as Gabriel took off walking down the room.

"The Vatican," he replied over his shoulder. "Soul Binding Operation HQ. Come on, we need to get to the vaults and the holy relics. This way."

Rows of switchboard operators bathed in the glow of dim lights orchestrated an underworld symphony, their hands dancing across vintage switchboards, connecting calls with practiced precision. Wires snaked along the walls like arteries, pulsating with the lifeblood of otherworldly communications as screens flickered with cryptic codes and surveillance feeds, mapping out a chessboard of clandestine operations.

"What are they doing?" asked Atlas as they marched past them. "There are thousands of them."

"They run things," said Gabriel. "They receive the death notices, they connect the souls to their chosen binders, they send out the seeker orbs, they retrieve our souls at the gates of Hell, they process them, and they pay your wages. They do everything." He counted each responsibility off on his fingers as he spoke. "You see, Atlas, this is bigger than you. Bigger than all of us. This stops, and everything stops."

Dim neon lights cast an ethereal glow on the determined faces of the operators, relentless activity at the end of every gaze. In this cybernetic ballet, every call signified a soul hanging in the balance.

They walked through huge wooden doors, leaving the noise and bustle behind, and out into a marble hall with an immense crystal chandelier hanging overhead. It was quiet here. Atlas headed through a small mahogany door to the right and down worn, stone steps lit by fire torches at intervals.

The air grew cool and musty as they descended, heavy with the weight of antiquity. Shadows danced along ancient walls adorned with faded frescoes, whispering tales of saints and sinners alike. Torchlight flickered, casting eerie shapes upon the rough-hewn stone, illuminating the path to the sacred unknown below.

Finally, at the bottom, Gabriel walked purposefully down a

small, claustrophobic tunnel, then along another that had hundreds of little arches, floor to ceiling. "This is the Vatican Necropolis, Atlas," he said. "The catacombs under the Vatican. The ones beneath even those in public view. It's where we hide all Heaven's secrets, artifacts, and the like."

He marched on ahead with Atlas at his heels. The place felt like it had no air, and Atlas could feel his anxiety bubbling. He could taste the dust in his mouth. He needed fresh air and to know the way out of a place in order to feel safe. This was not a good place for him. He felt his breath quicken and get shallow, knowing that the lightheadedness would follow shortly.

Gabriel took a sudden right and went into an even darker tunnel, at the end of which was a wooden door. Beside it, a man sat on a three-legged stool, looking out of place in the cavernous maze.

"Hey, Gabe," he said cheerily.

"Hey, Joseph," sang Gabriel back. "How are the grandkids?"

Joseph beamed. "They are good, thank God," he said. "Growing up so fast. Do you want in?"

Gabriel nodded, and Joseph got up, a large bunch of jangling keys connected to his belt. "It's one of these," he muttered to himself. "I'll get you sorted, Gabe."

Atlas was feeling increasingly panicked but after what felt like fifteen minutes and a hundred keys, Joseph eventually found the right key, inserted it into the lock, and pushed open the door to reveal a vast room. Along the two sides were rows and rows of shelves. Glass and wooden cases stood in the center aisle, housing whizzing and whirring trinkets, objects floating by themselves, and other items emanating gentle golden light.

A treasure trove of antiquity unfolded before them. Golden artifacts glimmered amidst the flickering torchlight, their surfaces reflecting the echoes of bygone eras. Jeweled trinkets adorned ornate pedestals, whispering tales of forgotten kings and queens, and ancient manuscripts, their parchment weathered by time's gentle caress, lay nestled amongst intricate relics.

"We'll take it from here, Joseph," said Gabriel, smiling. "Thank you."

Joseph saluted and closed the door behind them, Atlas peering worriedly after him.

"You okay?" asked Gabriel. Atlas didn't answer; just looked around the room. He was on the verge of another panic attack. He was miles from home and probably miles and miles underground, beneath crushing concrete. And there was no air.

Gabriel walked towards him and scanned his face. Atlas was sweating profusely, and his hands were shaking.

"Give me your unease, Atlas," said Gabriel, stretching out his hands. "Let me carry your burden for a while."

Atlas looked at Gabriel in bewilderment. "What do you mean, give you my unease?" he asked.

"Give me your anxiety," Gabriel replied. "Let me carry it and unburden you."

Atlas laughed gently. "You are taking the whole angel thing really seriously now, Gabe, aren't you? I thought you just took the job because it allowed you to come to earth and eat stuff."

Gabriel gestured towards Atlas's hands. "Put your hands in mine," he said gently, winking at him. "Come on. Trust me."

Atlas shuffled his feet and looked back at Gabriel awkwardly. "It's fine," he said, embarrassed. He didn't want to be standing holding anyone's hands, never mind someone miles below ground where there was absolutely no air. "I'll be fine," he insisted. "I just need a minute. It's a bit claustrophobic down here."

Gabriel also insisted.

Atlas tutted and placed his hands in Gabriel's. He immediately felt anxiety leaving his body, like it was pouring out through his fingertips. Calm descended from his scalp like warm water, pouring gently down his face, making his shoulders softer, calming his heart rate, and dampening the ceaseless volcanic acid in his stomach. He was able to take a deep, easy breath and felt himself smile. He felt serene.

"Better?" asked Gabriel.

Atlas smiled. He had never felt like this. It felt like peace. He smiled wider.

Gabriel smiled back and nodded in the direction of a tall, imposing mahogany cupboard. "There are some gadgets in here that you'll like," he said, walking towards it. "They haven't seen the light of day in maybe a century. They were remnants of the last war between Heaven and Hell, but I think the current events warrant getting them back out."

Gabriel opened the cupboard, and the room was immediately bathed in a pale blue light.

He curled his hand around a small, ornate silver ball and held it in front of Atlas's face. "This," he said, "can slow down time for humans, angels, and demons alike. A simple incantation said beforehand will allow you and your people to move freely."

He then pulled a thick, deep-red bound book down from the shelf. "This will help me turn souls into angels if I need to," he muttered, putting it under his arm and reaching for three dark gray egg-shaped objects. "These," he said, "are basically demon hand grenades. Humans won't even notice them going off. Please use these sparingly, as the paperwork following a demon cull is an absolute nightmare between upstairs and downstairs. I'm not even permitted to hand these out, but I don't suppose it will matter now that...well...all Hell's broken loose."

He opened a wooden chest with several gold chains inside. "This," he said, pulling out a long gold chain with a coin at the end, "will disguise your human traits and help you blend in with the demons and disappear. And this," he said, reaching up to a brass hand and pulling a signet ring off one of its elongated fingers, "emanates a stunning spell that will disorientate an attacker to give you time to escape."

He opened a drawer and produced a black leather box, opening it to reveal a golden dagger with a ruby stone on its hilt. "This can bypass any protection spell. If you need to...you know...kill anyone."

Atlas looked at Gabriel as he handed it to him. "Kill someone? I can hardly kill anyone, as that would make me a murderer. I don't want to end up in Hell, Gabriel. It wouldn't look good on my resume."

Gabriel dropped his head. "Atlas, I, of all people—an angel, you know—would never tell you to take another person's life. That's not a Christian thing to do or say. I would say to you that if you need protection if you are being attacked and have no way out, this can help you. Just don't let anyone evil get their hands on it, or they could kill you because it can bypass your protections, too."

Atlas tucked the dagger into his belt. "Right," he said as if it was the most normal thing in the world. He was so chilled out, he could sleep right there on the dusty floor. His mind drifted to Elsa and how, when she laughed, she threw her head back. He smiled at the memory.

Gabriel interrupted the pleasant memory. "Pay attention to where your mind goes when you give it a break," he said. Atlas felt almost tipsy.

"This," said Gabriel, pulling his attention back and taking a small purple crystal from a box, "is very important. Carry it with you always. I mean that. Never let it out of your sight."

He put it in Atlas's palm and closed his hand over it. "This is a Life Stone. If the worst happens, you hold it in your hand—or put it in someone else's hand—and say 'Domine, vivifica me' meaning 'Lord, grant me life.' It will pull you back to your earthly body straight away. Be careful that there is no one touching you because it can also pull souls back to earth with you. You don't want to be bringing back all manner of dodgy demons and ghouls. Don't ever let this out of your sight, Atlas, not for a second. This little thing would be extremely dangerous in the wrong hands. So dangerous I don't even want to think about it. I'm giving it to you now because of the dire circumstances we find ourselves in. It was used only once, many centuries ago, to bring someone important back from the dead after three days. But that's neither here nor there. It has been kept safe here since. Every evil being in the universe would love to get their hands on this, but thankfully, not many know it exists. Could you imagine who they could bring back to life with this? Serial killers, for example. Dictators, madmen, murderers? No, thank you very much. These are extraordinary times, and this is an extraordinary artifact. Guard it with your very life, always."

Atlas felt the warmth from the stone in his hand. "Well," he said. "Hopefully, I won't need this. But yeah, good to have, I suppose."

Gabriel locked eyes with Atlas and opened his mouth to speak, closed it again, and just nodded slowly. He closed the cupboard doors, and the room was immediately cloaked in darkness again. The pair walked to the door, where a golden goblet caught Atlas's eye. It was glowing, and he could hear a low hum if he strained his ear. He stopped and stared, utterly mesmerized.

Gabriel stopped and turned around. "Let's go, Atlas," he said, looking worried.

"That is so beautiful," said Atlas. "Can I touch it?" he asked, reaching out his hand towards the cup. "I just want to hold it, just for a second."

"No!" shouted Gabriel. He slapped Atlas's hand down and snapped him out of his trance. "Come on, out of here." He grabbed Atlas by the shirt collar and hauled him toward the door.

"What was that?" asked Atlas as they tumbled through the door, waved to Joseph, and set off back down the warren of corridors.

"One touch of that cup, and you'll have eternal life," said Gabriel. "You don't want that negativity in your life, Atlas. It's cursed. It draws people in. Did you hear singing?"

Atlas walked faster to keep up, "I heard humming," he replied.

"Yeah," said Gabriel, making Atlas dizzy with his fast-paced corner-turning. "You touch the surface of that cup, and you'll live forever. Only problem is, your body doesn't get the memo. Your skin rots, your hair falls out, as do your eyeballs. After two hundred years, you look like a bit of a nightmare, but you're still alive. Trust me, you don't want that negativity in your life."

CHAPTER SIXTEEN

Gabriel's calming prayer lasted until the moment they arrived back in Dublin. In the blink of an eye, they were back at the church, and Atlas felt his worry and fear descend on him again. He was glad for it, though, as he would need an edge when he went to get his mother back.

They were holding her in an abandoned police station in Bray. Bray rested approximately twenty kilometers south of Dublin, tracing the scenic coastline of County Wicklow. His mother used to take him there on the train when he was small. They would sit on the wall overlooking the beach and eat ice cream. He hadn't been back in years.

Kane Street Police Station looked even more ominous on a rainy, dark night than during the day. Weathered by time and neglect, the abandoned station stood like a silent sentinel on a dark hill at the edge of a long, narrow beach. Its once proud façade was now crumbling, and ivy tendrils crept along cracked walls, reclaiming the building as nature's own.

Windows—some boarded, others shattered—offered glimpses into a forgotten past. Seagulls circled above, their mournful cries echoing through the desolate streets. From where he sat in his car across the road, he could see that there was barely a single brick left untouched by graffiti. Atlas could hear a car alarm blaring from a side street and a dog barking nearby, despite the rain ferociously bouncing off the pavement.

Caliber looked at the scene and puffed out his cheeks, sighing dramatically. "What's the plan, Atlas?" he asked, looking worriedly through the rain-splattered car window.

"There is no plan," Atlas replied wearily. "We are going in there, we're going to get Ma, and then we're going back to the pub."

Caliber looked at him, concerned. "Atlas, are you okay?" he asked. But before he could hear his answer, Atlas was outside the car in the pouring rain, smoking a cigarette like a condemned man.

He checked his pockets for the items Gabriel had given him.

"You don't need to come in with me," he said when Caliber joined him in the rain. "You have done enough, and they are aware of the things that matter to me. I don't want to risk you getting taken too."

Caliber looked at Atlas, his lip curling upward.

"Shut up," said Atlas. "Don't make this awkward."

The dead man pulled him into a hug. "I'm coming in with you," he said, pulling apart and grabbing him by the shoulders. "If you go, I go. I've got your back. I'm not leaving. I'm staying right here."

For some reason—perhaps it was Gabriel's calming prayer wearing off—Caliber's words brought a lump to Atlas's throat and rendered him unable to speak.

"Come on, you," said Caliber, walking towards the station. "We might as well get this over with."

Atlas pulled a silver ball from his pocket and held it in front of him. "This thing will give us a few moments to escape," he explained. "It will slow down those demons and give us time to run. When you see me throw it, grab my mother and run like your soul depends on it. Get her to safety."

Atlas closed his hand around the silver ball, held it to his heart, and bowed his head. *"Custodiat eos, Domine,"* he said. *"Custodi eos a potestate artificii tui. Permitte eas ire velociter in nomine tuo. Amen."* (Protect those gathered, Lord. Keep them from the power of your artifact. Allow them to move swiftly in your name. Amen).

He returned the ball to his back pocket. “Let’s go,” he said, marching determinedly through the puddles toward the dark, foreboding building. He checked his neck for the protection amulets and took a few deep breaths to steady himself, an act which seemed easier now.

He had spent his entire life having panic attacks about dying, but he wasn’t afraid anymore. If he gave up, he would die. If he went into this station, he might die. If he tried to rescue his mother’s soul, he might die. But at least he would die trying, with his boots on.

Mr. Smith would be expecting him—he knew that—so there was no need to be covert. The quicker the Hell beasts dragged him to Mr. Smith, the quicker he would get Ma back.

Beneath the cloak of night, the abandoned police station loomed in the torrential downpour. Rain cascaded from broken gutters, drumming a melancholic rhythm upon cracked concrete. Weeds had reclaimed the perimeter, entwined with rusted metal fences like mournful lamentations.

Atlas took off at a run down the dark alley to the side of the building and up some steps to a rotted wooden door. He stood back and aimed his boot at it. It crashed to the floor with a bang.

He walked into the darkness, Caliber just behind him. All he could hear was the sound of his own breath as he inched forward into the blackness. In the silence, it was almost deafening until a low growl stopped him in his tracks. This was it. He hoped his protections would stand. He also hoped that the beasts waiting in the decrepit shadows of this building to pounce would understand that Mr. Smith wanted to bargain with him and not just eat him without question.

He could hear shuffling at either side of him as he moved. He knew they were close, as he could feel and smell their rancid breath.

He lit his lighter, and their twisted forms melded with the shadows, eyes gleaming with infernal hunger that pierced the darkness on all sides of him. Claws scraped against decaying floorboards as they moved, and the stench of sulfur permeated the air, mingling with the musty scent of decay. With ragged breaths, they growled, their sinister sounds echoing through the desolate halls.

"I take it you're the welcome party," said Atlas confidently. "Take me to Mr. Smith."

The beasts growled and made to swipe their claws at him, withdrawing and whimpering like injured dogs as they struck his protection.

"Yeah, I'm pretty much untouchable," he said to the nearest beast. "Take me to him."

The beasts turned at once as if they had heard a call inaudible to everyone else and began to march forward, Atlas and Caliber following them.

Large wooden doors opened into what looked like an abandoned courtroom. There was an ominous aura about the place. Torches lit the room, but darkness seeped through cracks in the wall. Tattered legal documents fluttered in a cold breeze. The judge's bench, now seemingly a gateway to infernal realms, exuded an eerie glow, casting an unholy hue upon the forsaken chamber.

Torn banners hung limply, their insignias warped by rot and time. Ghastly apparitions of lost souls floated ethereally around the ceiling, their anguished cries echoing through the chamber, now a macabre theater of lost justice, consumed by oppressive darkness.

In the center of the room stood Mr. Smith, triumphantly holding Atlas's mother. Her frail form trembled beneath his menacing grip as she met her son's eyes with a mixture of fear and resignation.

A twisted smile played across Mr. Smith's lips as he relished his power. His black shirt button undone, he exuded an air of calculated and sinister ease.

"Mr. Bishop," he snarled, emphasizing each word menacingly. "Does your mother not mean anything to you at all? Any other man would have chased the carriage down until their heart gave out and then would have gotten up and chased it again. They would have killed every man and beast on it. But not you."

His words hung heavy in the air like a pendulum swinging between hate and despair.

Atlas looked at his mother's face; she looked broken.

"Are you okay?" he asked her, ignoring Mr. Smith.

"Of course, she's not okay!" he roared. "Firstly, she's fucking dead. Secondly, she's in the company of demons wanting to rip her limb from limb! Her son has abandoned her to Hell! No one loves her!"

Mr. Smith composed himself slightly and continued. "However, we have made sure that she was very uncomfortable indeed. She has been tortured thoroughly and robustly."

His mother couldn't hold Atlas's stare. She shook her head and looked at the ground.

"So," said Mr. Smith. "You have come here to negotiate, I imagine. You want your mother back. I want you to come work for me, or indeed, just hand over all your powers and die. Shall we begin negotiations?"

Atlas caught his mother's gaze. "It will be okay," he mouthed.

"How will it be okay, Bishop!" shouted Mr. Smith. "Nothing is going to be okay! Stop telling your mother lies. Lie after lie. Time after time. It's all you are capable of. You have broken her heart. Look at her!"

Mr. Smith took a deep breath. "What is your decision?" he demanded. "Are you joining us, are you handing over your powers, or will I rip your mother's soul apart now? I haven't got all fucking day!"

Atlas reached slowly around to his back pocket.

"I have someone here who might help you make up your mind," hissed Mr. Smith, smiling. "Eddie! Come here."

Atlas's mother began to sob, and his eyes were distracted from her anguish to a dark corner of the room where a man walked purposefully forward. Atlas strained to see his face, as there was something very familiar about his walk, about how he carried himself.

"Hello, son," the man said as the light from the torches hit his sickening, grinning face. "Did you miss me?"

At sixty-five, he cut a gaunt figure, his once sturdy frame now worn and frail, the cancer that had ravaged his body having taken its toll. The years of alcoholism had etched lines of sorrow on his face, a testament to a life drenched in booze and regrets. His eyes, once sharp, were now dull with the haze of intoxication, betraying the violence that simmered beneath the surface. His voice was a volatile cocktail of bitterness and resentment, gravelly and harsh, dripping with venomous disdain for his wife and son.

Mr. Smith laughed maniacally as Atlas dropped his hand from his back pocket and stared at the man, at his own father, in shock. He had searched for him for six years, and here he was in front of him.

"Atlas," whispered Caliber. "Stay focused."

"I hear you've been looking for me, Atlas," his father said. "I didn't want to be found. I didn't want anything to do with you, you freak, or your bitch mother. Brings back too many crap memories, see. You both have the stench of death and tragedy about you. It's pathetic, and it's disgusting. I'm better than that."

His eyes ablaze with fury, fists clenched, and breath heavy with vengeance, Atlas stared at his father, the murderer he wanted to bind more than any other. A tempest of rage surged through his veins, seeking justice's reckoning. If he slit his father's throat right there, he could go to Hell, but he didn't care.

"Oh, Atlas!" laughed Mr. Smith. "You have thoughts of murder. About your father! How very unnatural. That's not how things should be. And here I was, thinking this would be a lovely family reunion. Kill him if you like: join me in Hell. I know of your dark heart. Do it!"

He smiled encouragingly at Atlas, who was frozen to the spot with undiluted rage.

"When I found your father in the hospice, he was at death's

door. Cancer had ravaged his body, and he had but days to live. There was no fight left in him. You could have so easily bound your mother's soul to him and secured her place in Heaven. He was as weak as a kitten. But you didn't. You failed. Again. You let her down again. I got there before you and offered him his health if he gave me his soul. And that's what he did! Your father belongs to Hell now. He belongs to *me*. And your useless mother will never see Heaven!"

Atlas's father laughed. "Too late, son," he jeered. "You've let your poor, brainless mother down again! You've done nothing but let her down your entire worthless life. Look at you, standing there with your lip quivering. Boo hoo! Just like you were that night I snuffed out her worthless life. I would have done you too...yeah... I would have killed you too, you sniveling little cretin, except I could hear the cop sirens and didn't want to get banged up for something so stupid as killing the both of you. I did the world a favor. Look at her!"

A tornado of fury churned within Atlas as he faced the man who shattered his world. His rage was almost unfathomable. His eyes burned with anguish and betrayal, and his soul screamed for the justice that had been denied him. Atlas could hear his heart thundering in his chest, louder and louder. He wanted to plunge a knife into the old man's chest, watch his blood spill out all over the floor, and see the panic and horror in his eyes as his life slipped away.

"Atlas," crooned Mr. Smith, reading his mind again. "Stop your whining and answer my question. Are you joining me?"

Atlas moved forward and looked his nemesis square in the eye. "Fuck. You!" he snarled slowly.

Mr. Smith nodded at Atlas's father, who produced a knife and drove it deep into his mother's chest. She fell to the floor like she had that horrific night, gasping for breath, her throat emanating a horrible, wet gurgle of blood and breath.

"Ma!" shouted Atlas, surging forward, but Caliber held him back.

Mr. Smith moved forward, blocking Atlas's view of his mother.

He could still see his father's smiling face, however. "Your mother has died a hundred deaths since she came here, and when I take her soul to Hell, she will die a million more."

His father pulled her up by the scruff of her Sunday dress and slapped her face hard. She awoke with a shock, scanning her surroundings and descending into sobs once more.

"Will you join us, Atlas Bishop?" Mr. Smith said and moved forward, circling around Atlas. "To save your poor mother from this nightmare? Do you even want it to stop, Atlas?" he whispered, now so close Atlas could smell his whiskey breath. "Will you join us?"

Atlas glared at him, staring straight into his dark eyes. "Fuck you, Smith," he said. "Never!"

Mr. Smith's expression turned thunderous. "Then it's war," he growled. "You are no match for me. You will all lose. Everything. Your world falls on Saturday."

He waved his hand, and a wall of flames rose up between them, sending Atlas staggering back. With a sinister grin through the flames, Mr. Smith traced arcane symbols in the air, each stroke igniting more flames. The air crackled with dark anticipation as the ground quivered beneath them. Then, with a thunderous roar, the earth split asunder, revealing a yawning chasm of fire and brimstone. From its depths surged billows of smoke, carrying echoes of tormented souls. The courtroom became a gateway to Hell, a maelstrom of damnation.

Mr. Smith and his beasts marched down into the chasm, one by one. Atlas tried to run through the flames, but Caliber held him back again. He struggled to be free and saw his father grab his mother and drag her limp body through the chasm, laughing as he went.

"No!" shouted Atlas. "Ma!"

The chasm solidified, the firewall fell, and Atlas struggled free from Caliber to run to the middle of the room. Hell's portal had closed, and his mother was gone. Again.

CHAPTER SEVENTEEN

Atlas was drinking tea by the bar. He had told Varie that he needed a double whiskey, pointing at the bottle of Bushmills on the counter, but had got a mug of Earl Grey instead. It wasn't taking the edge off in the slightest.

When Varie stepped away to make a phone call, Caliber studied his face from the next barstool over. "Do you want to talk about what happened back there?" he said gently. "About your father? About your mother? About everything?"

Atlas shook his head again, let out a big sigh, and swallowed the last of the tea in his cup. "I need to think," he said, getting up and heading for the stairs.

He spun around before his foot hit the first stair, eyes bulging with rage. "That bastard!" he shouted. "That bastard has my Ma. Did you see him, standing there with a big smile on his face after stabbing her again and again? Fucking prick!

"She's in Hell now, and I'm never going to get her back. Why did you pull me back? I could have run through those flames, Caliber." He raked a hand through his hair.

"I didn't sign up for this," he raged. "Part of the reason I did this was to secure my Ma's place in Heaven. That's it now; she's in

Hell. There's no fucking point in any of this. I'm done. I'm calling Gabriel. He can kill me. I don't care anymore."

Caliber stood up and walked over to him.

"Atlas, your life hasn't been easy," he said. "And no one would blame you for walking away because this is hard. What your father did to you when you were a kid was brutal and wrong, and what he did to your poor, defenseless mother was barbaric and unforgivable. He is a monster. Sounds like he always was."

Atlas dropped his shoulders. "Yeah, and that means I am half monster, too," he said, sniffing.

Caliber shook his head again. "No, you're not a monster, Atlas," he said. "You are a bit psychotic sometimes when the occasion calls for it. Like when you do that thing with your thumbs in people's eyes. But you never, ever hurt anyone who doesn't deserve it—no one who hasn't hurt people themselves. You're a fucking monster hunter, not a monster, because you know—from painful experience—exactly what monsters are capable of."

Atlas stood up a little taller. "Right," he said, just a hint of defiance in his voice. "Maybe you're right."

"That's the spirit," said Caliber, thumping him on the arm.

Varie walked across the bar, still talking on the phone, before hanging up.

"You okay?" she said. "You haven't said much since you came back. What happened?"

"Mr. Smith found my father," he said. "Found him in Italy in a hospice and gave him back his health in exchange for his soul. When I told him I wasn't going to work for him building this army of darkness he was planning, they dragged my mother to Hell. Just normal, everyday stuff. You know, just another day in the life of Atlas fucking Bishop."

Varie put her hand on his arm. "I'm so sorry, At," she said, moving closer. "Is there a way to get her back?"

He shook his head. "I can't go to Hell, no," he said, dropping his head. "She is out of my reach now. I promised her I would keep her soul safe, and, as usual, I've managed to mess that up."

Varie dropped her hand and walked to the bar, taking a seat. Atlas followed her over.

"Did Mr. Smith say anything about the whole taking over the world thing?" she asked.

"He threatened me, said that I was no match for him and that the world was going to end on Saturday," said Atlas, rubbing his forehead. "Or something like that."

Varie put her hand to her stomach. "Right," she said. "That's a bit shit."

Atlas looked at her, her head bowed. Her face was different. There was more color in it: it was rounder. She looked tired as her hair fell down across her eyes.

"I am doing my best, Var," he said quietly, "to sort this out, but I've no help, and I'm taking on Hell by myself. It's a bit overwhelming at times."

He reached over the bar and grabbed the bottle of Bushmills from the counter, screwing the cap off. A gentle pop, like a whispered promise, sounded from the bottle, and the aromatic essence of aged oak and amber warmth wafted out. He breathed it in: it felt familiar and comforting. He raised the bottle to his mouth as Varie stared at him, a look of disappointment on her face.

"Sure. Get drunk," she said quietly, not able to keep his gaze. "That's your plan. Brilliant."

Atlas set the bottle down on the bar, and there was an awkward silence. The air thickened with unspoken tension, a palpable void stretching between them like a gaping wound. Words faltered, suffocated by the weight of shattered expectations.

Varie reached for the remote control on the bar counter and pointed it at the television. A lively sports presenter broke the silence from outside Croke Park in Dublin, talking about the match on Saturday. He said that it was a historic moment, England playing Ireland, and that over a hundred thousand people were expected at the event.

Varie gestured with the remote control. "This. This could be Mr. Smith's big moment," she said.

"Jesus," Atlas whispered. "It makes total sense. He said I was no match for him. Everything ends on Saturday. He sends those dark guys in there, everyone starts killing one another, and you're talking thousands and thousands of innocent people dead."

Atlas took a deep breath. "Gabriel!" he roared, making Varie jump.

There was a chewing sound from behind them, and they spun around to a bar table where Gabriel sat, resting his feet. "What's happening? All sorted?" he asked, spitting pistachio shells from his mouth onto the floor.

Varie stood up, gaping at Gabriel. "Who is that?" she asked, alarmed. "Where did he come from?"

Atlas edged past her and moved towards the table, pushing Gabriel's feet onto the floor. "Gabriel," he said sternly. "I think Mr. Smith is planning a super-killer event at a football match on Saturday here in Dublin. The bars, churches, and cinemas were only dummy runs. Also, he has dragged my mother to Hell."

Gabriel looked at Atlas with a slack jaw, pistachio nuts dripping from his gaping mouth.

"There will be around a hundred thousand people at that match on Saturday afternoon," said Atlas. "If he gets his way, he will have an army of tens of thousands. We have to do something."

Gabriel stood up, spitting the last of the nuts on the floor. He raised his finger, signaling he needed a minute, and disappeared.

Atlas looked at Varie.

"Did that just happen?" she asked. "Did he just disappear? Who the fuck is that, Atlas?"

"That's the Angel Gabriel, Varie," he replied like it was the most normal thing in the world. "He's a bit..."

His words were cut off by Gabriel reappearing beside him, gripping his arm.

"Right," he said urgently. "I can help you. I have authorization from the big man himself. We can't let this happen, but you understand that I have to keep my nose clean and work behind the scenes. That's the stipulations, and you know what he's like about his rules. How many souls have you got downstairs?"

Atlas looked at Caliber. "At last count, seventy-nine," he answered.

"That's not nearly enough," said Gabriel. "But it will have to do. We need to make an army for ourselves—an army of light, to challenge this darkness."

He let go of Atlas's arm and held out his hand. The red leather book from the Vatican vaults appeared in it from out of thin air.

"What the hell?" said Varie, moving closer to Atlas.

Gabriel opened his book, licked his thumb, and flicked over a few pages. "Right," he said. "These are unprecedented times and therefore call for some unprecedented measures. Atlas, I'm sorry about your mum. I know you, I know your heart, I know you're smart, and I know you'll figure something out with what you have in front of you. I have every faith in you."

"So, I'm making all your souls angels, beings of light, souls who can battle down the darkness with their very presence. We haven't time for the usual process, so we'll have to bypass a few laws and just assume that they are all..." he looked directly at Caliber, "... reasonably good people."

"What?" replied Caliber, surprised. "I'm going to be an angel? Brilliant! What exactly does that mean?"

Gabriel sat on the edge of the desk. "It means you are higher beings," he said. "You get a lot of privileges between Heaven and Earth. You don't get wings or anything, though. That's a Hollywood thing that people get really pissed off about when they find out. I mean, what practical use are wings anyway? They serve absolutely no purpose. They put wings on angels in statues and in TV shows, and then people expect it in real life, it's like..."

"Gabriel," snapped Atlas. "Focus. What will these angels do? Can they fight?"

Gabriel nodded. "Yes," he said. "If they need to. But their very presence should—if all goes well—suffocate the darkness and stop the violence from spreading."

Atlas noticed Caliber was sitting down in the corner. He mumbled something.

"What's that, Caliber?" asked Gabriel, turning more pages in his book. "Did you say something?"

Caliber looked to Atlas, then Gabriel. "Sorry, yeah," he said, clearing his throat as if to give his voice more strength. "I was just wondering if, being an angel, I could go to Heaven at some stage?"

Gabriel nodded. "Yeah," he said. "Yeah, you can go to Heaven any time you want. You'll have an all-access pass after the ceremony. We have an open-door policy for angels."

Caliber nodded and put his head down. "That's good," he said. "That's all... I wanted just to...my daughter... She's..."

Atlas moved across the room and put his hand on his shoulder. "You'll be able to see Louisa now," he said. "That's good, mate, yeah."

Varie looked at Atlas, who was talking to himself, and then back to Gabriel, who had just appeared from thin air and was talking about promoting folks to angels. "Sorry," she said. "I'm a bit lost. I'm getting half a conversation here, and I'm very confused. This is all very weird."

Gabriel placed his hand on her forehead. "God gave me eyes so I could see," he said. Varie pushed his hand away and shrugged him off.

She turned to complain to Atlas, her face moving from anger to shock, when she saw that he was standing with his hand on the shoulder of a man with a large hole in his head. "What is that?" she gasped, stumbling backward.

"Can you see Caliber now?" Atlas asked. "He was killed last week: shot in the head, as you can see, by Morrison. Do you remember I told you about him? It's okay. These are the people I help, Varie. Lost souls who need to find the one who killed them so they can go to Heaven. Mr. Smith killed Caliber's murderer, so he's kind of stuck now. If you look around, you will see the bar is packed with souls, all with various injuries. It's alarming at first when you see them—I totally get that—but you get used to it."

Varie had gone very pale.

Caliber walked towards her. “I don’t mean to scare you,” he said, putting his hands up as if to surrender. “I usually wear a hat, but I’ve left it somewhere. I sometimes forget a bit of my head is missing.”

Varie put her hand to her mouth. “I think I’m going to be sick!” she shouted, running to the bathroom.

“Righto!” said Gabriel, bouncing forward and clapping. “Let’s go build ourselves an army of angels!”

CHAPTER EIGHTEEN

Atlas sat at the bar and watched Gabriel place hands on each of the lost souls. He saw their wounds heal, their bloody and ripped clothes return to normal, and their faces brighten.

They transformed from horrific corpses into beautiful, luminous creatures. Every one of them looked serene, like angels were supposed to.

He watched as Caliber took his turn, the hole in his head closing over, the color returning to his cheeks, and his shirt—the one he kept telling Atlas his wife had bought him—was like new again. He smiled widely at Atlas, who couldn't help but smile back. However, when Caliber averted his eyes, Atlas's smile faded as the sadness over his mother consumed him again.

"Woooow!" said Caliber, pulling up a bar stool beside Atlas. "This feels so weird." He picked up the remote control from the bar and switched the television channel. "Cool!" he declared. "I can lift stuff! I wonder if I can eat things, too?" He stood up and reached over the bar for a packet of peanuts Atlas was sure had been left there since the bar was last open. Caliber poured them into his mouth. "Oh my God, amazing!" he said, spitting crumbs of nuts all over Atlas.

Varie appeared behind the bar. “You look good, Caliber,” she said. “Much better.”

Caliber smiled. “I feel much better,” he said. “I feel calm and happy and positive. I can’t think of anything negative, honestly.”

Atlas scratched his head and grimaced. “Caliber,” he said. “I’m really happy for you; this is great. But we have a mass super-killer event happening tomorrow, and the Devil is going to use it to take over the world. Plus, my ma is in Hell.”

Caliber smiled again, and, at that very moment, he appeared saint-like. He was glowing. “Everything will work out, Atlas,” he said gently. “All will be well. I can feel it.”

The new angel got up as Gabriel called everyone to the middle of the room and told them that they had to charge overnight. Varie laughed. “Like cell phones?” she whispered.

Atlas couldn’t muster the energy to laugh or even smile. A heaviness had descended upon him, weighing on every molecule in his body, dragging him down. A darkness had enveloped his mind, suffocating his spirit's vitality. Each hour felt like a marathon. His limbs were heavy with the weight of sadness, dragging through the mire of his current existence. Even the simplest task had become a Herculean trial, draining whatever bits of energy remained. Nothing really mattered anymore, not even almost eighty luminous angels standing in a circle chanting, with the Angel Gabriel leading the chorus.

“Have you a plan, At?” asked Varie, sitting on the seat in front of him. “Or are we going with the ‘charge in all guns blazing, and see what happens next’ method that has served you so well thus far?”

Atlas raised neither his head nor a smile.

“All we can do is go in and try to stop them, Varie,” he said wearily, tapping a cigarette on the table. “Plans aren’t really my thing, but I want you to stay here. You have the baby to think of now. I’m not putting you in any more danger.”

Varie shook her head. “I’m coming with you, At,” she said. “You’re not doing this alone. You’ll need all the help you can get.

You really think I am going to sit here on my own while you go off to save the world?"

Atlas raised a weak smile this time.

"It'll be alright, you know," she said, grabbing his hand. "It'll work out."

Her voice soothed his weary soul like a warm embrace. She held his gaze; her touch, tender and reassuring, caressed his hand.

But he pulled his hand from hers and stood up, severing the fragile connection. Silence reigned, heavy with unspoken words, hanging between them like a delicate, shattered promise. Varie stood, too, looking hurt.

"Yeah," he sighed. "Maybe it will for you; I hope it does. But when this is all over, and if I survive, I have no one. I have nothing. I work with corpses and murderers every damn day of the week. If I died tomorrow, no one would fucking care. So, maybe everything will be alright for you, but for me, not so much."

Varie pulled him into a tight hug. He tried to resist, but the warmth of her body against his disarmed him. He hadn't had a hug from a living person in years. He surrendered to it and put his arms on her back as she hugged tighter.

"You're hurting, At," she said softly. "And I'm here as your friend. I care about you, and I'll go to your funeral when you die as an old man in your bed after a long and happy life, so stop whining about that. I'll be there, right? I'll even cry if you pay me enough."
He sniffed.

"Things look awful now. And I don't blame you for being consumed by darkness, but the sun will shine again. It will, Atlas. It will."

She let him go. "Okay?" she asked.

He nodded and managed a weak smile.

Gabriel came bounding over. "Okay, you two," he said cheerily. "This lot will charge themselves overnight by moonlight. They are doing a bit of chanting now, which will help them harness their power and grow it. By the time morning comes, these guys will be nuclear. Place them in the stadium and get them to move when they see aggression break out. Their light will be able to counteract the dark energy Mr. Smith intends to unleash. They can push back on his minions and destroy them. But we must be careful, Atlas: they can also be destroyed."

Atlas nodded. "If my mum were here, she would be an angel, too," he said. He felt a wave of emotion and felt he might cry, but swallowed hard and choked back the impending tears.

Gabriel patted him on the back. "It's sad, Atlas," he said. "We need to focus on this right now. If this goes wrong tomorrow, it's curtains for the world. The hatred and aggression will spill out over the world, humans killing humans, innocents lost in their millions. Hell will be on Earth, and Heaven will be empty. Cruelty and barbarity will reign. There will be no softness, no light. No hope. No love. Only hate. We can't have that; you must not allow that to happen. Are we good?" he finished.

Atlas nodded, regaining his composure. "Yeah, we're good," he said. "I'll do my best."

Gabriel smiled, clasped Atlas on the shoulder, then disappeared.

Atlas, on Varie's insistence, moved to the leather sofa on the periphery of the dance floor that was playing host to the chanting angels. She said he was tired and that he needed to sleep, and things would look better in the morning. She took the sofa opposite and threw him a blanket and cushion she had found upstairs.

Atlas let his head fall heavily onto the soft cushion as he tuned in to the low chant. It was repetitive and relaxing, and he soon felt his eyes slowly close.

He woke up three minutes later gasping for breath, startling Varie.

"Jesus! You still do that," she said, her hand on her chest and hugging her blanket closer up to her neck. "Night terrors. God, I remember those. Every night. Are you okay?"

Atlas nodded, looking away from her without answering and to the angels. He closed his eyes again and fell back into a deep sleep, dreaming of his mother walking in front of him, on fire, her skin melting from her face, of her screaming and screaming for help, screaming his name. He dreamed of running to catch up with her, reaching out for her, but never managing to grab her, his father laughing maniacally as she burned.

He woke with a jump again, suddenly ripped from slumber's gentle embrace. His heart pounded a frantic rhythm, echoing in his ears. Sweat beaded upon his brow, cold and clammy, as fear's icy fingers tightened around his throat. Gasping for air, he sat upright, throwing aside his blanket. He shook the disorientation from his head and looked to the dancefloor where the chanting continued, the angels glowing like moonlight now. He looked to the sofa opposite where Varie was fast asleep, her mouth slightly open, snoring gently. Her blonde hair had fallen over her face. He pulled the blanket up over her shoulders and she snuggled into the cushion, smiling in her sleep.

He hadn't been able to sleep through the night without whiskey in years. His parched throat yearned for the amber liquid, its seductive whisper echoing in his mind. It would bring relaxation and sleep, he knew that, but he needed to be sharp. Reason battled desire, a relentless tug-of-war between indulgence and restraint.

He got up and walked to the bar, where the bottle of Bushmills Whiskey still stood, untouched. Whiskey drowned the bad dreams, but he knew that he drank too much. He pulled down a glass from the rack overhead and unscrewed the cap on the whiskey bottle. He poured himself a glass, just one large one, and sank it. Putting the bottle behind the bar again, he returned to his place on the sofa. He put his head on his cushion, felt his eyes grow heavy, and was asleep again within two minutes.

Dawn's light through the stained-glass window gently caressed his weary eyelids as consciousness tiptoed back into his realm. For a fleeting moment, he savored the illusion of normalcy, stretching and smiling, until the weight of reality crashed upon him like a tidal wave. Dread flooded his veins as the memory of his mother's fate resurfaced, clawing through his façade of peace, leaving behind a trail of raw anguish.

Varie was behind the bar making coffee. He walked over, wiping the sleep from his eyes.

"How does one transport angels, ordinarily?" he asked, yawning. "A bus?"

She shrugged her shoulders. "Maybe," she said. "Do you know anyone with a bus?"

Atlas pulled out his phone and scrolled down to his mechanic, pressing the call button. "Hi, Frank," he said. "Yeah, it's me again. Listen, I need a bus. Bring it to the church on Jervis Street. No, I'm not at a party in a crematorium this time."

Atlas pulled the phone away from his ear to stop the loud laughter from the other end of the phone from hurting his eardrums. "Can you just get me a bus, Frank?"

Varie laughed and handed him a cup of coffee over the bar. He hung up and rolled his eyes.

They stood in silence, drinking their coffee. There was so much he wanted to say to her before they went out into the world, past Gabriel's protective veil, and into the lion's den, but he couldn't find the words.

The angels had stopped chanting and were standing, heads bowed, in their circle formation in total silence.

"It's so calming," said Varie, dreamily. "That stuff that they do."

Atlas looked at her and then to the angels. "What?" he asked. "Standing still?"

Varie nodded slowly. "Yeah," she said, her lips barely moving. "Everything is just so blissful."

Atlas stared at them, standing there, doing nothing. "Really?" he asked. Varie just nodded as if in a trance herself.

Atlas widened his eyes and started an inventory check. He pulled crystals from his back pocket and placed them on the bar. He pulled the dagger from his jeans and slapped it down on the polished wood, along with demon grenades, the life stone, and his binding rope. He took off the two amulets around his neck and placed them on the bar beside him. A wave of bliss suddenly rolled over him, and he found himself smiling at Varie like he was drunk. He had never noticed how beautiful the bar was—all the beautiful wood and the sun streaming in through stained-glass windows onto the floor. He took a big, easy breath and smiled some more. This was just bliss.

Caliber walked towards him. He was also beautiful, and when he spoke, his voice sounded like a song. "Atlas?" he said.

"Yes?" Atlas replied, noticing for the first time how comfortable his shoes were, so soft. Atlas ran his fingers through his own hair: it was so silky, not prickly the way it usually was. "Hair is great, isn't it?" he muttered, so pleased with himself that he had made this discovery. "God, I just love hair. It's really amazing how it just sits there."

"Atlas," said Caliber again. "Put these back on."

Atlas could smell coffee. He really loved the smell of coffee. It was warm and rich and reminded him of mornings. He loved mornings. They were the start of another wonderful day, a chance to start anew. He looked at Varie who was dancing in a circle, twirling her hands in the air. She looked beautiful as the sun shone in the window and set alight her hair like a dancing fairy. He laughed gently. He really loved fairies. They were so beautiful.

"Atlas," insisted Caliber. "Put these back on now."

He reached over and slipped Le Fondre's amulet back over Atlas's head. All his happiness disappeared.

"What the hell was that?" Atlas snapped. "I felt drunk, so happy. I had forgotten everything was crap. Take this back off me." He wrestled with Caliber as he tried to take off the protective piece.

"Atlas, no!" said Caliber. "You need to focus. We have serious work to do. That is our power you're feeling, our bliss. It's like dark energy, except light. Your amulet will protect you from it so you can get the job done. You can get some bliss later. There will be plenty left, don't worry. I'll keep some for you; now help me put this other amulet on Varie."

As soon as the necklace was over her head, Varie's face turned to thunder. "What on earth was that?" she asked. "I felt like I was doing LSD! I liked it. Can I do it again?"

Caliber widened his eyes and sighed. "You two need to focus," he said.

Atlas nodded quickly. "Right," he said, grabbing his equipment off the bar and putting it back in his pockets. "You're right. I'll see if the bus is here."

He walked to the back door, pulling a cigarette from behind his ear and lighting it before stepping out into the morning sunshine. The winter sun, a timid visitor in the frosty sky, caressed his upturned face. A gentle glow enveloped him, whispering promises of hope amidst the cold. In that fleeting moment, he found a smidgen of solace, a respite from the bleakness.

"Hi," said Varie from beside him. He hadn't heard her come out.

"Hiya," he said, throwing his cigarette on the ground and stubbing it out, waving away smoke from his mouth.

"What are you doing?" Varie laughed.

"The baby," he said, nodding to her stomach.

"Oh," she said, looking at her feet.

He looked at her in the sunlight with a heart full of warmth.

"You're glowing," he said, breaking the silence.

"It's probably the angel dust," she said, smiling sadly.

"No," said Atlas. "I noticed it even before you told me you were pregnant. At the hospital, even. You look different. Happy. Beautiful."

"Atlas, don't..." she said.

"I'm not flirting with you, Varie," he said. "I'm really happy for you. And you're right, everything will be okay."

They both looked out onto the street. There were fewer demonic beings there now: just one or two in the shadows where the sun didn't reach.

"You know," said Atlas. "That day in the bistro, I said some things you don't remember. I want you to know, in case I don't make it through today..."

"Atlas, don't..." she said again.

"No," he insisted. "You used to say I had no feelings and no emotions. And I did, I was just really bad at showing them. Everyone I ever loved was taken from me, including you, eventually. So, my default emotion was, and is, ultimately, anger. It's easier to sit with that than fear, and I'm sorry. I was an absolute nightmare to live with; I know I was. It couldn't have been easy for you. You were a saint to put up for me for so long, to remain my friend, and to care for me even after we split up. That takes a really strong person, Varie, and I want you to know I love you."

Varie nodded, her emotions strangling her voice. She pulled him into a tight hug, sobbing into his chest. He thought he heard the muffled words, "I love you too."

He took off Le Fondre's amulet and put it over her head. "Keep this on," he said. "It will protect you and the baby."

"No! What about you?" she sniffed.

"I'll be grand," he said. "I'm Atlas Bishop."

A bus pulled up outside.

"Let's get going," Atlas said, walking back into the church. "You go into the underground coach park, offload these angels, and we'll meet you on the stands. The guys know they have to spread out as soon as you get there, cover all the entrances and aisles, and battle down the darkness when they see it erupting. They'll hear it before it happens. It starts off with shouting and ends up with dying."

Atlas clapped his hands at the bar to gain the attention of the gathered angels.

"Listen, my friends," he said. "Listen, warriors of light. Today, we face the darkness head-on. But remember, within each of you burns a flame that cannot be extinguished. You are the guardians of hope, the champions of love. Let bravery be your armor and compassion your sword. Together, we'll illuminate the shadows and banish fear. For every heart you touch, a beacon of light will pierce the darkness. So go forth, my friends, and let your brilliance illuminate the world."

A chorus of determined faces ignited with purpose, stood in

front of him, their souls ablaze with the fervor of a shared mission. Atlas looked around at their faces, each one embodying resilience and hope. He could feel himself warming as they stood, ready to confront the shadows and unleash the transformative power of their collective light upon the world.

The angels walked in single file out the door and onto the bus. Atlas followed them on board and looked down the aisle at what seemed like a very odd day trip indeed. Angels were sitting on the seats, standing, holding onto the hand grips, and crouching on the floor.

"Are you ready?" he asked Varie as she started the engine.

She had a determined look on her face. "I was actually born ready, so..." she said.

He put his hand on her shoulder and squeezed gently.

"Keep that amulet on, always," he warned.

He looked at her one last time and got off the bus, heading for his own car and Caliber.

They raced through the streets of Dublin, past scores of scarved fans making their way to the ground, past bars with football fans holding their plastic beer glasses in the air and singing songs so passionately, arms around one another. They passed men and women dressed head-to-toe in their team's colors. They stopped at a traffic light and a family passed in front of them, excitedly chattering, all wearing Ireland tops, even the baby in the stroller.

Atlas felt sick. He hoped he could stop this.

CHAPTER NINETEEN

Atlas pulled the car around the corner. Croke Park's fortress-like arches loomed large over the small red brick terraced houses as if the structure had just landed from space. He watched in his mirror as Varie's bus of angels took a right into the service entrance.

"We'll have to park here and walk," he said. "It's too packed."

They pulled onto a side street and parked. Atlas checked his pockets for everything he needed and hoped Caliber's blissful energy would somehow help him pass security with a dagger down his jeans and his pockets full of demon grenades.

They took off at a fast walk to the top of a street, where they found a lively pub that had drawn a vast number of rowdy, drunken fans. They sang odes to England while wrapped in their flags. Caliber marched on ahead of him, weaving his way through the crowd, touching people on the shoulder and calming them. The throng parted like the Red Sea for Atlas as the angel forged ahead. In his wake, grown men were crying, professing their love for their friends, and hugging strangers.

Caliber looked around and smiled cheekily at Atlas as he walked ahead toward security.

They skipped the queue, and no one complained. Before long, Atlas found himself face to face with a burly security guard dressed in black, who asked for his ticket. Atlas noticed he had the letters "HATE" tattooed across the knuckles of both of his hands. He looked at Caliber, who stood between the two of them.

"This man doesn't need a ticket," the angel whispered into the guard's ear, the latter's face immediately softening. "You don't need to search him. He's clean. Let him in. He is doing God's work. Peace be with you."

The security man beamed at Atlas. "Go on, lad," he said, smiling at him like an old friend and standing aside. "Go on and do your work. Peace be with you." He congenially slapped Atlas on the back as he passed.

Atlas walked in and made for the stadium steps, taking off at a jog with Caliber behind him. As they neared the steps, they could hear the soft hum of thousands of people talking at once, some singing along with the pop song blasting out over the speakers. Atlas's heart was beating fiercely and erratically in his chest, but he didn't have time to worry about having a heart attack right now.

He reached the top and walked through the darkened tunnel into the light of the vast stadium. Thousands of people appeared before them, instantly engulfing them in a symphony of sights and sounds. The vast expanse unfolded beneath, revealing tiers upon tiers of seats, stretching like a grand tapestry toward the field below. A sea of humanity pulsated with anticipation, their fervor tangible in the air. The meticulously groomed emerald turf lay at the heart of it all, a canvas awaiting the brushstrokes of athletic prowess. As the roar of the crowd reached a crescendo, Atlas felt the electric energy coursing through every inch of this cathedral of sport.

Almost every seat was full, and the enormity of the task before them hit him hard.

"Jesus," he whispered as they scanned the crowd beneath them.

"Nope," said Caliber. "He's not here today, At. It's just us."

Atlas took his phone from his pocket and dialed Varie. He noticed that his hands were shaking.

No answer.

He rang again. Nothing. The crowd was jovial, the sounds of laughter, singing, and children's excited voices reaching his ears.

And again. Nothing.

"What the hell, Caliber," he declared. "Where is she?"

He followed Caliber's gaze to a commotion at the bottom of the stands just below them. From a distance, a section of the crowd looked to be compressing themselves into a circle.

A man shouted, followed by the sound of breaking glass. A woman screamed, and a child began to wail. People ran from the seats surrounding them, and Atlas could see fists flailing, men jumping into the fray, and a child racing towards them with blood running down his face.

"It has begun," said Caliber. "We need to move."

A blood-chilling scream from their right signaled that a demon had started his work within the crowd there as well. Atlas turned to see a man plunging a broken bottle into a woman's neck. He scanned the faces of those involved and noticed only malevolence and hatred in their eyes.

Chaos erupted in the heart of the stadium, a tempest of fury amidst the roar of the crowd. Bodies collided with primal force, each blow echoing like thunder against the metal stands. Anger and aggression fuelled the melee, a swirling vortex of violence. Spectators scattered, their screams lost in the tumult. The air thickened with tension, fraught with danger at every turn. Amidst the frenzy, fists flew, and tempers flared, painting the scene with raw brutality.

Screaming to the left. Shouting to the right. The entire stadium had come alive with fighting. The atmosphere was charged with hate: Atlas could physically feel it.

He tried calling Varie again. Nothing. "We have no angels, Caliber! Where are they?"

Caliber grabbed him by the shoulders. "Atlas, you go and get the angels; I will try to help here as best I can. Hurry!"

Atlas took off at a run, taking in the signs as he went. A man lunged at him with a metal bar, just missing his head. A woman swiped at him with a ripped beer can as he passed, cursing when her blow didn't connect. He ducked as someone lobbed a bottle at him, causing him to stumble over two old men wrestling on the floor.

Atlas continued running as pandemonium swept through the stadium—screaming, shouting, breaking glass, rage, and fury exploding all around him. He found the sign for the underground car park and took the stairs at a sprint until he reached the ground floor and what seemed like miles and miles of a dark parking garage.

Behind him, the stadium's fire alarm blared, but he ran, looking for the bus, panicked, his heart about to burst. His hope was fading fast as the screaming above intensified.

He leaned his back against a wall and caught his breath. And then he prayed.

"Divine beings, hear my call.
Guide me to the angels of light, defenders against darkness.
Grant us strength and unity in our mission to protect the world from evil's grasp.
Amen."

Atlas felt a warmth in his chest and watched as a ball of light separated from his heart and floated away in front of him. He ran after it as it led him down three flights of stairs, around corners of the vast parking garage, to the far end of the building.

He finally found them. The angels were surrounded by Hell's beasts—grotesque hybrids of demonic and human forms. Their sinewy bodies, complete with twisting horns and leathery wings, writhed with malice. Dog-like faces contorted into snarls of primal fury, their eyes ablaze with sinister intent. With razor-sharp claws and fangs dripping with ichor, they stalked around their victims with the promise of savage brutality, their guttural growls reverberating around the immense space.

He saw Varie in the middle of the angels' protective circle.

The stadium above roared with rage and chaos.

"Hey!" shouted Atlas, walking towards them, waving his arms. "Hey! Over here!"

The demons turned, growled, and moved closer to him.

A wave of screams from above rose and crashed like a tsunami.

"Hey! Come and get it! Over here!" Atlas shouted again, waving his hands and urging the demons to come closer, away from the angels.

The demons pounced in unison, charging him at speed. Atlas took off running across the dull, gray car park as dim fluorescent lights cast eerie shadows over cracked concrete floors. He ran on, breathing in the scent of exhaust fumes and tires as he tore around corners, the beasts at his heels, swiping at him with their vicious claws.

He reached into his pocket as he ran and pulled out a demon hand grenade. There was no pin, and Gabriel hadn't told him how to use the thing. Atlas threw it on the ground behind him in a rage as he ran on in between the cars, muttering benign curses at the angel.

The grenade exploded without warning in a puff of purple smoke. One by one, the pursuing demons burst into a bright red mist and were gone in the wind—every last one of them.

Atlas stopped running and looked at the scene, a mixture of bewilderment and pride on his face.

The roar of thousands of voices melded into a cacophony of chaos above him, reverberating through the stadium and jarring Atlas out of his daze. Shrill screams pierced the air, almost drowned by the thunderous stampede of frantic footsteps. Atlas took off back toward the stadium, hoping that the angels had been able to get there.

As he ran, he checked that his dagger was in place. The noise from the stands was thunderous now as he ran down the cement tunnel and emerged back into the sunlit arena.

The entire place was alive with anger, rage, and hate. Everywhere his gaze landed, people were fighting, dead bodies draped over the plastic seats in the stands. People lay bleeding in the aisles, and the field was a mass of clambering limbs as people took out their fury on one another. Players lay dead on the field as a police officer fired his gun into the crowd. A paramedic ran past them with a pair of scissors in his eye, shouts of rage coming from all angles. Below them, Atlas could see an angel moving slowly down the aisle, his hands held out by his side, an almost blinding light emanating from his form, dissipating the rage as it landed on those fighting.

He looked around the stadium at the light-bringers fighting back the darkness with such ferocity, bringing peace to those who'd had hate placed in their hearts. People who were attacking their loved ones with such brutality, who were spilling their blood, who were taking their lives.

There was so much death, so much pain. So much hatred.

Atlas put his hand to his head. It was too much to take in. The stadium looked like a war zone.

Varie ran towards him. "Thank God, At," she gasped, breathless. "I thought they got you."

He looked from the violence and blood and brutality to her soft face.

"Jesus, Varie," he whispered. "We are too late."

He watched the brutal spectacle unfold, a chilling numbness creeping over him, tinged with disbelief and horror. There were so many the angels hadn't reached yet. Each blow landed with sickening force, echoing through his mind like a relentless drumbeat. Helplessness washed over him, a suffocating weight pressing down, and he grappled with the senselessness of it all, a silent scream trapped inside his chest.

"We've done our best, At," Varie said softly, holding his arm.

"The angels will do their work now. There's nothing more we can do."

Atlas shifted his arm away. "I have to go, Varie," he said, "I'm sorry." He took off at a run across the stand, stopping only to look down the aisle at the dark characters wielding havoc.

His heart was pounding like a drum, adrenaline surging through his veins. With each step, he dodged debris and chaos, feet pounding against cold concrete. The stadium's sickening roar deafened him, but he pressed on, driven by fear and determination. Every step brought him closer to his goal, the stadium now a frenzied backdrop of desperation and survival.

"Atlas!" shouted Varie, running behind him. "Wait!"

Atlas ignored her and kept going. In the distance, he saw a light, growing brighter and brighter and then exploding, sending sheer white light and heat across half the stadium.

When his eyes adjusted, he saw his father standing over a felled angel, a blade raised over his head in victory. He met Atlas's gaze and began laughing. Atlas sprinted toward him, and he set off running, hurtling over chairs and bodies and taking steps two at a time up toward the service entrance to the roof.

Atlas burst through the roof doors after him and saw his father staggering towards the railings.

"Come back, you bastard!" Atlas roared after him.

His father just laughed and met the railings at speed, almost toppling over them. He spun around to see Atlas skidding to a halt before him.

"Look at the state of you," he sneered. "You're an embarrassment to the Bishop name."

Atlas laughed incredulously. "*I'm* an embarrassment?" he said. "Wife killer. Child beater. Murderer. Minion of the devil. You've some nerve."

Atlas moved closer, coming toe-to-toe with his father and looking him in the eye. A place he had wanted to be for many years, for he was no longer a frightened little boy.

"Do you miss your Mummy, son?" he grinned wickedly. "Well,

she's having a ball in Hell. I greatly appreciate the good work of those making her pay for all those years she made my life hell, the whining bitch."

Atlas stared hard at him as Varie burst through the door behind him.

"Atlas!" she shouted, surveying the treacherous terrain and high drop to the ground. "Come back!"

His father looked over his shoulder at Varie. "Is that your girlfriend, son?" he asked. "Are you not going to introduce me? Is she wife material?"

Atlas glared at his father. "I'm not your son," he growled. "You piece of shit."

"Let's me and you settle this like men," Atlas snarled, rolling up his sleeves. "I have no protection. Try what you can to hurt me. An even fight, but this isn't eight-year-old me you'll be fighting, old man. I'm ready for you. I want to make you feel pain. I want payback."

His father chortled. "You haven't a chance, you weak little boy. I'll put you on your back like I did when you were a wee boy. You used to pee your pants like a sissy when I punched you. You'll probably do it again now. You're no match for me."

Atlas swung a punch that connected with his father's jaw, his head swinging back but his body barely moving. He punched him again, this time hard in the stomach, but it was like hitting iron. His eyes were ablaze with righteous fury, mirroring his father's violent glare. With every strike, Atlas unleashed years of pent-up rage, each blow a strike of vengeance. His father responded and caught him with a savage undercut, sending him staggering backward. He lost his footing and crashed to the ground, sliding down toward the edge of the building. He heard Varie shouting his name as he skidded, gripping a safety ladder just in time to stop him from going over the edge.

"Not so big now, are you?" roared his father. "I can still take you, it's like fighting a child, you pathetic little boy."

Atlas rose to his feet and retaliated with a strong right hook, sending his father backward against the safety railing, dizzy and disoriented. It gave him enough time to take the dagger from his jeans before running at the old man and plunging the blade deep into his heart. As he did so, he could hear Varie screaming his name from behind.

He didn't care. His father gasped in pain, grabbing him hard by the shoulders.

"Who's the weak little boy now, you prick," Atlas whispered in his ear. "How is it to feel your lifeblood ebb away? I'm going to enjoy watching you die, you bastard. You ruined my fucking life."

His father's grip lightened, his face lost its rage, and the light in his eyes grew dim.

Atlas watched his face turn from anger to fear and finally sadness. He almost felt pity but quickly shook it from his head.

"Die, you bastard!" snarled Atlas, half crying, twisting the knife, pushing it further into his chest. They were face to face now, and his voice broke with emotion. "I fucking hate you," he hissed, his forehead falling against his father's. "Die, you fucking prick." he whispered, emotion choking his voice. Tears streamed down his face, a cathartic release of pain and retribution.

His father groaned, a final death rattle, as his eyes rolled to the back of his head. He was gone at last. Atlas pulled out the knife and plunged it repeatedly into his father's chest, over and over again, like the brute had done to his mother all those years ago. In the frenzy, he could hear Varie screaming for him to stop. She was crying and screaming at him, but he didn't care.

His father slid down his body and fell in a heap to the ground. Atlas stood over him, the dagger in his hand still dripping with blood.

He turned to Varie. "I'm sorry," he said. "I love you."

He raised the glinting dagger to his throat. With a flash of steel and a crimson cascade, the blade sliced through the flesh and sinew of his own throat. His eyes widened with agony, a silent scream echoing through the air, drowned by the gurgling rush of blood.

He looked from Varie's horrified face out across Dublin as his life gushed away. Rooftops sprawled like an intricate patchwork quilt woven with chimneys and satellite dishes. Slate-gray tiles glistened under the sun while wisps of chimney smoke danced in the evening breeze. The city's heartbeat pulsed below as his own slowed, a rhythmic symphony of distant traffic and murmured conversations framed by the silhouette of distant hills and spires.

He looked to the ground below, people appearing like ants at this distance. He leaned against the safety railing.

His legs felt weak. This was it. Death. He would embrace it. With the last ounce of strength he had, he threw his broken body over the railings.

Varie screaming his name was the last sound he heard, and the sunlight bouncing off her beautiful blonde hair as she leaned over the railing, hands outstretched, was the last sight he saw. And he was fine with that. He wouldn't have wanted it any other way.

He could feel his light going out as the ground rushed to meet him. He could hear his heart beating loudly, slower, then stopping.

That was it. All over. The end.

CHAPTER TWENTY

Atlas fell through the earth, traveling at lightning speed, through the ceaseless blackness and deafening silence, through ferocious, roaring fires, and then...nothing.

Walls of molten rock blurred past, their searing heat scorching flesh and searing the air. A cacophony of anguished cries rose, echoing through cavernous depths as the abyss below him beckoned. Gravity's grip tightened, dragging Atlas deeper into the infernal abyss toward eternal damnation.

His knees slammed into the ground, and his body crumpled around them as it caught up. Disoriented, he shook his head. The ground was moving beneath him, and he could hear faint voices.

A brutal kick to the stomach returned him to his senses. "Look what you did, dickhead," his father screamed in Atlas's face. "Now I'm stuck in hell! I hope you're fucking happy now."

Atlas gingerly got to his feet and coughed, dust from the floor disturbed by his fall mingling with the ash in the air. He looked around to see they were on an old train, rattling slowly, jarringly along aged tracks. Plush scarlet seats were tattered and torn, their once vibrant colors having faded to a morose beige. The air was heavy with the intensely suffocating stench of brimstone; the monotonous rhythm of the train's wheels echoed a funeral dirge.

Outside the window was a city on fire, the landscape unfolding like a nightmare. Rivers of molten lava snaked through charred valleys, casting an eerie glow over jagged cliffs and ashen plains. Grotesque creatures writhed in agony, their tortured forms illuminated by flickering flames. The air was thick with the stench of sulphur, a suffocating miasma that clung to the windows. Amidst the infernal chaos, screams of the damned echoed in a haunting chorus. The sky was a deep, blood red, and Atlas could see shadowy figures in the distance moving amidst the flames. Bodies hung from burning bridges as the train trundled over inner city streets, where rows of people were crucified along building façades, their faces contorted in pain. The agonized screaming was intense and relentless.

Atlas looked up at the train car, which was full of mean and angry people with dark faces. His gaze stopped at a frightened-looking man who was crying. The man looked back at him and got up, unsure if he should approach, before moving quickly toward him, grabbing his shirt with his fists and pulling his face closer.

"I'm not supposed to be here," he whimpered. "I don't know why I'm here! I'm scared. Can you help me? Please help me."

Atlas's father got up and pulled the frightened man away, pushing him up against the wall. "You're here because you murdered someone, you piece of shit," he snarled. "Like this piece of murdering shit here that's supposed to be my son," he said, nodding at Atlas. "Now sit down and shut the fuck up."

He let the man go and he scurried back to his seat, hugging his knees to his chest and crying.

Atlas's father approached him.

"Sit down," he ordered.

"Fuck you," spat Atlas.

"You're still an insolent little shit," said his father.

"You're still the world's worst father," replied Atlas.

"You're just like your mother."

Atlas smiled widely. "I know," he said. "Do you want to go again? I can take you, big man. You cried like a baby when you were dying."

His father rolled his eyes. "You're the same as me now, Atlas Bishop," he said. "A murderer. There's nothing that can take that away. That's a stain on your soul forever. You're a monster, too. Just like me. You're here to stay, so welcome to your new home."

His father looked out the window, but his initial joy and arrogance seemed to wane with every horrific sight he observed.

Atlas watched him, disgusted by how pathetic and small he was. His father was nothing but a weak old man. He wondered why he had feared him for so long, this demon who had haunted his nightmares for decades.

"I'll never be like you, Eddie," he said. "You're a pathetic excuse for a human being, the scum of the earth. And you're stuck here in the hottest holiday resort in the world. I'd be feeling pretty shit about stuff right now if I were you."

His father glared at him. "You're stuck here too, dickhead," he mumbled.

Atlas smiled wider. "Yeah, but I'll never suffer, knowing I took you out. I'd do that again and again. It felt so good, twisting a knife in your heart over and over, old man. Now you know what Ma felt. Hell doesn't scare me, asshole. Thanks to you, I've been dead inside since I was eight years old. To suffer, you have to care, and I don't. My work is done, and I'm the happiest man in fucking Hell, thanks very much."

His father glared at him. "Who got you then?" he snarled, pointing at his neck and his blood-stained shirt. "Who took you out?"

"None of your fucking business," Atlas snarled back.

The train entered a tall, dark tunnel, slowed, and then ground to a halt. Everyone in the carriage, mean or not, was afraid now.

As the train doors creaked open, a suffocating wave of sulfuric stench assaulted Atlas's senses, clinging to the air and his skin like a malevolent fog. A dimly lit platform stretched out before them, shrouded in a gloom that seemed to devour any trace of light daring to penetrate its depths. Shadows danced eerily along the cracked concrete walls, flickering with a sinister life all their own.

The sound that greeted them was a cacophony of tortured wails and anguished screams, echoing off the desolate walls with haunting resonance. The very air itself was imbued with the tormented cries of the damned, a symphony of suffering that reverberated through the marrow of Atlas's bones.

The landscape that unfolded beyond the platform was a nightmare made manifest. Whatever this place once was, the roof had long gone. In the distance, jagged obsidian cliffs jutted skywards, their surfaces etched with writhing tendrils of blackened flame that licked hungrily at the empty air. Streams of lava snaked through the ashen plains below, casting a hellish glow that bathed the landscape in a sickly red light.

Amidst the desolation, grotesque figures shuffled aimlessly, their twisted forms contorted in agony. Some were trapped in torment, their flesh rent and torn asunder, while others writhed and convulsed grotesquely.

Above it all loomed a towering citadel, its spires reaching toward the heavens like accusing fingers pointed at the very heart of existence. The walls were lined with rows upon rows of twisted faces frozen in expressions of torment, their eyes vacant and hollow as they bore witness to the unending horrors that surrounded them.

As Atlas stepped out onto the platform, he could feel the oppressive weight of despair settling over him like a suffocating blanket, each breath a struggle against the malevolent forces that sought to drag him down into the abyss. He had entered a realm beyond comprehension, a place where nightmares took form and reality itself seemed to unravel at the seams.

He looked around at his immediate surroundings. They were in a surreal version of Grand Central Station in New York. Its majestic arches were twisted into gnarled, skeletal forms, the once bustling concourse now a desolate wasteland littered with charred debris. Flames licked at the stained-glass windows, casting eerie shadows that danced with sinister glee. The air was thick with the stench of despair.

Atlas gazed up to what was left of the majestic infernal ceiling, black as night and seeming to move as writhing shadows scaled its walls. Passengers with brutal head injuries and missing limbs walked past them to catch their trains, and Atlas caught the gaze of a woman serving in a kiosk, who turned her head away to reveal horrific burns to her face.

He inhaled deeply, and it felt like he was breathing in fire, scalding his throat.

Silent, black-clad soldiers stood guard on either side of the iconic stone stairs, their batons raised. Their once-pristine uniforms now hung in tatters, stained with the blood of the damned, and their eyes gleamed with a sinister fervor, devoid of mercy or remorse.

Passengers ran the gauntlet, beaten relentlessly, and kicked down the stairs if they fell. They were shot at close range, their faces mangled, but still they ran on. Atlas's father was struck in the face by a black masked fist right before Atlas himself felt the searing pain of a swiftly-wielded baton across the back of his head. He buckled over in pain, and a guard kicked him hard in the back, sending him tumbling down the stone stairs. He felt the sharp impact of every one of them.

A figure wearing an officer's uniform stood waiting at the bottom of the stairs as Atlas landed ungraciously at his feet. His eyes were black holes, his cheekbones sunken, his uniform and hat dusty and torn. His flesh was barely clinging to the bones on his hand, which clenched a black cane. Every movement was a calculated step toward perpetuating suffering, his visage twisted into a demonic smirk that heralded the horrors he delighted in unleashing upon the damned.

He reached down and grabbed Atlas by the shirt, pulling him to his feet and up into his face.

"Atlas Bishop," he boomed. There was nothing where his eyes should have been.

"Yeah," Atlas managed, spitting blood on the floor. "How's it going, man? I'd say it's nice to meet you, but it's really not. Can you point me in the direction of my hotel? I'd like to freshen up after my journey."

The officer dropped Atlas and stepped back as five soldiers moved in. Their expressionless faces stared at Atlas momentarily as he painfully attempted to find his feet again. The officer cracked his cane on the ground, and two of the soldiers grabbed Atlas by the arms as the others moved in to beat him mercilessly. He felt every thick, heavy punch as it landed and reverberated through his body. He tasted the blood in the back of his throat. His head was thrown from left to right with each punch, and he could feel his brain bouncing off his skull as his neck muscles ripped.

"Maybe this will teach you some respect!" shouted the officer as the blows continued to rain.

Pain was now a constant companion. The soldiers held his arms in vice grips, and he couldn't fight back. His ribs cracked, and a searing pain shot through his body. He tried to kick out his legs and resist, but to no avail. He'd been kicked and kneed in the groin so many times that each blow was simply another beat in the relentless rhythm of his torture. Pain pulsed through his body from so many sources that his brain couldn't keep up. He let his body go limp, but still, they pummeled him. The officer leaned down into Atlas's bloody face. "You will learn, Atlas Bishop," he growled, "I will make sure of that."

Atlas groaned. "And what happens if I don't want to learn, dickhead?"

The officer raised his cane and crashed it down on Atlas's head. Everything went black.

Atlas tried to focus his vision, but the ground was moving too quickly beneath him. A fiercely hot wind made it impossible to breathe, but he supposed breathing wasn't all that important now that he was dead.

The ground, cracked and desolate, quaked beneath each footfall, a testament to the eternal torment that pervaded this accursed realm. A graveyard of bones littered the scorched earth, and shadows danced malevolently, obscuring the path ahead.

Atlas's legs ached as they were dragged along the ground over the rubble and skulls. He felt the vice-like grip on both his arms tightening before everything went black again.

A sharp, stinging pain brought him back to consciousness. A soldier stood in front of him, adjusting the black leather glove that had just made contact with his face.

"Stand up!" he roared. Atlas tried and failed to get to his feet, falling to the side as his legs collapsed beneath him.

They were standing on the steps of St Patrick's Cathedral, its huge spires piercing the fiery sky, twisting into a macabre mockery of its former grandeur. Its once-pristine peaks loomed like jagged teeth against a blood-red sky. The stained-glass windows, once aglow with divine light, now cast eerie shadows of torment. The air vibrated with sinister whispers and gargoyles leered menacingly from charred façades, their stone forms twisted with malevolence. There was a suffocating darkness swirling about it as harsh, fiery wind roared against them. Sand tore at Atlas's eyes when he blinked, ash burning his flesh.

"On your feet!" roared the soldier. "The supreme leader wants to meet you. You will show respect."

Atlas put all his effort into standing on his feet. The pain was ceaseless and he figured if he were still alive, he would have definitely vomited by now.

Surrounded by soldiers, he staggered up the steps, falling onto his knees at the top. To his left, his father—his smile now completely gone—moved to help him, grabbing onto his arm and pulling him up. Atlas wrenched his arm violently from the old man's hand.

"Fuck off!" Atlas roared into the wind. "Don't you fucking touch me! You're the worst person in this place, and that's saying something."

His father's head fell again.

They walked through the cathedral's massive wooden doors, and the magnificence of the building opened up before them. The pews stood empty, bathed in a sickly glow, while the echoes of unholy chants reverberated through the desecrated halls. Even this holiest of sanctuaries had succumbed to damnation. Its stone pillars stood tall, but many pews at the front of the church had been ripped out and, judging by the flames in one corner of the building, had been used to fuel a large bonfire on which several bodies had been scorched. They walked up the aisle toward the altar, which had been stripped bare of any holy relics.

He could see his mother standing there, head bowed, wringing her hands, a broken woman.

"Atlas Bishop, Supreme Leader," shouted the soldier as they neared and threw Atlas at the base of the altar. His weary bones crashed onto the harsh stone floor. Everything hurt.

His mother lifted her head. "Atlas!" she cried, "No!"

He tried to raise his hand to her but hadn't the strength. His battered and swollen head felt cool against the cold stone; it was comforting and eased his pain for a brief moment.

"I'm alright, Ma," he mustered.

He could hear her sob, then shout, "You leave him alone!" as the click-clack of high heels sounded closer to him. He was brought to his feet once again by unseen hands.

Atlas opened his eyes to find himself staring into the face of the Devil. A stunningly beautiful woman, her golden locks cascaded like molten rivers over smooth skin. Voluptuous curves undulated beneath the flickering flames, a tantalizing dance of temptation. Her eyes, glistening pools of black darkness, held the secrets of eternity and simmered with an evil intelligence. Her lips parted in a sardonic smile as she tipped her head to one side, considering her latest inmate. "Atlas Bishop," she purred, holding his chin up and staring into his eyes.

"Don't hurt him!" his mother cried.

"I'd keep your maternal instincts to yourself if you want your son to prosper in his new home." She dismissively flicked a hand in the direction of Atlas's mother, and the latter immediately doubled over in pain, dropping to her knees.

The Devil then waved her hand at Atlas and propelled him into a ceremonial chair on the altar.

"Let's talk, shall we, Atlas? Just you and me; no need for any intermediaries. I've waited a long time to meet the famous Atlas Bishop, so I'm sure that you and I can come to some sort of amicable arrangement."

"Yes," whimpered Atlas. "Let's make a deal."

The Devil's face reset as she marched over and straddled him on the chair.

"Poor man," she whispered, stroking his cheek. "What did they do to you? I do apologize on behalf of my staff. Sometimes, they get a little...over-enthusiastic. Let me make it up to you."

Her eyes glowed softly with infernal desire, drawing him into her abyss with a mesmerizing gaze. Her voice, a velvet whisper laced with promises of ecstasy, entwined around his soul like tendrils of smoke. With each gesture, she moved with a sinuous grace, her form a tantalizing mirage in the flames. Her touch ignited a primal fire within him, consuming reason and inviting him to surrender to the intoxicating embrace of damnation.

She kissed his forehead. "I have known you for an age. The bold, brave, brutal Atlas Bishop. I have wanted to meet you for a very long time. You have been doing a most excellent job. I can see why Smith hates you so much. He is so jealous."

She lowered her head to his and spoke again, her voice a whisper in his ear. "There is much light in you still, but also so much darkness." She ran her nails down his chest. "I can feel it radiating from your skin and seeping into mine. It's delicious." She ran her tongue along his neck. "Yesss," she purred. "I can taste it. Let me take your pain away, Atlas Bishop."

She kissed his cheek, his neck, and reached for his bloody hand

and kissed his palm. She gently sucked one of his fingers into her mouth, staring deep into his eyes, and swirled her tongue around his fingertip before pulling it out between pursed lips and moaning softly.

She stared fiercely at him, hungry. He was hypnotized.

"You're like me, Atlas," she whispered against his lips. "We are more alike than you think."

She kissed him hard on the mouth, rolling her tongue around his, pressing her warm body against his weary frame. He was totally, utterly intoxicated.

She pulled away and slowly spun around in his lap to face the room. "Yes," she whispered and licked her lips as everyone watched, transfixed. "Yes, I want you, Atlas Bishop. I want all of you. Together, we could rule Hell forever. Say you'll join me. Say yes."

Atlas felt some strength return to his body. He smiled, the taste of her lips still on his. The pain had dissipated, and his blood was flowing again. Atlas scanned the room. His father, standing to his left, had a disgusted look on his face. His mother was leaning on a table at the altar; weak, hurt, and still sobbing.

"You!" shouted the Devil, pointing at Atlas's father. "I have no use for you now. The sight of you, with your disgusting weak stature and your filthy nails, displeases me greatly. He has been brought to me, so I need you no longer. Your presence irritates me. Be gone."

She nodded at the soldiers, who grabbed his father by the arms and dragged him backward down the aisle. The large wooden doors swung open, and a gust of fiery wind blew into the church. Atlas felt the blast of heat from the fires beyond the cathedral's steps and stood up, gripping the side of the ceremonial chair for support.

His father struggled with the soldiers, shouting and kicking his feet against the ground in a desperate attempt to stop them from taking him. "You promised me eternal life!" he raged.

The Devil turned and glared at him. "I lied," she roared, her eyes gleaming. "You should know better than to trust the Devil, stupid human."

She directed her gaze to the soldiers. "Take him to the Seventh Circle! Make him pay for his Earthly actions. Make him suffer!"

His father's face betrayed his panic. "No!" he cried. "No, please!"

He turned to Atlas. "Son," he pleaded. "Help me!"

Atlas turned his back and walked to his mother, a woman broken by the man's terrestrial actions. He stood beside her, and they both watched as his father cried, pleaded, and begged to be shown mercy as he was dragged down the cathedral steps.

The doors slammed shut with a boom, and silence fell once more in the church.

"Why did you come, Atlas?" his mother asked him.

"It's okay, Ma," he whispered, reaching out his hand to take hers. "Everything will be okay."

She sobbed harder into her palms, and Atlas let his hand fall back to his side.

The cathedral's doors swung open again, and Mr. Smith marched up the aisle. Cloaked in shadows and wrath, he ascended the steps in purposeful strides, his presence commanding fear among the soldiers in the stagnant air. His eyes, seething orbs of malice, pierced the darkness with a fiery glare, reflecting the anger that perpetually burned within. Each step resonated with suppressed fury, echoing through the church like a thunderous lament.

"You!" Mr. Smith snarled, pointing at Atlas. "You ruined everything!"

He ran at Atlas and punched him hard in the stomach, lifting him several feet in the air and taking his breath away. He came forward again and kicked him in the face, feeling the steel from his toe-capped boot shatter his cheekbone. Atlas fell to his knees in agony, his head spinning.

He dragged Atlas to his feet, pulled a dagger from his belt, and held it to his neck. Atlas could feel the cold sting of its blade. "I can cut you a million times, Atlas Bishop, and you'll feel every single one. First your neck, then your balls."

"Step back!" warned the Devil, stepping from the side of the altar, her eyes dancing between Mr. Smith and Atlas. "Remove your filthy hands from him."

Mr. Smith immediately stepped back and bowed. "My sincere apologies, Supreme Leader. I did not know you were here. Please forgive me for the insolence. I am not worthy to be in your presence... I must..."

"Oh, stop your sniveling!" she said, walking toward him.

She grabbed his face tightly in her hand, her mouth so close that her spittle landed on his cheek. "You failed, Smith," she snarled. "Your plan for domination was brought down by a bunch of fucking angels."

She grasped Mr. Smith's head with her manicured hands and began to crush his skull. He screamed in pain and dropped to his knees, blood pouring from his nose and mouth.

"You think you can overthrow me?" she raged. She tilted his head to face her as she continued the torture, staring intensely into his face, wanting to see the pain in his eyes. Atlas tried to ignore Mr. Smith's agonizing cries but couldn't.

The Devil finally released her grip, and Mr. Smith collapsed onto the stone floor, writhing in agony with tears streaming down his face.

"You broke my nail with your fucking skull, you asshole," she shouted, kicking him hard in the stomach with the point of her stiletto shoe. He cried all the louder. She gave him one more dig in the guts with her shoe, then she walked over to Atlas.

"I'm so sorry you had to see that," she crooned, her hand caressing his chest. "I just don't like failures. You wouldn't let me down like that, would you? No, you wouldn't. Now, my dark one. You'll work for me, yes?"

Atlas looked across to Mr. Smith on the ground beside him, his body broken.

The Devil turned his face to her. "Never mind him," she said. "I am finished with him. He's done. I want you to take his place." She drew closer. "You are so very good at collecting souls," she whispered. "You are vicious, brutal, and heartless. Your soul is so black, so vengeful. You have all the secrets of Heaven, and I want them. We can use them; we can take over the world, Atlas Bishop. You and I, together. I know we will burn. I can feel it. I can feel that powerful dark energy flowing through your veins. I feel it everywhere. It's so strong and intoxicating."

Atlas nodded, and the Devil moved in closer.

"I know you have a beautiful, deep, dark side, Atlas. I can feel it. Give it to me. Say...*yes*."

Mr. Smith groaned from the ground.

The Devil spun around and kicked him again. "You are *ruining the moment*," she growled.

She walked to the front of the altar and bellowed at her guards. "Get up here and get him out!"

Atlas reached into his pocket with one hand and grabbed his mother's hand with the other as Mr. Smith looked up from the ground at him.

Atlas cleared his throat and the Devil spun around and flashed him a dazzling smile.

"Thanks for the job offer," said Atlas. "It sounds really brilliant, yeah. You've seriously tempted me—I guess that's your thing—and I've no doubt we'd have fun together exploring my dark side. I mean, I'll probably regret this on so many levels, but I'm not interested in working with you. This isn't my scene. This is a horrible, stinking, rotten, sweaty place. Do you ever turn the heat off? Jesus! Just no. But thanks anyway."

He gripped the crystal tightly and whispered, "*Domine, vivifica me* (Lord, grant me life)," and immediately felt a pull in his belly button.

The last thing he remembered was Mr. Smith reaching his hand out and grabbing his ankle.

CHAPTER TWENTY-ONE

Atlas slowly opened his eyes. Everything was white, and there was a bright light shining on him. Was this Heaven? He reached his hand up to rub his blurry eyes, and they met resistance. He pushed against what felt like plastic, looked to his left, and saw a zipper. He panicked and sat up, banging his head hard on a metal object, before falling onto the cold floor. He grabbed the zipper and yanked hard, pulling apart what he now realized was a body bag. He let it drop to the floor and felt his body with his hands to ensure everything was still intact.

Shouting "Yes!" at the top of his voice, he joyfully punched the air. "In your face, Devil woman!"

He looked back at the table he had just fallen from and the large medical light he had banged his head on. He peered around the morgue to be greeted by rows and rows of dead bodies.

An icy chill pervaded the air, seeping into every corner like a silent specter. Atlas wrapped his arms around himself and shivered, looking around to see if there was anything that he could use for clothes or heat. Fluorescent lights flickered overhead, casting harsh shadows across the gleaming stainless steel surfaces. The scent of disinfectant mingled with the faint aroma of death and decay. Rows of metal gurneys stood sentinel, draped with crisp, white sheets concealing their lifeless occupants. The silence was oppressive, broken only by the occasional hum of machinery or the shuffle of footsteps outside the doors.

In this stark chamber of death, Atlas realized he hadn't been able to save everyone.

The morgue doors swung open, and a young doctor in scrubs entered, staring in astonishment at the scene before him. Varie and two nurses followed, stopping short when they saw the formerly dead man standing in front of them, very much alive.

No one spoke for at least a minute. Atlas pulled the body bag up to protect his modesty and eventually spoke to break the awkward silence.

"Hello," he said cheerily as they stood like statues, mouths agape. "I know how this looks."

He expected someone to answer, but they didn't. They just stood there looking at him.

The fluorescent lights flickered uncertainly, casting eerie shadows on the scene. Silence hung heavy in the air, broken only by the doctor's ragged breaths.

"It looks mad, I suppose, from where you're standing," laughed Atlas. "I know, I know, that's how it looks. But listen, folks. I think I know what happened. I have very low blood pressure. Someone must have mistaken me for being dead and bagged me up. I just woke up! I'm totally fine. Honestly. I feel much better now."

Varie, her eyes red from crying, moved her mouth as if to speak but then stayed silent.

"Sir," said the doctor, scanning his face, "you lost every drop of blood you had in your body, and you fell three hundred feet off the top of Croke Park onto the concrete. Blood pressure wasn't your issue. Being...being....um...being actually dead was your issue."

The doctor stepped tentatively toward Atlas, reached out his hand, and took Atlas by the wrist to check his pulse.

"I don't know how to explain this," he muttered. "I can't explain this. You were definitely dead. I processed you myself. I was about to do the autopsy. You were, without a doubt, absolutely dead." The doctor looked as if he was about to faint.

Atlas pulled his wrist away. "Don't worry about it, mate!" he said, slapping him on the upper arm. "Everything's fine; it's all good. No harm done."

Atlas wrapped the body bag around his waist like a skirt and walked towards Varie. He moved his jaw around, discovering it was no longer broken. He checked his neck, and there was no knife wound. Brilliant.

"It was mad, Var," he said when he reached her. "I woke up on this train. My father was there, the prick. He's in the Seventh Circle now, being tortured for an eternity, which is a good outcome, I think. Everything was on fire down there, like *everything*. The Devil is a seriously strange individual; I could tell that Ma hated her." Varie just stared at him, not speaking. She was ghostly white.

Atlas shrugged. "So what are we doing then?" he asked. "Where are the keys, Varie? I'll drive. You're maybe in a bit of shock there, yeah?" Varie kept staring at him.

Atlas continued cheerfully, "Right. I need to get some clothes; I'm kinda naked. Can we, like, move?"

Varie looked at the medical staff and back at Atlas before walking after him.

Atlas's bare feet slapped hard against the cold hospital floor as he marched toward the exit. People stopped to stare at him as he struggled to maintain his modesty with the body bag. He just wanted to go outside and see the sky, breathe the air, then this would seem real. The nightmare would be over.

His eyes widened in awe as he saw the radiant spectacle before him. Through the sliding doors in front of him, sunlight was dancing upon verdant flower beds at the hospital entrance. A gentle breeze came in as the doors opened and closed, caressing his skin, carrying with it the sweet scent of the flowers and new beginnings. As he walked more quickly, he inhaled the crisp, invigorating air, filling his lungs with the promise of freedom. He practically ran through the hospital doors outside, turned his face to the sun, and raised his arms high in the air, allowing the wind to take his body bag. He took a deep breath of normal, non-hellish air and shouted "Yes!" at the top of his lungs before two security guards rugby-tackled him to the ground, and everything went black.

Whispered words from the corner of the room awoke him, and he felt a warm hand in his. He opened his eyes to be greeted by Varie's face looking at him from beside the hospital bed.

"Are you done with your amateur dramatics?" she asked, smiling. Caliber stood behind her, shaking his head.

Atlas smiled back at her. "How did we do?" he asked. "In the stadium. Did we stop it?"

Varie nodded slowly. "We lost a lot of people," she said sadly. "Around two hundred dead, many more injured."

Caliber stepped forward. "We did everything we could, Atlas," he said. "It could have been catastrophic. We lost one angel—the traffic warden lady. We also lost you for a time."

Atlas nodded, every bone in his body aching.

"Is that why you were being so weird this last while?" Varie continued. "Did you know you were going to do that? It was the worst thing I have ever experienced, Atlas. I don't want to ever experience anything like that again. I had to watch you die; do you know how that felt?"

Atlas looked at her, smiling sympathetically, even though he was the one who had died.

"Anyway, your plan worked," she said. "The plan you didn't bother telling anyone about."

Whispering doctors came to his bedside and spoke of their confusion over his condition. They talked about the catastrophic injuries Atlas had sustained that he couldn't have possibly survived—a slit through, total exsanguination, and blunt force trauma from the fall. They insisted that he was dead on arrival in the hospital and had remained dead overnight in the morgue. He was dead when the doctor was about to open up his body and take out all his organs. He was totally and utterly dead, as dead as dead could be.

Atlas looked out the window across the rooftops of Dublin. The sun was shining, and the city's enchanting landscape looked so beautiful. Below his window, a quilt of rooftops stretched into the distance, interwoven with the rich history of old and new. Cathedral spires breached the skyline, reaching toward the heavens in silent reverence. Christ Church Cathedral stood steadfast, and Dublin Castle's ramparts stood proud, guardians of bygone eras. Amidst the timeworn charm, modern glass buildings rose, reflecting the sun's golden embrace. Towering blocks of steel and glass mingled with centuries-old structures, harmonizing the city's past and present. His city. It was beautiful.

Atlas turned to Varie. "Where's my mum?" he asked. "Is she okay?"

One of the doctors leaned over and pressed a button on a beeping machine to silence it. "She just went for a cup of coffee, Mr. Bishop," he said. "She said she would be back shortly. She's very grateful that you are doing well now."

Atlas looked eagerly from him to Varie. She smiled widely and gripped his hand tighter.

The hospital door opened, and his mother walked in, dressed immaculately in a lilac trouser suit, her hair and make-up sitting perfectly. She was talking animatedly to the man walking behind her—a beaming Gabriel.

"Atlas!" she sang. "You're awake!" She scooped him up into a big hug. She was warm. She was alive. Atlas held tightly to her, his face snuggling into her warm neck. He could sense tears building in his eyes as he felt the energy radiate from her to him. He felt like a little boy again.

They broke away, Atlas still holding onto her shoulders. "You're alive!" he said, beaming. "You're actually here and alive. It's so good to see you."

She laughed, nodded, and hugged him again. "I am, yes. Thank you, son," she whispered. "Thank you for coming for me. You made a promise, and you kept it."

The doctors looked at each other. "Okay," said the older one. "Since everyone is here—I take it you are his parents and his wife—we should really talk about the situation here."

Ma sat at the edge of the bed, still holding his hand, while Gabriel stood beside the doctors with his head bowed and arms crossed, smiling. Varie turned to face them.

"We don't know what happened here," said the doctor, "but I think we are all in agreement that it was very strange indeed. It is not just strange but medically impossible, in fact, for someone to come back to life after having their throat slit, after falling from the equivalent of a seven-story building and being in the morgue with no pulse for over twenty-four hours. We have made a decision, and we are going to call in a team from London to assess you. This is some kind of medical miracle, Mr. Bishop. So we're going to keep you here for observation. Then, we are going to alert medical experts from around the world. This will change the world."

Gabriel moved forward and raised his hand to command the doctor's attention. "There's nothing strange here," he said calmly. "This man is absolutely fine. He just had low blood pressure, and that's why it was presumed he was dead. Someone made an administrative error in his charts. He wasn't dead. He didn't fall. He's fine to go home. No further tests are needed; no further investigations are needed. There will be no talk of miracles. Everything is normal, so wipe your computer records and release him now."

The doctors looked away from Gabriel to their notes. "Yes," said the older doctor, smiling. "Mr. Bishop, you are totally fine. We think it was just low blood pressure. Just make sure to drink plenty of water, stay hydrated, and rest up for the next couple of days. I'm going to sign you out now. You are free to go."

Gabriel threw Atlas a plastic bag full of his clothes. He got dressed and checked the pockets for his artifacts, which were all still there. Varie placed his protection amulets back over his head.

"Gabriel," said Atlas. "It's going to take some work to erase the memories of everyone involved in this."

Gabriel smiled. "I have a few angels on the case as we speak," he replied confidently. "There were a lot of things to tidy up. Heaven and Hell have been in negotiations—peace talks, if you will. The Devil blames Mr. Smith for going rogue; she said he was acting alone. Whether we believe that or not is neither here nor there. Both sides have signed a peace treaty, and all is well."

Gabriel motioned them all out the door and continued. "But you're not to worry about any of it, Atlas. You're to rest up and get better, Soul Binder. Your work is piling up again."

They walked together from the hospital out into the bright October sunshine. Atlas looked around at the gathered crowd. Everyone who mattered to him was right there. He allowed himself a moment to be happy and at peace. He had vowed to make the next part of his life matter. Having braved the depths of Hell and returned, his spirit was forged anew, ablaze with an unyielding resolve. Every breath was a reminder of the preciousness of life reclaimed. Each step forward resonated with a newfound purpose, a commitment to seize every moment with unwavering determination.

Though the scars of the inferno would no doubt linger, he vowed they would serve as badges of resilience, driving him to embrace life's boundless possibilities. He had suffered enough. With a heart now reasonably untethered by fear, he made a promise to himself to live each day to the fullest.

The air inside St. Michael's Boxing Gym was thick with the pungent musk of sweat and the tang of body odor, mingling with the metallic scent of blood and the acrid bite of ammonia. Heat radiated from the worn, canvas-covered ring. The sound of fists hitting leather punching bags echoed off the grimy walls, punctuated by grunts of exertion and the sharp commands of trainers.

Testosterone hung heavy in the air, fuelling the relentless rhythm of training.

In the smoky ring, tension crackled like electricity. With clenched fists and determination etched upon their faces, Atlas and Caliber circled each other, eyes locked in a fierce dance of rivalry.

"What are you going to do now, soul man?" asked Caliber, dancing lightly on the balls of his feet.

"I'm going to mess that pretty angel face up," said Atlas, swinging a blow at his head.

With every blow exchanged, the sound of leather meeting flesh reverberated through the arena, a symphony of aggression and raw power. Blood mingled with sweat, staining the canvas with the evidence of their ferocious struggle.

Mick from Gilligan's Pub watched from the ropes, a look of bewilderment on his face.

His brother Aidan joined him, unwrapping his hand protections.

"Is he doing that thing again?" asked Aidan quietly. "He takes it so seriously. Look at him ducking and weaving, pretending he's being hit. He's a madman."

Mick nodded in agreement. "Chatting and laughing away to himself, too," he said. "If this is what going off the drink does to you, I want nothing to do with it. He's lost his marbles."

"Atlas!" shouted Mick. "I hate to see you like this, son. A drink would do you good. Come on over at lunchtime, and I'll get you one on ice. You wouldn't be at this nonsense if you were still on the drink. Come on; it's been over two months! Do you not fancy a wee whiskey?"

Caliber stopped, and the two stood panting, the sweat dripping off their faces. Atlas smiled widely. He felt better than he ever had in his life. It had taken a few weeks for the haze of alcoholism to lift, but Caliber had been there every step of the way, and he was so glad for him. He had emerged from the depths of despair, reborn with a newfound clarity and resolve.

Each day was a triumph over the chains of addiction, a testament to his unwavering determination and the continual support of his friend. When the withdrawal symptoms had got almost too much to handle, Caliber had taken him here, and they had punched the hell out of one another until the anger and frustration had evaporated.

Every day that passed since his last drink, the weight of shame and regret had slowly dissipated, replaced by a sense of empowerment and liberation. The journey was arduous, fraught with temptation and self-doubt, but he found strength in his angelic friend.

The two hugged as Mick and Aidan looked on from the ringside, not able to see Caliber, but watching Atlas laugh, smile, and hug himself.

Atlas went under the ropes and jumped down onto the gym floor, the sun shining brightly in through the floor-to-ceiling windows. Life was very different now. Varie was doing well and starting to display a baby bump, while Atlas and Elsa were in the exciting early stages of a relationship. His mother was loving life. When there was happiness and hope, work wasn't so much of a chore. He didn't perpetually think something bad was going to happen.

His mindset had changed. Life was good. Really good.

EPILOGUE

Mr. Smith watched the scene from the shadows of the doorway. He was slowly getting used to being mortal again. Not that he liked it. He had cut his finger on a rusty nail a week ago and it had hurt like crazy.

He had cast himself from the Devil's infernal realms by grabbing Atlas's ankle while he held the Life Stone. He hadn't thought it fully through but knew he would have been annihilated for trying to take over Hell's unholy realm from the boss. So he now had to grapple with the unfamiliar confines of mortality, whether he liked it or not.

No longer bound by eternal damnation, he navigated the fragile realm of humanity with cautious uncertainty. He had to eat, drink, think, sleep, and he had human bodily functions. People didn't fear him. But they would.

Every heartbeat reminded him of his newfound mortality. Time, once an abstract concept, now ticked away relentlessly. He didn't have much of it left. Mortal lifetimes were puny and short, and he was going to leave his mark on this place.

He needed to make this new life he had acquired count for

something. He needed the magic stone that could bring the worst of Hell's souls back to life, back to Earth, and he was going to get it, even if it meant killing that seemingly unkillable bastard Atlas Bishop and everyone he ever held dear.

ACKNOWLEDGMENTS

I wrote this book in the midst of PTSD, struggling badly after witnessing someone being murdered on the street in Northern Ireland. I wrote it in the middle of the night when nightmares stole my sleep. I wrote to calm panic attacks and I wrote when the world shut down due to Covid. It was a beautiful, vibrant, dark, and lush escape.

I want to thank my husband, Brendan, for always encouraging my mad ideas and giving me the space I needed to create the world Atlas Bishop exists in, our kids for being little lights in the dark, and my mum, Gloria, and aunts, Kathleen, Margaret, and Mary for showing me that strong Donegal women are unstoppable.

And my late father, William J. Breslin, who instilled in me a profound love of stories and of life.

A heartfelt thank you to my editors, whose keen eyes and insightful feedback have significantly shaped this book. Your dedication and expertise have been invaluable, ensuring the story is captivating and polished.

To my publisher—the luminous, fierce, indefatigable Cassandra L Thompson from Quill and Crow Publishing House—thank you for believing in me, my vision, and for giving Atlas Bishop life.

I am also deeply appreciative of the early readers who offered their time and thoughts. Your feedback was instrumental in enhancing the reading experience.

And to you, readers, thank you for embarking on this journey with me. I hope this book brings you as much joy, excitement, and adventure as it brought me while writing it.

And lastly, to Atlas Bishop, who came into my mind and just wouldn't leave until he exorcised the demons that haunted me.

This book is for every broken person left behind whose fight for justice, closure, and peace began when their loved one's heart stopped beating.

ABOUT THE AUTHOR

Leona O'Neill is a Professor in Journalism at Ulster University after spending 24 years as a news journalist in Northern Ireland, a place that could never stand accused of lacking in drama. During her time as a reporter, she covered everything from terror attacks and murders to presidential visits and political scandals and literally everything in between and often allowed her many newsroom experiences to flavor her fiction writing. She is a weekly newspaper columnist, a Field Producer for many international news outlets, and an avid campaigner for journalism safety and better mental health in newsrooms. She is a Derry Girl, a Mum of four, and lives near Donegal, where she can often be found on a beach looking windswept and interesting with her husband and her dog.

THANK YOU FOR READING

Thank you for reading *Perdition Street.* We deeply appreciate our readers, and are grateful for everyone who takes the time to leave us a review. If you're interested, please visit our website to find review links. Your reviews help small presses and indie authors thrive, and we appreciate your support.

More Books from Quill & Crow

All the Parts of the Soul, Catherine Fearns

Blood Coven, Sabrina Voerman

The Ancient Ones, Cassandra L. Thompson

Milton Keynes UK
Ingram Content Group UK Ltd.
UKHW041818060924
447980UK00006B/479